RUZNIEL

Book One
The Laws of Magic

Ruzniel Book 1
Footsteps Press First Edition
Americana and PT Serif

Typeset by Drupath Hutingali

ISBN 978-1-908867-77-3

Any Resemblance to real Magicians, Ruzniel and Magical Folk is entirely on purpose and taken from the original translation of the Laws of Magic. The words of the poems spoken by Rimfelder are here republished with permission as are the excerpts from the Book of Derivations which is one of my most precious possessions. The descriptions of Damkina come from Hiesia and many of the incidental descriptions are taken from the long discussions I had with Vingura in his beautiful gardens.
How, you may wonder? That is another story ...

RUZNIEL

Book One
The Laws of Magic

Daniel Nanavati

artwork
Jennika Bastian

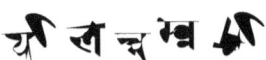

Chapters

Book Two: The End of the Universe

ᢌᢋ᭬ᢖ᭬ᢥ ᢓᢚᢧᢛ ᢙᢇᢧᢙᢋ

My heartfelt thanks for beta reading and proofing:

Serena
Kate
Marit
Angeline

Ruzniel speaks of three days,
The last in the universe,
When uncertainty holds sway
And time's changed into a curse.

For more than mere victory
Sangyma war across space
Sacrificing all glory
For Freedom to have a place.

These are not mythic pages
Encoding magic on Earth
but names, once lost to Ages,
That have gifted us our birth.

The opening of the ballad
'Ruzniel' by Daniel Benshana,.
No one knows how Benshana
alone knows this story.

Saturday

When we are born not only our relatives know.

Not only our neighbours know.

Not only our family doctors know.

Not only parrots and dolphins know.

The Sangyma, the most ancient of all magicians, also know.

They do not show an interest immediately, because, if a child is magical, the magic will not become apparent until they are eight years old. That is the age when the Sangyma, who discovered the laws of magic, always pay a visit.

They visit to test the magic in the child.

To find out how deep the magic flows in them.

To see how wise they are.

To see how trustworthy they are.

And most important of all, to discover which side they will take in the war.

They look for newborns all over the universe. They search for magical life with dedication and tirelessness. The Sangyma need, love and protect all life, because that is their calling. The lives of others are as important to them as their own, because they know Crilodach is out there, looking to kill all those who do not meet Its needs; all those who will not serve It. Many more worlds have fallen to Crilodach than have been saved from It, but that is not always because the Sangyma failed or because their magic has always been less than Crilodach's. As the Sangyma, being the great magicians they are, would tell you, 'to win a war you do not need to win every battle, you only need to win the last one.' (Although you would be very fortunate if they spoke to you in English.)

All the time, of course, they are also looking for that most elusive of all magicians, that rarest of all talents, the spellmaker.

Filvani, the wonderful Sangyma teacher, showed through his now famous formula, that on rare occasions in the life of the universe, someone would be born who could put

1

magical compounds together and create unique magic; new spells. They do not even have to think through the spell because magic, being a part of their inner energy, flows out of them like water from a spring. No pouring over books or endless experiments for them, just an immediate understanding of exactly the spell needed for the situation at hand.

The spellmakers have been born to fight alongside the Sangyma since the war started. Crilodach's soldiers fear them the most. Any new magic is unexpected and the unexpected can be dangerous.

All life is made of atoms from the creation of the universe. Filvani said that some of the atoms in the brains of the spellmakers have been part of many other lives stretching far back to this beginning of all things. These atoms spark ideas in the spellmakers that are as old as the universe; ideas that set them apart as magicians, as people and as thinkers.

The Sangyma treasure all spells, for when they use them they say they can feel the life–force of every magician who has ever cast that spell. To be the first to recast a spell that a spellmaker has created is to feel the full strength of the spellmaker. A rare privilege.

In all the ages only one Earth child was ever born with magical qualities. So rare was this event, they cloned him because they knew when a species gives only one child to the laws of magic, that child must contain all the magic in that species. The Earth was held to be one of the most magical planets in the universe, though humans were held in deep suspicion. In fact no human but one ever knew what the Earth became. Never knew that, had Crilodach ever suspected the true nature of the planet, It would have conquered the Earth before any other worlds. Instead It believed, as the Sangyma wanted It to believe, that the Earth had been destroyed in the titanic battle between the Sangyma Sanjava, Filvani and Fulminar against Crilodach's powerful general, Rataplan. Rataplan, who had done Crilodach's killing for so long his hands had evolved into claws. They said Rataplan's thoughts were so dark his blood had ceased to flow and he could not be killed. The Sangyma knew this wasn't true but they did agree that he was a brutal and merciless enemy.

Not all Sangyma visit the eight year old child at the same time. No room in any house is large enough to provide for them. But, eventually magical children get to meet them all, for like rivers running to the sea, magical people instinctively flow towards each other.

Well, they did when the Sangyma were all alive.

They have almost all been killed one by one, falling, despite their finest spells, into the endless traps set by Crilodach and Its creatures. In his books, Filvani writes that the second law of magic states,

श्रानाच चाऽ नो ऽॉाॉहॊॅॅॅ चॅॅॅॅॅॅॅॅ ऽॅॅॅॅॅॅ
ऽॅॅॅॅॅॅॅॅॅ ॅॅॅॅॅॅॅ चहॅॅॅॅॅ ऽॅॅॅॅॅ
ॅॅॅ ऽॅॅॅॅ ॅॅॅॅ ॅॅॅॅॅॅ

which, translated from the Ebiric, the magical language of the Sangyma, means –

'Magic Can Be Neither Created Nor Destroyed Merely Changed From One Form Into Another'

Since this is true, we may assume they are still out there somewhere, in some form. Perhaps they are living in some person, animal or building near you. You never know with the Sangyma. They have all kinds of secrets. Some very respected authorities on the subject of magic say that when they are dead the Sangyma are, in fact, at their most powerful. That probably makes more sense to you than to me because everyone seems to know more about magic and magical people than I. The universe has many mysteries but a mystery is only an unknown yet to be discovered, so those who know don't find such things mysterious at all.

There are many other creatures the Sangyma have to guard the universe against, all pursuing their own devious plans and desires. Filvani explains their existence in the ninth law of magic,

ॅॅॅॅॅॅॅॅॅॅ ॅॅॅॅॅॅ ॅॅॅॅ ॅॅ ॅॅॅॅॅॅॅ
ॅॅॅ ॅॅॅॅॅॅॅॅ ॅॅॅॅॅ

'For Every Spell There Is An Equal And Opposite Spell'

This means that whenever a magician is born, a malicious enemy springs up to fight them. However, Crilodach is more powerful than any single Sangyma, because It is unique. It was not born.

All but six Sangyma have died in the endless battles against Crilodach that have spanned different times, many places and almost every world. Wars to protect the people who needed to be protected and to give new worlds a chance. Wars that have split families, pitted friends against each other, thrown up traitors as numerous as the stars along with heroes as bright as suns. Skirmishes testing defences in far flung places; civil wars testing resolve in parts of space long forgotten; worlds clashing against worlds for supremacy, using every excuse to kill; down to the mighty battles referenced in Filvani's books on the laws of magic. Behind them all, Crilodach plans Its triumph. It has never changed. Crilodach has never evolved. Sangyma magic, the most ancient of all weapons, has had to constantly adapt to Its cunning.

Spells, like light, travel at a constant speed. There are those who say if you can catch up with a spell, you can see when, where and who created that spell – a dangerous and terrible thing to do if the spell was created in battle. To see the images of the fighters, to smell and hear the spell working away protecting, killing, helping, hurting and who knows what else, is terrifying. Surfing a spell like that is not a wise thing to do but some have tried. If you ever find someone who says they have, ask them about their feet. People who have know all about singed feet.

If I told you how to recognize a spell you may try surfing them yourself and then you would be off on your own adventure. So I will tell you how to do that another day, keep you here, and save your feet.

Speaking about days, this was a Saturday. Saturdays are rare in the Sangyma calendar coming round only once every three years, which makes them good days for secret meetings. This was a warm, breezy Saturday. Tegriel had been on a long journey taking nearly three weeks and he, whose memories went back further than any other Sangyma, was tired. He had had to go the long way round to avoid Crilodach's spies, who could be counted upon to be everywhere. If he had been able to use magic, he would have communicated with his mind, or travelled to the meeting place within a second. But if he had done that all would have been for nothing; all the fighting; all the lives lost; all the planning; all the hopes; all the work would dissolve as if they had never existed. When everything is at stake the wisest magician takes the greatest care. And though he knew this, and though he knew travelling without magic was his only choice, he also knew that nothing makes you feel older, faster, than not being able to do what you know you can do.

That also makes you incredibly irritable.

The dusty shoes make you feel neglected.

Sweat dripping down your neck makes you feel very uncomfortable.

Dirty clothes make you itchy and feel in need of a constant shower.

His eyes hurt and his legs hurt. Most of all his backside hurt from sitting in too many bumpy vehicles, astride dozens of horses in saddles that had seen better days, and from the hard, wet, wood bench, on a fishing boat that smelled of herring and nothing else, which he had once sat on for half a day.

At the beginning of Tegriel's journey the mountains, strewn by a forgetful giant, had been hard and unforgiving on his feet and hands. He had stumbled several times and grazed his knees. On another planet every one of his toes had been stubbed on a rock and his knuckles ached from hitting razor-sharp outcrops along the way. Even on this world he had managed to hit his head on a low branch and heard bells ringing in his ears for the rest of that day.

Now, as the suns reached their varied zeniths, crossing beams of light like swords, he stopped to stare at the wonderful view of the far-reaching landscape spread out before him. No matter how desperate the situation, nor how pressing the matter to hand, Tegriel had always had the time to stop and stare at nature. He took in the delightful green moon that never disappeared day or night, and the low lying clouds that twisted themselves into strange shapes that reminded him of places the locals had never even heard named. The natural world was as important as food and drink to him.

He was almost at his destination. He was glad that his journey was nearly over. He sighed a little because the times were equally extraordinary and terrible. He was about to meet his fellow Sangyma and bring them tidings as full of achievement and sadness as any news could ever be, but then, as with everything in his long life, he embraced the challenges. But in embracing them, lay huge dangers they would be extremely unwise to set aside.

Filvani's eighth law of magic states that,

'A Spell Is Always Two Things At Once'

Sometimes they can be far more than two but most assuredly a spell is never just one thing and one thing only. The spell cast to make a bowl of soup is not simple but actually the same as the spell to make a planet. And before you ask, yes, there are creatures who will boil up and eat planets. The Sangyma have always been able to think of three things, and do two things, at the same time. Their magic enables them to do this, so even when they are hiding from their enemies they find great difficulty in just doing one thing, and in thinking just one thing, at a time. (This is quite the opposite of all other living beings.) So taking time to fill his mind with the view enabled Tegriel to concentrate and not to betray himself by his thoughts for so much as a second. For if he did, in that second Crilodach's agents could strike him with all the virulence their undying hatred could pour forth.

His best strategy lay in moving along with ordinary people, travelling in crowds. That way he blended in, but oh, how many times had he wanted wings! Blending in he vanished from his enemies, or so he thought. He had left his home and gone through three disguises on the way to try to fool prying eyes. His cover story here was as a man going to see his sister and his first born niece.

"Lovely child," he told anyone who asked, "image of her mother mind you. Image. Not a bad thing either, she got the looks in the family."

He smiled. They smiled. He nodded. They nodded and did not like him at all.

He was suitably dressed, carrying a small bag over his shoulder with changes of clothes and some money, but not too much. He never knew how much to create for these rare kinds of journeys. He put down his strength despite his age, to a good vegetarian diet and the fact he did not drink. Sangyma do not have to work out, magic is physically such hard work they keep their muscle tone all their lives.

He headed down to the valley where the other Sangyma were gathered. He had no wand or staff because he had never had either. He thought magicians who had staffs rather odd and those with wands even odder. Both can get broken in a fight but if you fight only with your mind, that will only break when you do, as the fifth law states,

'The Power Of A Spell Is Exponentially Increased Or Decreased By The Power Of The Mind That Casts It'

Even when he stumbled he did not stop himself from hitting the ground. He had had to accept a helping hand more than once, which was a novel experience for a magician who had spent his life being called upon to help others.

All in all they were the longest three weeks of his long life. Doing something magical every day was second nature to him. He particularly liked getting a glass to fill with water and float over to his mouth whilst he kept reading. Not being able to do that was like having his hands tied behind his back all day. Every day. Every night. Sangyma dream and he had to make sure he did not inadvertently dream something that gave away his identity.

The other five Sangyma would be making similar journeys from various places. None of them would use a drop of magic. He knew they would be anxious, after all they had waited for his news their whole lives. Spellmakers are extremely rare but this spellmaker's birth, coming several years after he had met the Ruzniel Tobia, meant only one thing. As he had prophesied, the end of their war with Crilodach approached. Zaqui, the defining moment of their universe, through which the new universe would be created out of the ashes of the old, was coming. The universe was shrinking. The battlefield would soon encompass so small a space they would be fighting nose–to–nose. Zaqui, being a force of nature and not a person, ruled them all and could not be stopped.

Long ago Tegriel had chosen this meeting place knowing, even then, what was going to be. His fellow Sangyma had not questioned his certainty. If they had ever doubted him he had proven his worth a thousand times, rarely being wrong about Crilodach's plots and intentions. So they all made their way to this long prearranged meeting place, to discuss their final plans, which, with his unmatched foresight, Tegriel already knew. The time had come to share his final ideas.

Tegriel knew things because of his special magic and to try to understand how that could be, when he had never explained himself to the others, would be like trying to make sunshine smile. The place of sunshine was not to smile, but to give smiles. Tegriel knew the time when his power of prophesy would be explained, though some of those he was meeting today would not be alive to discover his secret.

Survival was not the point. This battle would be judged as won or lost only by what came afterwards. Actually all battles and wars have been won or lost by what comes afterwards but sometimes those who win, in the joy of the conflict being over, miss this fact. This is why the Sangyma, although they had won many battles, never held victory celebrations. You will never see a Sangyma marching whilst waving flags, that's not something they feel comfortable doing. By looking into their eyes you can see they remember their friends and all those who have fallen in battle. Across a Sangyma's eyes walk all those they have ever known. Most magicians are generally happy people but because of these vivid memories, their eyes are always sad.

The most important thing, and the reason for all the secrecy, was to ensure Crilodach did not know about the child. If It suspected for an instant that this spellmaker, born on the eve of Zaqui, would wield the power to stop Its cherished plans, It would move to kill her with all of Its might. Then things would have finished too early and all the many fallen would have died for no reason. The birth of this child, and of her reaching eight years old, was the 'afterwards' of every battle, on every world, the Sangyma had ever fought.

Since no magic had entered or left the universe since creation, they had to explain why the available magic in the universe was getting harder to find. The Sangyma were certain enough magic was still available for their fight, only hidden, and finding those hiding places was not something that could be done with ordinary spells. Tegriel had told them all that this child would be the most powerful spellmaker they had ever seen. When they discussed amongst themselves how Tegriel could see the future when the laws of magic specifically state that the future is uncertain, Filvani shrugged and pointed out that the study of quantum magic is particularly useful in this regard as is an understanding of magical relativity. The first will tell you how strong a spell needs to be, the second will tell you the time anywhere in the universe. Filvani would then smile at his joke. But the point was clear, nothing about Tegriel can be entirely explained by observation. They had to wait for Tegriel to explain this magic of his to them, if he ever would.

That morning Tegriel had said goodbye to his latest travelling companions who had been a group of actors who performed for a good dinner and a place to sleep, and set off on a particularly narrow pathway. The path ended in a tall standing stone, from where the long valley he had stared at when admiring the view opened up before him. He walked through a glade of maple trees and down into the depths of the wood, along leafy pathways to where a bright stream was bubbling up from the ground. He looked for the line of red stones he knew was his marker. Seeing them ahead he bent down, washed his face and sipped the cold water. Then he stretched his arms and giving a slight yawn, descended the valley slopes until the suns were a mere glitter through the trees. The birds fluttered and the odd blue-furred fox came out and licked his fingers. A peaceful place. A quiet glade. Tegriel knew two Sangyma would die here and he had to allow them to because of everything that would come after. But his heart was as heavy as lead at the thought.

Then he heard the movement of a man splashing water and humming softly to himself. He peered over a mulberry bush.

Fulminar, who had arrived two weeks before, was sitting by a pool in the twilight, his grey trousers rolled up to his knees, soaking his tired feet. There are those who say Fulminar was the greatest of all the Sangyma. Everyone has their favourite Sangyma (truth to tell the men mostly like the proud woman Sangyma, Zananto). Many are the arguments over who has the fastest eye, the quickest wit, the funniest jokes. Tegriel saw his oldest friend. A sudden desire welled up in his throat to warn him, to apologize to him for what was going to happen. But he controlled the impulse for he knew the result of telling him would be more disastrous than losing him. Without looking up, Fulminar greeted him in his rich, deep voice that always sounded as if he were singing not speaking.

"Welcome, welcome at last!"

Tegriel sat down beside him, their arms around each others' shoulders.

"We've been working too hard," Tegriel told him.

"You look a little tired," suggested Fulminar, frowning a little. "Not keeping up with your vitamins?"

"While you look a little fatter. Not keeping up with your magic?"

Tegriel poked him in the stomach and they laughed, as if

their laughter could ward off the sorrows that lay ahead of them.

"I do a lot of running around," complained Fulminar. "You would not believe how those Ruzniel keep me busy."

"I can imagine."

"No Ruzniel companion for you still, I suppose?"

"Maybe one day soon. My life has always been too dangerous even for the best trained Ruzniel."

"Just one as a companion instead of several thousand would be a holiday for me!" Fulminar laughed, "But you should have a Ruzniel at your right hand. Does no good you endlessly trying to get things done all by yourself."

"Too many have been lost," Tegriel said, sadly. He paused. Fulminar looked at him intently and asked,

"The child?"

Tegriel breathed in deeply. He had wanted so much to say he was sorry to Fulminar; for not telling him, for not letting him prepare himself. He had been on the brink of giving in and saying as much when his friend asked him about the birth of the new spellmaker and almost with relief he responded, dropping his hands on to the ground,

"She is undoubtedly a spellmaker."

They both looked around suddenly, as if the words should herald an attack from an enemy in the woods about them.

"This place is too quiet," grumbled Fulminar.

"I took every precaution," Tegriel assured him.

"We all did but still ... smells trappish. Might be because I am getting old. I see danger in everything."

"You? Of us all you have kept your youth intact."

"That's because I found a woman to love."

"How is she?"

"She is here. Probably ready to tell me my fears are unfounded, that I always think the worse and I should be more like Gertis."

Tegriel wanted to confide in him even more, but instead he replied,

"I feel uneasy too Fulminar ... if anything happens, anything at all, get Zananto away immediately."

"But ..."

"No buts! Immediately. Please. It would be hard enough to lose either of you, but to lose you both would be unbearable."

"As you wish," Fulminar conceded. "Though you assume she would ever do anything I tell her."

There was a moment's silence and then Fulminar, knowing the subject needed to be aired further when they were all together, splashed his feet in the water and said,

"I like to bathe my feet after a long day or a long journey."

"As do I."

"Nothing like warm water for tired feet," Fulminar grinned, "and not the slightest bit of magic needed."

Tegriel dipped his feet into the water without taking off his shoes. Sangyma never take off their shoes. Shoes are like a second skin. With them a Sangyma can feel trouble through the ground from miles away. They weave them from Anio Cordium, a kind of flax that never wears out which grows in abundance in the marshes outside Motil, Ruz's second largest city in the east.

The two Sangyma sat there for all the world like two ordinary friends taking in a weekend holiday of fishing and sunbathing. But for the dust on Tegriel's clothes, you might have thought he had been lazing away the whole day by this pool in these woods.

"Any later, we would have given up on you," Fulminar joked, slapping him on the back. "I said you would be here never a fear, but the others were getting jittery, 'He is dependable', I said, 'there are too many dangers out there,' they all said, 'I know for sure he will get here,' I said."

"Another day is more than I could have stood," revealed Tegriel.

"Hard travelling?"

"Hard walking."

"We are here, safe and sound. Together. That is all that is important right now," said Fulminar.

"All?"

"Well a beginning at least, whatever else may come we can all face together."

"You and I have seen and been through much yet we have never been here before," said Tegriel.

"That we know of."

Tegriel looked at him, wondering if somehow he knew. He had been so careful never to betray the truth but Fulminar had always had a deep perception about why things happen the way they do.

"You still believe we have done this before?" Tegriel asked him.

"I have an open mind on the subject," Fulminar replied.

"If we have, how come we do not know what will happen?"

"Do we not?"

"Oh, and you are going to enlighten me I suppose on how deep my ignorance goes?" Fulminar twitched his nose and looked at his old friend.

"Well now, there is knowing and knowing. I cannot say for sure we will win, but I cannot say for sure we will lose.

So maybe there is something out there ... something I am feeling for, searching for. Something akin to a memory."

"I have a similar feeling but I have sense enough to know whatever the feeling means, we still have to fight for our lives."

"You have your prophecies."

"I am not always right."

"Enough times to make a difference. Enough times to make me feel your magic taps into something none of us have yet experienced," said Fulminar.

"The outcome is uncertain, so whether or not we have been here before, we must not lose the advantage we have sacrificed so many to gain," Tegriel said.

"I do not see any advantage in proceeding into the unknown, unknowingly, with little more than hope in what we have achieved so far as a weapon."

"Can you not?" asked his friend. Fulminar thought for a while and said,

"We might draw Crilodach out for once. When It knows how well laid our plans have been. About time I actually saw It."

"I am in no rush to meet It face to face again."

"I am in no rush for this beautiful universe to die, but that's going to happen and one way or another I will be there, so," he shook his shoulders and pulled a foot out of the water, "if I cannot avoid a bad thing I will make myself believe I am entangled for my own good."

"That helps?"

"Only me," Fulminar smiled. "Only me."

"Have you been here long?" asked Tegriel, closing his eyes for a moment, wallowing in his much needed rest.

"Two weeks," replied Fulminar beginning to let his feet dry on the grass.

"Two weeks! You must have run all the way!"

"Gertis was here first let me tell you, but then he is young and enthusiastic. A bit too young maybe. He has been chattering non-stop about everything under the suns. I wish the young would learn to be less enthusiastic about danger."

He hummed a little and looked at Tegriel quizzically, who replied,

"You know as well as I we are not chosen. I have no power to decide who will be a Sangyma. Besides, a little youthful energy never hurt anyone, least of all you."

14

"He makes me feel very old," Fulminar said.

"You are old. Almost too old."

"So are you. Which is why the journey probably raddled your bones. You look better for the foot soak mind you. Either that or my eyes are etching out the lines around yours."

"I barely remember you not having lines on your face."

Tegriel splashed his feet for a few moments, taking in the pleasant forest smells, then he added,

"Recently things have been too quiet. Makes me wonder what Crilodach is planning."

"As It always wonders what we are planning." Fulminar stretched his toes with a satisfied, throaty hum. "You suspect It knows?"

A worried look crossed Tegriel's face and then vanished as he again quelled his desire to warn his oldest friend,

"If It did, It would have been more active, not less. Crilodach is never one to let Its advantage slip. I think we may assume It is wondering why we have been so quiet. It i scared that we have found the way to survive the Zaqui as It fears."

"Hmm," said Fulminar rubbing his chin. "Crilodach must know Zaqui is close. It will know, as we do, that soon will be Its last and greatest chance of success."

"Those with appetites like Crilodach only see what is next on the menu. We have shown time and again It never sees much past Its nose."

"Maybe It is blinded by Its own nature, but you have also warned us never to take anything about It for granted." He yawned and Tegriel joined him, stretching his arms.

"Your yawns are catching."

"It is a warm afternoon with nothing to do but think and listen. They are always the most tiring unless you are Copret, who seems to find something to claw at even on days like this."

"How is the bear?"

"Doing well considering," said Fulminar, "but I will let him tell you the story. Come, I think we have a meal being offered if my nose is correct. I must say being able to conjure up a feast will be welcome after this. I have been eating bean-grass and water-sprouts for far too long."

"Bean-grass sounds delicious. I have been living on bread and goats milk." Tegriel stood up and brushed his coat lightly with his hand.

"Pity our stomachs have to suffer for our magic," laughed Fulminar.

They walked along together. Above the two of them, in the trees, the leaves were quietly moved as if something wanted a clearer view. Something Fulminar did not know was there.

They were not far from the others, who all knew Tegriel had arrived. They had decided not to disturb the two of them as they talked. The two, firm friends, whose long lives had seen more death and destruction, more hope and sacrifice, more love and determination than can be found on a million, million worlds, walked together. You would never have guessed all that they had seen to look at them now, walking along the valley, allowing the odd insect to land on their hands, exchange a few words, and then fly off. Two old men in a rather lovely wooded valley, pondering the events of the past, and planning for the events of the future, in as far as they were able. But if you could have held the dog Kalevala in your arms, as Tegriel had, as the first of the spellmakers died, or run with Fulminar as he looked madly for clues to finding a kidnapped Ruzniel, you would have understood that a Sangyma is always far more than they look, always feeling far deeper than anything they say and always more dangerous than you could imagine.

They marched into a glade speckled with silver birch and apple-trees. The sun played on the leaves turning them golden, flicking a mottled light over clothes, hair and eyes. A warm, thoughtful sunshine playing amongst ancient and thoughtful magicians. The wind blew through the twig-like branches around them, bobbing them up and down like seagulls on the incoming waves of a secluded beach. There was almost music in their sound. Birds sang but they did not make their tunes any more happy than normal. Even the animals knew they had to act normally. Crilodach's spies are very subtle. They could be a worm, they could be a rock, they could be a leaf. Just as the Sangyma, they too could not use magic for fear of giving away their position. But then, what was moving closer in the trees did not need any magic.

Filvani was the first to realize that the essential ingredient in all magic is time. Time to think, time to plan, time to act. Time, as he writes in his second law of magic, is a unifying energy,

हा ओ। ।व ।वव ओ य् ् सओ।ब व यहॊ ॊ।ॊ र
वहॊ ॊ ।व वा ओ वहॊ ॊ ।व ओ।वाव

'Time Is Its own Spell. Wherever There Is Time, There Is Magic'

Tegriel looked around at his closest friends whom he had not seen for a long while.

Filvani, white haired now, with his thin, long fingers that could turn the pages of the thinnest papers, sat on an aged oak log with his invisible books around him, a ream of papers covered with notes stuffed into his pockets. A scholar. Always writing. Always something to save for others to read. Always something to record. He was the only person who could claim to be a teacher of Sangyma. Although some said he was the least magical of all the Sangyma, Tegriel and the others often said of him, that his skills were beyond magic.

Sanjava, large and powerful, his long red and blue hair moving without his command, his mind watching everything, his hands touching the bark of a fallen tree as he took a step towards Tegriel. Inspecting the trunk for heaviness, you could almost see him thinking about tearing into his enemies' hearts by throwing it like a javelin. His hair was a weapon as sharp as a blade, every strand as strong as the toughest metal. His wisdom was legendary and many of his sayings are in Filvani's books. Sanjava saw all magic in colour, and had once said to Tegriel he thought he could paint a spell. Tegriel told him not to, for what he would paint would be his own magic and Crilodach could use that against him. As it was, Sanjava was brilliant enough to ensure his magic would be with the fighters in the final battle, even though he would be dead.

Zananto's quiet eyes followed them as they walked forward. She smiled, her white teeth catching the sun and lighting up her whole face which was framed by her curly, auburn hair. Her clothes almost danced in the light breeze. She was not a beautiful woman but anyone who has ever met Zananto will tell you, she is unforgettable. They say her memory is equalled only by Tegriel and her bravery only by the bears. The magic in her runs deep and no one, not even Tegriel, knew that she had laid down plans to provide them with a powerful force against Crilodach in the final battle.

The young Gertis ran up and dusted Tegriel's long coat. His youth belied a rapid and powerful thinker as swift in action as he was fast on his feet. Unusually for a Sangyma, Gertis was able to change spells after casting them and he had used the art on many occasions to confound his enemies. He would fool them by throwing a flower at them and in mid flight the flower would suddenly become an arrow. He was respected amongst the Sangyma for his powers though often criticized for thinking with his heart, more than his head. This was a trait that was going to get him into great trouble. But out of that trouble, and through his heart, would come a mighty army.

Tegriel's eyes looked around the other Sangyma, finally resting once again upon Fulminar. His forehead furrowed,

"Where is Breseut?" he asked.

"He did not return with me."

Copret growled his bear growl as he spoke, and his brown eyes burned. He had been sitting quietly on the ground behind a tree but now he got up and faced Tegriel. Many stories are told about Copret. He may be a brown bear but he is a mighty person. He is the most loyal of friends but the last adventure he went on with Breseut had ended in disaster. He carried the scars on his legs as proof. Breseut had been taken prisoner and killed himself rather than be tortured, for he carried in his head knowledge of this meeting which he knew the enemy must never uncover.

"You said they were all here!" snapped Tegriel.

"I did not want to upset you right away," conceded Fulminar, looking at the ground.

"We must be grateful he died by his own hand," Filvani said sadly. "Thus far the secret of your discovery is safe."

"Things are bad enough without having to endure the loss, one by one, of my only companions in this life," Tegriel told them.

"We all know the risks of what we do," Zananto pointed out, "There is no blame because you sent them on a mission that failed."

"I have sent so many who never come back," Tegriel said.

"Any of us could have been there instead of him," soothed Sanjava.

"And may well be before this is over," added Filvani.

The leaves rustled. Copret sniffed the air. Whatever aroused his interest in the trees had gone quickly. All was quiet above them.

"We are fewer every time we meet," sighed Tegriel.

He hugged them all in turn. He looked deep into Zananto's eyes. Would this be the last time she looked upon him as a friend? When she found out that he knew so much more than he ever told them? When she realized he had not spoken about Fulminar's death despite his knowing? That his words about Breseut were, though truly sad, not from surprise.

"The ways of the Sangyma are always going to be hard and lonely," Zananto told him, rubbing her palms together gently. "Our powers are our strength and our doom. Knowing that has never stopped us doing what has to be done."

"That's true of everyone who stands against It," growled Copret, who never spoke Its name if he did not have to. The bears were one of Crilodach's most antagonistic enemies. There was nothing they did not know about Its cruelty.

"How, then, could we possibly be different," she answered.

She held Copret's gaze. He wanted to sleep soundly, to sing and not be worried about who might hear his words, to walk freely even for a moment, without having to worry about other people's destinies. What a wonder, he thought, to be able to hibernate! So many times he had wanted to be just the same as everyone else but, to be so would mean forgetting so many things. He could never quite accept being ignorant of so much.

"Do not blame yourself," Tegriel told him, coming over and holding his arm. "I apologize if I seemed in any way to be criticizing you."

"We're still in the fight," said Copret. "We'll make a good account of ourselves in the names of the fallen."

"I do not relish combat as you seem to my friend," Tegriel said. Copret hugged his old tutor tightly.

"That's because you take victory almost as badly as defeat," replied the bear, "I never understand you. There's no relish in breaking bones but rather theirs than mine, I say, and rather theirs than anyone I love." He let Tegriel go before he squeezed the breath out of him.

"There is much more fighting to come," Tegriel told him.

"We were put here to do a job and we should do that to the best of our ability. Isn't that what you constantly tell me, Fulminar?" added Copret.

"Yes," nodded Fulminar, in agreement.

"Indeed we should," said Gertis thumping his right knee

with his clenched fist. "And if the time is now I am ready to do my bit."

"We gave up being free, to fight It. We gave up sleep, wine and song," added Copret, "family and happiness. We gave up being young." They all turned to look at Tegriel.

"Sacrifice for others, that was and is our code," he told Copret. "As one who is not a Sangyma we agreed if you ever wanted, you may leave us and be at peace."

"You know very well I'll never leave you," Copret told him. "I'd rather have my claws torn out."

"Then no more regrets," said Tegriel.

"Breseut is worthy of regret. He was good fighter and a strong friend."

"Then he was all he should have been," said Tegriel.

"I'm sorry," Copret said, dropping his paws by his side and sitting down again by his tree.

"Did you find out anything?" he asked the bear.

"We found no trace of It," he replied.

"That is very worrying," Tegriel replied.

"What did you send them to find?" asked Filvani.

"I had word that It might have found one of the Sagitæ."

There was something of a stunned silence. This was not the kind if thing casually said to the Sangyma, because the three Sagitæ were the whole reason for their endless war with Crilodach. These were the bejals It wanted more than any other. Bejals are any object that is, or is made, magical. They can be anything at all although, in the case of the Sagitæ, they happen to be jewels.

"You think Crilodach has captured one?" asked Zananto.

"We still don't know," added Copret bitterly.

"Once before It captured one," remembered Sanjava. "We stole that one back."

"Did you find what you went looking for?" Zananto asked Tegriel, breaking the silence that followed the depressing news.

Their faces all showed absolute concentration. They stood or sat waiting for his answer; an answer that was at once their challenge, hope and death. They were so quiet in that moment even the leaves seemed to be listening and whatever had crept closer, stopped moving.

"Yes and no," Tegriel told them.

"Always the two sided answer, when will you learn to say yes or no?" asked Gertis.

"When you grow whiskers," Tegriel answered.

"Not long then!" Gertis responded smiling.

"We are wiser but there is a catch." Fulminar said, leaning back against a birch tree, "Is she the spellmaker?"

"There is always a catch," Filvani said, putting down his book almost knowing what Tegriel was going to say.

A bird disturbed on her nest flew from a tree with a squawk. Zananto saw her flutter and lose a feather. She met Copret's gaze as he saw the same thing. They both knew Crilodach would go to any lengths to overhear this conversation but they felt nothing close to them that made them uneasy.

"The power we seek, the power we need, will no longer reside entirely within the Zaqui."

"Did I not say as much? Did I not show you the laws allowed for change?" said Filvani, triumphantly. "The laws never lie. We should have planned for this. Nothing can be taken for granted, the laws live their own lives and they will mutate if conditions allow. In fact they must. That is how they remain free. Continual change is the DNA of magic." He beamed.

"That makes our lives more difficult," complained Gertis.

"And Crilodach's," reminded Sanjava.

"You did warn me," Tegriel nodded at Filvani. "As you say, the power mutated."

"But not lost?" asked Gertis.

"As if," growled Copret.

"Not lost. The power became a person." Tegriel let his words sink in for they were very surprising.

"Another person? Is that possible?" asked Zananto.

"A great deal of power for one person!" said Copret. "Too much in fact. They cannot be ordinary in any way, shape or form. Such a power would kill any of us."

"I agree with you," Tegriel said, walking to an apple tree and taking a small red apple to eat. "Though in you or I the power would prove fatal to our weak bodies, this person was just conceived when the elements reached her and she was born able to handle and hold them. The power is in every one of her cells, in her skin and muscles and most importantly in her mind, and she is who she is because of that."

Boughs in the trees nearby bent with an unseen weight.

"An amazing turn of events," observed Sanjava, shaking his head, his brown skin twinkling in the light, "a truly amazing thing. Yet, why should we be surprised? To give the power to a thinking being who fights on our side makes perfect sense."

"And the last thing Crilodach might suspect," said Zananto, then she added questioningly, "As long as she is on our side?"

"Do you doubt her?" asked Fulminar, shooting a look at Tegriel just in case.

"You knew?" she asked Fulminar.

"More or less," Fulminar admitted.

"More than that," Tegriel paused and swallowed, "she knows already this has happened. Though she is only eight. She has many powers beyond her years. She knew what I was going to say before I finished and she knew many things that have happened that only the power in her could have given her knowledge of, because her family definitely did not know."

"I think we should move swiftly to guard her," said Fulminar.

"We already know her. She is the granddaughter of Wefdal Gentle," Tegriel revealed.

"Lilah!" Gertis sighed, "Oh, I knew she was special. She is so intelligent and graceful." He got up and did a little dance,

"Oh, that is wonderful," said Filvani.

"Lilah indeed," said Sanjava, "amazing!"

"But she has a baby brother. Born of the same womb. He may equally have some powers," suggested Sanjava.

"We cannot separate those born to be magicians," warned Zananto. Above them the clouding sky threatened rain.

"Separate them we must," insisted Tegriel, throwing away his apple core. "She must learn. The power is not for any of us to use. If she remains untutored she will fail. If the enemy finds her and turns her, all is lost. The whole of our existence would have been for nothing. We must ensure she becomes the greatest of all the spellmakers. We have no choice but to take her into our care."

"Nonetheless you must allow the brother to remember," said Filvani. "He must have the right to find her. He will be lonely and the hope of finding her will be his panacea."

"A man's loneliness is the least problem facing us," Sanjava told him.

"Is that wise? To let him know?" asked Gertis. "Dangerous

enough our knowing. A normal magician could be tortured, could speak to the wrong people ... anything."

"Filvani is right," smiled Fulminar, "the brother must not be left out. He will feel half a person all his life. We cannot allow that. Besides, if he goes looking for her, as he will if he does not understand, he may ruin everything. I suggest he is taught. I have a friend, Palik Tomil, in need of a new student. He will do well with him, and Palik will make a fine magician out of him let me tell you."

"Excellent choice," said Zananto. "I know Palik very well. He will not let us down."

"How old is the brother?" asked Copret.

"Three," replied Tegriel.

"I would still keep him in the dark for a while," Copret growled. "If you tell him now, what's to say he won't also become a target for Crilodach and as Gertis says, he may let slip information."

"I will tell Palik to tell the brother only when he asks to know," Sanjava told them. "What is his name?"

"Midrak," said Tegriel. "He is too young yet to be trained."

"No matter," Sanjava replied. "Palik will be ready for him."

"And we will tell Lilah she will see her brother again because she is bound to miss him. We must teach him as much as we can, otherwise he will not be able to stand with her when the time comes." Tegriel stopped talking as they all let the information sink in, then Sanjava went on,

"Zananto, you had better collect the girl. You are best placed to guide her as not only her teacher but her new mother. If I may I will go and get the bejal Bofindle for her?" He was asking their permission and all of them nodded. Bofindle was a weapon only the spellmakers could command.

"Copret, you had better get back to your kindred. There is work to be done still on Earth. We need to finish Trecrogo," said Tegriel.

"The blueprints are complete. We have everything ready to start growing the foundations."

"Gertis, you need to go and talk to Wei K'un. Tell him the time is here and that I sent you. He will know what that means and do what needs to be done. The cloned human being must be ready. A great deal rides on his shoulders," went on Tegriel.

"May I know what that means?" asked Gertis.

"Watch and he will show you, and no arguments, for your own good, and go in person. Do not transmit the message any other way. We must all be twice as vigilant now."

"Won't building Trecrogo give the game away?" asked Copret, scratching his ear.

"It does not even know we saved the Earth. It will not know what you are doing but as soon as It finds out It will be all over Trecrogo like a ravenous leech, and we need to meet It there head–on. With luck, Lilah will be ready," said Tegriel.

"I have some added plans for Trecrogo," Filvani told them, "I think I need to talk to Wei K'un, the clone being endowed with enhanced cellular structure has given me a way of controlling the power he will generate. I have written out the instructions here." He took out a handful of papers and choosing three, gave them to Copret.

"Excellent, get any other modifications in the plans straight to me, we work quickly once we get started," said the bear.

"No problem at all," Filvani agreed.

None but Tegriel knew that after a lifetime of learning and writing, no more papers would ever be written by Filvani.

"Within a lifetime matters will be concluded," said Fulminar getting up. "And this old Sangyma will be able to rest a little longer than usual."

"Within the lifetime of a spellmaker," corrected Zananto, "not a small amount of time."

"Perhaps not, but now we know she is here, we had best prepare swiftly," said Gertis.

"I will go immediately to Wefdal Gentle. May Crilodach never know of this meeting. It will destroy every planet in the universe to find Lilah." Zananto got up as she spoke and turned to them,

"My thoughts, as ever, go with you all."

"And ours with you," the others said together.

Then the enemy struck.

Razor sharp bolts, like burning steel spears, streaked down from the trees above them. Aimed directly at their heads and hearts, they came in thick clusters intending to kill everyone. The Sangyma instinctively protected themselves. The invisible books around Filvani were hit and burst into flames. For a second, distracted by his precious library being lost, he turned to quench the flames and the rain of bolts instantly intensified upon him, seeming to come from everywhere at once. Though the other Sangyma deflected most of them, one ablaze with tragic hatred, got through. Within a second they saw their friend, his cloak on fire, his hands outstretched, vanish into grey and black ashes. Understanding that he was dead his books showed themselves and stripped the text from their pages in harmony with the frenzied attack. They burned to wisps of smoke allowing the letters to find safety as a spell. From that moment on the letters preferred to come only when summed by the Sangyma. They would never again appear in books. The grey–green smoke from the books caught the breeze, circled the glade and seeped into the trees revealing the enemy, hanging from the trees upside down like bats, great silver arms swinging, bolts flying from all their long fingers. This was an invisible and deadly infestation of Crilodach's creatures. Magic did not make them invisible. Crilodach had found a way to make invisibility part of their nature. Being natural no spells were used. The Sangyma were taken by surprise, except Tegriel who knew what happened because of this battle. But such certainty as his is a bitter gift.

Magic particles contain a great deal of energy but to be more effective, they look for other random magical particles in the air, forming a chain reaction controlled only by those trained in the magical arts. The energy released enables Sangyma to travel across the universe at great speed. Using the connections particles have to each other, along with their words, they can summon up portals through which they can pass. The portals themselves vanish as they pass through these transitory gateways funnelling the Sangyma from place to place. They call these portals the Ossendark. Fulminar opened an Ossendark right next to Zananto as Filvani fell and his books transformed. He grabbed her arm, following Tegriel's orders,

"Hurry," he ordered her.

"No!" she refused, wanting to remain with her friends and fight.

"They can handle this, your task has been given you."

"I cannot leave them or you."

"These creatures may already know everything we said here. Lilah is in danger. You must go!" he insisted.

Zananto could see that Fulminar was right. As she turned away from the battle, bolts directed at her and Fulminar were thrown in vast numbers flying straight through thick tree trunks to get at their targets.

"Go! I will cover your escape," he promised.

She left them quickly, never to see any of them again. But as she vanished, she turned to see Fulminar fall protecting the Ossendark with his own body. What she did not see was Tegriel's anguish at the sight he had so wanted to warn Fulminar about, to let him know why he could not warn his old friend that in this place his body would die; that he knew Fulminar would fight on in another form.

Copret uprooted a tree and hammered at the flames engulfing the ground where Filvani had sat. Tegriel and Sanjava flew through the trees of the forest, gripping their enemies by their wings and throwing them against each other, shredding them into pieces, and then casting them on to the ground, where they were pierced by bolts from others of their kind.

Now, the whole forest was alive with these creatures. How had Crilodach known that they were meeting here? What manner of creature was It able to conjure up, that at this late stage in their war, It could still surprise them?

"None must escape," ordered Tegriel.

Gertis stood over Fulminar's fallen body and made sure nothing followed Zananto. Then, like a whirlwind, he ran about the forest tearing into the enemy and breaking their wings. Tegriel flew above them whilst the others made a prison of the trees. All day and all night they fought with deadly force and sad hearts. Never a word came from these creatures for Crilodach had not created them to have voices. The Baltimru, the only species to have killed two Sangyma in the same battle, would garner great fear in the years to come.

The Baltimru laid waste the forest with their fire and their bolts like steel. Blinded by the smoke from Filvani's books they missed their mark time and again but to have killed two Sangyma in the same ambush was already a great success. Once the Sangyma grouped together the Baltimru fell in heaps, like autumn leaves ready to be shovelled on to the compost heap. They tried to escape but Sanjava was everywhere and his hair embraced them like a giant web, strangling them as they writhed. Their strong teeth shattered in their mouths as they bit at the strands of his hair. They fired hot bolts at him but all their weapons passed through him as if he had been a ghost.

Unable to fly, unable to escape the creatures gathered together and attacked in one huge mass across the trees and across the glade. The ground burned at their touch. The Sangyma, who were hovering, met them with speed, power and anger. Copret made short work of those who were hiding from them, even though there were many tears in his eyes shed for his dead friends.

By the next night the work was over. The fires were out. The forest was ravished. Now at last Gertis could weep with Copret over the death of Fulminar and Filvani.

"How were we discovered?" asked Copret.

"Who knows," said Gertis to the bear.

"When I saw him I said to Fulminar," Tegriel told them, "that It had been very quiet recently. Obviously Crilodach has been secretly tracking us. Waiting. It has created yet more new creatures to fight us."

"It will seek Bofindle out," Sanjava told them.

"Zananto knows where best to hide Lilah but from this moment none of us must speak of them or try to find them."

They all agreed with Tegriel's good sense. They left the creatures rotting and cleared up the last remnants of their fallen friends. There is rarely much left to bury for the Sangyma vanish like the mist. What was left would be buried another day.

Copret went to his people. He told them of the deaths of three Sangyma. Such was the scale of the disaster that many a bear felt they had lost their own family. Then with renewed energy and determination they designed and completed Trecrogo which was to be the scene of the next test of strength against Crilodach. No one builds like the bears. Every stone was perfect, every wall plumb and the labyrinthine rooms and corridors were not only complex, they were internally heated. There were secrets here only chosen individuals could unlock, and one great secret that they hoped would herald Crilodach's defeat.

Wei K'un told Gertis about the boy who would be Trecrogo's keeper and Gertis learned a great deal about humans for the first time. Zananto made her way to Lilah, ate with Wefdal Gentle and talked to him long into the night before taking the young girl. Hidden in her cloak the girl was smuggled to Ruz and then to a secret place few had ever visited. Zananto never forgot how Fulminar died making sure she was safe. When people point to Tegriel's prophecies and ask for an explanation of why he is so accurate, no one can answer them. Tegriel either has a secret or is lucky. Though Zananto never learned Tegriel's secret, like Fulminar, she suspected the truth. And though she was hurt and angry she understood why, if he had known, he had said nothing.

One atom can be made to do a million different things. One atom can effect another the other side of the universe with just the right words. The Sangyma learned why this worked and what kinds of people could use this power but only one person, Lilah would ever have the power to make use of all the magic that can be created at one and the same time. Spellmakers, they say can cast a spell in the present that alters the past (though others say that is impossible.) Filvani was of the opinion that just because you cannot change events does not mean you cannot change time.

Through Zananto, Lilah was trained by the very best and given the bejal Bofindle, a weapon of mythical prowess, by Sanjava when she was twelve years old. She grew slowly, learning well, not ageing until she had mastered each lesson they had set her for her age. So she grew with the magic in her body. Magic strengthened her bones and muscles as her mind became pliable and subtle. Her limbs became swift, her eyes sharp and everyone who saw her said there had never been anyone like her before. To be in her presence was to be in her power. To be in her power was to be safe.

Palik Tomil accepted his charge with humility and patience. He taught her brother Midrak almost everything he knew before he died. By the time Midrak could create water, Fulminar was a myth in the fables of many worlds. When he was able to make a tree grow in a single night, Tegriel no longer greeted his friends. Sanjava with his great wisdom fell as Midrak held Palik in his arms and laid him to rest in the depths of his world, his tears erupting from his heart and falling like monsoon rain. When Midrak went back to see his family for the last time, Gertis was lost trying to free a friend from Hâgon, the prison Crilodach had hewn beneath Its lair Damkina, and when Midrak had spent ten years mourning his teacher, Wefdal Gentle told him he should go and find a Ruzniel companion, then practice his magic as he had been taught to do. Wefdal

Gentle sat stroking his grandson's hair as he sat cross-legged before the fire.

"In my lifetime five Sangyma have left us," Midrak sighed, shaking his head.

"A bad time, but maybe there are no good times. Just times. We must all face challenges."

"I'm ready," said Midrak standing up.

He had grown tall for an Ifari but his face was the face of a young man heavy with thoughts. His grandfather's hair was white as snow, his eyes were dimmed and he moved like a snail about the house. Only his voice was still strong with a hint of passing in the baritone. He could no longer hold a song and many things he should have remembered he could not. The Ifari live to be very old but Wefdal would not live to Zaqui.

"I will miss you," he told him, kissing his head. Wefdal raised his hand and patted Midrak's arm.

"I've missed you both. I wasn't allowed to see you grow up. Of all loses in the worlds that's my deepest."

"I'll try to find her," Midrak promised, shaking his hand.

"Palik said she and you would meet as adults. You cannot hold a magical brother and sister apart. Even so you will only find her if she wants to be found."

Midrak hesitated not wanting to go, yet knowing he had to leave.

"We will not see each other again will we?" he asked.

"There you are, wanting to stay as ever," smiled Wefdal, letting go his grip on Midrak's arm. "Be gone now. You belong to the laws of magic and they call you to a great cause. You go with my love and my wishes for your success."

Midrak went to the door. He looked back one more time at the place he had grown to know well; thought back to when he left Palik's home and realized his fate was never to have a home for long.

As he walked away from his grandfather, Zananto vanished in a vast ocean of lava surrounding the hidden prison of the three dragons brothers. She was laying secret signs for others to follow that would aid the success of their fight against Crilodach. With her death the enemy thought no Sangyma now lived. Facing only Lilah, for all her prowess, Crilodach believed It could tie her up fighting Its endless armies. It thought It had already won the war. Its dream of eternal life looked assured.

The Careless Star

Because they are always in the thick of the fighting, the Ruzniel have to learn from an early age about the beginnings of everything, the history of most things, the meaning of nothing and the likelihood of anything. They have to be able to converse in many languages, learn new languages within days and get on with people from all kinds of weird backgrounds living on all kinds of alien planets with unbelievable customs. They must diagnose problems, help find cures for unknown diseases, remain calm in all weathers and be dependable in a crisis.

The Ruzniel are educated, wise, friendly and always fair. They are the kind of people anyone would be happy to employ, though no Ruzniel in history ever worked for money. In fact on Ruz, their home planet, the Ruzniel all work towards one aim; to fight Crilodach and Its creatures. Everyone magical knows that Tegriel found the first of the hardy, noseless people who came to be known as Ruzniel in the depths of the past but no one is too sure how. The Ruzniel have just always been there.

So why, as Midrak stared about him, was Ruz, this fantastic place which had echoed with the teachings of their tutors since the Sangyma founded their vast, circular cities, completely empty with hardly a leaf stirring?

The Ruzniel do not mention Crilodach's name except softly, in special rooms, where they learn what It looks like and what It is capable of doing. They learn how to recognize Its creatures, which come in many forms, what they have done, what they smell like and where they are most likely to be found. They also study all that is known of the deaths of the Sangyma to learn as much as possible about Crilodach's fighting strategy and methods.

But no one here was telling these stories to wide-eyed Ruzniel children. In the cities which had been strengthened by the incantations of Fulminar, there was complete silence. Even the animals had disappeared. Midrak Earthshaker stood absolutely alone in the one place where there should

30

be no loneliness. He looked around.

"Hello," he cried out. His voice touched with a despair like the first rasps of a growing sickness that was taking hold of his body.

His call echoed down the mountain side, rolled across the streams and into the city finding a way to open windows, along alley–ways and across roads. He lifted his thumbs to his temples and between his facing palms, across his eyes, there appeared a silvery skein like the gossamer of a spider's thread. He looked deep through the magic that revealed everything that eyes cannot see, and saw a seemingly dead, empty world. Nothing was being hidden as far as his magic could reveal, for there was nothing to hide.

Midrak, looking at the lifeless scene before him, felt very miserable. Was he looking at the death of all spells? Ruz was empty and he already knew that emptiness expands to fill all the available space. This was not just a deserted planet, but a world waiting to die.

The walls of Ruzniel cities shimmer as if on fire, yet are cool to the touch; pieced together with an ancient certainty which left no marks to reveal how or why they glow, how or why they glitter in the moonlight and blaze in the sunlight. They shine deep into space like beacons promising safe harbour and friendship to new and old travellers. Unique lights that stick in the mind so that, when far away, visitors will remember them and find an inner strength to continue on into terrible danger. Everyone who has ever seen them knows there is no fear, no darkness and no tragedy that these lights cannot penetrate. They say Ruz is like a lighthouse in the darkness of the immensity of space. If you are ever lost, you need only look to this glow and you will find safety.

No longer.

Once you could have whiled away the years in learning, drinking in the teachings of the finest minds. Once you could have watched the visitors from many planets coming and going along the broad streets.

Magicians and wizards.

The rare spellmakers

Young and old Ruzniel.

Adventurers and weary travellers.

Those with many eyes and those with only two.

Those who come with news and great gifts and those who

come alone, poor, shoeless and are given food, solace and rest.

Those who come on purpose.

Those who arrive by accident.

Those who were rescued and need to be cared for until their nightmares are healed. Driven into panic and despair by savage mind–imps who can transform ideas into weapons while inside your head.

The cities held them all. Whether they were built in the mountains or by the seashore, in the valleys or on the plains. Cities like this have their own secrets. Their own hearts. Ruzniel cities think.

Never did he expect to find Ruz empty. Without the Ruzniel people the cities had become desolate, waiting for something awful. The perfume of the flowers was still strong, the air still sweet but the final storm was coming. Everything left on Ruz was only here because they could not leave.

The teaching faculty of the Ruzniel agree that all will be known one day but for how long all will be known is not revealed. Although time reveals all, all is not always very revealing because once you have all the facts you realize you can put them together many different ways, and only experience herself tells you the best way to join them up. No one has ever experienced everything and, most certainly, no one has ever experienced a universe without Ruz and the Sangyma.

At each and every turn and twist of their cities, the walls blend into the design as if the cities were made in one solid piece. Though they look hard as titanium, if you fell against them they would be as soft as a down pillow. Nothing in these cities was ever made to hurt anything of flesh and blood. These cities, grown on the hills and plains, were part of the essence of the planet; bonded into every vibrant, living thing. Grown as trees grow. Grown when the planet grew, cooling down when things were finding their orbit and their purpose. Grown from seeds buried in Losek soil, a magical soil found in only the rarest places. Only the houses were left to be built, everything else was grown out of Losek soil with the help of Tegriel's spells.

The gardens, rooms, halls and domes were stacked with signs of their magnificent heritage, stretching back to the beginning. Thousands of names have been carved into the stonework by students. Mosaics telling the stories of the travels and the sagas of 'companions' for all to see. Stories of wild places and strange peoples enclosed in pretty parks filled with ancient trees taken as seeds from planets so far away only the Ossendark could get the Ruzniel there and back.

Midrak lowered his hands. He knew he had to leave the mountain side and investigate. His spirit felt chilled. He was anxious. There was to be no sight–seeing, repose, or convivial laughter on this visit.

In one of the smallest, well kept parks, in the most important city of learning built near the only ocean on the planet, are the tombs. Whenever and wherever a Ruzniel dies their body is instantly materialized here. The first to know of these deaths are the tutors, who then tell the Ruzniel's family. Only the magician whom the Ruzniel accompanied may tell how they died and everyone has to wait, sometimes for generations, before they find out exactly what happened. Sometimes they never know, for even magicians can be murdered before they have the time to tell. Of all the tombs set in regular, well tended rows, seven bear no name, no phrase to suggest what these Ruzniel were famed for doing, how bright their art, how piercing their intelligence or how brilliant their magic. Even a six year old Ruzniel child can tell you about these graves.

These seven were the first to die. Their seven tombs are garlanded by natural springs whose clear water washes them, so that the onyx surface glows green in daylight and yellow in starlight. So strong is the aura around these seven, nameless tombs that every chosen Ruzniel has to come here when they have graduated from the years of learning, before they begin their lifetime of being a magician's companion.

Here they take their leave of home forever.

Here, for the first time, a lifetime of rumours are laid to rest. Here, they take their oaths and are told why such oaths were written and why they should be kept. A Ruzniel's oath may be trusted to the end of time. Magic would never work if a single Ruzniel lied. The oath, written in the same language Filvani uses in his books, begins,

> *'I stand upon the brink of everything, fixed to the compass points of hope and strength'*

And continues,

> *'Of purpose willing to traverse the length*
> *And breadth of the universe, conquering*
> *Loneliness, pain and armies at the flood*
> *To honour the laws of magic and those*
> *Whose spells keep the Sagitæ from all enemies.*
> *My body runs with magic not with blood.*
> *I was chosen to be the eyes and ears*
> *The strong arm, the tireless companion*
> *The unwavering, heart–strong guardian*
> *Of all who aid all that Crilodach fears.*
> *In memory of the three forever lost*
> *I pledge my life to this, despite all costs.'*

Here, where the graduates begin a life facing any and all dangers, they are told of the battles and defeats and of how the laws of magic came to be written by the wise Filvani and added to by the six–fingered Jobib the Blind, one of the only Sangyma to have known Rataplan, before he became Crilodach's general. Jobib was famous on worlds long since vanished.

The Ruzniel are told that during Zaqui, the end of this universe and the birth of the new, the true enemy may be difficult to recognize. Friends will turn against each other. All the worlds will be lost and made anew because Zaqui even has the power to crush the particles of matter in Crilodach. They are told that the balance of power in the new universe has to be decided in this universe. Knowledge, they are told, knowledge is the beginning of all magic but has to be rediscovered after Zaqui.

All Ruzniel seek across the ages and the void, in every planet and star, for the remains of a whisper of the 'three' who fought, but whose bodies never came back. To find out if they are imprisoned, if lost, if dead but nonetheless to find them and to know what happened. To uncover the truth of this great mystery fills their hearts.

Stories are plentiful of those Ruzniel who have heard a rumour in that solar system or a whisper in that galaxy. There is even one famous story of Bedic–Ra, who found the 'three'. His body is buried. He will never speak again. No one has ever heard his magician talk. To talk of Bedic–Ra is unlucky; bravado to even mention his name, as if you are merely pretending to be brave. They say that creatures were uncovered by him that mutilated his body so completely no tutor has ever dared to look into his tomb. They say the one who found him was struck deaf, dumb and blind.

"If you think you know, you do not know and when you know you will no longer think you know for you will know you know nothing." This is the first conundrum of great learning.

So saying, all new student Ruzniel frown and raise their shoulders in confusion. Many years later as they graduate they will understand. Knowledge is a feeling, not a set of facts. Wisdom is the seventh sense. The rarest sense of all. Wisdom is a magician's strength.

Above the tombs range the Purple Alps stretching for ten thousand miles, over part of which Midrak walked briskly downwards. Above this mountain range sets Eurthon, the moon, which lights up the slopes with a purple hue giving them their name. The Ruzniel have learned to make climbing a sport, for a strong body aids survival. Over generations they have developed strong shoulders and round eyes, two layers of skin and seven fingered hands. But all the mountain cabins he passes are empty. Climbing ropes are stored. No one greets him.

The freshwater spring that wetted the tombs of 'the seven' is dry and clogged with large, dead leaves, yellow and black and pale, along with broken hazel twigs. The moon is abnormally muted. The purple of the mountains has turned to a dusty grey.

How ominous to possess eyes that could not see a hint of the Ruzniel amongst so much beauty. Eyes that once, long ago, saw animation, movement and, with the right spell, the wafting, sweet perfume given off by the stone–work. Eyes that sought out paintings known for their quality, cloth known for hard–wearing versatility and tutors who remembered magicians from the distant past. Endless names of the great ... lost. Midrak sat down on a yew bench carved like a dolphin catching fish, and stared about him.

Months had gone by since anyone had touched anything here. No stores of food, no warm welcome, no friendly faces.

Everything had been hurriedly collected and taken away. As if everything living had needed to be rescued.

Could the Ruzniel be dead? What could have killed them? Why had he had no warning of the tragedy? Why had he not heard any magical calls for help? He coughed softly as a little dust caught in his dry throat or maybe he was stifling a sob for a dreadful sadness filled his mind. Would his own next step take him into the nothingness into which the Ruzniel had vanished?

He knew the fall of Ruz signalled Zaqui. Thousands should be here searching, looking … unless they already knew? Unless he was the last to know? He shivered. He blinked at the brightness of a nearby star, brighter than when he had arrived in the Ossendark not half an hour earlier.

He looked down and saw a thin wisp of smoke curling slowly upwards, moved by the lightest of breezes, blending into the grey sky so well as to be invisible to most eyes. He felt a rush of delight.

"Someone is living in this desolation," he said to himself, "Now I may be able to get some answers."

He closed his eyes. He saw the column of smoke in his mind. The smell. The curling wisps around his clothes. He looked down into the smoke, though his eyes were tight shut, and saw the light of a makeshift fire with crossed, neatly cut pieces of wood crackling away. The cold wind of the mountain side vanished. He felt the soft, warm breeze of the plains filling his hair, giving way to the close, warm smell of vegetable soup being cooked. His clothes felt as if they had just been ironed. His toes curled at the pleasant sensation of the fire warming his feet.

He opened his eyes. He was standing in a small room with an open roof through which the stars twinkled. The light from the fire flickered as a young female Ruzniel with long, auburn hair blew on to the flames to make the soup that was now bubbling and filling the room with the delicious smells, cook faster.

She rested on her heels as she stirred, the light from the flames flashing off her olive skin. When Midrak appeared above her fire she showed no astonishment. He gently came down and stood before her. The light of the flames flickered across his face. She asked softly, in a calm voice, without raising her face to look at him,

"Who are you?"

"I am a student of Filvani," revealed Midrak folding his arms.

"Why are you here?" she asked him, resting her hands on the ground and looking up.

"To seek the path of the Sangyma."

"Where were you schooled?"

"In the land of my forefathers by the eyes and hands of Palik Tomil, appointed by none other than Tegriel."

He held out a hand and on his palm the face of Palik Tomil appeared, smaller than life size but discernible none-the-less. She looked at the image and then back at him,

"What do you want of me?"

"Of you, I do not know but of the Ruzniel I wish to find a friend, a companion, a seeker of the three."

"You have found such a one in I."

She gave him a slight smile and reached over to find a second soup bowl from her small rucksack, to serve him a meal. Midrak sat down in front of the fire and made the flames rise slightly higher. The soup bubbled happily. He warmed his hands by the fire and asked,

"How long have you been here?"

She looked puzzled, furrowing her forehead finding remembering hard,

"I'm not sure, I may have been here months, I can't remember. My supplies are nearly all gone, but I may have had only a day's worth or maybe a year's."

"You know you are a Ruzniel?"

"Sure."

Leaning forward he passed his hand over her eyes. She was not in anyone's power, neither hypnotized nor drugged. She was not lying. She seemed content, unafraid of being alone, at home in his presence. These things were all normal. But Ruzniel are famed for their memories, you simply never meet one who says, 'I can't remember ...'

That he should meet a unique Ruzniel along with an empty planet made sense to Midrak. He sat back, looking about him, getting some idea of where he was. Magicians find when they reach Ruz, that, to welcome them, the cities imprint a map in their brains so they can never get lost. A very useful device that only lasts whilst they are on Ruz, once they leave they lose the map (some Ruzniel, with dry wit, say they lose their sense of direction too.)

"What do you recall?" he asked her. She did her best to

answer him,

"I'm at home in this huge city by myself. I ... walked here and knew I should light a fire though I wasn't all that hungry despite not eating much. As though I were showing you where I was." She began to fill a soup bowl, "As if I knew the time to move on had arrived. I'm unable to bring my mother's face to mind. I know I've brothers but I don't know their names. I recognize the stars above, though I almost feel that I'm seeing them for the first time. Particularly the closest one. I should be lost, yet feel I'm not. As if I were in some kind of dream."

"There is a veil over your memory. An enchantment perhaps?" Midrak suggested, taking the soup from her with a smile.

"I don't know," she shrugged.

"Your supplies may have been growing to suit your need. Certain magicians can provide such sustenance. Very useful if you have to wait a long time for someone to arrive."

"I guess."

"A power is at work here that chooses not to be known to us. Nonetheless, we have been brought together for a purpose, or perhaps in your case, you have been left behind for a purpose." He sipped the vegetable soup,

"This is delicious, thank you."

"Is anyone else with you?" she asked. She did not fill her own bowl.

"We are alone for the moment," he told her.

"I feel very strongly that I've been waiting for you. Does that make sense?"

"Nothing else makes more sense. Perhaps we are to wait for others, perhaps we are to go on alone. Time will tell us all, if we are not first informed by whomever has drawn us together." He took a breath, put down his soup and looking directly at her, asked,

"Do you remember your name?"

"Tobia."

"Well, Tobia this is not the way I was told I would gain a Ruzniel companion." She started packing up her small bag of belongings,

"Maybe not," she said, "but you have one nonetheless."

"How are you so sure?" He looked at her intently, his fingers caressing the ground where he sat.

"I just am."

"Does your insight tell you where everyone has gone?"

"There's a great deal of silence in my mind."

He filled her bowl for her. She held the soup warming her hands before sipping it without a spoon.

"When your memory clears we shall know."

"Perhaps remembering isn't important."

She was looking at the stars with a wistful air, seeing something that was only slowly making sense to her. Like a warning light materializing out of the dense fog at a great distance.

"An entire race has vanished! That must be important. And the Ruzniel of all people, of all times." said Midrak, "A new universe is being born."

"I'm confused," she admitted, "I've the sense of being part of something and not a part of anything. Have all my people just gone? Are they safe?"

"Are we?" he asked.

Midrak picked up a stick, poked at the fire waiting for the sparks to fly upward then threw the stick amongst them. The flames flared along the bark and ate deeply into the wood. The warmth spread out and dissipated into the emptiness of the night. He looked up. The stars were changing. His face hardened. He looked into Tobia's eyes,

"Tobia, if I commanded, will you follow?"

"Yes." She had not hesitated in her answer.

"I do not command you. You must accompany me only if you wish to."

"I'd rather follow you into a volcano than stay here. I sense an imminent danger." She got to her feet, "As if something were getting closer and closer and I had to get away to survive. For the first time I feel fear. I think you brought the danger with you."

"I have yet to make enemies who even know my name." He turned his head and looked at the shadows.

"Magicians have countless enemies just because they are magicians," she said.

"Running away from fear never makes one a good companion."

"I'm not running away. In fact, if I stayed here all I might find is my death. With you I will find worse things."

Midrak lightly scratched his left ear. This was a true Ruzniel answer.

"Where were you before you found yourself waiting for

Tobia

me?"

"I've vague dreams of places. Things I know must have been but I'd never recognize again. Faces that aren't quite faces, words that don't run into sentences, feelings that don't make any sense. I feel like an ember of wood carrying only a remnant of the immense fire of which I was once a part."

"Are you the last Ruzniel?" His voice trembled slightly as he spoke, hardly able to believe he was asking such a question.

"Surely not?" she replied.

"Perhaps the Ruzniel left because that was part of a plan, but what plan? When did you last see a tutor?"

"Maybe months ago, perhaps just five minutes ago," she shrugged.

"The power that brought us together must be strong for you to have lost all sense of time."

"I know someone died."

"I am sorry."

"When we leave here perhaps my memory will improve."

"Can you feel if the power that brought us together is here now?"

"When all the colours of light are mixed together they create white light and you can longer discern one colour from the next. All you know for certain is that all the colours are there. Ruz mixes so many feelings together they just become life. Impossible for me to isolate one, I'm afraid."

"I understand," he said.

"We must leave Ruz soon," she warned him.

"The senses of the Ruzniel are equal in every way to those of the Sangyma. Very well, we will get ready to leave."

They walked back to the room Tobia had found herself in before she had lit the fire. Midrak looked about him and touched the shimmering walls,

"Is there anything special about this chamber?"

"I walked through here before preparing the soup. I awoke on that stone slab," she pointed at the floor, "and for a moment I thought ... nothing. A strange and awkward moment. My mind was completely empty, like the city."

"You saw no one?"

"No one. Then I thought there was magic here I couldn't do anything about, so I thought I'd better eat, but whether that was the meal we've just taken or another, I don't know."

"What was this side–chamber?" he asked.

"I can sense laughter here. The talking and teaching, the times of joy and making of new friends. Exchanging names, writing in books, There is animated arguing and suppressed excitement. A place filled with enthusiasm and drawings, paints and music. See here, in classic Ruzniel script is the third of the laws," she read allowed,

'Every Atom Is Made Of Coloured Particles And Space; Within Each Space, There Is One Quantum Of Magic'

"This is a classroom for first year Ruzniel students," he realized.

They moved on, hand in hand along quiet corridors that flowed into each other, like all roads. Their shadows played over bright walls. Tobia's shoes padded softly along the floors. To Midrak, Tobia seemed small, fragile and lost, lacking the decisiveness and power he needed in a companion. Yet he knew that even Tobia might prove the very person he needed. How could he pass any judgment before he knew the whole truth? Before he grew to know her better?

They finally came to a large, windowless room which smelled as sweet as a rose garden and seemed to Midrak to be the centre of a maze of doubts. This place throbbed with voices and yet they were the only ones here. He let go of Tobia's hand.

The ceiling was low enough for him to reach up and touch. The hexagonal room stretched away with more hexagonal rooms leading off from the sides. A hundred entrances and exits, corridors like the ones they had been travelling down, leading off who knew where? He lifted his hands and whispered a few words to his fingers. Between his hands once more, stretched a thin web as if made instantly by a spider strung with fine craftsmanship between his palms, shimmering silver and white. He had set the same web to catch lies not flies on the mountain side. He peered deeply through the skein at each and every corner of the room.

"Such spells won't help you here," came Tobia's voice.

Midrak clapped his hands together and the web vanished.

"All there is to see you can see with your own eyes. The incantations laid by Filvani forbid magicians to be fooled by anything in Ruzniel places."

"Are you beginning to remember now?" he asked her.

"Things just come to me. As if I've never been in any doubt that they're true but when I try to remember, to fix them in my mind, I find I can't," she told him.

"The only spells Palik Tomil has not taught me are those of the deepest Sangyma magic, the others I know well. You must have been touched by a Sangyma. Your forgetfulness must have a purpose. See here," he pointed and read the seventh law engraved on the wall,

'The Spell Of A Sangyma Moves At A Constant Speed Through All Space'

"Do not give yourself a headache trying to recall anything. Knowledge will come when you have need. We must tread, for a while, with the lightness of butterflies."

The stars shone like scattered seeds waiting to burst into flower. The cool evening air funnelled into the corridors and blew her clothes against her skin. Midrak's flowing garments did not move. In all weathers they stayed unruffled. Only his hair lifted slightly to allow his ears to hear the minutest sounds. The breeze brought the scents of many flowers and conjured in Tobia's mind the smoothness of red petals and blue flower stems and small twenty leafed, mauve herbs. Midrak listened for any messages born on the breeze. Nothing came to him. He lowered his head.

"What are you listening for?" she asked, following his movements as a cat follows a mouse's tail.

"Something that is not Ruzniel."

"Maybe what brought you here was Ruzniel."

"Do you possess the power?" he asked, turning to look down at her.

"Certainly not."

"The city." He passed his fingers over his lips in thought, "Does the city cast such power?"

"I don't think so. Maybe you're here without a reason."

"There is always a reason for a magician being on your doorstep. If there were no reason then every cell in my body would have fought my coming here. But nothing in me said my journey was anything less that normal and essential. I must look deeper."

They left the chambers and found themselves in another open courtyard. Here were seats dotted around, each in the shape of a letter of the Ruzniel alphabet. All thirty-six characters were represented.

"This place has some significance?" he asked.

"There's some kind of power here, an atmosphere of calm and deliberation. Different to the rest of the rooms. People visited this place on special occasions. They did not live here. Only special ceremonies and festivals were conducted here," she sounded like a tour guide as the words bubbled out of her.

"This is what I need," he told her.

He sat cross-legged and began breathing in and out like a Buddhist performing yogic exercises. Tobia stood quietly to one side by an old, dry fountain and stared up at the large star which for some reason worried her. The star was new. But how could she, who remembered so poorly, think that? Above her the star grew nearer. She leant against the paper-thin bark of a birch tree brought back from a planet called Earth, her lungs filled with sweet air and the sweetness travelled to her mind. She felt as if her insides were bigger than her body – and she remembered.

They lived by the bridge over the white river. The detached house was circular with a high, domed roof. Far too high for Ruzniel of normal height but her father, Medase, wished to put in a second floor. This was something unheard of amongst the Ruzniel. He never got around to finishing the house and her auburn-haired mother complained about all the wasted space, which they had to heat. She suspected he just liked having a roof line that was higher than any others nearby. The windows were circular, not the modern square ones preferred by Ruzniel with no eye for the charm of traditional building methods. The door opened by a handle, not a sliding panel and the fountain was brushed copper, not steel. All in all their home was singular and stood out from every other building except for the Academy.

A certain number of Ruzniel had to forgo working with magicians to marry and bring up children, so her father had never attended the Academy. Her father liked the old stories and the older ways. He loved the tradition of presenting the six year olds to the tutors, from whom a few would be chosen to attend the academy. They were allowed to play in the park and the tutors watched them, seeking out those who showed instincts and characteristics that were most beneficial in companions. In all the ages of learning none chosen had ever failed to graduate.

But even those who were not chosen, had special skills. Medase had a special skill for painting. The delicacy of his fingers made his work wonderfully intricate and fine. Every leaf of a tree, every hair of a dog, every shadow on the skin, every nuance of colour in the eyes, was painted with the accuracy of a high resolution photograph. He was chosen to decorate many of the best places including the Choosing Rooms where he worked letters of the alphabet into the benches and ornamented the walls with the stories his own father had loved. He had spent many months working in the very courtyard in which Tobia and Midrak found themselves, trying to sort out their puzzle with too few pieces.

Her father met many magicians doing his work because he was asked to work in the private areas of the Academy. He listened to everything that was said in his earshot, and always kept his own counsel. He was never known to gossip. The tutors, over many years, came to see Medase as part of the Academy, often missing him when he was finished in one place before setting up to paint in another. He was in all respects part of the fabric of the Academy so much so that on occasions tutors would walk by him and say,

"Look here, Medase, what do you think about this ... ?"

They would seek his advice on some matter of importance to them. He was too modest to ever reveal if any of the tutors had ever taken his advice, though once or twice he had come home with a particularly satisfied look on his face.

One wet morning when Tobia was six, he decided to take her with him to work in the Choosing Rooms as a birthday present, to mix his paints as he finished his major work on Tegriel and Sanjava. A fine portrait drawn from the memories of those who had seen them. Ruzniel memories were always excellent and every line on their faces would be so exact, once you saw the finished work, you would recognize them the moment you met with them. You would even expect Sanjava to have a rich deep voice and Tegriel to have a tenor voice that sounded clear as a tenor bell. For, like all great Ruzniel painters, Medase could show you in his paintings what people sounded like in real life.

Tobia had been filled with excitement and passed into the Academy as if in a dream. Every stone seemed to call her name. The courtyards were animated and pulsated with learning and wonder. Chosen Ruzniel were busy at sports, or in the library or sitting around talking about some point in the laws. The presence of the highly over-dressed tutors, walking and talking as they went by, filled her with pride, especially as they all nodded at Medase in greeting.

"Well, Medase, what have we here? Your daughter?"

The speaker was a tutor with a fine, fluted voice and kind, green eyes that could draw the best out of his students without a cross word passing his lips. He approached them from the solid iron doorway that led through a hall into his private chambers. Medase was delighted that such a person would welcome his daughter,

"Tobia. She's six today. I brought her to see if painting may be her gift as well. I'm unsure what her special skill is, she excels at so much."

The tutor looked at her and nodded but as they walked away his gaze followed them. He could see there was something strange about her. He had told her years later how he had stood there for quite a while, trying to figure out exactly what, and so been late for his next class.

She and her father worked all morning. Her fingers were quickly covered with paint whilst her father's remained clean. Each brush was used for one colour only and she saw how he allowed wet paint to mix in some areas of clothing and waited for other areas to dry where he needed clarity. As she looked, shadows came to life, mouths seemed to speak, eyes seemed to look at her; there was age in these faces brought out by brown, movement caught in blue and yellow, magic surrounded by pink and grey. Gold in the skin, red upon the hair and glazes making the figures spring from the wall as if alive. Yet, behind the figures in the painting was the threat of nothingness, cold and unwelcome, as if Tegriel and Sanjava stood between her and emptiness. They were caught by her father's magic, mighty, yet lost in their work to all else. She looked at the painting from close and far with intense, wide eyes. She discovered that day that her father was a great painter.

Before lunch the tutors ran in, animated with excitement. Without saying a word they busied themselves preparing the room. Medase put down the paintbrush and put his finger to his lips, telling her to remain quiet. Together they watched from the trellis on which they sat.

The best clothes were brought out and hurriedly put on, then seven graduates were brought out and placed into a semi-circle. Always seven were called, a tradition suggested by the number of the first to be lost in the war. Eyes looked around, feet hurried, hands brushed down and smoothed their clothes. There was noise but no talk, as if heartbeats were communicating with each other making words unnecessary. Then as quickly as the bustle had begun they all stopped moving. Everything went quiet. They all stood stock still, waiting. Tobia held her breath.

A man dressed in satin robes and silk floated in and looked down the line of graduates, turned and went back, stopping in front of each one and holding their gaze for several seconds. Tobia's eyes opened wide. She recognized him. He was behind her on the wall larger than life but caught exactly as he was by her father. The firm mouth, the oval face, the slanted eyes and the curly, cropped hair outlining his skull. He stopped in front of each one but never said a word. Then he took two out of the line and looked at them for a long time, undecided which to choose. He asked no questions nor acknowledged the tutors. The silence sat like a hat upon their heads, always there but easy to forget. So much was going on. All their brains were racing.

"Is that really Tegriel?" Tobia asked in a whisper, wanting to know so she could tell her mother the moment she ran home.

Medase closed his eyes in fright. Not only was speaking forbidden during the Choosing, whispering was pointless in the presence of a Sangyma; they heard everything. The Sangyma turned and seemed intrigued to see them and the painting on the wall. He floated over and studied the painting. He touched Medase's hands.

"This is a fine gift."

Medase swallowed. He had never been addressed by a

Sangyma before and simply said,

"Thank you," before catching sight of all the tutors and graduates looking at him with astonishment. Then the Sangyma's gaze fell upon Tobia and his eyes opened wide.

"Who are you?" The question came out almost as if he felt he should have been introduced before.

"She's my daughter."

The Sangyma put up his hand to silence Medase and spoke softly,

"Daughter of Medase do you have a name?"

"Tobia," she replied firmly.

He looked austere but she knew the inner gentleness in him. She could sense his calm and power. He stretched out a hand and gently took her chin and lifted her face to his. She was not even remotely scared and met his gaze with almost as much interest as he met hers. She counted his front teeth as he spoke,

"You are six," he divined.

"I am."

"You were not chosen. Why?"

"I wasn't brought forward because my family have special skills."

"Will you enter the Academy now?"

"I don't know," she shrugged.

"Then know. Had you been trained Tobia, daughter of Medase, you would have been my choice, young as you are! You must learn the ways of Ruzniel companions. You must study hard. To help you I shall give you a gift which you will find invaluable. You will forget when the time comes to forget. You will remember as and when you need. Your memories will hold the key to your actions. Sometimes you will remember things you have never known. Things only I know." He stopped speaking and looked around at the astonished tutors then back at her, "I wondered why at this late hour I finally had need of a Ruzniel. I was meant to meet you. The fire that burns inside you Tobia will one day help to create wonders."

"I'm not sure ..." she started.

"Understand only this," he said, his voice clear inside her head although no one else heard anything he said, "Your mind and mine will ever be close. Remember this name, Lilah, remember and find her. She will be a sister to you. She is a spellmaker. The foremost of women. Taken from her family ages since she has learned all that may be taught. She has a weapon by her side that cannot be beaten. She has a brother, Midrak. He will search for her. He will come here. Be his companion. Take him to her. The journey you take together will change history."

Her mind was dizzy. She did not see him float away. She did not see him clap a hand upon the shoulder of one of the two Ruzniel and tell him to prepare to leave. She did not hear him order the tutors to place her in learning. She did not see him leave or hear her father whisper into her ear as he stroked her hair,

"That will teach you to whisper in the presence of Tegriel."

"What was that about?" she asked.

"That," said the slightly overweight etiquette tutor Dram, walking over, "was the first time any of us have seen one chosen before they've graduated. Medase, her path is set. She must come to the Academy."

"He saw something in the girl he liked," said Antel, well known for his photographic memory of history books.

"Something he needed," suggested Celium, the foremost woman tutor at the Academy, who was never one to make a point lightly.

"No, by the tone of his voice and the gift he's given, this is something we all need. She's chosen indeed," said Dram, rubbing the back of one hand into the palm of another as he always did when he had reached a decision.

"Why did he take Tullival? Why not take the girl and train her himself," said Dram.

"Fool," muttered Celium, "do you question the ways of Tegriel, the oldest Sangyma alive? He was here at the birth of the universe, he knows things we'll never know. Up to now he's always kept his silence but I feel the time of silence is over. The girl's chosen. That's that. She may well become the greatest Ruzniel that ever lived."

"You think he's been waiting for Tobia all these ages?" asked Antel. "Maybe that's why he never asked for a companion before."

"That may be," said Dram, "who knows his plans? He was ever the hardest to work with and for, never ready to give any hint of how his mind worked."

"He doesn't even like visiting Ruz much he's such a loner," said Celium.

"He said little to give me the impression she's that

important. She's obviously special but that doesn't mean we'll finally find the three," said Dram.

"All in good time," suggested Antel

"He gave a gift to my daughter," Medase said, grinning from ear to ear, "My daughter. The first in the family to go to the Academy."

The tutor they had met when they had first entered nodded slowly at Medase, who was so filled with delight he didn't hear him murmur,

"A great thing and yet a terrible thing at the same time. The three haven't yet been found. We've no answers and within the life-time of a Ruzniel already six years old, great events are forming that may change everything."

He walked away perplexed. She did not know him then but she would grow to know and love Yomiel for his wisdom, care and his unrivalled knowledge of the laws of magic. He would become a second father to her.

Tobia shook herself out of her reverie and looked around feeling a slight chill. The first thing she noticed was the star looked even bigger. Advancing upon Ruz at an incredible speed. She realized this was the danger she had felt for so long. She was sure now. She looked over to where Midrak was still meditating. She had been chosen to be Midrak's companion. She had been trained. She had stayed here to meet him. She had been chosen years before by Tegriel himself. How had he known Midrak would come? What did she possess that no other Ruzniel had ever possessed. She jumped up and ran over to tell Midrak the news.

Midrak was deep in a trance but he heard her soft feet and awoke. His eyes were shallow for a while whilst he came back to her, until he said,

"I cannot find anything."

"I remembered something just now." She told him what she had remembered and he got up and put his hands on her shoulders.

"Forgive me," he said, resting a hand on her shoulder.

"What for?"

"For not trusting you enough. So my Ruzniel companion has been chosen by Tegriel himself. I could wish for no greater and no better."

"I don't like what's happening. Look at how large that star has become in the past hour."

"That," realized Midrak, "is because we are drawing closer together. See the other stars falling away. I understand now. Ruz is going to die as a planet. Tobia, the Ruzniel have gone for that reason and you were left behind because Tegriel knew I was going to arrive. But with such imminent danger, there must be yet another reason why we had to meet here and not a safer place."

"I know where Lilah is to be found."

"Lilah?" he gasped.

"Yes."

"Tegriel has told you about her?"

"Only that she's your sister and a spellmaker," she replied.

"She is the reason I became a magician. All the learning in all the worlds would never reveal where she was until Zaqui was close. She has been shielded by the Sangyma. Tell me everything he said to you about her."

Before Tobia could speak further events that had been building up in front of their eyes all the time came to a head.

First came a murmur that was mournful enough to silence the half formed question in her mind. The murmur harmonized with a low rumble deep within the planet. The gravity of the star began to pull the world apart. The wind picked up and reverberated uneasily against the buildings. The grass changed colour. The sky became dark blue, then grey, then black. Shadows appeared and vanished as if on a passing train. Then the ground wobbled like jelly. For seconds the buildings in the city shivered and shook but stayed firm.

Their own feet felt as if glued to the ground. Without a sound, the seamless thrust of the core of the world sent shock-waves pounding through the city and the buildings were pushed upwards and fell back like so many leaves, crumbling into dust and rubble. Then came a roar as they had never heard, as if thunder had been but a small fire-cracker. As if the sea lashing against the cliffs and turning them to pebbles was but a tiny waterfall. As if whirlwinds were welcoming spring breezes. After the roar came a heat that threatened to burn the hair off their heads. Soon their eyes were clouded by the fog of hot dust. In the darkness everything was noise. Around them the wind swept away stone, suddenly molten and hot, unrecognizable as home, flowing like a river of water into the blackness of space towards the immense star. The cities themselves, being living buildings, cried from the pain of their death.

Midrak placed his hand on Tobia's shoulder and levitated off the ground. In a twinkling they were on the Purple Alps overlooking the destruction. The soil had become a sea and the lower slopes of the mountains turned to water and flowed into the holes opening up beneath them. The sky was a third full of the star and two thirds full of dust. Still the ground shook and blew great clouds into the air which touched clouds of dust pouring from the star as atoms flung themselves in their billions and billions towards each other, and the world became one long explosion, eating everything. Midrak looked and saw one building on the far side of the plains still standing and he gestured,

"There, Tobia, there is strong magic there. That building withstands the end. Come, we will go there. That may be our way out before we are killed."

He closed his eyes and even though she did not, she still saw nothing until they appeared in the central chamber within the building. The mountains had vanished. She had lost her bag of provisions.

Here was sudden stillness. Silence. As if the room were grieving the loss of the Ruzniel heritage. The roar outside was now a distant thudding, as if her ears had been blocked. A fire burned in the darkness and the air was sweet and thick. There was no dust. They could breathe easily.

"Do you know where we are?" he asked her.

"No idea," she told him. He walked forward and a high voice spoke quickly but firmly,

"Who are you?"

"Midrak Earthshaker," he replied, stopping in his tracks.

"You are late," the voice reprimanded him.

"I did not know I was expected."

"Come towards the fire. Tobia stand where you are."

Midrak came forward but hearing a small cry of alarm he turned. Tobia had gone.

"Where is she?" he asked, angrily.

"Safe. You will join her. First, before the final destruction of Ruz, I must talk with you."

"Who are you?"

"I? They called me Fulminar many ages ago."

"Fulminar? The Sangyma? But you ... you ..."

"Were killed. Indeed I was. Just after we knew your sister's power and decided to teach her all we knew. In my death, my spirit was able to come here, to be with the Ruzniel where I have lived on ever since. Here, at the very root of their civilization my essence has been, following them through their streets and walls, even from beneath their feet. Looking, living, guarding. Here I have stayed. Watching and waiting for this day. You have much to learn and know yet Midrak."

"Palik told me to come here. He prepared the Ossendark to open when the time came for me to leave my grandfather. Nothing is as I expected but I trusted Palik and he had his orders from Tegriel himself."

"I have dared not speak all these years for even here the Sangyma may be overheard. My place was to be secret and quiet. The star tearing Ruz to pieces is not a natural phenomenon. This is no dying sun but was sent by the enemy to destroy the Academies. They did not know I was here. They did not know I could save the Ruzniel and the learning. The triumph of my silence is that they are safe until the end."

"How can you live here?"

"The spirit of my mind is in the very fabric of the stone. Now my time has finally come. I chose all those aeons ago to allow my magic to be used to protect and train the Ruzniel. I have survived without my bodily form living as spirits live to fulfil my promise to these strange and wonderful people. Whatever can be accomplished by my presence has been done. Quickly now, so you understand all that has been told to you at this time, what is the fourth law, Midrak?"

"*Magic cannot of itself pass from the unlearnèd to the learnèd,*" recited Midrak.

"Tegriel many years ago gave Tobia a magical gift."

"She has told me," said Midrak.

"Ah, she has begun to remember. Good. Heed her words. Sometimes she will not know what they mean herself but heed them well. Part of Tegriel is within her, for his body, too, is now dead. I am sending you to another place. Lilah is there. She knows she is to find you there and one other. That other is called Rimfelder. He is a poet. Words will be your ally in the days to come. Wherever we can help all our strength will be with you. You will find guidance in strange places, death everywhere and in your time of victory, the knowledge of defeat."

"That I understand."

"Palik Tomil was a wise man. I know he would have schooled you well."

"Fulminar, your knowledge that lives in these stones, can you not live again in flesh and blood?"

"I can but there is no time to prepare the spells."

Fulminar's voice echoed for a mere second as Midrak made a decision that would almost cost them their lives.

"Then use me. Let us go together to the end. Let us face what is to be, as one."

"You are not mentally prepared for the effort of clearing your mind for mine to join you. The preparations take months to ..."

"I did not know I would find such a one as you but I am certain I cannot let your knowledge vanish, now of all times. Come, Fulminar, let Ruz go. As Tegriel is a part of Tobia so become a part of me."

"But in this time, under these conditions what you suggest is far more dangerous than normal. I am revealed, the enemy knows I am here. They beat upon the winds and scream my name. Their power is intense."

"We must try. We are called upon to fight, let us fight as one."

The room exploded. The essence coursing through the stones could no longer withstand the forces of the planets colliding.

Midrak cried out as his body was buffeted by the explosion and his blood boiled as the spirit of Fulminar coursed into his mind and with him came the deadly peril that would almost kill them, the Lazab. Deadliest of the mind–imps. A sinister enemy that had been waiting for this moment for a long time, hiding in the darkest shadows so small an ant would not have noticed them. Ruz died even as the Ossendark taking Midrak to safety closed.

Midrak, his ears still deafened by the explosion, focussed his eyes and found himself standing up to his ankles in a stream running green and thick from foul–smelling pollution. The ringing in his ears blotted out all other noises. The acidic smell brought tears to his eyes and a cough to his throat. He tried to wade out to the bank on unsteady feet and looked up at the sky to see a single, evening sun a safe distance away.

He had a splitting headache, a dry mouth and a feeling of infinite sadness. He was tired. So very tired his legs barely had strength enough to hold his body up. He felt drained, weak and powerless. He collapsed, dying and unconscious, on to the muddy, unknown ground.

Trecrogo

As Tobia cooked soup on her small fire, far away, Demeter had promised himself the biggest bonfire. What he ended up with was pretty big, and some of the logs had been so heavy he had had to drag, rather than carry them over. The wood did crackle in a very satisfying way, just as a camp fire should. The ash gave off a pleasant fragrance. The hazel gave out a lot of heat. There is something warming about seeing sparks swirl and jostle upwards, even when you are not cold. As if you have created your own friend in a strange country and they were enjoying your company. All-in-all his efforts had probably made the biggest bonfire seen on this world in a long time.

Chloe was standing, idly twisting a sycamore twig in her hands, as the light from the flames flickered over her young face. She thought he had made a pretty good bonfire, which was the whole point for Demeter. He only wanted to impress her. He thought that was important if he was going to pass the test and he wanted very much to pass. He had waited his whole life, all twelve years, for this and he wanted to do well. He did not mind the scratches and blisters he had on his fingers and arms from the branches. He didn't mind sleeping in the open or being lost. He just wanted to pass.

He thought trying to catch sparks in his hands would impress her too, so he was spending a lot of time uselessly dancing around chancing being burnt. She was far too clever to be impressed by him trying to show off. He had no idea of that yet but then he had so much to learn about people and places, his being wrong about Chloe almost all the time was hardly surprising. She knew he would be wrong, of course. Her knowledge of these things was deep and instinctive, which is why she had been chosen to be his teacher, despite being the same age. She sat down.

The sparks rose unusually high into the night sky. Odd ones flew sideways and evaporated in the misty, night air. The fire threw out bits of burning ash trying to catch the wings of the flies and moths attracted to the blaze. The blissful warmth permeated their clothes. Not that the night was cold but being alone and outdoors and more or less lost made them both feel in need of some comfort.

Demeter, for now, felt safe. His mind was occupied by the fire and what Chloe thought of him. He had forgotten his aching feet, his tired legs and his moaning about wanting more to eat. Chloe did not feel safe. She was wise to be on her guard, not because this world was unknown to her as far as she knew, but because, and this she definitely did not know, they were going to be involved in a truly momentous battle in less than a day. Knowing something like that in advance would only have made them more anxious and left them unable to enjoy this warm bonfire, over which Demeter had laboured for several hours. The last bonfire they would ever know.

Chloe lifted a long, twisted branch which was burning at the end, smoking where the sap still sizzled and bubbled. Demeter threw another armful of small branches on to the heap.

"The sparks make patterns. Have you noticed?" he asked, rubbing some dirt off his hands and scratching his chin. The fire made his blue eyes sparkle. "They look like burning flies. Look," he pointed suddenly, "they're dancing too."

"I don't think you're growing a beard yet so you can stop scratching," she replied, using the stick as a poker.

Demeter looked at the mud on his knees and sniffed. That's what happens, he thought, when you scramble about in fields collecting fallen twigs and branches then drag them over to a dry-stone wall to build a bonfire.

"The fire makes the stars look brighter," observed Chloe.

"Yeah, right," he said, sitting down.

"They look brighter," she insisted, waving the burning stick in her hand.

"Nothing will ever make the stars look brighter. They're dying, you know that."

"I don't have to believe that if I don't want to."

"Yeah, well, if you don't believe what's obvious to everyone else, you're just being stupid."

"Oh really?" She turned away from him and drummed her fingers on the stick in her hand.

"Well no, not really, but you need a good reason to go against what everyone else says," he said quickly. She pursed her lips, replying

"How about the, 'they look brighter only you're too blind to see', reason?"

"How about you're just being difficult and for the sake of being right?"

"I think they look brighter," she insisted.

She looked upwards. The fire throwing her sitting shadow far behind her where the shape blended seamlessly into the shapeless night.

"Well you're in a minority of one."

"Good," she hugged her knees. "That makes my life perfectly simple."

"And lonely." He stared up at the stars wondering if she were right after all.

"One can't be lonely in a minority of one as long as one likes one's own company," she argued.

"Well, I'd be lonely without you around."

"Not the point," she said flatly.

Chloe breathed in and looked at Demeter in the darkness, the colours in his clothes being played with by the wavering light of the flames. He was the oddest clone. He was so human in so many ways. Well, he would be, she kept saying to herself. Being a clone from a people long vanished from the universe was not a new experience, but this people of all people was strange. There had been a ban on cloning humans for ... well, as long as she could remember and though she was only twelve Chloe could remember a long, long way back because she had been taught to remember other people's experiences. This is something which doesn't take magic but can be a very difficult technique to master.

Her people, the Terika, had been chosen by the Sangyma D'beiht (pronounced Date by his father) who had married into one of their families. The Terika had always kept themselves apart up to the time D'beiht joined them but after that they agreed to train those whom the Sangyma chose. Their distance from other peoples and lack of military prowess made them uninteresting to Rataplan. So they had developed a series of unique tests meant to teach clones a great deal in the shortest time.

Demeter unnerved Chloe at first. She had been apprehensive about meeting him, but now she was getting used to him. She still kept her distance though. She had heard how quickly male clones attached themselves to the women who took the test with them. After all, she was his first experience of company so she had to be understanding.

She was no wiser as to what was going to happen than he was, a fact which carried immense dangers. Her cousin had died when her clone found a hidden explosive. He had smothered the explosive with his body, thinking he would protect her, killing them both. They had had to change the test because of that, but no one could change the new ruling that Demeter had to be on his own, with one person his own

60

age. She stuck out her bottom lip and blew the hair from her eyes,

"Well, I guess I wouldn't like you not being around either as long as we're all alone out here, but that isn't to say I like you being around all the time."

"That's a given," he agreed, kicking a stick with his heel.

"I suppose you must feel uncomfortable, seeing as you're the last of your kind."

"Terrified. This universe is so wild, open, dark and vast." He stretched out his hands into the darkness and went on, "These hills go on forever and the sky seems so much bigger than I could've imagined, as if I've been eaten up by the day and regurgitated by the night. The bonfire doesn't exactly make me feel any better."

"Let the wood burn down then."

"I thought you'd appreciate the warmth, as long as we're stuck in such a strange place."

"We're not stuck. Wei K'un said we're waiting. Waiting is part of the learning experience."

"Yeah, but he forgot to tell us what we're waiting for. We walked all week and look at this place, hundreds of miles of – what? Open countryside, valleys, high hills, woodlands, rivers and not so much as a bird. Not a bee or another person anywhere. Just flies, moths and millions of beetles. Apart from the berries we've been eating, this planet is inhospitable."

"You sound as if this world's unknown to you. This is supposed to be exactly as Earth was. I find the countryside rather beautiful."

He rolled on to his stomach feeling the fire warm his shirt and replied,

"That's not the point. I mean wouldn't you like a few other people around? A few other faces? Not that I'm fed up with your face, not at all. But this place has been around a while so where are the people? Where are the animals? How can you take a test surrounded by emptiness? Where's the challenge?" He dug his fingers into the soft soil as he continued, "I could understand if we had to grow or find our own food but we don't even have to do that. Have they deliberately kept this place empty?"

Chloe knew he was right, and she knew more, she knew why they had kept the original Earth empty of humans. They were never going to clone more than one. She allowed a spider crawling on her shoes to crawl on to her hand. She followed his wanderings along her fingers with her intense, purple eyes,

"I know you're fed up waiting but, you have to understand, patience is a maturing experience. I've had to remind you of that far too many times already."

Demeter hated counting days when there was nothing to do. Hours felt like years so days were the longest things. He feared that the test might be having to live here for months. He felt sick at the thought.

"We were left with a, 'you'll find out everything in time.' Who wants that? I want to know now. Sometimes these magicians say things that have no meaning at all like, 'in the end all things are one', great. I really want to hear about the end of things. These magicians come into your life and speak mysterious thoughts, tell you, you have 'something important' to do, you get all excited and then dumped. Left alone on a deserted planet. A test. A test of what? If I was born for some reason I want to know what and I want to know now." He sat up, "This is so unfair! My time might come and go and I'll never know."

He threw a stick into the centre of the fire, felt the heat on his finger-nails and hurt his eyes staring as the flames happily burnt the bark.

"You can't expect people to tell you everything one-two-three."

"Why not?" he asked.

"You need to find things out for yourself. That's the whole idea of the test."

"I didn't ask for any of this. I deserve a little help. Maybe a lot of help."

"Be creative. No one told you to make a fire, you did quite well without matches. Be as creative about why you're here. Make up a few stories for yourself. Keep your mind free of complaints. Complaining never helps anyone. I'm allowing you in my corner of the field this evening and you brought the fire. Now, you've made me sad. I wish I'd never asked you over."

He looked at her. She shivered slightly as a draft of cool air blew down across the valley, along the walling and up her back.

"I'm not a normal person like you. I work in a different way," Demeter told her.

"A more stupid way or a better way?"

"Well I'm sad too. The fire makes me that way." He paused and looked at her, "What do you do when you get sad?"

"Things come to me when I'm sad. Strange things. Strange thoughts. Don't know why they just do. Odd things I've never thought of before, old things I've thought about many times. Wicked things I wish might happen but I know never will." A smile played over her lips, "I guess sometimes childish things."

"Nothing useful, though, like how to get hold of Wei K'un and get him to get us out of this place?"

"Maybe that crossed my mind," she rubbed her ankle.

"For real?"

"No."

"Then why'd you say so?"

"Put another log on the fire, the stars are getting dull and the sky needs a little painting." Demeter did as he was asked, then said,

"Do you think he's forgotten us?"

"Since when do magicians forget things?"

"Well you can't expect him to remember everyone. No one can, anymore than you can be expected to know everything. I always suspected half his mystery was the way he used to say 'you won't know yet' or ' time will reveal all', as if he secretly knew already. I'll lay odds he knew nothing. Just stringing us along, making us feel awkward and ignorant. He had that way with him, as if he were hiding a bunch of stuff in his clothes and all the time laughing to himself. I don't think he was a very pleasant person."

"He was as he wanted to be. Magicians can remember, believe me they are trained to. Besides even a human being like you doesn't forget people."

"What exactly does that mean? I'm a perfectly ok human aren't I? The cloning was perfect. I look like those films I was shown. Everyone seemed pleased with the result, or were they all lying to me?"

"Not saying much if you are."

The spider had crawled up her arm now and was busy getting lost in her hair.

"See, that's another thing. Everyone always goes quiet when I talk about my humanity. As if I'd reminded them of something bad. Am I suffering from some disease that made me odder than anyone else? Because if I am, the Terika are pretty odd too, let me tell you."

"How would you know what odd was?" she asked him.

"I may be cloned but my feelings aren't. They developed over the past twelve years just like yours."

He looked at himself in the fire–lit darkness. His hands and legs were just like Chloe's but her face shone. He knew his did not. Her eyes shone too, in a way that seemed to make them unreal, as if they lived independently of her. He was sure her eyes were magical but he had never had the courage to ask her about them. And there was something else about her he had noticed. She could blend into the background. She could be standing a few feet away from him and he would lose sight of her. He found her spooky. She did not vanish often for which he was very thankful. She found being almost invisible a very useful way of observing him without him realizing. Seeing how he was changing, how he was developing. Sometimes he appeared to be lost in thought, which was not something her people ever did, and she found watching him, almost hearing his brain working, fascinating.

"I wonder if I'm just what we're supposed to be like," he went on, "Not having human parents teach me means I never know exactly how I should act. What I should say. What I may become. You're all so sure of yourselves. I don't think I'm sure of anything much. I try to be, but living with you people is difficult. Just when I'm certain of something you vanish, or change shape, or worse, speak. I'm sure human beings didn't do that."

"How are you so sure?" she asked him.

"I can't keep up with you all. You think so fast."

"That's just your age."

"Is not."

"Is too."

"I've grown used to you haven't I? If that were my age I'd never change until my age did and I've changed. I don't change or vanish or speak in riddles and I expect the unexpected. I don't challenge the weird. I agreed to come on this test. I'm sure that was a human thing to do."

"Oh?" she stretched tiredly, "how are you sure of that?"

"I've always liked adventures for as long as I can remember. Did humans like adventures?"

"Who knows," she said.

"Do you have any idea?"

"No."

"Helpful tonight."

"Though," she added thoughtfully, "Wei K'un told me once you were a strange race given to meaningless, terrible wars yet great acts of selflessness. Whatever that means. I know enough to know you must be exactly what you feel you want to be. Though your race vanished from the universe there are still many stories told about them. They had quite an impact one way or another on other peoples. At least, some few of them did." She rested on her arm, her face facing the fire as she lay on the ground, "The special ones," she ended.

"He told me many races breathed a sigh of relief when humans lessened in strength," said Demeter. "When I asked him why he said, 'because too many of them interfered in other peoples' lives, and rarely to any good effect'. He said we were presumptuous, nosey and interfering nuisances who believed our right to know something overruled every other consideration. Yet, he added, some of us were given to acts of incredible brilliance."

"He used the word interfering?"

"Yes. Our greatest failing, he said, was we never just passed something by, we always got involved. As if we knew how to do things better or wanted to do better. We had this ability to solve problems and so we thought we could always solve problems no matter what they were. More often than not, we were the problem because what we found was only a problem in our minds and not to anyone else."

She was thoughtful for a moment,

"You don't think he put us here to stop you getting involved in something do you?" she suggested.

"Involved in what, I'd like to know?"

"Exactly my point."

"What does that mean?" he asked, biting his lip.

"Well, how are we to know what you're not to get involved in, if we're here and uninvolved?"

"None the wiser, and out of the way you mean?" he said.

"Yes."

"Would Wei K'un do that?" he asked, wrinkling up his nose in disgust.

"Nothing to stop him. Though, to tell you honestly, they would never have cloned you, or kept back the material to clone you, if they hadn't thought you vital."

"Me? Vital. That's a laugh. Took me all evening to light a

simple fire."

"Lighting fires may not be what you're particularly good at and the time taken to do whatever you need to do, might not matter."

"Oh, come on! You don't keep the 'vital' in the dark. You don't keep the 'vital' uninvolved. You don't put the 'vital' on an empty planet and walk away without waving."

"You're here to take the test, once you've faced and lived through the dangers you'll be better prepared."

Sparks flew out of the fire and fell near Chloe. Demeter immediately got up and stamped them out on the ground.

"They wouldn't have hurt me," she told him.

"Can't be too careful," he responded. "I thought Wei K'un was meant to be looking after us? I mean we should be protected from any dangers that might kill us."

"All night you've been saying there's nothing here. We've tramped around for seven days and not even had to cross a raging river, now all of a sudden you're whining about dangers."

"You brought up the possibility," he complained.

"This test could be anything, you knew that when we started. Anything. All we know is, we must continue east, which we've done." She frowned. He should be ready to know how dangerous the test can be but he seemed really put out by the thought. She continued,

"Nothing has happened yet so we'll just keep going east until something does."

"What if we end up where we started?"

"Then we'd have walked around the entire planet and be even more tired than we are now."

"That might take years," he moaned.

"You'd have had the time to grow up then, wouldn't you?"

"So would you."

"Yes, I guess I would. Maybe that's what we're supposed to do."

"Since when?"

"Since you suggested we might have been abandoned."

"I never said that," he grumbled, knowing he had.

"Then what did you say?"

"I said we shouldn't be abandoned."

"Kindly stop standing over me, go over there."

She pointed deliberately at a spot a few feet away. He walked away and sat up against the stone.

"All this talk of not knowing, of not trusting Wei K'un, of growing up alone. You're rambling," she told him.

"Would you like that?" he asked.

"What? Rambling?"

"No just the two of us being stuck here for years."

She decided to change the subject quickly.

"You know, I think there are less stars in the sky than earlier. The long line that was there, the Wand, they're definitely brighter than before. And look there, where a circle of stars are vanishing one by one."

He strained his neck looking upwards,

"For once I think you're right."

"Then for once you're thinking."

"There, look! I swear a star just vanished," he pointed.

"Which one?"

"Well I can hardly show you if the thing's not there now. Look where my finger's pointing." She stared at the emptiness.

"If you can see a single star vanishing things are speeding up." Then she added, "At last! Look, the dawn is beginning to rise now we'll be able to walk on. You've talked all night."

"Half the night was taken up with making the fire," he reminded her.

"You're going to be tired all day."

"I'll live."

The first hints of light flowed across the wakening land like an incoming tide, and the hidden slowly came to be seen. As they watched the last of their fire burn out, the night melted away into shadows cast by trees, rocks and old walls no human being ever built. They both looked ahead of them out of the valley and on to a huge plain that was the flattest thing either of them had ever seen. A vast savannah devoid of all animals. What kept the grass so short with no grazing animals around neither of them knew. The tree line along the valley side suddenly vanished as if the last, tall trees were too scared to drop seeds upon the open ground. Or perhaps the soil was poisonous to them. Or, perhaps, there was magic at work.

They both walked the last few miles towards the savannah and without a word started to trek across. Drawn, as ever, by the sun that cast special shadows for them to follow. Shadows which swept away from them although there was nothing to cast any shadow, anywhere. On this plain their own bodies cast no shadows. Chloe walked with a firm, small step which Demeter, an inch smaller, always followed. He would never grow any taller. He watched her arms swing as she walked and her sharp eyes narrow as she looked far ahead.

After they had walked for three hours Chloe stopped. For days she had been the one pointing things out, as Demeter always missed the obvious. He looked, but so often only ever saw things at the last minute. She despaired of ever teaching him anything. He had always been like that, as if something had gone very wrong in the connections in his brain.

Why did she have to teach this boy everything?

Was Wei K'un testing her as much as Demeter?

Truth to tell, right now, she was unsure of this assignment herself. She tried to fight the uncertainty. She knew if the teacher was unsure, the lesson could not be learned. She could never admit to such thoughts out loud. She rarely said anything out loud about her doubts. She always felt that would show weakness. She had to be strong, if not for Demeter then for herself.

Why Wei K'un would be testing her left her mystified. Not surprising as she had no real idea of the forces gathering who would join them shortly. The thought that this was no test had not yet entered her head. She would guess that later on during the day when at last she would wonder just whom Demeter was cloned from, and begin to understand that the human being whose DNA they had kept secret and alive, had been no ordinary human being, and that Demeter's were one set of shoulders upon which the fate of everything rested. Now, however, as the smell of the camp fire dissipated from their clothes and the sun was hottest, she saw something for the first time that opened up this future for her. Unexpected, huge and standing directly in their path.

"Do you see anything ahead?" she asked him softly, stopping in her tracks.

"Lots of grass and a heat haze."

"Anything else?"

"No. Oh wait a second, yes." He screwed up his eyes trying to focus, "Something almost shimmering in the distance. Your eyes are far better than mine I can't make out whats there."

"A building. A big building. A huge building. Looks like a mountain even from this distance. Come on, this is the first sign of any life we've seen."

She grabbed his arm and pulled him after her, excited at seeing something that might be their destination. A building spoke of people, civilization, hot food! Traditionally, as Chloe knew, anything that seemed strange had the hidden tasks inside which Demeter would have to tackle. At last, she thought, they would soon be finished and home. She could not have been more wrong.

The building, as they approached after walking all morning, turned out to be a huge stone wall, rising sheer out of the Losek soil stretching in both directions for as far as they could see. Along the rounded side, small stones were jutting out on the wall's surface. A set of steps curled slowly up the vast, smooth, circular side until they too vanished from sight. The wall was so large the sun's movement visibly tracked across the surface. Some parts were always in shadow.

"Dangerous way in," said Demeter, looking at the steps. "Narrow. No hand rails."

He looked at her as she stood looking at the steps. He knew that look,

"Me first or you?" he asked.

"Do you have a head for heights?" she asked him. He replied looking upwards,

"I really don't know."

"By the time we get half way up there you'll feel like you're on the side of an exposed cliff. How's your balance in a high wind?"

"If you think we should be climbing up there, to find out what's inside, we have to go whether I'm scared or not. Unless you think someone is going to open a hidden gate down here, come out and see who we are first."

"Tests are never that easy."

"Let's get going then," he said.

"You first."

"Why?"

"If you slip, I'll have half a second to catch you."

"But you'll be behind me. What happens if you slip?"

"You'll have half a second to say goodbye to me. Now go."

Her voice was full of authority. She pointed up the steps, her face the picture of determination. The small, stone steps were flat. Every one of them was the exact same size. Their feet fitted them well. They held out their hands against the wall as they went. As they got more used to the climb, they leant slightly into the wall, with just one hand each, letting their other arms hang by their sides. As they got even higher, they turned closer into the wall and began using two hands again. Having both hands against the wall, even though there were no hand holds, made them feel safer.

They walked up the steps circling the wall but though Demeter looked down, he never saw any steps below him so he knew they had not encircled the whole building, or so he thought. The idea that the steps were vanishing from behind them as they progressed did not occur to him. Not a single window greeted them as they continued their climb upwards and after a few hours his legs were feeling like lead weights. His knees ached. His fingers were tired of the feel of stone. The sun beat down on them. He was hot and sweaty despite the breeze. He stopped climbing. He was breathing heavily.

"You have to keep on," she told him, "there's no way we can sit on these steps to rest."

"You know, I think we're so high the wind is deafening me, I thought you said we couldn't stop."

"I did. Now move."

"I'm tired," he moaned.

"Do as you're told. This is no time to argue."

"We'd be in the clouds if there were any."

"Keep going I said, if there's a storm and we're caught here we'll be blown to our deaths."

Demeter shivered. He began to climb again muttering to himself,

"What happened to patience?"

"Everything has a place," she replied, prodding him in the back. He forgot she could hear better than any cat. "Go," she insisted.

By the end of the afternoon, with the sun beating down, their legs feeling like jelly and panting hard, they finally reached the last step and lifted themselves over a parapet on to a large, stone floor with thankful sighs. They sank down on their backsides for a few minutes, grateful to have managed the steep climb; feeling exhausted. Then curiosity filled them both and they sat up, surveying the scene below them from their high elevation.

"I can't feel anything but pain in my legs," he moaned, rubbing his knees. "Another step and they'd have fallen off."

"That was a tough climb," she agreed. "We're certainly

not going down again," she said, as she leaned over the side and looked straight down. The last steps were sliding into the wall below them. Demeter gulped in shock.

"Good thing they didn't do that when we were on them."

"You don't understand much about magic, do you?" she told him.

"Why? Does that look good to you?"

"That's meant to be. The steps were put there for us. Now no one can follow us up. Which you'd have realized if you could think logically."

"I gave up thinking after the first ten thousand steps."

"About the same time you gave up counting them?"

"How do you know I was counting them?" he asked.

"You moved your lips."

"My back was towards you how do you know that?"

"Look at that view," she gasped, purposely not answering him.

Hundreds of miles of the countryside they had been walking through all week, spread out before them. They could even see why they had not seen the building long before they actually did. The valley they had walked in meandered, tucked under their line of sight. They slowly stood up and saw in the distance, over the hills, the mountains beneath which they had walked. Wei K'un had chosen their path well. This building was meant to come as a surprise.

Around them, on the vast roof, were many stairways vanishing into the unlit corridors below. There were no sounds and no movement. They were as alone up here as they had been on the savannah. The stones were warm because they had been heated by the sun for several hours. That was not the only comfort, there was also the smell. A sweet smell. Like a rose garden. Chloe felt as absolutely safe as a teddy bear must feel being cuddled by a child.

"Well this feels good. Even though we don't know who built this place or why yet," she said.

"What now?" asked Demeter.

"We should try to find a way in."

"You look as if you half expect us to be attacked."

"I don't know that I do, and I don't know that I don't."

Demeter wiped some of the sweat off his forehead,

"I thought you knew everything about the test. I never anticipated I wouldn't live until you mentioned everything being dangerous. Now you tell me you can't even recognise danger one way or another."

"Are you still harping on about that?"

"I'm not harping!"

"Everything that lives has enemies. None more than human beings. We ought to go inside," she said.

"What if we get lost?"

"Do you know where we are right now?"

"No, do you?"

"No, but I've a hard time thinking people already lost can get lost."

"They can get more lost!" he argued.

"We might also get less lost. Come on, which of these stairways should we take?"

"You're asking me?"

"I just did."

"How about that one."

He pointed to the nearest staircase. There were no signs or directions. She looked for runes on the stones. Nothing. They walked down.

"You know if this goes all the way to the ground and we find nothing there, I'm going to feel very stupid," he muttered.

Whatever else he was thinking of saying he never said for, quite unexpectedly, the stairs ended and they walked into a large, round room, lit by lamps that came on as they entered. There was a long table running down the longest wall, with several matching chairs in ornate oak. Smells of spices and fresh water were everywhere. As she looked she could almost hear the voices of the bears who had worked here. The clatter of metal on stone, the bustle of thousands moving around a city of stairs. Walking to and from their homes, their places of work, their friends, their parties. Skipping up and down stairs, along stairs, across stairs. Broad staircases and short steps. Some made in stone, some in special woods that can hold spells. She could almost hear the stone cutters and the carpenters. Almost but not quite. But one thing she found strange. None of them had lived in this walled city after they had completed the building.

"Is there no one here?" asked Demeter.

"I don't think there is," she answered, somewhat wary and yet entranced by what she saw.

"Is an empty building any use to us?"

"Everything is of use to you when you don't know where or what you're doing. The tests may not involve other people. On the other hand, others may be coming who are not here yet."

She walked around the table and gently caressed the walls with her finger tips,

"The work that has gone into this place is immense," she stated.

"A stair city."

"That's a fair observation."

"Escalator city would have been better. Whoever made this place put in too many stairs. My muscles felt as if I were floating by the time I finally reached the top."

"Which should tell you a thing or two."

"Such as?"

"A place so high is built for defence," she told him.

"You do know where we are then?"

"No, I've never been here before."

Demeter looked puzzled and then he shrugged,

"I know, I know. My test. My learning experience."

"Well?" she asked.

"I would like to learn to sit down once in a while," he replied.

"Take a chair, maybe the legs will grow wings and fly you out of here."

"Do chairs do that?"

"Some do."

"Well, that would be something I suppose," he said.

He flopped down on one of the chairs, half hoping, but nothing happened.

Chloe looked around and walked some way down the room which was so empty and tranquil. The first rush of memories which the stones had let out, like a vivid aroma, evaporated as she moved around. The stones were like sensitive flowers that closed at the brush of her feet and the sound of her breathing. She reached out to them and they gave her ideas of great bears following blueprints to the letter. Fitting stones side by side to within an atom's width. Taking care the stairs were exactly where they were supposed to be and every step the correct size.

She realized that she and Demeter were to complete what the bears had started. This seemed to her to be the test. Then she bit her lip. If she was right, why had they not been sent straight here? Why had they had to walk for days to get here?

"Well?" he asked, breaking into her thoughts.

"Well nothing. Come on we'd better look elsewhere."

"More stairs I suppose," he complained.

"Lots more."

"I still wish someone was with us to tell us what to do."

"I've told you ten times a day, you have to work things out for yourself."

"What chance do I have if you don't even know what's going on?"

"That thought did cross my mind."

"See, you've no confidence in me at all," he said.

"That's not true. I agreed to accompany you on this test. I must've had some hope nothing awful would happen to me."

"I thought you chose to teach me."

"No way, you're not that important."

She turned away and walked down the hallways. He followed her like a lost lamb.

"Anything can happen," she warned.

"Is nothing an anything?"

"Sure but not very challenging when we're inside an unknown building that resonates with mystery."

"Right now, I find nothing a challenge that's much easier on my aching legs."

"I like things to happen. Don't you think life should be filled with challenges?"

"You can have too much of the things you enjoy."

"Challenges are icing on the cake of living."

"Look, walking that long dangerous stairway entrance was challenging. Staying outdoors in the night was challenging. Being bored and staying cheerful is challenging."

"No, the challenges must be extreme. Like wild creatures biting at you, imprisonment by magic spells. Besides your things aren't at all challenging, they're everyday. The real challenges are ..."

"Oh I've heard all about magic and the Sangyma. Like chairs with wings I suppose. I never saw Wei K'un so much as conjure an orange. I'll bet magic doesn't even exist."

"Magic and science spring from the same understanding of atoms. But whereas science explores the atom for raw power, magic emphasizes that power only ever changes our power to change."

"Oh great, now you sound like he used to when he wanted to be mysterious."

"Strange things do happen and someone or something is always behind them," she insisted.

"Sure they do and explainable things happen too, and I like the explainable."

"Then how do you explain the unexplained things?" she asked him.

"Things waiting for an explanation."

"The universe doesn't sleep waiting for you to find things out. You're so boring. Not like other clones at all. At least they have imaginations but then we've never taught a human before."

They had walked passed all the doors that were around the room.

"I have an imagination," he defended himself, "I imagine being home, away from this place, having a sumptuous warm bath and a hot drink."

"Hmm, well at least you're displaying the selfishness they said was the mark of your species."

"I'll make you a drink too, if you like."

"Too late! Come on we'll go down here," she suggested.

"No, I would go that way instead."

"You arguing?"

"Just suggesting that the other way seems better to me."

"You haven't chosen the way we've gone once this whole week and now you think you can argue with me just because we're in a building? I'm the one who got us here, not you."

"I just feel mine is a better way that's all."

She stared at him. She sniffed. Chloe knew to trust people's sincere feelings. He was annoying and often seemed lost but for once his face was showing no confusion. Maybe this place was talking to him in some subliminal way.

"Ok," she consented, "lead the way."

For most of the day they walked the stairwells and rooms of this massive city finding nothing but more passages and rooms, more stairs and halls. The air was refreshing, though still. They explored until the sun was falling outside which they did not notice because the rooms were windowless and well lit. Chloe did not tell him that she fully expected to run into trouble around every corner and was quite disappointed when nothing happened.

In the late evening when they happened upon three staircases in a row Demeter chose the middle one. He had chosen all the ways they had walked never hesitating once. This time he hit the jackpot and Chloe felt that without him knowing, he had definitely been guided by some instinct tied to this stair city.

This building and Demeter were made for each other, as if this place were his natural home. She had heard of such empathy before, as if places carried a fingerprint only certain individuals could decipher but she had never thought such a vast, secret place could be one of them. This perfectly made, impregnable fortress filled with secrets and magic, was his birthright. Chloe felt awed. She realized for the first time that whatever was going to happen was going to be extraordinarily big.

They entered a small room and at last they found a glassless window set into the wall, low and broad, looking out on to a twilight sky. They saw the sun going down and realized they had walked right through the building and were looking out of the far side. Beneath them was an ocean lapped against the walls. They had walked miles without realising. The sea was calm. Above the water, for the first time, they saw a stream of long, thin clouds, lazily floating. They were both so relieved to see the outside world, like meeting an old friend after so long seeing nothing but stone walls, they stared for a long time, even after the night had fallen, when the depleted stars came out and the water sparkled as the light was caught in the waves.

As Demeter watched the stars coming out, Chloe walked around the room and saw the charts that were hanging from the walls. She looked at them, tracing her fingers over the words. These were the first writings she had found in this place and she drank in everything they revealed. Demeter heard her gasp. He turned to face her.

"What have you found?" he asked.

"I don't believe this!" Her finger-tips were tracing across the images and letters.

"You don't? I thought you believed everything?"

"What makes you think that?"

"Well, anyone who believes anything is possible must believe everything. Otherwise if they ever said 'I don't believe that' they're saying, 'not possible', aren't they? And they can't say that."

"The more you talk the more sense you make. That should worry me but somehow doesn't."

"You're warming to me," he joked.

"Or becoming indifferent," she argued. "Look at this. Do you know what this is? No, silly question you would never know what this is, want me to tell you?"

"Please," he nodded.

"Ok, this is a chart about the birth of worlds. Here look, at the top is a sun, this is called on this chart Ketanya, now the sun breaks in two and here is born Herat and Rathe, from Rathe comes Teh'ra and from Herat comes Arthe. And look here ... here is the one that amazes me here, this is the last world born to this family of planets ... Earth."

"Earth?"

"An important world known throughout the universe, the home of so many great beings, famous magicians have fought here and terrible people were born here. Your homeland. Well of your people. But this chart is new. Look. Earth vanished aeons of years ago, and here on the chart this loop and circle what does that look like?"

"The walls of this place."

"Exactly, this building is on the planet Earth, not a planet like Earth as I first thought."

"Wait a minute we're on one of the most magical places in the universe?"

"Most important," she corrected, "This is the worst!"

"Worst? I thought you would have loved to be on such a important world in the universe what with all your talk about challenges."

"I am but Earth, the real Earth, isn't supposed to exist anymore."

She rushed from one chart to the next, her fingers following the patterns that made no sense at all to Demeter.

"Oh good we're dreaming," he said.

"We're here but ... here the planet is destroyed. Exploding when the sun in the solar system cooled and died. But that's just stories. The Sangyma hid the truth."

She ran her eyes over the charts darting from one to another. At that moment she looked exactly like a scholarly, second year Ruzniel, finding something new about magic that overturned everything they thought they knew about the universe.

"The stories of how humans were expelled from Earth are real. People have always said this world had been blown to pieces. Earth was a place where there are more beginnings than endings. The only such place in the universe. But the Sangyma themselves saved this world. We're on Earth. Earth was saved. I've been walking all over a world Crilodach doesn't know still exists. With a real human being."

"You weren't expecting anything like this were you?" he said.

"This is no test. We weren't sent here to test you at all."

Her words rang like bells in the room. Her voice had deepened slightly. The import of what she was saying sank into his brain as if the words were water flowing into a glass. He felt them inside himself and his confusion and loneliness congealed in his stomach and formed a knot. He was shaking. They stared at each other for a moment, her purple eyes almost glowing, and swiftly darting from the charts to his face, as if his face were part of the message. Part of the charts.

"This is the real thing," she said. "This is the planet on which your people evolved. This is your home. From here humans went to other planets and worlds. Here was found the Tree of Life, hidden since the dawn time, from where magic flowed outwards like rivers. But to protect the magic the Sangyma expelled the humans and they, cast out, began an odyssey which took them to many places until they died out. They were too unruly. Too clever. They would not share with others. Many sided with the enemy. They did a terrible thing here though I don't know what. The charts say nothing. This fortress must have been built after they had gone. Who knows when. And who really knows why the Earth was hidden. Why no one was allowed to live here anymore."

She sighed. Beneath them they heard the sea lapping against the walls of the city and for the first time Demeter thought he could feel the memories in the stones, the builders walking about. The talk and excitement of a people long ago dead who left their fortress perfectly intact and waiting for ... him?

"Wow," he said slowly, "then this place is like ... mine?"

"Not a bit of it! But bringing you here makes sense, for whatever we're supposed to do, you will have an instinctive understanding of this planet. That's why you found your way to this room. Why you seemed so sure of where we were going for the first time since we were left here. Why we had to spend a few days here first and not come straight to this fortress."

"There's a reason for that?"

"To acclimatize Earth to having a human being living here again."

"Oh, of course, nothing to do with me finding my legs."

"And you too I suppose."

"Who's this enemy we sided with?" he asked her.

"Don't let that worry you. Don't be eager to know about It or meet It until you have to."

"Not sure I'd get anywhere without your help," he told her, "I don't know how to read those charts or even which way up they go."

"True. That must be why I'm here with you. At least in the beginning. Until we've found out how this place works."

"Eh?"

"Come on," she ordered taking down the charts and rolling them up without saying any more.

"Why? Where are we going?" he asked, confused.

"I need more light and a long table. We're going to go back to that large room we first entered. There we can lay all these out and see them properly."

"More walking."

"You are such a moaner."

"What do we do when you have read these?" he asked, his arms filled with the charts as she rapidly rolled them and threw them at him.

"Then we'll be able to work out why this place was built and what the fortress is here to do."

"Exactly, I was wondering about that part. I mean what can a building do?"

"All depends upon who the designers are, who the builders are and what materials they used."

"All adding up to what?"

"A purpose," she said, as if he were really stupid.

"So this place has a purpose?"

"Most definitely." He clung to the charts and peeping over them said,

"Is that why we're here, to find out what this fortress' purpose is?"

"Better than that."

"Really?"

"Stop being dense. They don't need us to come along and find out what the purpose is, they already know. But obviously they're not the ones who will use this place otherwise they'd still be here. We're here. They're not." She rapped him lightly on the head with a rolled chart, which she then added to the pile in his arms.

"Oh I see, we're the ones who'll use whatever this place does."

"Or be used, yes. Looks that way."

"Or be used?" He did not like the sound of that at all. "Are you saying this place is alive?" he asked.

"Not only a mind has self awareness, there are lots of things that know they exist." Demeter looked around wondering what a building's eyes looked like,

"Presumably we also need a reason to use whatever this fortress does."

Chloe stopped on the stairs and looked down at him. She breathed in,

"Yes we'll need a reason." She was quiet for a moment. "And we'll need allies. Time. Knowledge. And most of all we'll need you to think straight."

"Really? More people? Is that where Wei K'un has gone, to get more people?"

"I don't know. All I know for sure is that we must learn all about this fortress. Once we know how things work here we can await anyone, or any thing, that turns up."

"You sound like this is going to be hard."

"For you, certainly."

"And not for you?"

"For me all things are hard, my life was not supposed to be easy. But for you, this is a great challenge. No, don't ask me I don't know exactly and won't be drawn. Come on, we have to get to that table and work on these charts if you want to know." She stopped.

"What's the matter now?" he asked, almost bumping into her. She was looking around very lost.

"I don't know the way back."

"Oh that's easy we go up the next steps, right, third staircase on left, second right, third left, fourth right, down a set of small steps, seventh left second right, up a long stairwell, along the passage, second left, fifth right, ninth left, eighth left, fourth right, left hand stairs, back to that long passage and by that time we're half way there and then

..."

"How do you remember so well?"

"Just do."

"Is that the way we came?"

"I've no idea. All I know is, that's the way back."

She looked at him and for the first time that he remembered, Chloe let her face break into a slight smile. His innate knowledge of the way back confirmed everything she suspected. Their destinies were bound up with this place.

"You go first. I don't remember all the numbers."

"Ok."

Demeter knew what she meant about this place being alive. He could sense the memories held by the stones and feel himself getting more and more comfortable within these walls. He felt a great power residing here. This fortress was a weapon. He also knew the fortress controlled the sea. He wondered a great deal about what kind of enemy they might be facing. About magical planets that are supposed to have vanished, and about how he was completely ignorant of the enemy he might have to fight. He thought about how human beings were so bad they had to be eradicated but the planet they evolved upon was magical enough to take centre stage in the universe. He also thought about Chloe.

Chloe was also thinking deeply.

At the long room beneath the parapet, they unrolled all the charts and put them together on the table. Demeter looked but he was unable to discern anything useful in them because the alphabet was strange to him. Even Chloe was having problems. But the charts all fitted into a pattern with the animals drawn to represent parts of the sky. Chloe hummed to herself as she walked around the table looking, stopping every now and then to get her bearings.

"This is definitely the Earth," she said.

He could feel the awe in her voice as she said the word.

"Why is this fortress empty but for us?" he asked her.

"Because no one else is here yet."

"If that's true then by your logic, we're meant to be here first."

"What do you think?" she asked.

"I don't know, you're the teacher."

"Not all the time. You should know more about this place than me."

"Well I don't."

Demeter went and sat on one of four large chairs set along the walls and stuck his chin on his knees, wrapping his hands around his feet and gently rocking on his backside. He looked at the floor. There, near the chair, were four slots in the floor. He looked at them and saw they were the only slots in the stone. Everywhere else was smooth. Even he knew, those slots must gave been put there for a purpose. He got down from the chair and stuck his finger in them one by one, circling them and then looking at his finger. They were spotless. Not a piece of dust in any of them. That was odd enough, he thought. One in the corner was near the chair leg and he could see the base of the leg looked the size of the slot.

He got up and pushed the heavy chair sideways and forward and found the legs slid into the slots with ease. Slotting down, as if set in cement, the high back broke at the seat and showed a hinge which folded down forming a small table. Chloe heard the noise and looked up.

"What are you doing?"

"I didn't break anything!" he whined.

She walked over and touched the chair. She looked around the room and saw three other chairs that were exactly similar.

"Lets have a look at the others."

They found each chair was near such slots. Chloe immediately tried to push one, but found she couldn't budge any of them. Only he could move them. They responded only to his touch. One by one Demeter pushed them into place while she stood close by him. Each was hinged and the high backs all folded flat, until they formed the four corners of a large rectangle, around the room. No sooner were they finished then the table soundlessly, suddenly split in two. Each section moved until each side had slotted over the chairs on each side. Then, in the space left between them, the flooring opened, turning downwards, revealing a new staircase of bright red stairs each decorated with dragons and lions. Two of the charts fell from the table on to the steps. Demeter looked at Chloe and then stepped forward on to the first step to retrieve them. They walked down. The walls were etched with the same writing as on the charts. Demeter picked them up, rolled them and slid them on to the floor which was now at forehead height.

"Well done," she congratulated him.

"What did I do?"

"You've helped to unlock the key to this fortress. I might have been reading for hours to work out there was a hidden set of steps beneath the table."

"Just luck," he admitted.

"Never be indifferent to your actions, they all have consequences. We now know you touching something might help us." Demeter laughed at her,

"Or I might blow the whole place up," he said, slapping the side of the wall.

The stone he hit quivered and the wall reverberated so violently they thought for a moment he was going to be crushed. They both ran back up the steps in terror, Demeter slipping and bruised his leg in his haste. He clambered out as the roof opened up above the table, and the stairs moved like an escalator for several seconds until a single, short beam of intense light shot into the air from beneath them, filling the room with a blaze of blue. They put their hands over their heads and lay stretched out on the floor fearing to look. Then, with a slam which reverberated through the room and forced them to cover their ears with their hands, the roof closed. The stairs stopped moving, the sounds dissipated. Slowly, they got up. They looked at the stairs and the roof and then at each other, their ears still ringing. They were breathing hard with alarm. Their hearts thumped like rocks inside their chests.

"What was that?" he asked, amazed.

"Any of several things. Maybe a power surge, maybe a short circuit or ..." she hesitated, "maybe a signal."

"Sent to whom?"

"I've no idea but I guess we may well find out soon enough because now they'll know we're here."

"Will that be a good or bad thing?"

"I hope the charts can tell us. I won't beat about the bush, you must have some inbuilt connection with this place. Everything you touch does something. Why I wasn't told I don't know but maybe ignorance is a weapon too. Maybe that's what the stories about the human race are all about, that sometimes you need not to know. Maybe what we're here to do battle with and whatever we're here to fight, is watching us. Scanning brains to glean information. Be careful, OK! Be very careful until I get to grips with these charts and work out what's happening. Better not touch anything else for a while."

"Until you say the word I'm not leaving your side."

Chloe took a deep breath and went over to the charts and stared at them. This was going to take a long time and she instinctively knew sleep was out of the question. Her eyes never wavering, she made connections, moving the charts, double checking, going back over her work to make sure she was doing things right. These charts were made to be hard to decipher and even as she looked she knew they could lie to her if they did not trust her.

She saw a new look in Demeter's face. A determination. An intense interest. She was glad. He was beginning to focus on the events of the past days and understand there was real work to be done. He had finally taken the first step on the journey to whatever he had to become. More than that, he had suddenly begun to grow up. His mind was alive to the power of magic.

Rimfelder

Rimfelder paced his room like a tiger baffled by the bars of a steel cage. He was bursting with pent up energy, as if a spring were coiled inside him which he longed to release in some kind – any kind – of action. He had no idea what to do. The battle, though over, still raged in his head, ringing with all the shouts and battle cries of the desperate fighters. His brain was still afire with the unwelcome spectacle of the previous day, when they had stormed the city and won their freedom. He wanted to be far away but, to be separated from everyone he knew, frightened him. He could not stop thinking. He could not relax. Daylight was becoming a torture to him because shadows transformed into vivid memories.

His world was in confusion. Everything he had grown up knowing had somersaulted in the last week. There were no certainties in their new–found freedom. Anything he did not understand became an immense worry. Why did there seem to be less stars in the sky than yesterday? Yesterday? Could he really count the hours back to when everyone had been oppressed by the tyrant? When he had been a criminal, watched and hunted, by the tyrant's guards? Yesterday seemed years, not mere hours, ago.

Riven with anxiety he needed to sleep but he was scared of his dreams. Fidgety, yet longing for rest, watchful of everything through eyes still red from tears, looking for clues he could not find to a puzzle he did not fully grasp. He knew something was going to happen that was dreadful and terrifying. But for the life of him he could not imagine what was going to happen, or what could be more terrifying and deadly than what had already taken place. Anything? Everything? Something was coming. No, 'she' was coming. But who was she? He did not have the energy or time to sort out his troubled thoughts.

The battle they had fought to conquer the city had filled him with such bitter images. How could one sit still after that? The sight and smell of his first battle. The sounds that drown out all other noises. To see and feel the blood and the anger in others and in yourself, the sense of the tides of battle as hope flowed into despair then became victory within the same night. He had never seen anything like their fighting before. The vivid picture, painted on the canvas of his mind, underscored everything he could see, everything he could feel and everything he could hear. He had never been a soldier yet he had been right in the middle of hundreds of fighting Arvernat. What mighty warriors they were. He did not believe they were troubled by thoughts like his.

This was the picture that was engraved upon his mind, a red canvas hanging behind his aching eyes, mirror-plated upon his retina. Not only did he see their bloodied images in his memory but wherever he looked, there rose out towards him mis-shaped bodies turned into ghosts by the weapons of war. Dead arms and faces. Broken bits of people still in pain even after death, or so he imagined. In every shadow and crevice of the walls he saw the living, dying and wounded, twisted by the art of war into broken puppets that no longer moved. The running feet, the flaying hands, the wide eyes, open mouths gasping, all seemed to be sewn, like a memorial tapestry, into the very air he breathed until his chest hurt and he coughed out sorrow with every breath.

He closed his eyes. He still saw the faces, the terror in hundreds of eyes, the agony of their wounds, their deaths and the final reluctant joy of victory torn from the fallen by those who survived. A friend cut in half. Tears of agony in the wounds, smashed grimaces from once handsome faces, eyes sparkling in the moonlight which lay plucked from heads strewn across the grass like beads from a broken necklace. The smell of burning skin, the feel underfoot of muscles moving as he ran on the dead to get to the breach in the wall. His own shock at what he had done. What he had become.

He had walked with the dead. His shoes were still covered in their blood. His hair was sticky where his scalp had been running with sweat. He could not forget. His hands were curled, still trying to clutch weapons that were no longer in them. The battle was over but peace had not yet come to the poet. Peace would never come to him again.

He was too hurt to stay by himself. He understood that all wars scar you even when you are not wounded. Memories etch those scars in you for all time. You can never give those memories to anyone else. Only those who lived through battle know what he now knew. Everything else is just stories. Imagination. Fantasy. All these deaths were glued to his heart and fought against his sleeping with the ferocious energy of all those who want to live, of all those who had not wanted to die last night. There was no portion of the ground outside that was not red with the blood of his friends. He groaned to himself. There was nowhere he could go to escape these images. To escape this feeling of dread. To escape her arrival.

The rebellion of the Arvernat, the genetically engineered miners who lived below ground, had been short and bitter. The preparations had taken months and been carried out in such secrecy that even he did not know about them until the last few days. Until a few days ago the Arvernat had been his enemies as much as anyone else who lived under the watchfulness of the guards and their tyrant leader.

The tyrant had genetically created miners to excavate the mines. Huge men and women, their skins tinged green to give them protection against the cold below the surface, and the eerily adapted, photon-emitting cells in their eyes enabling them to see in the dark. The ores they unearthed were the raw materials of all the things the people in the cities, the Tsarbo, took for granted; building their homes, laying down the roads, even keeping them warm in the winter. They also provided the raw materials the tyrant needed to make weapons and keep the army strong. The people only knew what the tyrant wanted them to know. They feared the Arvernat. Rimfelder had feared them, until they had saved his life.

The Arvernat, in their turn, were kept apart, never allowed to see the sun except in the few secret places they had made for themselves. Places they had to crawl on their stomachs to reach, when they had the time. From these carefully hidden holes in the ground they learned to count the stars and watch the sun rise and set. They worked out their world orbited the sun and from precise measurements in their long tunnels they learned their world was round. They thought the Tsarbo and tyrant were in league to keep them enslaved. The Tsarbo told their children the Arvernat were dirty, dangerous, green, ignorant and no better than beasts. A good dog was worth more than all of them put together and there were many hundreds of thousands of them.

The mines were vast complexes. They stretched deep down for hundreds of miles, but there were no official entrances or exits on the surface. None that the Tsarbo ever saw. There was an entrance from the inner sanctum of the tyrant but no ordinary people ever went there. The people of the cities did not know how vast or how deep the mines ran but they feared how dark they were, how filled with their enemies and how different they must be from the cities. They were terrified by the difference. Trapped in the tyrant's grip by their own imaginations.

None of the Arvernat ever survived above ground long enough to meet and befriend anyone from the cities, and no one from the cities had ever been brave enough to dig a deep hole and find out who lived below them. Mutual fear was their breakfast, dinner and tea. They lived as enemies.

The Arvernat got their name from the largest of the mines in distant Arvern, a mountainous region set above the lakes. Their children were told nothing about the cities because the adults knew very little. Few of them had even seen the outline of them in the moonlight. None of them had ever managed to see inside one or walk the streets or touch the stone houses. Some children would creep along those secret narrow passages, which rose upwards through craggy rocks, to feel the rush of fresh air, the coolness of cold rain water and count the stars. Inside their own scooped out holes, which were their homes, they only ever had warm water to drink and the atmosphere was stifling and hot. The first of the children who crept along these passages began to love the fresh air. To crave the sunlight. To live beyond their imprisonment. To dream of living outside.

The few who had tried to get away and live on the surface had been found out, hunted down and killed.

The Arvernat were forbidden to be above ground.

Forbidden to eat the food prepared for the Tsarbo.

Forbidden to meet or marry any but their own kind.

Forbidden to learn to read or write.

Forbidden to stop working unless to eat or sleep.

They had become accustomed to the ignorance of almost everyone on this planet but they never accepted their fate. The children who had crept along those passages and seen the stars planned rebellion. They knew they were worth better treatment than they received. They knew they were the equal of anyone else on the planet. They knew they had been genetically engineered. They knew what fate was expected of them, and they cursed the tyrant and planned to rid themselves of their chains. They had seen city children playing in the fields. They had longed to hold hands and dance, to run and play hide–and–seek, to stand and sing to their parents without a guard whipping them for not working. Among them was one called Tethval. He would become their leader.

The science that created them had to make sure they had brains. Without brains they could not take orders. Without brains they could not handle the huge machines with which they dug into the planet. Without brains they could not communicate with each other. Their brains were sharp and clear. They had learnt about freedom because they had imagined walking in the fresh air, resting from work and laughing with friends. They had imagined deciding for themselves when to awake and when to sleep, when to eat and when to work. In their imaginations they were a different people. Not slaves but noble and proud. Not slaves but free and easy with each other. Not slaves but citizens. The rebellion was their way of finding their dreams, of making what they only imagined, into reality. They had no other way. No one would listen to them even if they tried to talk to them. War was their path to freedom.

If they had survived the people of this world would have told and retold the stories of their rebellion for centuries to come. But they would not survive. The universe only had three days left and their world not even half a day.

Rimfelder's eyes were heavy with tiredness and dark shadows were creeping down towards his nose. His hair was unkempt. He found the room unbearable. He opened the door on to the street. He tried not to look at the dirt and the squalor which Tethval and his men were clearing out with their great strength. They were heaping the spoil into huge piles and carting the rubbish away trying to make the place habitable, to limit the risks of disease from the refuse and the rats. They had never known about the poor living conditions in the city. The people were there with them, carting wheelbarrows and stones, working on the walls to repair the breech. Everyone had found liberation from the tyrant. The war, so nearly lost, had brought them all together. The Arvernat and the survivors were at last united.

The vanquished army, realizing the rebellion had freed

them from tyranny, were now helping the very mutants they had so bitterly fought but a day before, fought almost to standstill. They had faced each other for a day and a night. The battle had been close and vicious. Thousands had died. Thousands more had been injured. Thousands of the Arvernat had thrown themselves against the impenetrable walls of the city. Too many deaths for Rimfelder to contemplate. He had been with Tethval and multitudes of the Arvernat. He had seen their blood pour into the polluted rivers. With the tenacity of a crocodile holding living prey, memories clung to him even more tightly on the street than they had indoors.

Anyone who has been in a difficult and bloody battle wonders how they survived but Rimfelder wondered what he had survived for, and he knew deep inside, there was more. He knew something was approaching. Immense. Impossible. The expectation was driving him mad.

They were working to inspire a sense of normality in the city. Hope was in their hearts but he still could not bear to look at their faces as he passed them. He did not wish to catch anyone's eyes. He saw so much more in every face than the small smile, or nod of hello. Calling to him from every place, from every cobble and brick, from every child and adult face from every grave, were voices of the dead which he heard clearly. Victory brings to some a feeling of elation, but to the poet there was a deep sadness in everything he touched. Death, which lies behind all living things, was no longer forgettable and hidden but visible, even enticing. In his own death he could forget. His pain would dissipate. He would lose his fear. The faces of his many lost friends would welcome him. He was at home with them. He missed them. He could not go on living, feeling like this.

In all the activity, he alone, of them all, felt useless. Dread had taken over Rimfelder's heart. His existence was death and destruction and for the first time in his life he was lost for words. The war was not over yet. The turmoil in his brain resonated with all that was to come.

"Are you still moping for that something just out of reach?"

The imposing form of Tethval suddenly stood in front of him, with his thick muscles and light green skin. The strong lights in his eyes were muted in the daylight. His wide mouth half smiled. He respected this man who had never wanted to fight but had done so all the same when the Arvernat needed him. This poet who had been taken prisoner by them and had, when he had seen their true worth, when he had looked at their preparations and seen their weapons, joined them. Rimfelder respected Tethval for his courage and sense of purpose. His natural authority. A hardness, born of suffering, which really longed for an excuse to be kind. They were different in many ways but they understood each other. They liked each other.

"I don't know," Rimfelder shook his head and looked at the ground. "There are no calm thoughts in my mind. No words. No images that draw me to write anything. Just a continuous feeling of dread. I can't stop mourning."

Tethval took him by the shoulder and hugged him close. He spoke softly,

"Your sadness is beginning to get the others down. They look up to you. The first of the Tsarbo to befriend us."

He sighed at his friend.

"Why don't you go on a journey? Take the news of the liberation to others. If there are others. There's much to find out about our world. Much that we've been forbidden to know. Follow the roads. Find out where they lead, to other cities or countries. There were plenty of other mines, maybe they've all been liberated now the tyrant is dead. They may even crown you for bringing them the good tidings."

Rimfelder appreciated the offer but he felt a chill run through him. What would he find on such a journey? More suffering, more cruel images to stain his heart?

"Leave here?" He spread his arms wide and looked around the forlorn city, "I'm not sure. Maybe all I need is some work to occupy my mind. I'm too alone with my thoughts." He looked at the men working busily and added, "I don't seem to be needed here. Maybe a journey would do the trick."

He watched as people carried water out to the working men and they rested awhile, joked and talked. How could they talk? How could they work? Why were they bothering? Tethval slapped him on the back,

"Of course you're needed. They'll talk of your part in our fight for generations. The first of the Tsarbo to join the Arvernat. No one can take that away from you. You were and always will be the first. In fact before we took the city you were the only one. The guards here say they saw you. The sight of you standing shoulder to shoulder with me, made them think, maybe they were on the wrong side, for the first time. Many had heard of Rimfelder the poet. Several knew your work. You were better for us than a flag. You were a message of hope, a window upon a new future."

"I'm not sure to what side, to what world, to what cause, I belong anymore,"

"You've seen too much death close at hand. Neither a pleasing sensation nor a pleasing sound and the smell is beginning to permeate everything. We can't bury the dead fast enough in this heat," Tethval said.

"There are more graves than people to tend them and provide them with new flowers, if they can even find any flowers in these wastelands. The clogged rivers, treeless wastes, even the mountains seem bare of even so much as a little snow. The clouds drip rain, the air gives us breath sparingly ..." Tethval interrupted him,

"Look at the sunshine Rimfelder. Sunshine. And no one can tell you not to walk here or there, no one can tell you not to go and meet friends. We can't take away your memories, not one of them. Liberation, Rimfelder, write about that. The old tyrant is dead. Did you expect we would free ourselves without cost? There's always a price to be paid in sacrifices but we redeem that price by living on. We take back some of that price by taking what the fallen also fought for and making sure their children enjoy what they gained for all of us."

"Life's tainted. Tainted with blood, loss, pain. Living is no longer pure," he replied.

"Purity!" Tethval put his head back and laughed out loud, "I wish I were you. Here am I talking about stonework, houses, new hospitals, roads, fresh water and food supplies to keep people alive, and my friend looks at his feet and talks about purity."

"Someone has to," Rimfelder said.

"At the appropriate time. Not now. We have to build. That takes dedication, as well you know. We can't all spend our time looking for words and images. Nations are built, not dreamed."

"They're dreamed first," Rimfelder reminded him.

"And second? What comes second? Or don't you get that far in your musing?"

"What can be built upon the loss of so much life except a tombstone?"

"Something that will not enslave others."

"Nothing can come from blood but more blood. Now we know how to, we'll end up fighting ourselves if we've nothing else to fight."

"You have no faith in our sense of purpose?" Tethval looked hurt.

"In you always. In me not so much, you see I found something out on the battlefield."

"What?"

"I found parts ... exciting. I found I could disregard people dying around me as long as I could stay alive. I found part of my nature responds to battle. When we found out the tyrant had fallen, for one brief instant, I was happy."

"And that scares you?"

"I can almost see myself enjoying another fight."

Tethval was going to answer when there came a shout from the end of the street.

"Tethval!"

Pashtul, his daughter, who called to them was tall, lean and tired. She had been sent out with others to glean any food from the untended fields, preparing to plant new harvests and plan a new rotation for crops as the synthetic foods plants would have to be shut down. She hurried over animated and excited,

"Father, I've found this girl. She's a stranger."

Tethval looked at his daughter and then at the small, Ruzniel girl. So did Rimfelder. At first they both thought she was wounded and had had her nose cut off but they soon realized she had been born that way. Of the two of them Rimfelder felt a tinge of expectancy and dozens of questions at seeing Tobia. Tethval would not have recognized a being from another world but Rimfelder, taught to be aware of the strange through his own life as an outsider, saw at once.

She was looking intently at them all, as if she was searching out someone in particular and was disinterested in anyone else she met. She stared at Tethval but she looked longer at Rimfelder. Tegriel's inner being soothed her. She had materialized almost beside Pashtul and for a few moments both of them had been disorientated. She had looked around at her new surroundings and wanted to wait for Midrak, but the women had scooped her up almost immediately, for every life had become precious to the Arvernat. At first Pashtul had thought her a child. Only later did she realize she was another species entirely and she hurried back to find her father.

"A young child," Tethval smiled.

"A traveller," said his daughter. "She appeared from nowhere. Right by my side. As if she had just popped out of the ground. I couldn't leave her there, though she doesn't say much. She didn't try to stop me bringing her here."

"A traveller," repeated Rimfelder.

"You're welcome to our city," Tethval went on, "have you come to help us?"

"I don't know," Tobia replied. "I don't know what you need. I'm not a traveller," she looked around, "I'm a Ruzniel. I'm waiting for Midrak and a woman called Lilah. Is she here?"

"Who's Midrak?" asked Tethval, bending his knees and crouching so he could look her in the face.

"He's ..." she stopped talking.

A feeling of caution filled her. This was a strange world of which she knew nothing. The tall, imposing Tethval seemed gentler than his looks. Rimfelder was obviously deeply troubled. All around her she saw the signs of men and women trying to piece together shattered belongings. Ruined buildings, gauged earth, burnt soil. She had walked with Pashtul through the battleground and seen the scarred walls where several fruitless assaults had been made to enter the city. War was not rare in the universe. She wondered if something here was what she and Midrak had been brought together to combat, or if this place was of no importance at all except to those who lived here. Since she did not know what the war was about, or which side she might have supported or who had won, if indeed anyone had, she decided to be cautious. Always a very good strategy when you find yourself in the middle of things.

"... coming soon I hope," she ended quickly.

"You called yourself a Ruzniel. That's a race of people I presume?" asked Rimfelder.

Tobia nodded. She was in a very distant place for them not to know about her people. Who were they that had never heard of Ruz? She looked around. She looked upwards. The sky was clear. There was no imminent danger of attack here. But the enemy was everywhere. Time was counting down for them all at the same pace. Then Tegriel's presence calmed her fears. He knew these people. Tobia was safe.

94

"You have nothing to be frightened of here," said Tethval, sensing her unease. "We've been in a battle for our freedom. Things are as rough and awkward as you find them, for all of us, but we wish no harm to those who come here in peace. You find us unprepared for guests but more than ready to be good friends."

He offered her some water from a finely blown glass bowl.

"Thank you." She liked him. She did not accept the water.

"Could you not tell us more about why you're here?" asked Rimfelder.

"Personally, I'm here because, obviously, I must prepare for Midrak's arrival and unless I'm wrong Lilah will be looking for us."

"And who's Lilah?" asked the poet.

"She's Midrak's sister," is all Tobia would say, much to his annoyance as he was sure Lilah was the woman he had felt he was going to meet. Rimfelder felt Tobia's coming was the beginning of the awful future he knew awaited all of them.

"Prepare? How?" he asked.

"Learning a little of your ways so I may advise him when he gets here so he doesn't upset anyone. So he knows where you fit into the scheme of things whilst he's here." She smiled. Tethval stood up.

"This is a fine guest," said Tethval. "Not only one who appears out of nowhere but one who sends advance notice expecting a shattered people to provide accommodation no doubt. Does he come to help us?"

"Or to fight us?" said one of the men nearby.

"He will harm no one," Tobia defended him.

The assurance she gave did little to lessen the fact that they really knew little about each other. The atmosphere was still heavy with enemies who may or may not be difficult to recognize. Victory did not mean rest.

"He requires no room for rest. I assure you, when he gets here, he'll have the most honest and best of intentions," she insisted.

"That's what I've been sensing," said Rimfelder, "the arrival of someone important to us. Someone who'll help us find a way forward."

"Well," said Tethval, "I'm well disposed at the moment to travellers but I warn you now little lady, we'll defend ourselves if there's need. We've lost many friends fighting for our freedom. I do not intend to lose any more. You pose no threat to us I think, and I hope your friend Midrak doesn't, but people who send others to prepare the way for them usually have a high opinion of themselves. Here, we've the same opinion of everyone. We're all of the same high worth."

"Be assured Midrak takes from no one. Once you know him you'll pleased to give him much but he'll accept nothing because he needs nothing. You've nothing to fear from him unless you attack him."

"And if we did?" asked one of the Arvernat.

"He would stop you if he had to," she answered.

"There, Hurian we're answered. We have our first guest and our talk has turned to fighting. We've had enough of fighting," said Tethval, realizing there was no cause for them to argue.

"This Midrak may bring messages from others," said Rimfelder, tentatively, "Others who couldn't contact us before because of the tyrant. We're becoming one amongst the peoples of the universe. We'll take our place amongst the planets. For, unless I guess wrong, you, Ruzniel, aren't of this world." Tobia met his gaze.

"No I'm not but we're all of the same heart if we fight for justice."

"Be assured of that," the poet replied.

"Do you really think," asked Tethval, "that we have a place amongst stars at last?"

"I'm unsure but I hope so," said Rimfelder.

"May we offer you anything while you wait for Midrak?" asked Tethval

"I would like to see more of your world," said Tobia.

Tobia was given into Rimfelder's charge, something they both found acceptable, and she walked with him, out of the busy city, across the muddy battlefield and along the polluted river bank. Rimfelder wanted to get away from the broken city as he thought a quieter place would be better for talking. She breathed through every pore of her skin. The still, dry heat made her clothes sticky. She had the air of someone who would wait a thousand years if needed. The absolute confidence that Midrak would turn up in his own time.

"What exactly has happened here?" she asked, stepping over the stones that lay in her way.

"Liberation," he replied. "A small word in need of a great

deal of explaining. We were under the tyranny of a machine. A fighting machine which fed on our ignorance and took over our lives."

"How do an entire people become enslaved to a machine?" she asked.

"That's a question I continually asked. I see now the answer is, slowly. Step by step as everything seems to happen. Hour by hour. Day by day. The tyrant arrived one day from the sky before I or my mother were born. On a mission from another world to investigate life, to analyze and send messages back to those at home, but somehow those who sent this tyrant made the machine able to think, to react to any of a number of given situations. Almost a living machine. The tyrant landed near here and found a rural, simple people and began to manipulate them. Not at once. Somehow the people were unafraid and so the tyrant began to learn about us, secretly developing the idea of conquest."

He stopped walking and sat down on a large stone moving his hands in expressive gestures as he spoke.

"All very simple to begin with. Collecting samples, moving slowly within a few miles' radius of the landing. Sifting and digging out knowledge of who we were and how we lived. One or two brave souls gave a rock or two which the machine broke up, taking the rubble through holes beneath the robotic arms. The tyrant never did anything else. Never said anything. At night giving out such a lovely warmth that slowly on cold evenings, the people began to tell stories while sitting nearby.

The tyrant must have listened. Beginning to learn our languages. Months went by, maybe years. The area around the landing became a special place, seemingly never too cold nor too wet. Children were allowed there but told to show respect for the visitor. The site was a place where people wanted to be, more than a mere novelty. Other people heard about the tyrant and visited so they put up a few wooden walls for protection but the tyrant rolled right through them and they realized the visitor wanted to see and meet everyone who came.

I don't know when the tyrant first spoke nor to whom. But the words were perfect. Then the change took place. The tyrant seemed to have learned a great deal more about our world than we knew ourselves. We had never had a great science, or much of an interest in things outside this world but this machine had dug into our soil, charted our stars and observed our rainfall and humidity and understood our weather patterns. Like all those who possess greater knowledge than others, the tyrant was faced with a choice. To educate us or use the knowledge to gain power over us."

"The machine asked for many things of which we had no experience. Designing houses far stronger than our own. The people learned how to heat them with electricity and have light at night. The first things the tyrant taught us were novel and welcome, that was the cleverness of the tyrant's plan. They began to do anything the machine asked. That was their great mistake. Sometimes people are ready to love those most dangerous to them. To show respect to those who deserve none."

"Soon, the local people relied upon these gifts. So they built the first of the cities. Others visited and then they wanted their own cities. There were no walls at the beginning, but large, clean pathways and detached houses with indoor drainage. There were those who said no, they wanted to keep to the forests but, saddest of all, many of them were killed. Some by the machine and the growing number of armed men protecting the precious knowledge the tyrant was imparting to us. Some by their own friends and neighbours because the gifts the machine gave were so useful. So wanted. More wanted than the unspoiled land and forests. So the people were split, and those closest to the machine had power over the others, which they enjoyed. The people did the machine's work. The corruption was complete. Then the experiments started."

"Tethval and his people, the Arvernat, were created to mine the ores used to build the second generation of cities, and once built, the tyrant imprisoned the people inside them. Tethval's people were hard pressed, enslaved from birth but they began to plan, began to think of freedom. The people in the cities were taught that the Arvernat were all dangerous and so they created their own army, trained by those who had killed their own neighbours. How could anything good come from such men and women."

"The guards fought the Arvernat. We, who should have been on the same side, spent our time killing each other. For years, generations I think. And the tyrant cropped the very ground from beneath our feet. Shattered our environment. The few Arvernat who tried to escape were killed and brought to be displayed in front of the people. I shudder as I remember now but even I, as I stood and looked up at the hanging corpses, thought them ugly and terrifying. Suspicion and loathing were our meals, and all stories were of older days, when the world was free and we slept well at night. We believed the tyrant saved us from the Arvernat. If not for the guards they would have taken us over. We believed the Arvernat were the cause of everything bad that afflicted us."

"You changed your mind about the Arvernat though," Tobia observed.

"I never would have. I would have gone on the same way all my life but as with all these things you sometimes need an outsider to tell you what to do. To show you the path that you would never have seen for yourself. Sometimes things are just too close-up to see clearly. A few weeks ago, no maybe not weeks maybe only days, a boy appeared. So much has happened since and so quickly I lose track. He came from the same world as the machine. He was brought here by a wondrous process I don't understand. Nor did he, because he didn't travel through space but through a mirror."

"He was magical."

"He said not. He said someone had shown him. He talked about his world and ours being in some kind of harmony. The two sides of the same mirror. He alone was able to break the machine because he was not of our world and he disrupted the way the tyrant worked. Walked right through the machine like a ghost because he didn't wholly exist in our world. All the sophisticated weapons the tyrant had designed were useless against him. They passed right through him but his presence interfered with the tyrant's delicate, electronic circuits. So simple. Yet his was an act of the greatest bravery because he was all alone. Our army was still outside the walls."

"He found his way into this city, evaded the guards and met the machine. Whilst the rest of us stormed the city walls and tried to fight our way in, losing many lives in the process. Butchery, Tobia. Bodies heaped upon bodies. Butchery from which came freedom."

"He stood up to the tyrant as though he were the mightiest amongst us instead of the weakest. As we were beaten back and faced defeat even though we were strong, armed and determined, he was the one who brought us victory. Without any weapon but his own being. At the very moment of our defeat he turned our failure into victory and did not kill a single person."

Rimfelder stopped speaking for a while. He had not spoken to anyone about how he felt. He had not had the opportunity but somehow he felt this Ruzniel knew and he felt able to talk to her. He wiped his mouth with a light- blue handkerchief, changed position on the stone seat, and continued,

"We're a different people now. Experience you see has changed us. Manipulated us. Our visions of this world are no longer the same. We've no innocence left and the boy, Robin, has gone home, also altered in his way. No longer just a child. A hero to us. Whether or not he will come here again I can't tell you but we want him to. He's a part of us as much as we're a part of the universe. Each and every one of us. Equally. He told us that there were people in his world who would have acted in the same way as the machine, so that maybe the tyrant reflected their characters. Or maybe the truth is that everything in the universe takes advantage of innocence." Tobia, who had listened carefully to his every word, replied,

"Our thoughts always change after we've come through a time of trial. I'm sorry we couldn't have arrived sooner, we could have helped save lives. Midrak would have been able to break down the walls, but maybe Robin was meant to help you and not us."

"That you're here at all is strange enough. That we should have received any help is marvellous enough. Who knows what's in the future. I believe now that these things have a purpose beyond that which I see."

"There are few people with the knowledge to know the purpose of things. Filvani collated the laws of magic because he knew that the way of the universe was to exploit the living. That people want to be stronger than other people and the only way they know how to be, is to conquer them. But the strength of friendship is often greater than armies."

"What laws?" asked Rimfelder, sensing, at last, certainty in the confusion of his mind. Tobia knew Ebiric, the sweet, lilting language in which Filvani wrote the laws of magic and she quoted,

*Laws That Guide The Hand And Eye; Explain Why We
Live; Prepare Us To Die; Make A Continent Of Our
Hearts; A Nation Of Our Minds*

"That's beautiful."

"Midrak will explain more to you, but the laws of magic
brought Robin and me here."

"You know a great deal about other worlds. This Midrak
of yours must be a very powerful friend."

"My people have travelled all over the universe which is
why I was surprised you've never heard of the Ruzniel. As
for Midrak yes, he's powerful but not like your tyrant. Power
does not dictate his actions."

"You must know him well."

"I know his kind," she explained, smiling.

"Don't be surprised about anything that happens on this
world," he explained to her, "I've come to think we exist
outside time. Like an island that floats to nowhere. The
tyrant wanted us cut off and we've become used to living
this way. Though I thirst to know what's out there, who's
out there, what they've been doing whilst we've been in
chains. Such devastating chains." Tears welled in his eyes
and he fought them back. She told him,

"The essence of ignorance is always suffering. If you had
known other worlds you'd have been empowered by their
knowledge. We're all linked. Your tyrant knew that. What
happens in one world effects another."

"I can see that," he nodded, "and what I can't see, I feel."

"Robin's arrival may have saved time. Precious time.
We're not here by accident and if we'd come and had to fight
a battle here first, other battles might be lost. Everything
happens for a reason."

"Other battles?" Rimfelder's eyes opened wide as she said
this and he leaned forward, "I've had the dread that there
is more to come. Is that why you're here? To lead us to yet
more slaughter?"

"There's more to come, of that you may be assured.
However, this time you will neither be in ignorance nor
alone."

They looked back to see the city with the huge gash in the outer walls, where the breach had been made, exposed and raw in the sunset. Made by the explosion caused by Robin that had ripped the machine asunder. The last of the graves had been filled. The smoke that curled upwards but a day ago was now replaced by white clouds ribboning the sky. The evening sunshine cast long shadows. There was a great deal of noise and movement as Tethval's people carried on working, their eyes sending out beams of light in the growing darkness, until the view looked like a thousand, thousand torches were weaving in and out of each other. Snaking along pathways, going in and out of the city. A strange and beguiling sight to Tobia. Not least because some of them had been born with different coloured eyes and amidst the white, were blue and amber.

"Do you understand what you see now?" he asked her.

"Yes. Of how this fits into the scheme of things of which I'm a part, not at all. But things are never revealed all at once, just as not everything happens in one go. They say the universe takes billions of years to get even little things started."

"Will Midrak know the answers?"

"He may."

Her eyes looked at the view wondering if Lilah was among the many people she saw clearing up after the battle.

"I wish to understand so much," he said. "The great scheme of things. Why did this happen to us? Did we have to suffer?"

They started on their return journey. They kept on talking. By the time they came back she had learned all about the great battle and Rimfelder had learned that her world had been ripped to pieces. He knew something about the Sangyma and she knew something about a world that had never heard of any of the things she had been brought up knowing.

Tethval met them again with an optimistic smile and large hands outstretched to take his friend by the arm and press Tobia lightly on her back guiding her along the road.

"What have you learned about each other?" he asked.

"Much," said Rimfelder.

"Well, I think you should come with me. I don't want to alarm anyone but they found a body upstream. They thought he was dead but he's had some kind of seizure. Anyway, I wondered, as I don't recognize his clothes or his look, whether he might not be your Midrak."

"No!" cried Tobia in panic, her face momentarily covered with an agony of shock.

"We don't know. Only you can tell us. Come and see."

They led Tobia into a row of tents in which several hundred men and women were being treated for a variety of wounds. Some could move, and called out to them as they went passed. Most were swathed in bandages and being cared for by the nurses as best they could.

On a bunk by himself lay Midrak, softly breathing. His face was wet as the nurses had wiped thick gunk from his eyes and clothes. His hands were in fists and no one could prize them open. His eyes were tight shut and every muscle in his body seemed to have seized up. He felt like solid stone.

"Midrak," Tobia told them, softly.

"Is this the patient's companion you told to me about?" asked a doctor, looking at Tethval and then at Tobia.

"She is," replied Tethval. The doctor spoke to Tobia.

"I'm Bearus, and if you have any idea what this man suffers from I'd be pleased to know. His heart rate is steady and he appears to be asleep but his blood pressure is through the roof and his head's red hot. We're at a loss as to what to prescribe. His muscles are so tight they would break a needle if we tried to inject him with anything."

"You don't need to worry," she told them, "He'll heal himself. Whatever happened to him hasn't killed him. We can only wait. He may have induced this state in himself. If he has, trying to help him is futile."

"If we wait he might get worse."

"Believe me, his powers are greater than yours Bearus. He'll live. We can't interfere. We must give him the time he needs."

She hid her real fears. Even she knew this should not be happening to Midrak. But she needed to be alone with him before she could begin to find out what this was all about. Pashtul came over to Tethval and whispered in his ear. He looked at her and nodded and then turned to them and said,

"Another traveller comes to us. Maybe we should all go and find out who she is. I wonder if we have a hotel amongst any of the ruins in this place, we might need one if this keeps up."

"Are you coming?" Rimfelder asked Tobia, as she leaned

over Midrak searching his face for clues.

"No. I wish to stay beside Midrak. He may have need of me. He'll ask questions when he wakes. I should be here. If she is the one whom I'm here to meet she'll find me."

"You're a good friend," said the poet.

"Ruzniel have been companions to magicians for aeons. We are another set of eyes, another set of ears. Wherever there have been battles for justice, magicians and Ruzniel have always been found, side–by–side."

"I hope he gets well," wished Rimfelder.

"So do I."

"I'm very glad you came Tobia, very glad."

Tobia did not hear him. She was repeating to herself,

"So do I," looking intently at Midrak's pale face and closed eyes.

Rimfelder walked out into the dusk. Tobia raised her hand and touched Midrak's left eyelid and his eyes opened suddenly. The eye was glazed. Nothing was looking out of them that she recognized as Midrak. Something was in him that was alien to him. Something strange. She sensed a battle going on within him. He was being tormented. Something terrible had infected him.

"What are you?" she asked, aloud.

And though she heard no answer from Midrak's lips, she thought she could faintly make out cackling laughter. Then his head slightly turned. The staring eyes looked directly at her.

Her blood froze.

Lilah

The red-haired, black woman looked as if she had been made from a single piece of highly polished ebony. Her skin shone even in the dark. She was a presence you felt as much as saw. She had deep, black eyes that were wide, soft yet piercing. There was no whiteness in her eyes at all and she blinked but rarely. She hardly moved her head but gave the impression that she saw everything no matter how far away or how small. She gave the conviction that she had seen you long before you had seen her. She gave the feeling that she could see right through you. Telling her your name would have told her more than you knew about yourself but nothing she did not already know.

She was so poised that, as she walked, you would think she had been trained to walk on a high-wire. She had perfect balance and co-ordination. She did not slow her pace when going uphill, her legs did not tire faster going over rough ground. She seemed rooted to the worlds upon which she walked in a unique way no one else could equal.

Her breathing was deep, long, and so slow you could not see her chest rise or fall. Even as she walked she had such control, she was never out of breath and could run vast distances without breaking into a sweat. Her hair moved slightly with the breeze as if the strands were there to feel movement and sense changes in the atmosphere. Long, curled and graceful like a natural antennae around her head and ears. Hair that should have fallen all over her face but somehow never did. Her arms were long and muscular. Her fingers were elegant, ending in perfect nails that caught the light like diamonds. She was fascinating.

As they looked, the three Arvernat felt uncomfortable. Each saw someone they had known but could not recognize, yet felt they should. They knew she saw into their hearts and could recite all the lies they had ever told, one after the other. She was a presence as much as a person, she was the known more than the unknown, a friend more than an enemy, magic more than a woman. Her aura appeased their

Lilah

fears, yet awakened their understanding to depths of
ignorance they had never touched before. She seemed to say
without words,

'I know all that you are. I know who you have been. I

challenge you to become all that you ever dreamed you could be.'

They were instinctively in awe of her. She was important. Powerful. Without her once saying a word they were half in love with her. She made them feel that somehow, existence could not be complete without her. That all the questions they ever had about who they were, could be answered by her, in her own time, in her own way and the answers would be the only truth they would ever know. All they had to do was wait. So in silence they waited.

She stood quietly near to them, as the fresh clouds crossed the sky, saying nothing. Filling them with a quiet confidence. To be beside her was to be safe and untroubled. She was dressed in a pure white dress threaded with fine gold, rich, purple twisted cord in her hair, her gold throat–necklace of interlaced snakes crafted to her skin in one piece that could not be removed. She looked at them and then she looked around them. Speaking was unnecessary. The four of them had found out that for all the languages in the universe there are some things no one can actually say. They did not even know if they had found her or she had found them. They certainly could not be said to be guarding her, she was not in their power. Their hands hung by their sides, their work forgotten. The past few days suddenly seeming far away. Their very lives seemed to hang in the balance. The Ossendark, through which she had travelled, closed seamlessly behind her. Lilah waited. They waited. The planet waited.

The evening cast deep shadows but none was as dark as this woman. She transcended darkness. She wrapped evening and night in folds and burned with the promise of stars yet to be born. She was inner–light, she was dreams and comfort. Yet she was also storm and whirlwind, death and creation.

Lilah was more than all of these. She was unlike any that had gone before her. No spellmaker would come after her in this universe. Her long years of training, her own ability and her brilliant mind, combined to make her the most formidable opponent and most precious of friends. The three Arvernat men did not know this, they simply understood, as a dog understands, the movement that means 'go' and the movement that means 'rest'. She would never ask them, she would never order them, but they would follow her without regard to their safety.

They stood among the mass graves that had just been filled. So many were dead. They had started by burying them one by one but by the end of the first day that become six to a grave, then ten. They had just emptied a cart of the fallen. Friend and foe together. The cemetery now swept up the hill and over, well down into the valley out of sight of the city. They were on the very last grave. On top of this pile of bodies, lay a child. Fair haired. Small. Out of place in war.

Lilah walked towards the grave in time to her heart-beat. The Arvernat moved back to give her room. In the few minutes they had stood in silence the men had forgotten the direction she had walked from, had forgotten their names, their families, their work. She had become everything. And yet they knew she was transient, that she would walk away and their lives would be their own once again. That she would become their past, as elusive as a passing day recaptured by fleeting memory.

She looked at the corpses. She looked at their wounds. Finally she spoke. A cool, strong voice filled with emotion as though this had been her own child. She reached out and her white sleeves trailed through the dried blood and dirt but when she took her arm away no marks were upon her clothes, but her heart was scarred. Her eyes glistened with the child's tears.

"If I had arrived sooner I could have saved some of these people."

Her voice was full of sweetness. Restful. The men did not respond. The scene said all that needed to be said. Strangers meeting on a battlefield seem to guess and understand what is beyond them in ordinary life. The pain, the hurt, the empathy with others. The sharing of grief makes an unbreakable bond. The closeness of death rips away all that is unnecessary in the living. This is the one moment when life is free and unfettered. The greatest of all ironies is that this most precious of moments should be found stuck in the teeth of the brutal jaws of war.

The breeze picked up. Cold air blew the hair of the dead where they lay. A last hint of lives lost. Lilah stood up and turned away from the men for the first time in what seemed to them to be hours but could not have been more than seconds. She moved along, leaving them, and they were filled with the desire that she stay but they were too respectful to make such a request. After these precious few minutes, they would never be able to love another and yet she was untouched by the encounter, or so she seemed.

Slowly, she gave them back to themselves as she left. Like a gift. Knowing she could own them forever she allowed them freedom to be themselves and not her slaves. She had found them as grave diggers, she left them masters of their destinies. Filled with dreams given to them by her own silent emotion as she walked away.

She walked on towards the city, towards two other men who were coming hastily to meet her. One of them as green as the tall grass in her homeland, as green as others who walked the battlefield picking up arms, swords, knives and broken shields. Making sure the field would one day be safe for children to play upon. The other equally tall but thinner, somehow lesser but she knew no less clever. No less thoughtful. His clothes more ragged, his face longer but his stride; there was something about the way he walked. Purposeful and restless. He was anxious to meet her. His mind was full of noise. His heart full of hurt. She liked this man. He was an artist. He created. Suffered for the suffering of others. Filvani's hidden books had taught her the power of words and this man was a poet. She was here to collect him. A special place was his in these final days.

The light from Tethval's eyes picked out her white dress. She knew his name. Lilah was not one to arrive without knowing people's names. She knew all about this world. All about their peoples. Something in her had been alive when this world was created and been aware the day the satellite arrived and began to plan a tyrannous take–over. Times lost in the vastness of time and space but not lost to the magic of the Sangyma. Inside her head the songs of the universe sang in constant refrain. Like all spellmakers she tapped into that song to find out what was happening and where. A giant harmony of knowledge to which she was always linked. Sung from the tops of hidden towers only she and Tegriel knew existed, a mystic stream of knowledge,

'Matter Is Neutral, Only Thoughts Are Good Or Evil'

So wrote Filvani. But she knew the universe was not that

simple. She looked at the battlefield and heard the songs of war and peace, rebirth and fate, time and the selfishness of violence.

Lilah was her own song. Her song was added to the great song of knowing. That was spellmaker magic, to create something nature had not thought of before. The two men approached her, one already in love with her.

"Welcome," said Tethval, stretching out a hand slightly awed by the sight of this woman who was not dressed like Tobia or Midrak, "Have you come far?"

She looked at him and without touching his hand accepted his greeting with the merest bow,

"I was brought here by the Ossendark."

Her voice was coolness in heat, softness in granite, purpose in the unfathomable. As she used words so their meaning became known to them, even the ones they knew seemed fresh. Popped from a blister-pack, like medicines, to give them ease and soothe the clamour inside their brains.

"Why?" asked Rimfelder.

She looked at him as he spoke, her eyes going from his feet to his head taking in everything about him. This was the poet. She had wondered what he would be like. There was more that interested her about him than she had expected. The voice was nervous but not from fear. His body was strong, his heart loyal. His eyes swam with suffering.

"You may not understand," she suggested.

"Try us," Tethval suggested. "We're learning fast. You're not the first to visit us."

She stared at him, her black eyes being met his an intense and deep gaze. Unlike others who looked into the lights of the Arvernat, her eyes were not affected by the brightness, not cowed by their searching.

"You have had a hard time," she observed, looking around.

"There's more to come isn't there?" asked Rimfelder.

She knew the poet would have a sense of what was to come. Given the terrible decision she would have to make she did not lie to them but replied,

"There is a greater battle to come. One that yields no reward, but one we all fight. Our one consolation will be the knowledge that, in order to be victorious, one does not have to survive Zaqui."

"That sounds ominous," Tethval said, wanting to turn his head away from her deep gaze but finding he could not.

"More than a battle, we are engaged in a struggle," she continued, "Warriors and children will fight with equal merit. All the philosophies of all the worlds will bow before this struggle, will show how well or badly they prepared their nations and races for the greatest encounter with magic. A battle of ideas as much as peoples. A single atom may tilt the balance, sway the last drop of blood to fall on to our side. A second, saved now, will be spent a hundred times then."

Tethval was taken aback. At any other time he might have given a nervous laugh or taken to arguing but there was something about her that made him realize she was not pretending, not playing, not exaggerating. She was telling them the facts. Rimfelder also felt the truth of her words. Giving her name first or explaining who she was, was utterly unimportant. They had to understand. Prepare. She was telling them their lives had changed more completely than they had realized. That everything they knew was irrelevant and everything they had fought for, was already lost.

"Recruitment might not be that large here. We're not born for fighting. We carried on our war only to secure our freedom. We've already had enough of killing," answered Tethval.

"Freedom has come to you too late," she said, softly.

"But come when there's a choice to be made," replied Rimfelder, "that can't be too late."

She looked at him. His voice was filled with a gentle spirit that had been traumatized by the revolt. He was a soldier of the heart. One of those rare people who is never ready to kill others, but always prepared to die for them.

"Where are the others you spoke about?" she asked.

"First, what's your name?" asked Rimfelder.

"Lilah."

He and Tethval caught each others eyes. He had known for sure she must be the woman Tobia had mentioned. Her words brought all his fears to vivid life. What had they been saved for? The same question everyone who survives war feels. She had given him an answer that he hated but would embrace for her sake.

She seemed to enter his soul. She smiled at them like a mother seeing her children become grown-up. She now knew Tobia and Midrak were here. If there was one secret desire inside her heart then surely to meet her brother again was that desire. She was content to know they would be together, that the great task for which she had been prepared did not exclude family. There are times in magicians' lives when they can rest. Danger only comes to them only every so often. That was not her fate. From first day to last her way would be incessant war. Her hardest task was never to lose her love of other people's lives. Like Tegriel before her, she did not think a Ruzniel would live long in her company so she forfeited their wisdom and had no companions. She was also curious to see how Tobia worked and acted.

"You lead the people called the Arvernat?" she asked Tethval, jumping ahead of Rimfelder who was about to tell her their names.

"We've no leaders," answered Tethval.

"But you speak for them," she said.

"We speak for no one," answered Rimfelder, "we came here to meet you when we were told you'd been seen."

"If other strangers are here do you not think I have been sent to meet them?"

"Why here? Why now? Why us?"Rimfelder asked.

"The answer is the same for all questions Rimfelder, because this is necessary."

"I'm not sure they will be of much use to you. One of them is small, a Ruzniel girl devoted to the other and the other was fished out of a stream almost dead. He appears to be in some sort of coma," replied Tethval.

"Take me to them," she instantly demanded.

"Well ..." began Tethval.

"Why do you hesitate?" She was slightly angry.

"We don't know if you mean them harm," Tethval said, valiantly. "They're our guests. We should look out for them."

"Come to that," added Rimfelder, "we've only really spoken to the Ruzniel. She's been honest and friendly. I'd not like to see her harmed and, even though she mentioned you by name, we don't know you." Lilah was grateful for their words.

"You have a fear of me yet you challenge me on their behalf. Not knowing my power, not knowing my past. You are both brave men. I am sure all your people are the same but since I have no time for these niceties ..."

From nowhere in her hand there appeared a metal stick, perfectly cylindrical and about as long as her arm in length. Burning with a russet warmth the stick was capped at both ends by thick bands of gold ornately carved with playing monkeys. The stick fitted her grasp as if every inch were made for her fingers alone. They could not see where the stick began and her hands ended. She held the weapon for a second in front of their eyes and then, balanced on her palm, the stick shot into the air like a tree, growing up and up, bigger than a tree, than a mountain, until the huge presence dwarfed the city and disappeared into the clouds. Now the weapon grew sideways blotting out the moons and stars. They stared. But for the light of the Arvernat eyes and the light that emanated from Lilah nothing else could be seen. Still her open hand was touching but a small part of the great staff which must by now have weighed millions of tons. Everywhere the Arvernat stopped what they were doing and looked up wondering what terrible thing was happening.

Rimfelder gasped as he watched the light from hundreds of eyes play upon the smooth surface of the edifice that had grown out of her hand. Tethval stepped back, looking instinctively on the ground for some fallen weapon to defend himself.

Men came running up behind him, hastily armed. There was fear in their hearts and then suddenly the metal stick was once more small in her hand. Then the weapon vanished and they were standing in the battlefield with work to be done and the open, night sky above them. The only thing that had changed was their attitude. Men, who had been running, stopped. When she spoke everyone throughout the city heard her speak, though she never raised her voice above a whisper to Tethval and Rimfelder.

"Had I been an enemy you would have been the first to know," she smiled "and Bofindle, a mighty bejal that once belonged to a monkey king, would have obliterated your city more effectively than a hundred battalions of the enemy and far faster. Time is short. I have to see the others."

"If we don't take her I think she'll take herself," said Rimfelder. She replied,

"We cannot sit and eat together or spend the days talking. I cannot train your men in new ways of fighting or help you use new weapons. We must learn everything about each other immediately and proceed forward immediately. Instinct is our friend and if you have no instincts you cannot deal with me."

"Come then," conceded Tethval. "This way."

They set off towards the city and the men who had run forward parted to let them go by. There were a few who whispered as they passed.

"Who is she?" But they did not seek an answer, for they spoke out of awe.

"Tell me Tethval," she asked as they walked, "You were mutated into your present form?"

"Yes."

"By a machine that bred you to work the mines."

"Yes. The tyrant came here ages since from a planet called Earth."

"I have heard of that place." She was silent.

She knew at this very moment Chloe and Demeter were there coming to terms with powers they had never dreamed of possessing. Discovering the fortress Trecrogo, which they at first mistook for a city. That Copret was on his way to join them. That Wei K'un had been trapped by Rataplan and died before he revealed Demeter's existence. Events were racing and she was scared that Midrak would not be able to move in time to join them. She had to know why he was hurt.

"The Earth was been believed destroyed a long time ago. That machine must have fallen through a time–line to get here in order to create you. No mere machine could do that alone, there must be something else manipulating events."

She knew the fight with the Arvernat was raw and new and that the Earth had had no inhabitants for aeons. Could Crilodach play with time? How? She knew of only one way. The Upala could use time. Though the Upala had been captured by Crilodach long ago there had never been any evidence It had tried to use this exceptional bejal. If Crilodach had mastered power over time, they needed to be very frightened indeed.

"Is there's another force behind what happened here?" asked Rimfelder.

"Nothing is as you thought," she replied.

"Including people," observed Tethval.

"Most particularly people," she smiled .

Maybe, she thought, the best place to hide a brother and sister's meeting from the enemy, is on a planet It disregards because It has already fallen into Its grasp. A planet to which It pays no immediate attention because news of the liberation of the Arvernat had not yet reached Its ears. She hesitated, as if she thought she should tell them this. She decided not to.

Maybe she had wanted to tell Rimfelder and Tethval that she was hiding. Maybe she had wanted to tell them that if It found her It would attack because Its imperative was that she die and It would spare no effort to kill her. Maybe she wanted to tell them she brought them more danger than they had ever faced. That they faced extinction as much because she was there, as because of Zaqui.

Maybe she wanted desperately to tell the truth but knew that would do no good. They were all going towards the same place and knowing what and when that was, would not change a thing. This had been her life. The one thing she had to carry wherever she went. Whatever she did. Her fate was to see people sacrifice themselves without ever knowing if their pain and loss would achieve anything. She was like fire, for sure, in this war, but inside her she had already sunk a well of tears shed for all that would be lost before the end.

She kept silent. These few hours she gave them to believe their lives had a future were precious to her. They were the only gift she could give them. She gave as willingly as she would have given real years to their lives, if she had been able. Even she did not know the wonder that awaited them all. Nothing, as she herself had said, is as she thought.

"Here," said Rimfelder, as they walked into the city, "is our makeshift hospital."

"Bearus where are the strangers?" asked Tethval of the doctor who was binding up an Arvernat's leg wound.

"In there." He pointed to a closed door.

"Why was he moved?" asked Tethval.

"The young lady asked us to move him. She wanted him to be alone."

They all walked to where he had pointed and opened a door which led to a smaller, warm room with two windows looking out on to the streets. Midrak lay on a bed, his clothes dried. Tobia was wiping his forehead which had broken into a continuous sweat. The Ruzniel turned as they entered. Lilah and Tobia looked at each other as if there were no one else in the room.

"Who are you?" Tobia asked.

"She's Lilah," revealed Tethval, wondering why she did not know the very person she was here to meet.

"That might be her name, but I asked who she was," said

Tobia curtly.

Tethval did not try to answer for Lilah a second time. Lilah walked over to Tobia. She looked down at her brother. Her lips were drawn tight at the sight of him fighting whatever enemy was within him.

"An enemy of the enemies of the Sangyma," she recited.

"Why do you come at this time?" Tobia continued, touching Lilah's hand lightly, feeling her fourth metacarpal under her warm skin.

"There is a battle to count the stars."

"Zaqui is coming?" Tobia asked, standing up.

"Yes," Lilah told her.

"We have places we must go?"

"All the places that ever were or ever could be."

"I'm content," she replied.

Rimfelder felt as if his heart would break because their voices both were filled with mellow sorrow, like a far away, wistful song in a strange language filled with emotion that brought tears to his eyes he did not expect.

"Where did you come from?" asked Lilah.

"Ruz."

"Home? I was told the Ruzniel cities are no more."

"You're well informed for the destruction only took place a few hours ago. Even as we left, they were destroyed. I think that's why Midrak is ill. I don't know what happened to him as I left first, I didn't see. I'm sorry."

Tobia stopped. They all noticed the calmness of the woman had altered slightly. She seemed almost unwilling to look at Midrak again. The look in her face lasted but a moment. Then with no small effort she spoke,

"You have no need to apologize. How long has Midrak been your magician?"

"Since we met on Ruz."

"How did you meet?"

"I waited for him. He was sent to Ruz by Palik Tomil. We met. We talked. I began to remember."

"Began to remember?" asked Lilah.

"I seem to have forgotten so much, but things come to me now and again. Most of the time I'm unsure of anything." Lilah nodded, understandingly.

"You must be the daughter of Medase. I am pleased to meet you. I have been told about you. You bear essential knowledge about Tegriel, do you not?"

"I may."

"In good time we will talk. Now, I wish to tend my brother."

"Your brother?" Tethval sounded genuinely surprised.

"Yes Tethval, Midrak Earthshaker is my brother. The time has come for families to unite. I must save his life as only I am able to do."

"Your brother's dying?" asked Rimfelder.

"He may, without assistance," she said.

"Come," said Tethval to his friend, "we should talk outside."

"We'll come back," Rimfelder told her, leaving with his friend.

Tethval and Rimfelder left them. On the other side of the door they stood close together, looking along the lines of wounded as the doctor tended to them.

"What's on your mind?" Rimfelder asked.

"This Zaqui. She isn't telling us everything," said Tethval.

"Maybe she can't."

"Or maybe she's deliberately keeping things from us," whispered Tethval.

"I'm afraid, my friend, we're in the midst of another war next to which ours was a sideshow. In some way of which we're ignorant, our victory matters in the scheme of things."

"Will we win this greater battle?"

"Can't afford to lose, I think. You remember, when you looked out at the stars from your hidden tunnels you told me you wondered if other peoples suffered as the Arvernat did."

"Yes. With so many stars we thought there must be others."

"Now you know they do."

Rimfelder looked at an Arvernat who had lost an arm. He was again filled by the sense of loss and sacrifice that had almost overwhelmed him before the strangers had arrived. Now he knew, through Lilah he would find his answers but he was scared by what they would turn out to be.

"How can she be sure of all this?" asked Tethval.

"You don't like the sound of her warnings. Neither do I but somehow, I can't deny her words. Whatever the truth is we've still to live on. Whatever the future holds we've still to go forward. Always forward." Tethval took a deep breath as if trying to taste what fresh air was left to him and said,

"You believe she knows though?"

"Knows what?" asked the poet.

"The truth."

"Do you doubt she does?" Rimfelder asked him, surprised.

"No. No I don't," said Tethval. "I have a fear unlike any I've felt before."

They came to a window looking out over the hills and they both stood looking at the mixture of beauty in nature and suffering in people. Their lives had been built on that coexistence.

"In the battle," Tethval said softly, "I faced the shimmer of swords, the strength of enemies. I felt their breath, heard their shouts and even gave way to their victory. The fear I felt then is not this emptiness. Being in ignorance is worse than fighting with only my bare hands."

"She may know our future," said Rimfelder, with an innate understanding, "but what a fearful burden she lives with because of that. She may know who'll die and how. She can't save everyone from themselves. Think of the weight of choices, the terrible choices, always on her conscience. Perhaps, even worse, there's no choice, maybe there's only loss."

"Perhaps that's why she has that way with her, that sense of peace yet tremendous power," said Tethval.

"Maybe." Rimfelder rested his hands on the stone sill and looked outside, "The tragedy in worlds must be the same for all who feel."

Tethval looked at him and wrapped his arm around his friend's shoulder,

"If inner pain is the price of your friendship, I'll gladly pay."

In the private room Tobia hovered behind Lilah. Midrak's face was a mask. His eyes closed. His skin hot. His lips flaking. His dry clothes still smelling slightly from the polluted water into which he had fallen. One of the many men milling around had heard the cry of pain then the splash as Midrak rolled from the ground into the river. He had run over in time to haul him out before he drowned.

Lilah gently rubbed his temples with her long fingers. Tobia watched. Slowly his eyelids opened. Very slowly. Midrak was not opening them, but Lilah with her force of will. Lilah looked deeply into his blank eyes. For a long time there was silence. Her black eyes burned with questions. His eyes softened. Tobia saw them take on the look of warmth and feeling. Then Lilah growled in her throat and the eyes went back to their milky, deathly glaze.

"You heard distant laughter," asked Lilah.

"Yes. The eyes that looked at me were not his alone."

"I thought for a moment the distance he had been forced to travel might have sent him into a coma. That, perhaps, the speed at which he had had to leave made a difference; that sending you first weakened him unexpectedly; any of several ideas but his state has been induced to stop his mind falling into madness. He has done this to himself. Something attacked him on Ruz. Something invaded his brain. Something is trying to take over his thoughts and control his mind."

"What?"

"What indeed and how long do I have to find them? We cannot move him while he is like this, yet if I stay and help him I endanger our plans. Time, time, time." She sighed. "Not yet. Ordinarily he would not have survived this long, there must be a greater power in him. He holds a secret, a secret we may need."

Tethval and Rimfelder, fearful that she would never tell them what was really going to happen to them, came back into the room and heard her last words. Tethval asked,

"May we help in any way?"

She turned to them, her face deeply serious.

"Tethval, how many fighting men do you have here?" she asked.

"About two thousand. A few more lightly wounded. They're all busy right now burying the dead on the battlefield."

"And warrior women?"

"About fifteen hundred, again they're all scattered around the city and surrounds."

"Could you find more?"

"Our runners have been gone since first light to try to find other cities to bring them the news. There are others like us. Possibly they'll come to help us rebuild and gather together to celebrate. At least that's what we've asked, but we don't know who else is available. There is a great deal of chaos and uncertainty."

"Can you send out more messengers? Tell them to muster here as quickly as they may. Tell them the fight is not over. The enemy is coming back. If they stay where they are they will be destroyed. They must muster here without delay. Tell them there are more Arvernat. Thousands more." She had spoken rapidly and after a small pause she ended, "We will need every one of them."

Her words fell in the small room like bricks. No one moved.

"Am I going too fast for you?" she asked them.

"I'm confused," replied Tethval.

"When you look up at the stars what do you think about?" she asked him.

"I thought them glorious when I caught a glimpse of them."

"There are many worlds and many peoples around those stars," she told him.

"As Rimfelder has been telling me."

"Not that I know," added Rimfelder.

"The end of all these worlds, everything you see and many things you cannot see, is coming soon. Zaqui. All you see, all you are thinking of, everything you have known, everything you have never known. There will be a great cataclysm and eventually, from the Zaqui all life will be born anew. In this cosmos every atom has been forced to make a choice, to be part of the tyranny of Crilodach, or be part of those who fight It. There is an unevenness in creation. We have been able to fight against enslavement, to stand in Its way so It has never truly ruled everything. Still, It has managed to grasp at victories over too many places, peoples and worlds. Now, in the final days, there is a vital struggle going on to ensure It does not rule in the universe that comes after us. The plans of the Sangyma must be greater than the essence of Crilodach, or future galaxies will all be ruled as you have been ruled. Worse. There will be no freedom for anyone. Nothing but torture and pain. Nothing will evolve that has an independent mind. Anything birthed will have been created for the delight and pleasure of Crilodach and the monsters It creates. For eternity! If they rule in the new universe they will always rule for there will never stand against them anyone or anything strong enough to tilt the balance. This war is the most important of all wars. This is the fight for which all the others have been training grounds. We shall never live through anything like this again but from us will come others. We are their strength and they are the fulfilment of our promise."

"The end of everything?" Tethval repeated.

"Everything," she affirmed.

"Is there any way to prevent Zaqui?" he asked her.

"Zaqui must not be stopped. We must fight to see all the rights and the choices created again, for others to share. We have no greater task. We must have no greater wish."

"And your place in all this is where exactly?" asked Rimfelder.

She looked around the room and then at her brother, resting her hand near the pillow on which his head lay,

"I have been trained for this. I am one of those charged with fighting the slavery that would engulf us all from enemies you barely know, many that we have met before, many we have never known for they have bided their time only to appear at this moment. Enemies that will use every weapon they can against us. Enemies that have fought with us on a thousand battlefields in a thousand worlds and others who have never fought us. I cannot tell where all the skirmishes will be. All I can tell you, is that we know our own strength and we have been guided in this purpose by great minds."

"This man here, your brother, is he one of those great minds?" asked Tethval.

"He is not, though the other is," she replied.

"The small one," smiled Tethval.

"No, the one inside my brother."

"What?" asked Rimfelder.

"There is one of the Sangyma within the mind of my brother. Somehow on the journey here his mind has been attacked. I do not know why. His ordeal must be terrible. The struggle immense. The only way to save him and bring him back before the mind–imps, known to us as Lazab, strip his mind and leave him dead is for me to enter his mind. To do that I need to know that, out here, our enemy will be checked when It sends Its army to attack you. For they will arrive soon. In healing my brother I must drop my mask and It will see me. If they overrun you and get in here before I am finished not only will we lose Midrak, I shall die, so shall Tobia."

"Even minds are battlegrounds," said Rimfelder, stunned.

"They are the first battleground," said Lilah, "but after we finish here there is another prepared. A planet which was saved from destruction to which I must go."

"This enemy comes just for you?" asked Tethval.

"Yes, Tethval It does. I am sorry for that. It might have disregarded you but for me being here."

"And in disregarding us we would have found death from It anyway?" he asked her.

"You would," she assured him.

Tethval closed his eyes for a moment and then opening them said,

"Better to know than not."

"You can't enter his mind unless ..." began Tobia. She stopped speaking, and then continued, "Unless you've mastered arts that even the Sangyma barely know. Are you such a master?"

"I am Tobia," Lilah replied.

"But the arts were lost so many generations ago. Who taught you?"

"Their names themselves are charms and I may not speak them. Tethval, when I go into the mind of my brother my body will remain here in this room. If anyone comes here they could kill us both and walk away. If armies tried, if host upon host tried, they must be stopped."

"But we don't know what we're to face. How many, how strong," said Tethval, every inch the soldier.

"Indeed you do not but Bofindle does."

She took out the small metal stick which grew to her height, and laid the bejal on the floor.

"When needed, Bofindle will fight for you. The bejal's magic knows what to do."

"May I?" Tethval asked, bending down.

"No. Anyone who touches Bofindle without permission will burn to death. Leave well alone. Bofindle knows how to work. Will you fight for me Arvernat?"

"You have said in saving Midrak's life you expose us to the enemy," Tethval said.

"Yes."

"And in defending you we buy nothing for ourselves but hopefully deny the slavery we were forced to endure to others in a future world."

"I am sure others will face the same slavery but we hope not everyone."

"And we're going to die anyway whatever we do?" Tethval asked.

"Yes."

Tethval looked at the floor. Then he looked at Lilah,

scratching his chin. He wished things otherwise.

"Then that must be enough," he said.

"Thank you," she whispered, knowing he could have been angry but now he saw. He understood. Now he had chosen his side. He was an ally. She knew how he felt. She felt the depth of the loss inside him. She knew there was nothing she could do to help him.

"I will prepare," she said.

"Do you have to go alone?" Tobia asked.

"I know you feel your duty is to be with me but I cannot hold on to you in Midrak's mind, and fight the Lazab I will find there, at the same time. I need all my strength. Even now Midrak and Fulminar are fighting, and whatever is holding out against them is strong, stronger than one mind–imp should be. I am hoping I can tip the balance. Without Midrak we will lose Fulminar and without the knowledge Fulminar holds we will be the weaker. My brother has found a Sangyma, that is an unlooked for stroke of fortune, and I must rescue them both."

"Then I'll stay here and be your last defence if all else fails," Tobia offered.

"We won't fail," said Tethval. "If all we have to look forward to is death, what is there to lose in fighting. We have tasted so little of freedom. For our first challenge to be our last is a tragedy."

"There's no end to the bloodshed," said Rimfelder.

"Creation demands life for her art, you should know that Rimfelder. Go now please. I need to be alone with Tobia and my brother."

Tethval and Rimfelder walked out of the room. This time they walked passed all the wounded men and on to the streets. There was a surprising warmth in the night air. They both felt older.

"I'm not sure we should have allowed her to convince us to leave her alone so easily," suggested Rimfelder.

"Why?" asked Tethval, trying to look calm despite the turmoil, sadness and determination that filled him in equal measures.

"We really know nothing about her. And the more we know the stranger life becomes. Sangyma, enemies, ancient arts."

"Tobia seemed to take Lilah's news in her stride and she's no fool. She knows a good deal more than we do about these things."

"And who is she? For that matter who is Midrak and why should we worry about him?"

"If she's right, we're about to have another battle. This time with unknown enemies, and this time we're fighting for everyone not just for ourselves. We certainly have become one with all worlds, the spearhead of the oldest war in the universe."

"Maybe that's the real reason why you were created," suggested Rimfelder.

"Why?"

"For this battle. Maybe the tyrant thought the Arvernat were needed to mine ores but all the while the true reason for such strong and powerful people in their thousands was to fight this battle to save Midrak and his sister. Perhaps we're going to learn the true reason for everything. The real purpose to our lives."

"So, my friend, you've found reason and purpose at last! In the very thing you thought denies all reason and purpose. War. Not how we fight to live, but when we choose to die for others."

"A terrible reason," Rimfelder said.

"One that suits you though. Fits you like a second skin."

"And you? Have you found a reason?"

"The Arvernat are my reason. Purpose is a matter of luck. Once freedom was my cause and now, within a short few hours, I fight for Midrak, Lilah and Tobia whom I've only just met."

"Then we're fighting for what? Power? The truth?"

"As fighting is all we're to know the fight has become the truth."

Rimfelder fell silent and let Tethval go forward greeting his men and organizing the runners and defence. News that the strangers had arrived had travelled amongst them all. They had been waiting for Tethval's orders, as if they had all instinctively understood what was happening. They quickly organized themselves. The battlefield emptied, walls were guarded at every point, and though they tried to get the ordinary people to safety most stood their ground with the Arvernat, even the children. Everyone just knew they had to face the new enemy together. An hour passed. They still waited.

The sky was bright and clear, the heat from the rising sun was cooled by the breeze that swept over the hills making them think nothing in the world was wrong, as if liberation changed the weather, the smell, the feel of nature herself. But you cannot lie to the eyes of the Arvernat. Tethval had told them as much as he could of what was coming. What he said made little sense but they all trusted what they had seen and heard of Lilah. The Arvernat, who had struggled all their lives in the mines, secretly suspected their freedom was a mirage, that their achievement was hollow. Her revelations confirmed their fears and Tethval's words instilled a new certainly in their minds. This was to be a war to the death. Knowing strangers were amongst them who needed to be defended gave them added courage. No one complained. No one suggested the battle ahead could be avoided by telling the strangers to leave. They all knew, without being told, that this fight had to be fought. Here. Now. There were no options. This battle was theirs as if by right. They prepared for the worst. They saw every movement as their last, every sound as the arrival of their enemies and the beginning of their renewed struggle. Though none of them knew exactly what the enemy was that was coming, they knew It was coming for them. Battle-hardened, they waited to fight. Somewhere, in the depths of the night, they waited to die.

Some looked up at the sky, some way into the distance, some at their feet. One or two coughed slightly and the noise echoed along the still ranks. Several sipped drops of water and others fingered the battered spears and swords which had never been far from their sides. Some had not yet been cleaned from the day before. Each of them, as they waited, looked for a while at the graveyard they had spent long hours laying down. They remembered as the sun rose a little higher, as the breeze gently ruffled hair, there had been a time before war. Seven thousand Arvernat eyes looked, three and half thousand Arvernat hearts beat. The breach in the wall they had made in their own fight was now their greatest weakness. Tethval concentrated four hundred Arvernat behind the breach expecting any attacking force to aim straight for the gap as the easiest way to get into the city. So little did he know about what Crilodach created. So little did he suspect the violence that was about to be unleashed upon them, the anger that would vomit hatred across their world greater than any they could have ever felt from the tyrant.

The attack began almost without beginning. Small humps appeared in the grass as if moles were busy underneath. But these were not made by moles. Hundreds appeared in seconds. Stopped. The piles of soil, dark and rich, looked as if the ground had contracted a disease. Then they appeared in the graveyard of the recent dead. They grew higher. Bones lifted from their graves, stuck up at awkward angles catching the air. Cleaned bones. Bones which had been surrounded by bodies just a few hours before. Cold, broken and bare. Stripped of flesh as if eaten. Arvernat eyes saw and hearts felt heavy as their chests tightened.

What manner of creatures ate the dead?

They gripped their weapons tightly. No one moved. Mouths were set in anger at what they saw, showing their growing determination. Had they known what was coming some might have fled. Some might have asked Tethval how flesh and blood could withstand the monsters Crilodach sent against them. Some might have run to try to make sure a few Arvernat lived on. But they did not know. No one ran. That imperceptible bond of warriors, that glue of purpose and mutual reliance, flowed down their ranks forming a second wall.

The smell of perfume blew across the city as if the enemy were ridding themselves of any sweets left in the ground before erupting into their onslaught. Ridding themselves of anything pleasant. The planet became the enemy. The ground that should have become a playground for their children, a garden for food, became instead a shroud. Out of that same ground rose the primordial stone. Liquid, hot and gigantic. Multi-coloured. Twisted into hideous shapes, mountains, pebbles, rock and mineral became alive. Grotesques born out of a mind alive with hate. The very elements of worlds, inhuman, unstoppable, unfathomable, unthinking, driven into life by the hater of life. Raw-edged, sharp and pulsating. Their own world came to kill the Arvernat with an unmatched power to destroy and a deep desire for victory that was Its version of lust. Crilodach had reached out to take the only thing It ever wanted; everything.

All around the hills the slopes quaked and heaved as tall, thin, misshapen, molten creatures rose up, hands like mallets, silent as the grave, slow and ponderous orientating themselves to the purpose of Its mind. The hills vanished, liquefied in seconds into a gouged, rugged plain crowded with living malice.

Tethval's eyes were transfixed by the scene. His people watched. For generations they had been forced to mine underground, to hack into the stone beneath the surface. They saw the granite before them, they caught sight of the diamonds in their fingernails, hard and swift to cut through bones. They saw the larval deposits of stone that even dynamite could not break, in the muscles of the roughly formed army before them. Near enough to smell the familiar stink of the mines. Walking. Groaning with the agony of birth. Strong. As vast as an ocean. Mercury in the eyes as if they needed eyes. Osmium toothed. Their heads ablaze as gases oozed up from the chemical interactions bubbling through their massive forms. Flooding the distant horizon until there was nothing else for the men in the city to see but the enemy.

They all knew they did not stand a chance against such an army. Such a foe. That the steel and stone walls could not protect them. The smell, heat and fog given off by the army in front of them would have shaken any other group of men into instant submission. But the enthusiasm of liberation burnt strongly inside the Arvernat and Tsarbo and not a single one there took a step back; nor spoke one word in fright. If each of them had stood alone upon those walls, they would not have run. The chance to run had gone. The reason to run had gone. This was the end.

But if the ground around the city produced an army, why did the ground beneath their feet stay firm? Why was not everything rising out of the ground in the city? If the enemy could, surely they would have grown out of the houses and streets first? Right in their midst? Unless the enemy was playing with them. Tethval did not see play in the liquid metal eyes and malevolent grimaces of the stone warriors. If they could have flooded the city they would, but they mustered in front of the walls, encircling the city because something stopped them from being inside. He knew the army before them had no fear of them. Perhaps they wanted to fight the hard way. Perhaps the sight of the blood of the defenders was part of their battle plan. Whatever was keeping this mass at bay was the defenders' only hope. His mind thought of Lilah and Midrak. He gripped his sword with both hands, sure that any weapon he used would break on first contact.

"I never dreamed such a thing," whispered Rimfelder.

"You don't have nightmares?" asked Tethval.

"I will now."

"If you're ever allowed to sleep again," said Tethval. Rimfelder felt his stomach churn at the words. Tethval continued,

"I've seen such things in my dreams. The Arvernat know the unyielding nature of rock. We always wondered if our mines were alive in some way."

"What do we do?" asked the poet.

"Nothing. They must come to us. Leaving the city would be fruitless, they literally control the ground and would swallow us up in a second. We're prisoners."

"They'll just swarm over the wall," said Rimfelder.

"We'll fight hand-to-hand."

"In all the years you mined the ores of the world, did the rock ever fight back?"

"Never in this form. But I think this is but the image of our real enemy. It turns the planet against us to test us. It does not appear Itself, just as Lilah told us."

"We can give up all hope of reinforcements," Rimfelder said.

"We can never give up hope."

The ocean of stones that marched like an army reared up. Shoulder upon shoulder, forming ramparts as high as the walls of the city and yet higher. Beyond them uprooted mountains blotted out all light as they glided towards them ripping through the thin strips of cloud that withered in the sky. The defenders set their feet firmly upon the walls.

"People, hear me," shouted Tethval, "Do you see how the ground rises against us? Do you feel our planet's might and power? Don't let these feelings and sights confound your hope or drain your strength. Look, how the city at our feet remains untouched. The strangers who came here today knew we would be fighting for our lives. They've given us powerful, unknown weapons with which to fight. Without them we'd already have perished. Fight, as only you know how. Let us face the enemy with the same resolution with which we won our freedom."

The first of the army of stone dropped like bombs upon the walls. Arm to arm men grappled with them. Launching themselves forward they gripped the stone warriors and felt the heat from the core of their planet. But even as they fought the stone men grew stronger. Muscle to muscle like titans the Arvernat sweated. These were a people who were used to breaking the stone into pieces. Hammering and cracking the rock. Flesh to stone. Cries of pain filled their mouths as fingers broke and wrists cracked but others took their place as the first men fell, hammering into their enemy with anything that came to hand, were their last acts of defiance.

The army washed over the walls like a hideous flood breaking upon the walls and washing away the weak defences. The Tsarbo stood no chance. Tethval's people were trodden under foot and flattened like so much paper. The enemy made no sound. No roars or cries, they just came on like a torrent of hard, quenchless, dry stone. Implacable. Passionless.

If the enemy could have laughed, their merriment would have been a roar but the only sounds were from the defenders. Their shouts and calls. Their cries as the enemy's hard footfalls and pounding might fell upon flesh and bone. Anything that was of the city rippled as if hit by a quake, creaked and blew into dust but anything that was of the stone enemy was utterly silent. Only living beings felt anything. Only living beings cried in agony and died with the names of those they loved upon their lips. Falling, vanishing, clambering like ants over their new enemy to stop at least one of them.

Tethval and the others were forced back, wounded and reduced to waiting for the ground to heave up and swallow them. None of them had anything left to give. The enemy came on and the mountains closed in around the city walls caked in blood and dust and then suddenly they all stopped. The Arvernat watched, their lungs heaving in the darkness. Tethval lit his eyes and the lights played over the rough hewn surfaces of the stone so close he could have blown the dust off them. An enemy that only bled shadows.

Bofindle, as if from nowhere, flew into the air. The ancient weapon glimmered and shone ruby red. Like a spear thrusting mercilessly into the army of stone shattering a long line into bits. The bejal reared upwards until the brilliance emanating from the weapon's sides replaced the sun. Club-like Bofindle beat them back into the ground as long ago in the hands of a Spellmaker the bejal had beaten stars into place and once thrust Crilodach Itself into the ground. Rolling over the stone from side to side with a rolling-pin action used to crush them to dust, flattening out like a road flowing into the horizon. Bofindle disappeared into the distance destroying every enemy along the path. The enemy broke, shattered and vanished. When they struck at Bofindle their stone arms fragmented into dust. They jumped on to the bejal to be blown to smithereens. Bofindle was to them as they were to the Arvernat — unbeatable.

Running along Bofindle, from far away, came men and women using the bejal as a road. They came in their thousands, flying down the magic road. They leaped into the city to cheers. Some of their runners had gotten through. Arvernat eyes were no longer lit as the sun began to shine through the dust and light penetrated the battered city streets.

Then Bofindle wrapped around the city like a band. Close into the walls repairing the breaches made by the enemy. As high as the highest point, setting like a skin. The bejal held the city in a safe grasp. Nothing could get through or over this impenetrable magic.

"How many of you are there?" asked Tethval

"Eight thousand" said a woman, "no more. The others are dead. We thought we were done for a few seconds ago, before that weapon of yours blew the enemy into oblivion. I wish your weapon had come earlier. We were over a hundred thousand."

"This staff is no weapon of ours. The other Arvernat ..."

"Gone. We're all that's left. Those that tried to fall back into the mines were swallowed whole. Not even given time to shriek out. There's nothing anywhere eyes can see, but a quaking mass of stone. The world's ripping into pieces. As if huge hands were gouging out giant fistfuls of plasticine and modelling these creatures."

"Look," called Rimfelder. Tethval turned and watched in amazement at the scene outside the city.

Before them the enemy, like spoiled children distraught at not getting to their toys, were breaking up everything around them. Land just vanished. Cracked and crumbling into dust; dust into nothingness. Where once fields had filled their sight, grey swallowed up everything. Bleakness followed the grey as empty space took over the planet. Gaping holes appeared in the ground through which stars could be seen. Streams of debris vaporized as the atmosphere dissipated.

There was a storm. A rage of creaking and wildness. They felt drunk as the city moved like a ship caught in a hurricane of waves. Around their heads a maelstrom fought with the stars. Few of them could keep to their feet. They fell on to their knees. Some sat down and held each other. Hands braced against each other. People tied themselves to anything heavy. Winds tore their skin. Blinded the eyes. A raging torrent of noise filled their ears until the pain was so extreme they had to cover them. One person standing beside another could not hear the other shout. The sky was blotted out with dust. No one could tell which was worse, the stone army attacking or their rage at defeat.

Then silence. Only the heavy breathing of their comrades coughing and the rapid clearing of dust. Only each other. Nothing moved beneath their feet. The walls did not quake. Bofindle was still there. The houses that were standing before were still standing. They lived. Covered with dust but they were alive.

"You alright?" Rimfelder coughed, waving his hand in front of his face to try to clear the air.

"Breathing," replied Tethval brushing the dust from his eyes. "Just."

Their bodies ached, their heads rang with the last blasts of the enemy and their mouths were choked with dust. They got up and looked about them. Their world had vanished. Bofindle surrounded the walls, burned ruby red but all around them was open space. No world existed. The city was all. Like a bubble, held in open space. Once there had been a living planet here, now that was torn into space debris. Above them the sun burned as brightly as ever but even they could see the pull of gravity from their own world had been lost. Other planets in their solar system had begun to shift their orbits.

"Blown away," gasped Tethval, barely able to speak.

"What power can do such things?" asked Rimfelder.

"We may know one day. Right now my guess is we're supposed to be dead but aren't. We have the strangers to thank for that," said Tethval.

"Tethval there are many things we have to be thankful for but what I've just witnessed isn't one of them. All we've known, all we've fought for just vanished in a twinkling of an eye. We don't even know the creature who did this. How can we give thanks?"

"There are powers beyond us. Our struggles have little meaning to them, isn't that what Lilah told us? Maybe we're all victims of forces we know nothing about and can never control. At least whatever we do from now, and whatever happens to us, we have powerful allies."

"We've nothing. What could possibly be left for us to do?" asked the poet.

"Who knows. Maybe Tobia will tell us."

"Tethval we were powerless just now. We can't fool ourselves. We were powerless. If we're alive only because Lilah stayed to help her brother when they go ..."

"Hush," said Tethval. "This is not something we should speak about."

He smiled a strange half smile and Rimfelder couldn't help but note that his friend was now ready for anything. Whatever was coming, the Arvernat would not flinch.

A little while before Bofindle had saved Tethval and the others, Tobia, sitting alone, looked at Lilah, her own eyes suddenly growing tired. She realized this was no normal sleep.

"Can't I witness what you're about to do?" she asked, softly.

"To enter the mind of magician is the most dangerous procedure one can attempt. The skills I am going to use are not for the eyes of others."

"And if I sleep for how long will this room remain unguarded?"

"A few minutes."

"A lot can happen in a few minutes," she yawned.

She curled up on the floor and drifted into a dreamless sleep. Lilah watched as Tobia lay on the floor and closed her eyes. Her breath came softly. Her eyelids moved gently. Lilah went over and looked at the prone Midrak. His forehead was etched and lined, his mouth identical to her own, his nose angled slightly, the cheeks thin and worn. She touched the skin on his neck. He was cold. She took his hand which was warm. A thankful sign. His hair was still tangled from falling into the stream. For a moment her thoughts were of long ago and far away. Two young children hugging each other goodbye and neither understanding why they had to part despite all the explanations adults were giving them.

She sat on the floor by his bed. Her body relaxed, her back straight. Time remained silent, for this was not the place for time to speak. Then her body drifted slightly above the floor, and somewhere inside Midrak her spirit moved. Midrak opened his mouth but said nothing. A warmth filled the room. The two bodies were in perfect harmony. Heart beat to heart beat.

Tobia should have slept on but the magic seeping through the pores of the universe was already marching towards the city walls, hungry and alert. Knowing they had prey. The enemy's creatures only move when they sense blood. They need no leaders because they only have a single command inside them. You only need leaders when you need people of different opinions to do the same thing. As a general leads an army of free soldiers, or a dictator leads a country of individuals. These creatures are neither individuals nor a country.

The moment Lilah had concentrated upon Midrak the enemy had sensed her. You cannot hide such a powerful being as Lilah for long. It knew where she was. It smelled her in the city. The mountains were sweeping towards the walls in Its need to create an instant army, but It sensed she was inside the room and with the subtlety of a hunter It looked for ways to attack her there despite the powerful spells that protected her.

The room became hot and the doors impassable. Around them the bricks bubbled and blistered and the walls became alive with a thick, white, soup of matter. A soup that now slid down the stone and congealed on the floor. Tobia awoke to find herself covered with the thick glue clogging up her nose and stifling her mouth. As she opened her eyes in fright, the soup seeped under her eyelids. Her arms were pinned and, barely able to get up, she kicked out as the room closed in on them all. Then she lay as if mummified, her breath slowly being drawn from her.

A voice called. Though not her voice the call came from her. She found herself lifted and sitting in Lilah's lap as Bofindle, called to her aid from deep within her, seared into the ground and the walls burnt white hot and the hands reaching out, sent to grasp them all and strangle them, stiffened as the mighty weapon held their purpose at bay.

Half formed bodies rising out of the glue tried to scream as they were checked. Twisting in grimaces of pain, dissolving as quickly as they had been created, they vanished back into the walls which gave off the smell of charred skin, that soon turned to the smell of lavender as the creatures decayed. The heat dissipated. The hands reaching out vanished. The glue evaporated from her face and she gasped, gulping in warm air and rolling off Lilah's lap almost hugging the ground in fright. The doors could be opened again. Tobia opened her eyes. The enemy had done some of Its work well.

She was blind.

Her mind was racing. Bofindle became small and slid into her hands. She did not burn at the bejal's touch, for Tegriel's spirit was now fully awake within her. The weapon allowed her to hold on. The bejal felt as light as a feather and slight enough to slip behind her ear like a pencil. In a million ages only Tegriel and the spellmakers had ever been able to fight with this mighty weapon. She felt the bejal's strength enter her and she no longer felt afraid. She raised herself to her knees. Already she could hear the call to arms of the men and women outside and instantly her training took over. She forgot about herself. The enemy having failed inside the city was summoning up more energy. Those outside needed help. The room rocked with the first assault.

"The city's in danger" she said, "Go."

She opened her hands and Bofindle tilted upright for a moment as if listening. She listened too. Her mouth slightly opened. Unsteady on her feet.

Bofindle rolled like a bird diving into the water and flew through the walls as if they did not exist. Tobia turned her head and did not fall over, her balance was just as good as if she were sighted. In her new darkness she looked to where Midrak lay and found inside herself, Tegriel's eyes. The eyes of a Sangyma. The deep eyes of knowing. The kind eyes of understanding. No longer did she require light in order to see. Now she saw with magic. The magic particles that were in all things. She saw them within herself and felt everything as if the minutest thought had become part of her very being.

Suddenly she knew that some magic was indifferent, and could be swayed by whomever had enough power. Some was immovable and could be used only by a chosen few. With Tegriel she had become a mirror, reflecting the universe and catching the reflection with her mind. She sighed. Sighed for the ignorance that had been part of her life. For the tragedies that were to unfold before her in the days ahead. But in the sigh she also heard another sound. A gentle voice that she had not heard since she was six.

"You're with me?" she said softly.

"Part of me, Tobia, only part of me," replied Tegriel, "but before this ends you will find the rest of me and when you bring that part of me which is in you to my body, you shall see me again and we shall walk and talk as we so briefly did once before. Only this time I promise we will have more time."

"I must find the rest of you?" asked Tobia.

"In time, Tobia, you will find me. I have confidence in you. Your inner strength. The mind I saw when you were a child. You will find me but there are many losses to be had on the way and infinite danger. Everything we have helped to grow will be torn to pieces. Everything we cherished will be left stripped and desolate. There will be no sleeping. No going back. No home to return to. Never once must you stop to cry or allow sadness to break your spirit or your purpose."

"Midrak is here."

"I know. And with him is Fulminar from Ruz but, somehow, Lazab have entered his mind and are stopping Fulminar and Midrak from fully joining. Lilah will try to bring them back to us before those mind-imps kill them both."

"Do you think she will succeed?"

"No one else could. Not even I. Only her spirit would ever be allowed to enter Midrak's comatose mind without killing him. The resonance of the magical spirit in her is in perfect harmony with Midrak. They are brother and sister. Besides she wants to succeed, and wanting is a great magic."

"I see outside this room," she said, holding on to the back of the broken chair with a light touch, "I see Tethval and Rimfelder fighting for their lives. The mighty Bofindle bringing in a new army across a road, and more I can see outside this world. Faces. I hear languages. A thousand, thousand places and everywhere they say Crilodach's name."

"Armies are not what is needed in the coming battles. Armies need to see their enemy. We have only ever seen Its minions since my first battle with It. It has the cunning and the strength of creation in Its flesh. It is as old as the first atoms and as young as Its latest plan. But we have planned long. We need to draw It out from Its lair. Get It alone."

"We're so few."

"Do not count strength in numbers. Our enemy does that. See they throw entire planets at us, they tear at our minds but we stand firm. They will twist and turn but we will hold It by the tail in the end."

"We dare not fail," she said.

"Once before this battle was played out, before this, our universe, was made, and those to whom we owe everything held the enemy at bay. The Sangyma could not have been created if that battle had been lost. Now, in our turn, has come our time to fight for those we will never meet."

"Like them, for the sake of those who are yet to be born, we must not fail," she said, for now she knew as much as Tegriel and understood Lilah's task.

"The greatest weakness of our enemy is that we, few as we are, know what It wants," said Tegriel.

"Do we know how Crilodach was stopped before?"

"It was not stopped, merely weakened. Little enough can get through the death and birth of universes. Only three small pieces of the previous universe exist in this universe. Three cosmic jewels. The Sagitæ. These are the bejals that It craves."

"They hold the answers to surviving Zaqui?"

"They may. For we've always believed those cosmic jewels did not survive by accident but held some message for us to use. But such is the virulence of the enemy they have hidden themselves away. I could never reveal what I know of them without revealing the secret of my power."

"Have we failed you in not protecting them?"

"No! The Ruzniel succeeded in a million ways. As the universe shrinks we will have to be quick to snatch them up before It does. But there, I think, you will be helped by the spellmaker, the poet and by the strange light in Zananto's eyes whenever I talked about the Sagitæ."

Tobia sat down, her legs weary and her mind on fire.

"All those years ago you hid yourself in me."

"What better place? Whatever goes on outside Tobia, let your mind be restful. Let your mind be a haven. A calm sea. A quiet day. Whatever noise and violence comes to those around you, I will be here, and you will find and hear me."

"I'll do my best," she said.

Tegriel stopped talking. Outside the sounds of the battle

and the planet breaking up filled the room, and inside her mind she saw everything, like a film, for now she had been made a part of the fabric of creation. She heard the heart beats and the cries of the Arvernat. She felt the heat of battle flowing across the city and tension like a cord binding them all together. Making them all one in the madness. Her being was integrated into Tegriel and all he had been. Before she had only been creation's child, with her own parents and her own people. Now, as befitted one soon to fight for all life at the end of time, destined to travel where no Ruzniel had ever travelled before, she was being shown the mind of a new mother. The universe was calling to her and her true calling began to take her over.

The Lazab

Lilah felt that stuffy, sickly smell of mucus that sticks behind the eyes and drips from one's nose into one's mouth. The kind of curdling sweetness that seeps deep into your belly, makes you retch with a vomit that will not come. A clogging, oily feeling, heavy and rich, saturating every breath she took. Involuntarily, she put her hand to her nose but that did not help. The putrid tang wafted from every direction. She stood still for several moments as she forced herself to get used to the stench that stuck to her clothes and hair as if a plague of insects were burrowing into her skin to lay their eggs. A dense fog of sickness. She had to physically cut through the mess, like going through brambles, as she moved forward, where every step oozed with the slimy sickness that had invaded her brother's brain. She floated but the illness became an inescapable part of her. Sucking at her, sticking to her clothes, latching on to her lips, folded into her hair. She looked closely at Midrak's dying brain dripping with the fæces of the Lazab.

The colours of the cells should have been bright, glistening grey and white with health and ideas. Instead they were flaccid and ugly. The grades of ginger in ideas, the vibrant yellows of joy, the pure translucent greens of memories, the purples of spells and those fabulous, sparkling blues of a magician's inventive mind were covered over with a brown, mottled mucous, stinking like filthy, damp shoes. White pieces of fluff were limply strung out like old cobwebs twisting into every thought he had, polluting him with the insane ideas of the Lazab. Freshness was almost dead. These were not moulds growing in his brain, these were the detritus of the Lazab invading his very being. Taking him over.

Lilah knew she had to hunt them down and find their lair. To find the very place where they were strongest. Their leader would be there. There the smell would be lethal and the fog deep. The creatures would have traps set and executioners at the ready. Only there could the Lazab be killed before they killed her brother.

As she took away her hand from her nose and slowly breathed in, she smelled the exotic, noxious gases which rose off everything. A poison that covered her face and skin with an unwelcome oily film that stuck to her fingers. Emanating from every cell and circling round her, either too lazy to race anywhere or too sure of their power to rush their morbid work. They had time to explore this magical mind and watch Midrak fight for his life before fading into insensibility when they would take him over. The Lazab were certain Midrak would descend into their manufactured madness. Take over the brain and you have everything. But Lilah was made of strong magic and so was Midrak and hidden in his mind was Fulminar. The Lazab were not in charge yet. Not quite yet, but they were getting close. Very close. Lesser magicians would already have succumbed.

Lilah studied the struggling, intersecting thoughts around her, with alert, unblinking eyes. She floated above the cells of her brother's brain for she knew to touch anything could hurt him if he was not prepared. First, from the shock and second, from recognizing that she was inside his thoughts. Besides, floating meant she did not interact with the poison. The creatures would not be alerted for a little while to her presence. Although that ignorance would not last more then moments a spellmaker only needs a quiet second to develop a successful strategy. She knew from what she saw they had already made themselves at home. Once they knew she was here, the Lazab would guess who she was. Whether or not they knew Midrak had a sister and whether or not they knew who she was, she had to move quickly. She could feel the enemy outside in the city drawing close. The cries of battle contrasted starkly with the withering silence descending upon her brother's brain.

She clenched her hands and spoke briefly under her breath, calming her heart. Blood pumping in, blood pumping out, in unison with her brother. She would seek out his inner thoughts. Find out where in his coma he had run, to make his stand against the Lazab. He had not given up. Not yet. She did not communicate directly with him. That would give too much away too quickly to the enemy. She had to feel him out. Follow the sense of who Midrak was, allow him to sense her presence first in his remaining feeling, then as an idea, finally as a certainty. Giving him greater strength by letting him know he was not alone. To add her strength to his, to buy those precious moments that would help him defeat the madness eating his brain away.

She could already see blood seeping out where uncaring, sadistic steps had ripped and gashed the delicate veins. She knew what to do. She raised her fingers as she passed–by and the lesions healed. The trained mind of a magician should not be coarse, unwelcoming or oppressive. Thought activity was barely audible but with her acute hearing she could just make out her brother's quiet voice, overcast with the vile gloating of the ravenous Lazab.

Suppressed laughter was everywhere. Echoes came to her like the moans of tormented victims, resonating down dark corridors from dread dungeons and along ice–cold walls. Such mournful moans in dead languages from dry throats and swollen tongues. The groans of the tortured. Words of pleading that were not her brother's but echoes of other victims, whose minds were no longer their own, replayed to fill Midrak with an overwhelming sense of hopelessness. For the Lazab had learned from Crilodach that just as fighters will take heart from a hero refusing to capitulate, so they will fall more readily when they see others surrender. So many had fallen to the mind–imps they could not be counted. Like broken shells strewn across an endless beach.

She swallowed once. The creatures were imitating Midrak, talking in his voice, but substituting their own convoluted thoughts. She began to realize the cunning of what she was dealing with, as the laughter and merry making filled her ears. She did not know how many mind–imps Crilodach had created, but the Lazab were their most vicious and virulent strain, and they had travelled in their thousands to make this conquest into a party.

A putrid reek of gangrene rose from the cuts, adding to her nausea. Their laughter was debilitating. Their strategy was to make him unsure, fill him with fright and keep him guessing and all the while, as he struggled, the disease which would kill him was spreading. Eating him alive brain cell by brain cell. Chasing away his strength and will, sapping him of his thoughts. Shrinking his brain. Stripping him of the knowledge of who he was. Killing his memories. Forbidding him hope. They did not need him alive. They could manipulate the husk of a person with supreme skill and use dead victims to transport them to places where they could find new brains to invade. Manipulating the dead was the Lazab's special skill.

She drifted forward aware that the Lazab now knew she had arrived. They felt her mending the cuts and healing the disease. They moved to replace them but her magic was strong. The laughter was higher but the words which had come to her had changed. These were not the foreign, strange and ancient words of madness she heard but the mocking words of welcome. They could only have entered Midrak's brain because he had not been prepared to defend himself. She was prepared. The Lazab would not be able to take her by surprise.

Around her the enemy permeated the remaining space in Midrak's brain. Each and every thought he attempted was being blocked. He was trying a thousand different ways but the enemy was everywhere, breeding with rapidity, to stem and stifle his every move. The voices intermingled. She drifted forward, deftly swinging her body this way and that to avoid the ribbons of thought and counter-thought running like streams all around her. She couldn't move with any ease. Everything was trying to close in around her. To stop her. Possess her. She gritted her teeth. Her heart beat firmly. Her strength was now her brother's. The laughter suddenly welled up into a roar. The Lazab knew they were working together even without speaking to each other.

Their passion for madness and her devotion to healing were now in open conflict.

The enemy had anticipated someone would attempt to save him. Expecting someone to try to save his life they had come together like a small army setting sentries up all around his brain. How had they managed to take Midrak over so swiftly? She touched her fingernails together gently and the fragrance of oranges rose all around and beneath her as she continued on. Every cut healed more quickly. Midrak was trying to reach her. The laughter had stopped. Did they now know who she was?

If they knew, did they suspect her power?

Her knowledge of them?

Did they feel any fear?

The gangrene caused by the Lazab had done a lot of damage. If Midrak's brain was eaten away by too much, even after defeating them, saving his sanity might be impossible.

Midrak was too weak to stop whatever the Lazab were

doing to cause this damage. And now she knew why. The strong feeling she had had that the secret power in her brother was Fulminar was correct. But she also knew her brother had not been ready for their fusion. The sudden influx of incredible magic had sapped his strength and left him unable to stop their invasion. An opportunity that the Lazab had been waiting to spring, watching for, planning for, for who knows how long. Chancing their own death in the destruction of Ruz for the rare chance of killing a Sangyma. So well had they planned that Fulminar was imprisoned somewhere in this maze of thoughts. She didn't have time to tread all the caverns of Midrak's mind looking for Fulminar, she had to move on.

She shared the last seconds of Ruz in his thoughts, realizing her brother was sending her the information she needed. Over and over he was repeating simple things, revealing the crucial events. Telling her just how many Lazab she faced. Concentrating on her was keeping him sane enough to stay alive. She saw Midrak accept Fulminar's request, felt the ground heaving as they joined and there, sweeping up from the hidden corners in the darkness, the Lazab. Cunning in their every instinct. Malevolence in their being. Attaching themselves to Fulminar's life force amidst the roar and clamour of the dying planet. Their speed was incredible. Even she was shocked. Never had she seen anything move so fast, with such a single-minded purpose. For Fulminar never to know they were there, they must have been hidden long before he died in the clearing all those years ago. The enemy had planned long and set traps only on the off-chance Its creatures would find a use. A brilliant strategy for Crilodach with Its endless resources. For all that, the Lazab were only a disease, only a virus. They could be destroyed.

At the source of their magic she would be able to work out the power of the spells they used, by multiplying the speed of their spells by the time is took to create. As Filvani writes in his fifteenth law,

'The Power Of A Spell Is Equal To Its Speed Times The

Once she knew this she would be able to destroy them. Even if she lost her brother in the process. At the very least she could ensure Fulminar survived.

Always, she had to choose who could live and who die. Her heart was lead because of this. Yet Rimfelder had moved her. His innermost thoughts, longing for rest, were so like her own. For peace. For an end to all the choosing. An end to fighting. Somehow, she found comfort in thinking of him. A man riven with sorrow yet still loyal to the living.

She moved on, anxious to be done. Thoughts tumbled towards her like weapons thrown to distract her. Thousands of thoughts jumbled and begging for attention, seemingly from Midrak and Fulminar but all from the Lazab:

"Go back, we can handle this."

"Don't come any closer you'll make things worse the Lazab will kill us with poisons."

"Who are you? Why are you interfering?"

"They're like a sea you'll never succeed they bubble from the depths. As you cut down one, more spring up."

"Save yourself."

"Don't you know Zaqui is coming. We're already dead, leave and save the others."

"We're fine. We'll win. We don't need your help."

"Tobia is blind go and help her."

"Look the stars are bleeding, worlds are dying two magicians don't matter."

"Go left."

"Go right."

"Stay there we'll come and find you."

"Careful if you go down there you'll destroy us all!"

"They're like the sea. The Lazab can't be stopped."

"Why have you come to waste your time here?"

"Fulminar has already died you're too late."

"You are but a third magician for us to eat alive."

"Go back we can handle this."

"Tethval is dead, Rimfelder is dead, Midrak's body floats in a void. Inside him is an ocean of nothingness."

"Why do you interfere?"

"We're a sea and we're flowing into everything."

"You're too late!"

"I don't need your help."

"The universe is not built of energy but magic."

"Go back you're too late."

"Fulminar is dead."

"Tobia is blind!"

"Hear us laugh at you, you can't find us; you can't heal everything with orange blossom, you're trying to buy time but you have no time."

"Midrak is ours."

"Tethval is dead!"

"You're at the end of time, you're too late."

"What good do you do?"

"You'll be overtaken by us in your turn."

"We're a sea."

"We're fine go back we can handle this."

"There are many others to save, two magicians don't matter much."

"Why have you come to this scene of death?"

"What do you hope to achieve?"

"Go that way you'll find us."

"You can do nothing here."

"We're a sea. We bubble up from the depths."

"You're insignificant and powerless before us."

"Go right."

"Go right."

"Go right."

"Help us."

"Help yourself."

"Go left."

"Go."

Thoughts crossed her mind that she should not put herself in danger for a brother she had never known. That maybe she was wrong to try. That she was worth more than him. That Fulminar was too old for the fight as he had been tricked so easily.

These were not her thoughts.

These were the thoughts of the Lazab. They flooded the brain around her with their unique form of mad confusion, their insidious voices pretending to be reason. Always pretending. Listening to her brother's message had allowed them perilously close to her own mind. Their mind games were restless.

The Lazab delight in creating madness for their own pleasure. Creating lifelong suffering in a mind, tormented by their presence. A million, gushing words for every one from their victim; a thousand bubbling ideas for every one of their victim's. All causing mental chaos designed to unsettle, unnerve and eventually rule the mind of their victim by breaking them into pieces. Lazab are parasites.

How had they hidden away in Ruz for so long and survived without being discovered? What had they fed upon? Had Crilodach bred a new kind of Lazab, meant for one brain alone, able to survive for generations waiting for the right time to spring into life? Maybe even born only when the chosen host was ready. She shivered. Somewhere there could be a swarm of Lazab waiting for her.

Maybe they had been waiting for the rich pickings to be had in Zaqui. Like fish caught in an ever more shallow pond, living beings would be corralled into an ever smaller space as Zaqui came closer. In such a small space the minds to be eaten would be numerous and readily available. If only she had had the time to find Fulminar. To formulate a two-pronged attack against the Lazab. Nothing Crilodach ever made could withstand a spellmaker and a Sangyma working together. She lifted the veil around her by opening her mouth and in a firm strong voice she called out,

"Midrak. My brother. I am close."

She knew he would not be able to answer. She knew the Lazab would not be able to resist the temptation of sparring with her.

"He's not here" whispered a rasping voice in her ears made up of many individuals.

"Where then?" she asked.

"In our prison. In our traps. In our hands. Not here. Nowhere any more. Limbo. Our home. Our home here in the brain that was your brother. No more your brother now than we are. No more living than the disease with which we have infected him. No more magician. No more man. A nothing."

The voices dripped with pleasure. Satisfied by their achievements. Many Lazab, many more than a thousand as far as she could tell, joined as one to give them enough power to trap Fulminar as well as destroy Midrak. Their combined power had enabled them to swamp Midrak's mind so completely that Fulminar would never be able to fuse with him. She stopped for a moment. She had to keep them talking while her spells sought them out. Her voice was without fear,

"Where's Fulminar?"

"Weak. Tired. Too long keeping secrets in the world of the

Ruzniel. Too old for our game. He should have died years ago but he chose to live as a shell on Ruz. Now we put him to our ears like a shell and hear him crying his sea of tears. Wrapped in his own shame. The last of the Sangyma. The least of the Sangyma. Hiding away from us in Ruz but we find everyone eventually. We seek all, we find all. We know our time and our time's come. No one can escape us. No one can evade us by dying. We're here to stay. We're the plague that cannot be cured. We're playtime and wakefulness, we're the gods and demons in all things, we're the mighty creatures of your nightmares and you're nothing before us. No one is anything. You all belong to us. All your arts, all your thoughts will belong to us. Time is our father and mother. We're born to rule your every second. We're your inevitable future."

"What is Crilodach to you?" she demanded.

"Our mother."

All victories begin with knowledge. All spells are founded upon their need to exist. Find the right environment and the spell will be created. A magician's art is to discover the spells that exist. Magic is life and life is everywhere. Even Crilodach's magic. If Crilodach had given these creatures life and nurtured them, she knew how to fight them.

You have to look within yourself to know which path you will follow with magic. There is no middle way. No compromise. Death would be her weapon and reward. To want a reward and to fear death were the two greatest enemies of all. She moved on, oblivious to the myriad voices, unheeding of their incessant requests, indifferent to their pounding laughter.

The synapses of a magician's brain mutate with time. They are never the same from one moment to the next. A magician cannot think of the same thing the same way twice. The synapses which course through your brain, are invisible in a magician. The course of thought no more substantial than the noise of the spoken words of a spell. Though words have their greatest power in poets. The thinking part of a magician's brain, the cauldron of ideas, is awash with infinity. There are no stray thoughts in these minds, nothing half-formed. The colours in the ideas and notions are all purposeful. The thickness of certainty, the delicacy of understanding. The shyness of a new spell, the swiftness of an ancient command. The sparkle of a new idea, the heavy canvas of decision. Their invisibility had slowed the Lazab down. A spellmaker like Lilah is able to see into and through anything invisible.

The Lazab, born from the belly of a galaxy long since evaporated, destroy a mind by short-circuiting ideas. They leave their vomit everywhere and the contours of the spells are forced to move around the contagion, interrupting each other. Striking each other, sparking as they strike each other, until the magician can no longer think straight. Like a species over-breeding the mind-imps cannot permit anything else to inhabit the ground on which they feed. They corrupt the flow of the inner-life. Their laughter permeates every tissue until the brain cannot pierce the noise. The hideous, continual noise. The Lazab were beginning to find out that powerful magicians can never be forced into total madness, they live or die. No middle way. To be able to kill is a skill, but to enjoy the killing is a madness. All Lazab enjoy their work. They, too, have no middle way.

As the mind starts to die thoughts ramble where they should not go. Lost in a vibrant confusion every little idea becomes a mountain to climb, each minor incident a calamity. Reason drifts upon a raft in a wide, wide sea of anxiety unable to drink their salted thoughts without dying. The absurd becomes the normal and the normal becomes the offspring of insanity. Midrak was killing himself as slowly as he could, in the hope of defeating them before he died. He sensed Lilah. Knew who she was but all he could do was repeat the same things over and over in the hope she would hear. He did not know if she could. So he watched her move and in his secret way he guided her steps. With the subtlety of a spider avoiding the dew on a leaf. With the brilliance of her healing helping him he followed her and focussed upon her. She became his path. Through her he could see. Through her he could feel again. Through her he cut through the chaos. Through her he could find himself. Through her he would live.

She knew how to defeat them. She had to try to give his remaining thoughts as much power as she could. She had to stabilize the damage caused by the Lazab. She had to start to destroy them. They knew she had to destroy them. If she left one behind, that one could hide away and act as a spy for Crilodach helping It uncover all their plans. Worse maybe able to breed a whole new horde to infect Midrak at a later stage in their final battle with Crilodach.

"Where are we?" teased the voices.

"Everywhere," she replied calmly.

Listening. She breathed in and wrapped herself in a cloak of purple and green woven with silks from her fingers with the speed of a star finally dying.

The cloak stopped the incessant laughter from the Lazab. The deceit of the Lazab could not penetrate such delicate fibres. Frustrated by their inability to fathom her thoughts they might be scared enough to reveal themselves The Lazab doubted themselves for a second, like a parachutist on the edge of the void, momentarily seeing all the potential for death. Midrak sensed her inside her cloak, understanding what she was trying to do.

"Come then, witch, come find us. We're rich, we're poor. We're few. We're more. We've time to play with you. All the time left in the universe as everything falls into our hands to be reborn in our image, not yours, witch. Reborn for our pleasure. You've no time. You've no place. You'll die first and we'll watch. We'll count your kind down one by one. The Sangyma, the Ruzniel, the magicians, the Arvernat, the poet. All of you one by one."

The first region of the mind of a magician, at the base of their brains, is small. This is the place where the magician first realizes magic is in the universe. This rounded area, called the magibellum minoris, is filled with the potential of many futures. From here their strength flows into a large section of individual thoughts, the magibellum majoris, where different ideas pour into their muscles and their spells make thoughts into action. This secondary region is a place where no thoughts live, only raw power, bright and vital. Power flowing through them and out of them. Here where there should have been nothing because the Lazab were blocking Midrak's thoughts, Lilah found a black stone object set upon a pedestal. Or rather a perfect replica of stone and black marble. She stopped.

"Do you speak?" she demanded.

The stone creaked slightly, but did not move. The surface shone like a moonlit pond. She stared. The stone slowly unwound, snake-like, growing to touch the skin of her hand. The touch was cold. Colder than ice. Suddenly the stone was all about her, closing in to crush her. Hardening again, black and threatening. She lifted her arms and felt great weights trying to force them down. Her eyes blazed as she wrenched the sides of the stone and tore into the hard shell, to find an incredible softness. Bleeding from her scratches. The Lazab were laughing but no laughter came from the stone. She stopped. She breathed in. Then she let the stone set with her inside. She was no longer cold. Fulminar's voice came to her,

"You know how to hurt Lilah," he told her.

"I did not recognize you for a moment."

"You cannot recognize anyone here. They have changed the forms of everything."

"What happened?"

"The enemy destroyed Ruz. I was there at the last. Midrak found Tobia just in the nick of time. I was selfish Lilah, I should have died but I saw a chance to continue the struggle by becoming a part of Midrak. He asked me to. I wanted so much to continue to the very end. To give a roundness to my existence. I was so entranced by the idea I did not see the Lazab. Did not know they had crept up on us as we spoke." His voice sounded wretched. He went on,

"I thought I was hidden deeper than I needed to be. I forgot Its cunning. I thought only of living on. As if in escaping death once, I thought I had gained the right to always escape. I forgot to look everywhere before making my move. At the point of crisis, when I opened Midrak's mind to my own, as Ruz fell, when I could no longer hold the small part together in which we talked, they flowed into him with me. Laughing like children entering a sweet shop. I tried to turn back, to stop myself but I was too late and as I twisted and fought, Midrak cried out. The shock was too much for him. I thought we were all dead there and then. Where are we now?"

"A dying city kept alive by Bofindle," she answered.

"And who is here?"

"Me and some fighters who have no idea of the times we are living through. They have just fought for their liberation from their own tyrant."

"Liberation has come too late for them. And for me. I should never have attempted to stay alive."

"How can you say that? You are needed. Wisdom must not be lost. Do not blame yourself. My brother should have realized and been more careful. He was right to want you to be part of him. You are just that we need."

"Had I let him go the Lazab would not have had an opportunity to invade his mind. Now, for all my efforts, I am relegated to hiding in his brain and cannot help, whilst they play in the higher reaches of his thoughts preventing him from moving on. We are losing time. Every second weakens our chances."

"Which is why you can help me now."

"I have to fight for my own existence here. Their numbers have choked off all the paths to communicating with your brother. They have left this place empty and cold, already, I fear, the brain of a dead man. I can only move to finish the spell to join with our brother and only defeating them will enable me to live."

"This is not an auspicious way to meet."

"We should expect nothing less. Can you handle them alone?"

"I think so."

"Zananto taught you well," he said.

"She did."

"You know Zananto was my love?"

"She spoke of you. I know your body fell that fateful day when Tegriel brought you news of me. She told me things. Some of which I should not have known but we became friends. She was proud of you. She told me all the stories of your long existence and she wept as she talked about the loss of your body and how for a long time she thought you absolutely dead."

"She should not have told you that."

"I was a daughter to her. Mothers tell their daughters many things," Lilah explained.

"What else did you learn from her?"

"All the arts of Tegriel, all the arts of Fulminar, Filvani's laws and all the arts of creation. Birth and death are my hands, light and darkness are my names, time and nothingness are my virtues. In me the oldest arts of magic have found their voice, their hands and their eyes. I am ready for the future. But even I cannot see all things clearly. For some reason some things are being hidden from me. I cannot believe the enemy hides Itself from me or overcomes my powers of perception. This is something other than It. Some other source of power against which I may have to vie for victory. Or maybe in hiding from me, this magic also manages to hide from our enemies. I do not know. I take comfort from Bofindle, nothing may withstand such a bejal."

"I understand you perfectly. The Sangyma always had the same feeling of things being hidden. As if we had a role in a play but we did not know the ending. I always thought the Sagitæ were responsible for that," he told her.

"I agree with you."

"Save Midrak. That is what is important. I will look to myself you must concentrate upon your brother."

"Are you hurt?"

"Your hands are powerful but my thoughts are deeper than cuts or blood. Until I can fuse with Midrak fully, I am still in danger of dying, but he is the one who must be saved. I am a secondary consideration."

"I shall save you both."

"Do not think of me when you fight the Lazab, no arguments do not think if me at all. I know what I am talking about. Do not look for me or expect me. The less you think of me the stronger you will be."

She floated upwards, the protective shell opened again to allow her to depart and she left the spirit of Fulminar. She found herself in the intertwining regions of her brother's brain where memories and spells meet. The Lazab had clustered around. They had seen her. They knew where Fulminar was hiding. They had gathered and waited for her to come out. Like bats they clung to the very air and she felt the spiteful claws of their venom, like acid drops, everywhere she turned.

The noise was so loud they hurt her ears. Laughter. Spitting. Shouting. Cursing. The coarse din of a nation going to war. The storm was like a sharp, continuous blast of intensely cold air, all ice and noise, freezing out everything that was warm and alive. They knew she was a danger to them. Others fell into the web of Lazab madness as readily as rain falls from black clouds but Midrak was strong. They began to believe Fulminar had brought with him some spell or other they could not find, to strengthen Midrak's will to stay alive. They suspected if they could kill her they would win the day.

They spat at her and tore at the webbing about her skin. Their darts were poisoned, their mouths open and gaping, they tried to eat her with gaping mouths, to beat her with flat, spiky claws, to confuse her with their clamour. Their burning webs wrapped themselves around her. From all directions they sprang. Like confetti spilling from a thousand hands.

She was smothered, weighed down, drenched in their bile. They clapped and jeered. She let them envelop her. She knew the fastest way to find their leader was to let them take her where they wanted her to go. Where they were strongest. Most numerous. Beings like this always had a leader. There was always one greater than the rest, one who commanded. One who was stronger or faster or had had the luck to kill the previous leader. When the enemy came in large numbers they were always led. They could never think for themselves.

She was not scared of them. She had been trained to fight by those who had stood alone in the dark, in the desert of hopelessness and still fought with everything they had. She was a spellmaker. They did not know that yet, but they may as well have captured Crilodach Itself for all the victory she was ever going to let them taste. They were about to feel anger as they had never before experienced.

She pretended she was more tired than she was. She let them lead her, tearing at them only once in a while to remind them she was alive. They bubbled with joy at her feeble struggling. She heard their laughter. She felt them drag her upwards. Upwards. Their numbers grew. Their laughter and glee filled everything. The stench grew. The sides of all Midrak's thoughts had a green tinge to them, the excreta of the enemy splattered thick like paste. She listened as they jeered and sang. They cat-called and spoke in a dozen languages. They took her deeper into their hive. Continuously pulling at her. Like a weird circus act of misshapen tumblers and acrobats. Then she saw one through the webbing. Through the smallest slit in the rotting stench which covered her.

This one was a naked figure with no real face. No strong body but the sickly pale, thin body of a figure used to hiding. This Lazab's hands were large, like blobs and everything they touched quivered as if a cold touch of death had swept out from them. As if water had passed the lips of a thirsty woman but she never swallowed because her thirst had decayed her to the bone. This Lazab slid around, listening to their laughter as if laughter were food and the feast had started. He was not only laughing. In his large hands were pieces of Midrak's brain that had died. He was juggling with them occasionally taking a bite and swallowing, his flabby lips sucking at the small pieces.

Lilah was sick at the sight but she controlled her anger. She was feeling out her enemy. She knew she had yet to find the leader. The mind–imps were all gathering. He waved them all on and they started to drag her again, going past this sentry to their inner hive.

She let them drag her on. Over the soft surface of the mind which was hardening as their grip increased. Setting like cement. She let them think she was powerless. Unperceived by the mob she let drops of oil run from her hands which seeped into the hurt and the cuts. She no longer even tried to get free. She let them think they had vanquished her.

Finally they brought her to a large chamber. The centre of their hive. She heard and saw her brother. Saw a mass of thoughts without a face twisted into thick knots. Bright as sunshine and covered with webbing. With thousands of hands grabbing all at once. Surrounded by Lazab dancing like revelers at a sacrifice, as Midrak's mind fought them off, brandishing his magic, burning with light, slicing into them and though he killed some, ever more came. Born from a vile womb. A demanding, fearless, dancing rabble of agonies.

Before them all their leader sat. The one she had needed to hunt out. The one she had to defeat. She was hauled up towards him and the webbing from her face pulled away. The jeering lessened, the Lazab closest to her looked wary, waiting for orders. Others licked their mouths. They had never seen this before. Another, disembodied magician, inside the mind of one of their victims. They were unsure how to kill her. All they had ever done was eat minds. Yet here there was someone who was not mind, amongst them. She had the body of a woman and yet she was all magic. They dribbled in expectation of this new taste.

The leader breathed out and his breath filled the chamber. This was the stench which had filled her nose since she embarked upon this journey. And the thick, coldness of his breath vibrated. And the vibration quivered with sneering, and the sneering filled everything with a chill echo. This vile Lazab was the strongest ever known. He let out a deep throated growl. Two eyes slowly emerged from this ugly body. Large and grey. They blinked. He looked around. He stared at her. She stared back.

"Lilah!" gloated Debroc their leader, "Well, well this a good day. Midrak ours, Fulminar is trapped, and here in chains is Lilah. The great champion of the fools who stand against us. Tied, trussed and ready to eat. You will suffer more than the others. You dare to try to undo what I've done. You a mere woman. They did not even send a man to fight me. Me, the greatest of the Lazab. Debroc the mighty."

He laughed. All the Lazab laughed and beat their hands together. Mind-imps are huge chauvinists.

"I was not sent," she replied, slowly.

"You're a fool to take me on alone."

"I am ready for your death Debroc," she told him.

"As I yours. Your mind will die. We'll torment you for as long as we can. Crilodach will be pleased with this work. You're a prize. This day I've a great champion trapped, her body stranded on a world destroyed. The remnants held together only by Bofindle but that bejal is outside and can't enter here without killing your brother. That's exactly what you don't want and now can't stop. You should've brought the Bofindle with you. That would've beaten us. That would've flattened us. Without your mighty weapon, you're nothing."

"I am never nothing," she warned him.

"Weak and puny woman. Not even food enough for one meal. With you trapped Bofindle will play no part in events. We'll creep out of here into your body. We'll take our time. I'll keep you here. See already I've dispatched two of my best. They'll creep. Cling to your clothes. Slink into your ears. One in each and they'll eat their way through, whilst you're chained in here. You'll feel them. Slowly they'll go. You'll feel them eat out your eyes and blind you, feel them consume you until only one piece is left. That piece is my feast. What a day! What good work. What fun work. A shame this deed was not accomplished long ago then I, Debroc the mighty, could bask in my glory for longer."

"Always thinking of how grand you are. What are you without your orders and your betters? Not even meal enough for one spell," she said.

"I'll live after Zaqui. You didn't think we could do that did you? You didn't think we knew how, did you? You who've striven for generations to find the way to survive the end and oversee the birth of the new universe. We're the ones who've discovered how. I've been promised my place for

154

destroying Fulminar but joy, oh joy, I've a magician and a spellmaker as well. Now my place will be great indeed! Your capture'll make me greater still. You think we're fools but you're the fools. Pathetic little martyrs. Self-sacrifice is all you know. Selfishness is our strength. We're never caught out, never held up, never weakened by duty or feelings. We're tireless in this universe and in the new we'll be in control. Minds'll be created just for me to enjoy. I'll gorge myself on a million like you, no a billion! I'll keep a piece of you back and take you with me so I may create you again and again and each time I'll kill you slowly. That'll teach them to send a woman to harm me. A woman to break me. That'll teach them all."

"You would not have the wit for this," Lilah argued, "Your little army of Lazab is nothing but a side show. Crilodach has a universe to rule and whatever It has promised you It will never deliver. You're Its lackey. Crilodach uses such as you for sport. It promises you eternal life so you will do Its work."

"Crilodach is not my master," shouted Debroc.

"If It knows how to live on, It is too selfish to share. Wherever you end up depends wholly upon where It decides to put you," she argued.

Debroc smiled his toothless smile. Those who eat brains do not need teeth to chew.

"I'll be inside them. My mind-imps even now have plans. I don't care which side wins or loses for each side has brains. Each side has thoughts and as long as I'm inside the mind of the victor, I'm victorious."

"You would seek to invade Its mind?" she asked, wondering if the Lazab had gone quite mad.

"I'd infect any mind and stay there. Wait to see what happens. See the universe die. I could be inside anyone. Anywhere. Waiting. Watching. Do you understand? As you all betrayed yourselves and danced your battles and killed and maimed, I've danced from one to another. I've taken my chance here and there. My mind-imps paving the way, a safe haven for a little while and then another and then another. Always the same dance. Always I'm inside someone. Eating away. Sometimes slowly, sometimes quickly depending upon my whim. Waiting for my victory. I'll bring you to Crilodach, the most powerful of Its enemies and I'll dance into Its mind and wait for everlasting life. Those that sought to rule me will be ruled by me."

"The enemy you pay court to is too dangerous to ever be used."

"I've no friends. Why shouldn't I make everyone my enemy? I've been vilified in many planets. I'm told I drive people mad. Me. What do I do but give them thoughts they otherwise wouldn't have had? They should enjoy my stay, they can do nothing to evict me. But they try to rid themselves of me so then, I do little more than remind them of the thoughts they ought not to have. A little game. Have you seen Midrak's thoughts?"

Debroc was enjoying this moment. Everything was pointing to victory. Before her eyes the Lazab joined and made a circle and inside their blankness there appeared lights, and in the lights figures. As they merged and came together, she started to move her fingers along the webbing. Playing the strands like stings. She had heard enough, the time had come to act.

The thoughts of her brother opened up before her. She saw him calling her. She saw his face, his eyes opened wide. Fighting off madness as his mind was plagued with alien laughter and endless words from the Lazab. Then she saw Ruz exploding; Tethval's home planet under siege and shattering to bits. Blackness and laughter. She saw Midrak as a boy killing a bird. He had never done that. She saw him as a man crying over a dead Ruzniel. She saw him making magic in Ruz and floating towards Tobia. Then she saw her face. A young face, rippling in water where he had cast a spell to see his sister. She heard Debroc laughing.

She saw Tobia blinded and Lilah grew even more angry. A deep down anger that she had had to learn to control when she had been a teenager. The anger that had made her so formidable a fighter when she had learned to channel and focus such a rage that whole planets would crumble at her shout. The anger that gave her the strength to fight without rest, to hit out without softness, to move without drawing breath. The anger that had made her perfect to be the finest spellmaker ever to have lived. This is what made her uncompromising in defending what she knew was right. Determined in what she knew she had to do. All she had had to learn from her teachers was subtlety and patience and she had learned both. Her anger spread through her every pore, saturated her skin in sweat. But this was not normal

Lazab

sweat. This dripped on to the webbing they had covered her in, changing the chemical make-up of the strands. Realigning the atoms and rebuilding them so swiftly the Lazab were unaware of what was happening. This was a nano spell.

"Your picture show is over," she said.

"I make the rules," screamed Debroc.

"You have done all I will allow," she told them.

"I am laughing at you. You trussed up and awaiting death, allow nothing."

"I wonder at your stupidity at laughing when you should be running," she told him.

"Watch her you fools," he cried, sensing the web was loosening.

More webbing was flung around her. Inside her fingers strummed until the new webbing she had created began to vibrate. Hitting a high note. A single, soft, continuous note. She strummed her fingers so quickly no one could hear when one note ended and a new one began. She strummed. Always the same note repeated.

"Stop her!" Debroc cried again.

The note played over and over. The fresh webbing they stuck to her, changed instantly and vibrated. The note played on as her fingers strummed.

"Stop trying to entrap her within webbing. Stop. She's using that against you! Go to her body. Quickly. Invade her mind."

The webbing was now so thick they were blocked from getting to her. They had cordoned her off from their claws by their own stupidity.

Lilah smiled and played faster until the Lazab began to fall off their perches with the vibrancy of the tone and Midrak's whole mind resonated with the single, high note. The Lazab leader clapped his ears with his hands and screamed but no sound came from his mouth anymore, or if any did the single note downed out the sound. The note unsettled them, but such was the perfection of the spell that the note at the same time strengthened Midrak and Fulminar. Shattering the Lazab's effectiveness and giving a clear path to her other spells. Midrak's thoughts unwound. The tight knot spread out. The Lazab fæces vanished. The green turned to living tissue once more. The Lazab fell on to their hands and as they touched the reborn mind they melted.

What was left of them evaporated as spells in the oil she had dripped from her fingers sought them out. Midrak's mind strengthened and sharpened. Colours blazed in every corner.

Suddenly Lilah was unbound. How she had freed herself none of them could see. The thick webbing was draped over her arms and still she played. Standing softly upon a single idea. She threw the webbing down but the note played on without her fingers strumming. Everywhere she went the Lazab vanished before her and she ran with long steps. She ran like the wind through the mind and behind her came Midrak's lightning thoughts repairing his mind, and when she knew he was in control she stopped running. Now Midrak's mind was a dangerous place for her. She could not stay here once he had regained control. Two magicians cannot let their essences meet in the same place without fusing. If they tried, one would die.

She looked back. She had not seen what had happened to Debroc the mighty. She had to go quickly before her presence became dangerous to Midrak. She lifted her fingers for a brief second, placed them together and swept back to her body. She opened her eyes. She felt the Lazab close by her ears that had been sent to eat her brain. She intoned quietly to herself. She felt them no more. She sat up, uncrossed her legs and her feet lightly touched the floor. She looked about her. She could see where the battle had raged in the room. Then her thoughts turned to Tobia, and what she had been shown by the mind–imps.

"Tobia?" she called, softly.

"I'm here," she answered from the door, "they tried to get to you. But for Bofindle they would have succeeded."

"They have blinded you?"

"I'm alright. I no longer need light to see. Tegriel shows me the way. Look."

She walked around the room with ease and took Midrak's hand. Midrak opened his eyes. He was groggy. His head hurt but he was awake. He let out a small groan and then he turned his aching head to face Lilah. For a long moment they stared into each others' eyes. His face broke into a pale smile. He raised himself on his elbow and was sick on the floor. He coughed and cleared his throat.

"I think I will hear that music in my head for the rest of my life."

"That music will help you heal more quickly. Like a charm," his sister told him.

"Thank you," he said.

"How is Fulminar?" she asked.

"He is with me now. His eyes are my eyes. His strength returns. I have a terrible headache but we have succeeded. The Lazab are dead. I need some time to repair the damage to my brain but we can do that as we talk."

"Your eyes Midrak, one of them is a different colour to the other?"

"One of my eyes is now Fulminar's. He will see everything I do and hear everything I hear. I feel stronger carrying him with me."

"I am glad he survived. When you feel like getting up we must go outside," she said.

"Outside?" he looked around the room, "Where are we?"

"On the remains of a planet. We have leave here."

"I am ready," he agreed.

"How did you manage to call me?"

"Call you, when?" he asked her.

"To come and find you here on this world."

"I did not." Midrak sat up. His head spun and he reached out for Tobia who steadied him.

"I have spent enough time in the netherworld. Come Tobia." He stopped and looked at the Ruzniel again. "Tobia, your eyes."

"I'm alright," she said softly. "Truly I'm alright." Midrak tried to rise to his feet but they buckled under him.

"I must be a little more careful whom I let into my mind in future."

"A few hours' rest," suggested Tobia.

"No, we must go now. A few hours is too much," said Lilah. "We must get to the others and finish this once and for all." She put her arm under his and lifted him up. He steadied himself. He took a step with her help.

"That's enough, I must do this on my own to heal faster" he said.

She let him go. He rested against the wall and then with his hand on Tobia's shoulder and Lilah by his side, he walked out of the room.

Outside was devastation. If any hearts felt uplifted by seeing the brother and sister together none of them cheered for they were all too tired, traumatized and unable to see any future for themselves. As she looked around knowing what was coming one thought filled Lilah's mind. If Fulminar had called her here he would have said. If neither he nor Midrak had, what or who had brought her here to find her brother? What deeper magic was in play? The time was finally coming when the Sagitæ would reveal themselves. She knew they were involved somehow. But she could not feel them. Not yet.

Copret

Chloe carefully pinned the last chart to the others, flattening the whole layout with the dry, clean palm of her hand, biting her lips she was concentrating so hard, because she was so scared of making a tear. She liked things to be just right. She had to stretch over and strain her arms because, like all the other bits, this final part was much wider than her. The paper they were drawn upon felt smooth and warm to her touch. Any creases vanished on their own. If she had been asked she would have described them as friendly maps. Each of them had felt different. Some were even furry which really unnerved her for a moment. All their colours were vivid and obviously hand painted. Gold leaf edging was finely fixed so they married up exactly and as they met they glowed into each other as if they were happy to be joined and then their perfectly cut edges vanished, making them seamless. The bears had designed these charts carefully, for smaller hands than theirs but no less clear eyes.

She stood on a chair, looking down at what she had accomplished. The charts could be put together many different ways so finding the right combinations had taken a lot of effort. The details on the maps were intricate and small. Though she had noticed as you began to peer at particularly small areas they did seem to become bigger as she looked, as if they automatically magnified to suit the eyes that looked at them. This would be very useful for people who usually need glasses to read small letters. In fact most things in this fortress seemed to know you were looking at them. Even Demeter had noticed nothing seemed to remain the same for more than a minute.

Demeter was also changing before her eyes. She had made lots of tut–tut noises as she worked. Demeter had tiptoed around like a scared cat with wide open eyes. He had been badly shaken by his experience on the stairwell. Once, when he had disturbed her she had snapped at him sarcastically,

"Haven't you got a stone to push."

One thing Chloe would not tolerate was being distracted when she was concentrating. He did not know if everything in this place exploded at his touch but he had the tentative desire to try again and a delicious fear of what might happen when he did. Once or twice he had stood on the top of the stairwell and looked down, counting the steps, wondering why nothing had happened to Chloe when she had tried the same thing. He had an imperfect sense of his own power. He felt special. He had never felt this way before, frightening and yet welcoming at the same time. What kind of power had been given to him? He had a longing to learn. What held him back was not wanting to try anything without Chloe being next to him. Without her he could not overcome his fear of not knowing what to do. Was this the test? This anticipation. This uncertainty. This longing to see his new-found powers in action.

He had taken to sleeping on the side of the parapet overlooking the sea. Half way through that first night he had rolled into the walling with a thump. He awoke with a start, his nose hurting from the bump. His heart was thumping in his chest as he was half awake and scared in case he had accidentally set something off again, and a little disappointed nothing happened. He had not slept for the rest of the night but did not feel tired when day broke. He would never feel tired again.

Chloe was so engrossed in her charts, he could not find the right time to tell her he was half-way between euphoria and terror. He kept telling himself to 'get a grip.' What if he had fallen over the edge during that night? Could he fly? The ground was a very long way down. Yet somehow, and he did not know how, he had the strangest feeling if he had, the fortress would have saved him. This impressive building felt like part of his family. Strange. The stone felt alive. The longer he walked around the stronger the feeling became.

His heart raced as he passed other rooms and doors because the stone turned different colours as he drew closer. Worse still, he recalled she said that what he had done might be a signal. To think he might have summoned someone but he did not know who, why or very much about how, made him feel queasy.

What if he had summoned a 'something'?

What would have to do or not do when 'they' arrive?

What will 'they' say or not say to him?

Did he do something wrong or right, or mostly in-between?

Wherever he turned his mind raced with questions to which he had no immediate answers.

He became watchful of everything. Even noticing the spiders' webs that hanged in some corners of some rooms. He watched them being made by large blue spiders with nine legs. He counted the strands. He counted the spiders. He became an expert in how they started to make their webs, something he had never noticed before. He even learned they could jump. He wondered if they could talk.

He needed to eat but not because he was hungry. He realized his mind was hungrier than his stomach. The power in him was being released slowly and the fortress was calling him. He knew that he would never leave this place. He did not think that was a good or bad thing, just the truth. If you had looked at him now you would have noticed that the young boy was walking round with a very straight back and an assured step he had not shown on the journey through the valley. Demeter was becoming proud of his effect on the stone, as if he had come-of-age. Though he still kept his hands off the walls and one eye on Chloe. Thinking himself special did not change the fact that he disliked the thought of showing himself to be foolish in front of her.

Chloe looked intently at her finished work from her perch on the chair. The charts on the table showed her the skyline from the roof of the building. Finding the stairs they had climbed to get in had been her first success. Then she had found the window and even in these charts the room was shown with the charts on the walls but now as she looked, the charts had moved from the room, and were now shown across part of the floor in the room they were in. She saw the stars as she had watched them the night before and triumphantly she had pointed out to him how hundreds were missing in the sky. When they vanished they were swept from the charts as well. Where one was missing on the charts a brown mark, like foxing, appeared.

"They're keeping track of events in real time," she said, under her breath.

The sky was changing fast, as each and every hour more and more foxing appeared. More importantly for her was the discovery that this fortress had a name. A name she remembered Wei K'un using once without thinking and she instinctively understood he had been mistaken, so she said not asked him any questions. Demeter came in and stood by her side looking at the huge map set out in front of him.

"Its done," she told him.

He touched the paper lightly and a slight breeze wafted over the room and suddenly the maps became three dimensional and the fortress appeared translucent. They could see inside, around, and above from where they stood rotating the whole hologram with a flick on their fingers. For a second he worried he had done something wrong but she was smiling.

"Beautiful," she said.

"Everything's fading away in the sky," he said.

"Yes everything is."

"I don't think that's anything to crow over," he said flatly.

"I'm not crowing but your observation is right and that's important because now we have to plan for the future we know is coming."

"You think there's one?"

"Course. Why don't you?"

"Everything's vanishing?" he said. "That's a pretty empty future."

He stopped walking around the hologram and faced her across the split table, looking through the image towards her and seeing the universe move across her face.

"Even," she replied, her fists on her hips, "more because of that, than for any other reason."

"Your plan's what then?"

"I haven't gotten that far," she admitted.

"Will you ever?"

"The charts are here to show us what's happening. We can work on our response from there."

"I don't even know what I can and can't do, how can we form a plan?"

"All I know is the charts are beginning to make sense. Anything that makes sense takes us a step or two forward in the test."

"I think we need to leap forward," he said. He kicked one of the chairs and the three dimensional map vanished. He grimaced,

"I ... I'm sorry. I'm still nervous."

"That's ok I don't suppose this is easy for you but this is hard enough to do on my own without you telling me as much."

"I feel I'm close to something incredible but can't for the life of me see what. I feel really ... dumb," he said.

"We all get that way sometimes."

"You feel dumb?" He didn't believe her.

"I took most of the night to do this. I should've only taken a few hours."

"I should be more help but I don't like touching anything."

"I'm surprised you touched the charts then."

"I couldn't help myself. They looked so lovely. Least they didn't explode."

"Is fear the reason why you close your eyes before you put your hand out to touch anything?"

"I'm a coward."

"You should be braver. The light didn't kill us just unnerved us. Touch the charts again. I want to study the hologram."

He did as she asked. He bent down until his eyes were level with one corner of the table, and looked at the image closely.

"Unnerved's an understatement," he said, "I feel like the only things I can trust are you and ... you. Seems all the charts say is 'you're here' and by-the-way 'here' is disappearing."

Looking across the top and down into the fortress staring at the countless stairs she replied,

"Your turn to do something will come, don't worry."

He had walked round and was by her chair as he looked up and said,

"You're always so positive."

"I'm almost a month older than you."

"That makes no difference."

"The Terika aren't ordinary people. We've come from a strange past, one where we've been taught to do things a certain way for a reason we've never really known. I don't know why we teach clones. We just do. We do other things but our families have always said this was very important work. Perhaps so we could be of the best help to you."

"To me?" His voice was filled with disbelief.

"Who knows," she shrugged.

"This whole set of tasks takes some getting used to," he told her scratching the back of his head.

She hadn't told him everything she knew. She was unsure herself how much he could take in, in one go. She was not completely sure herself. She could see the difference in him yet he was still so unsure of himself she felt she had better leave key elements of the story out. She had been even younger when her aunt had told her the epic stories about the universe. She had always enjoyed knowing about the Sangyma and shivered whenever Crilodach's name was mentioned. Like a knife wound that pulled at unseen scars in her heart, the name made everyone chilly and uneasy and brought back all the nightmarish stories their aunts told them when they were small, in the dark night when the shadows veiled the eyes. As if fear of Crilodach was something inborn; something that did not have to be learned; something every living thing shared.

How children were gobbled up whole. How armies sank without trace into space. How gases swirled around towns and transformed themselves into creatures with sharp teeth. Worlds devoured whole, blood drunk in barrel–fulls, lives ripped apart in their millions. They were always told the most innocent looking animal was deadly if they came from Crilodach, and anyone, even the most beautiful and handsome of creatures, was an enemy once they had given themselves over to It.

She did not tell Demeter that Crilodach's name appeared in the charts. The unmistakable name. The whispered name. She knew the charts were not Its creation, so she and Demeter were not Its prisoners. This fortress was nothing to do with It. This place was their haven for the moment. Despite that certainty, It was there in their future and she knew, somewhere, It would appear and she would have to confront her old nightmares. The nightmares of her people. She could not show her fear. She had to be strong. Firm. She had to be in command, for Demeter's sake. For the sake of all creation. That was her test.

Until she was sure, she kept these worries to herself but she forgot Demeter was changing. He saw her eyes were troubled and he in his turn knew she would confide in him when she wanted to. He trusted her enough to give her space. He had changed enough to guess at some of the truth. At another time he would have assumed the charts were showing something that was not happening. That the stars were not disappearing. He would have assumed they were the test. But the Demeter who would have thought anything in this fortress would mislead him was already gone.

Here, in these charts, Chloe noticed the writings showed through the three dimensional image created by Demeter. Swirling calligraphy thick with ancient inks, rounded and elegant, swiftly moving across the table. Not a drop of ink out of place. Not a letter obscured. Each line ending in a gentle swirl. Each line beginning just so. The ink thickening where needed, translucent where necessary so she could see what lay beneath the letters. Pictures of places. People. Animals. She looked at the layout and her brain buzzed. The ink was a story. A scribe's passion for the unfolding of an epic. Zaqui. The ink flowed like time. For at the end of things time, like ink, can come in a thick amount or a thin amount depending on who is casting the spell and whose power is being revealed. As Filvani famously explained the manipulation of time changes the effect of spells but those are very complex pages only a few could ever understand.

The words of knowledge, of laughter, of pain and hope, the words of warning and, in the centre of everything, the fortress. The building they had called a stair city when they first arrived but now she knew the real name, Trecrogo. A magical fortress. The centre of a coming war. Built by the great bears sent to the Earth after the humans had been destroyed and their planet hidden. Bears that knew how to ask rocks buried in Losek soil, to build themselves together. Bears that moulded spells into the blocks so they would withstand the assaults of the enemy. Mighty black, brown and grey bears with great strength. Communal, thoughtful, intelligent and dedicated animals. Female and male working with equal strength and speed. Thousands of these great creatures spent decades building to a design drawn up by their elders. How every day they set themselves the tasks to complete and by every evening they achieved their aims. How the sun and moon helped them. How the rain was mixed into the stone blocks, how the Earth joined the blocks together to the proton, in seamless rows. How they rested and played at night, and then carried on again under the sunlight. Year upon year. Never thinning their ranks. Never sleeping too long. No one was hurt in this magical building. No one was buried under Trecrogo's foundations, for these foundations were not rooted in the Earth at all.

Trecrogo took power from beyond this world and was built to be a citadel for the few defenders who, in the last three days, would stand against It. Tall and powerful, open as a book; closed as a mountain. To their enemies the fortress would send out fear, to their friends Trecrogo would instill boldness, hope, strength and wonder. To their enemies the fortress would look dark and austere, to their allies every stone would shine with all the colours of the rainbow.

But deep within Trecrogo's structure was the secret that the fortress was not built to resist an onslaught alone. The main purpose was something quite different. Something Crilodach would not be expecting.

There were no eyes that could see where Trecrogo ended, no clouds that could float above the parapet. Yet the fortress had a certain height and the circular walls spanned the plains and seashore. They were inside a living building. Almost breathing. Thinking. Waiting with them because Trecrogo's story was being told within theirs. Waiting for the war to come. No longer waiting for the one to come who would unlock this immense power for Demeter was now here. Still waiting for Copret and the gathering of the allies. Still waiting to find out how many of those named would survive to reach this final battleground.

"If the stars are disappearing," he had said that morning, when she had been searching the skies, "how come we're still here."

"Not our turn yet," she replied, flatly.

He had looked at her. Suddenly he had that strong sense of fate that comes to all clones. The realization of knowing that you have been designed and not simply born. She stared at him. Even the air he was breathing was giving him knowledge, infused with the breath of the bears who had built Trecrogo. He was still a young boy outside but his mind was almost near manhood. He felt strong. Able. His mind was grappling with new ideas and possibilities. He was trying to understand so much and slowly, he was achieving his goal. That first beacon was working on him even though he was unaware how. Trecrogo knew he was here. Trecrogo was opening up the bears' secrets. Trecrogo, which had stood almost empty since the last of the bears had left, was awakening. And, far away, Lilah was aware they had arrived. And alive within Tobia, Tegriel knew they were there. And even further away, the last to know where a group of magicians only Rimfelder was destined to meet.

Chloe could follow the stars as they moved and vanished, so she had some idea of how much time they had. Precious little. Last night she had looked at the sky and seen two stars vanishing one after the other. She had given them their names. Inwarth and Gearin. Gone, and with them went the peoples of six worlds. They too would vanish from the face of history in their time. Some of the peoples may know, some others may have found out too late but how was Trecrogo going to save everyone? What would they live on? Where? For how long?

She looked at the charts. The answers were simple. Nothing, nowhere and just two more days. They were no more than pieces in a jigsaw. Death and life are two sides of the same knife edge, to exist is to be cut by the knife when death takes all. In every part of the universe and in every world and for every individual there were battles going on even as she stared at the hologram. In her mind's eye she saw them. Great wars and little wars. Nations were dying, people were running, leaders were being found, leaders were being lost, women, men and animals were strewn across the stars. Across seas, in valleys, on mountains and plains, in ships, cities and space, all were convulsing as, led by events they did not even see, did not even know existed, they fought to extinction.

The battles, like Tethval's, were but ripples created by the greatest war of all. She saw her fight was for freedom. For other peoples' freedom not her own. The defenders on Trecrogo would pay the price for that freedom. Just as Lilah had explained to Tethval, she saw she would get nothing for fighting. No memorial, no lasting name, no epic tales or rousing songs sung to her. Nor would Demeter who was the vital part of the jigsaw.

She knelt down and felt the thick paper on her knees as she traced her fingers over the symbols. Trecrogo is the place of the 'gathering'. She scratched her nose. What kind of gathering she wondered? Then she looked at the table that had split into two, long pieces. She stared. Suddenly she was inspired. She ran round the room and looked at the chairs set against the walls she could not move. She squeezed under one of them but saw nothing underneath the seat so she tried to look at the back. Her head couldn't get between the chair and wall so she reached up and with her arm slid her hand along the back between the chair and the wall and finally stretching with all her might, her head almost at right angles to her body her fingers felt what she had thought might be there. Words carved into the back. She was sure they were names. She crawled out and sat on the chair triumph in her eyes.

"Ok, so if they're names and I can't move one because that's not my chair maybe mine is one of the others." She tried them all but none of them moved for her. She bit her lip.

"Demeter!" she called.

He had found a very comfortable place to sit where nothing moved, shone or tingled when he moved. He got up when she called. She looked at him. His skin was shining,

"Do you know ..." he began.

"Not now." She held her hand up and pointed, "try to move one of these chairs."

"You sure?"

"Yes."

"Have you tried?"

"Now, not next year," she insisted.

He shrugged. Demeter was not at all keen to move anything but he went dutifully to each one. None of them budged until the fifth one, which, when he took the arms, lifted off the ground. Instinctively he let go as if the wood had bitten him. The chair dropped forward on to stout front legs, balanced for a moment and settled back. He ducked underneath the seat for a second wondering if he had set anything off. Nothing happened. Nothing exploded. He looked up at Chloe from the floor.

"I don't think the chairs do anything but move under tables," she told him, "like chairs are supposed to do."

"I was worried about ... you know."

"Don't be," she said.

"Just being careful," he defended himself. "I'm still not used to the stones changing colour as I pass them or the endless music."

"What music?" she asked, as he rose.

"Can't you hear? This low repetitive tune. Very lovely to listen to."

"Not a note."

"Well I'm not going mad. I know I'm hearing music."

"Never said you weren't."

"You're looking at me as if I were funny in the head," he said.

"I am looking at you the same way I always have."

"Exactly."

He rested his hands on the back of the chair filled with that queasy feeling again because she couldn't hear the music.

"Stop worrying," she told him.

He took a step back. She looked at him. Music. She wondered. Maybe Trecrogo was doing her job for her.

"Well I'll be," he said. She looked at the back of the chair he had moved, "That's my name." She was shocked.

"I can read!" he said.

"That doesn't make sense. I mean the name is ok I expected a name but I thought I'd be the only one to move the chair with my name on. I assumed because I couldn't move any of them I wasn't amongst those gathering at this table."

"Gathering?" he asked.

"This fortress is for a gathering. Others are coming. See they'll all have a chair each. We move each other's chairs and not our own. I wonder why."

"To make sure everyone is who they say they are," he said simply.

"How d'you work that out?" He leant on the table,

"Just that maybe the chairs are a matrix of people and because we're all meshed as a group, we'll rely on each other to be here. So if someone else could move the chair with my name on, that not only means I'm here but they are too. Two people have to be here to give them both their seat. Could be any two people I guess in case one doesn't get here."

Chloe could see the logic but she was surprised to hear Demeter suggesting such an idea. She had thought him too dense before but obviously he had a better brain than she had assumed.

"You know that for sure?" she asked.

"Just an idea."

"But I tried and none of the other chairs moved so where's yours?"

"There are more to try but maybe I don't need one."

"Why wouldn't you need one?"

"Maybe I'm the only clone."

"That makes no sense. I guess we'll have to wait for the others to even know who they are."

"I wonder if he's one of the others?" Demeter said.

"Who?"

"There's someone walking towards us."

"How do you know?" her voice was suddenly tense.

"I can see him. Ever since I touched those charts I can see everything just as they appear on them. The whole fortress and everything around." She gasped and sprang at him taking him by the shoulders,

"Why didn't you tell me."

"I was going to but you stopped me to move chairs," he defended himself.

"That's not as important as a visitor."

"You insisted."

"How could you be so dumb?"

"Don't moan at me."

"Who else is there to moan at? You should've shouted me down. The moment you saw them coming you should've told me. We could be in danger. He could be anyone. Where is he I can't see anything in the charts."

"He's still outside walking towards us."

"I'll run up to the parapet and look."

"He's far away."

She did not hesitate any longer but swiftly ran up the flight of steps with Demeter behind her.

"I think you should know he's not human looking," he shouted as they ran and then added, "He'll take ages to get here."

She got to the parapet and looked out across the plain. There walking at a brisk pace along the same path they had taken, was a bear still at some distance away. Large and powerful with silver-grey hair around his eyes, he walked towards them and surprising them both, he waved to them. He had seen them. Chloe waved back.

"You know him?" asked Demeter.

"No, never seen him before in my life."

"But you both waved to each other."

"I was just being friendly because he was," she said.

"I can do friendly."

"I want you to be very careful."

"I have been."

"No, not of Trecrogo, of this bear coming here. We don't know who he is or what he wants."

"OK," said Demeter putting his hands up with his palms facing her, "Two things, Trecrogo?"

"Is the real name of this place."

173

"How long have you known that?"

"Most of the night."

"Thanks for telling me," he complained.

"I was hoping you'd find out for yourself. Does knowing make a difference to you?"

"I don't know. Some things seem to make a difference some things don't at the time but later, yes they do."

"I'm sorry. In future I'll tell you things as I find them out, alright?"

"Thanks. Second, what do you expect me to do with an unfriendly bear?"

"Nothing. Something. I don't know if he'll attack us. If he does, be ready for him."

"That is so unfair."

Demeter looked at the advancing bear with something approaching terror. What could he do if this giant attacked them? They had no weapons he knew about. Then he said,

"Chloe, have you noticed something?"

"Lots of thing. What in particular?"

"Well we're pretty high up here aren't we?"

"Sure," she said.

"And that bear must be, what, a mile-and-a-half away?"

"About that."

"Then how come he looks like he's five minutes away at most?"

"I guess that's another of the Trecrogo's attributes, those who stay here are given sharp and far sight. I think we're growing into this fortress, or this fortress is growing into us."

"I know what you mean. And that bear can see us which means he's got pretty good sight too. Looking at us from his point of view, he doesn't know us, does he, so why did he wave?"

"He may know us. Never assume anything. We may be known to many people we've never met. Besides, his being here and alone means something just as our being here does," she explained.

"He knows us but we don't know him?" Demeter shook his head not believing himself to be that famous.

"Could be. I mean he waved so he's expecting someone to be here right? And he's walking towards us so this is where he wants to be."

"I guess." He scratched his nose.

"Which one of us is going to stay here and welcome him?" she asked.

"I can see you're itching to get back to your charts."

"Only to see if there's any mention of this bear in there. Bears built Trecrogo."

"They did?"

"Yes."

He held back from saying that was something else she had not told him. He looked at the advancing bear. He looked at his shoes.

"Then maybe he's one of the architects," he suggested.

"Maybe, though they left a long time ago. I don't know how long bears live. I don't think he's dangerous to us but we can't be too careful."

"From his size I wouldn't like to be anyone he's dangerous to." He shifted uneasily on his feet and added," If I scream out will you come immediately?"

"Of course I will. If he attacks I'll need to defend you because I don't want to end up having to handle Trecrogo alone."

Demeter screwed up his nose,

"I could so go off you," he told her.

"If I thought you were in real danger I'd tell you but to tell the truth, since you let out that beacon I've been expecting someone to appear. Now just stay calm and keep your distance for a while. I have a feeling ... ," she stopped, not sure how to tell him.

"About?"

"That Trecrogo will always help you somehow."

"If he attacks me I'm running away as fast as I can," he said.

"I wonder if you will." She stared at him. He could not see how his skin glowed.

"You think I'd stay around him when he's angry? Have you noticed how large he is? He could take ten like me with one claw with no more effort than you'd take to launch a kite into the air."

"You don't know what you'll do until bad things happen and you have to put them right."

"I'd run."

"See what the music tells you."

"Tells me?"

"Of course. If you can hear music and I can't, then

Trecrogo must be communicating with you on some level. I think your powers are emerging even though you are, as yet, unaware of them."

"I'd need to be aware of them for them to help me."

"To be honest I'm not worried. No bears ever fought for Crilodach."

Demeter stood by the top step and looked out at the oncoming bear whose strides were even and long. He held his head high and his arms were swinging with ease and grace. This was a bear who knew exactly where he was going and what he was doing.

"Powers," thought Demeter out loud. He puffed and blew his hair up from his eyes. The test was supposed to be taken with Chloe. Now he was going to face this bear alone.

"I'll run," he said under his breath. He looked around at the empty parapet around him. "Only problem is where to?"

All morning he stood watching as the bear walked closer and finally arrived at the base of Trecrogo. Shifting the load he was carrying on his back, he started to walk up the steps which came out to meet him, then vanished behind him as he climbed them. Taking two at a time at an even pace, he never wavered or stopped. He looked ahead all the time, his bare claws and strong legs lifting his huge body upwards. Where Chloe and Demeter had taken all day to climb up, he reached the last few steps in less than an hour. But then for Copret the steps would have lifted him as he walked. For Copret all things made way. As the mighty bear neared the parapet, Demeter heard the song he was singing. His voice was mellow and pleasing, unusual in bears who are not known for their singing. The tune was the same as that Trecrogo was playing in his head. Standing on the edge of the walling like an ant overlooking a vast cliff, Demeter spoke as the furry head and shoulders got to within earshot.

"Please stop there," his voice trembled.

The bear looked up, judging Demeter's shining face and reading his eyes. Copret had narrow eyes for such a big bear. The wind caught his black fur edged with silver, and made his face glow and sparkle in the sunlight as the hairs moved like waves across an ocean. He stopped as Demeter had asked. He smelled of dry forest floors. His breathing was even and constant, showing no signs of breathlessness from the hard climb, and smelling of warm, honeyed milk. Demeter swallowed uncomfortably. His heart thumped. He felt he had insulted the bear by making him wait.

"I admit I'm a little late, I had to collect something for Lilah," Copret patted a small pouch tied with red string on his hip. He smiled. His white teeth glittered. Demeter did not smile back though he wanted to. He wanted to move out of the bear's way and let him pass but he resisted the urge. The bear was impressed with his determination but Copret knew a thing or two about the human Demeter was cloned from, and knew he had not been chosen in haste of without the advice of the Sangyma.

"Unsure of me little fellow?" he said, in a growling voice.

"I want you to tell me who you are?"

"Before you let me come up to rest my legs?"

"I realize you're in danger standing there but I'd like to know. I've a friend to protect."

"I think you're an excellent fellow to protect your friends, but this bag is heavy and I've walked a long way today and I would like to sit down, if you'd be so kind."

"Then speak quickly and I'll let you rest."

"There's no way you'll let me up now?"

"Not until you tell me."

"I'm one of the faithful," replied the bear, hiding his grin.

"Which one?"

"Copret. You must be Demeter.

"Chloe said you might well know me."

"Wei K'un told me you were both sent on ahead."

"You know Wei K'un." Demeter began to feel awful, the way you do when you realize you have made a big mistake.

"You might say that," smiled Copret, "we've never actually met but we've talked often. May I come up now? I'd like to drink and rest. I fear you may attack me at any moment from your advantageous height and strong though I am the fall would kill me."

Demeter looked at him and saw a twinkle in his eyes at his joke. Demeter's weight would never have been enough to dislodge Copret from the two steps he was standing upon.

"Please do," said the boy.

Demeter stepped back from the wall without a shadow of fear. Copret finally mounted the parapet in one bound, so swift and fast Demeter knew he could have jumped up at any time he had wanted to during their brief conversation. He took the bag from his back, took out a bowl and drank in large gulps for so long Demeter was amazed the small bowl could hold so much water or that he could carry so much in his bag without spilling any.

"Would you like some?" Copret offered.

He handed the bowl to Demeter who walked forward and took hold carefully, half fearing something would blow-up. The bowl was well worked gold and silver and fitted his hands as if made for them. The empty bowl filled with clear water as he looked. He stared. He smelled the sweetness and he sipped. Once he had done so he felt light headed.

"That's delicious."

"Best water there is," smiled Copret. The bear sat down and looked at Demeter as he drank. Copret nodded in satisfaction.

"Good, you are whom you say you are."

"Am I?" asked Chloe, coming towards them from the stairwell. "Would you like me to drink the Xandyc water so you may see my true self as well?"

"No, little one you don't need too. I apologize for testing your friend but I must be sure. Trecrogo is no place in which to find the enemy in control."

"Another test?" moaned Demeter, "I'll never be free of them."

"Life is a test," said Copret. He scratched his face and patted Demeter on the head. "For the faithful even death is a test. Are any of the others here yet?"

"Who else do we expect?"

"Midrak and Lilah amongst others. Let's see here, have you found out how Trecrogo works yet?"

"No, are you going to teach us?" asked Chloe.

"Indeed I will. I'd have been here yesterday but I was held up. However we hoped giving you a week's journey time would acclimatize your bodies to the earth."

"There's a lot more to do," she told him.

"Then let's get on little ones, the sooner you become masters of all you have to do the better."

"This place is dangerous," said Demeter.

"Not to you," said Copret.

"We had a run in with some kind of beacon when we were first here," Demeter told him.

"That signal was meant for me," the bear smiled.

"We'll show you the charts," suggested Chloe. "I've been reading them. Your people built Trecrogo."

"They did, indeed. The chief architect was a member of

my family, along with thirteen of the stonemasons. They laid the sea walls. Took months of discussion with the sea to work out the correct route but they did the work and the sea was very pleased with the results."

They took him over to the stairwell and he looked down. Copret scratched the side of his hairy face with his huge paw and grinned,

"Well now seems to me if you don't know the central power system you have a lot of learning to do." He looked at them both. "I think I came along just in time, you two might have been at this for months."

"At what?" asked Demeter.

"At discovering who you are little fellow."

"I'm a clone."

"Ah, but of whom?" asked Copret.

"You know?" he asked.

Demeter's eyes widened. He had always wanted to know. Copret smiled and his teeth shone and Chloe noticed they were edged with gold.

"Many ages ago, on this very planet, there was born a brilliant and clever man to a woman not much older than you, Chloe. During the last days. This world was already degraded, not as you see the place today filled with green and trees. Then all was arid, wasted. Wars and ignorance had left all but a few dead. Most of those who had died were killed by my people. I know that sounds terrible, but the human beings had to be stopped. They had killed a Sangyma. Yes, I see you raise your eyes in wonder and horror. They were not exactly allied to Crilodach but they were not allied to us either so we were sent to stop their foolishness. They attacked us. Blindly. Fearful more than angry. They were born fighters. They had done little else in all the millions of years of their species. Fighting and killing. They attacked us with all they had. We fought back with all we had.

Except this one woman. She came to one of my ancestors and sat with him and talked. She was bright, clear headed and listened as she was told of the Sangyma, those cosmic jewels the three Sagitæ and the laws of magic. She listened. She followed us. She left this world with her son in her arms and came to live with us far away, even as we secretly moved this planet so none would know the Earth still existed. The magic of the entire human species was held in her child and that made him very important. We set off a vast explosion and under Its nose we spirit the planet away and built this place, where the magical core of the Earth could exist without Crilodach ever knowing. Our task was to build Trecrogo whilst everyone else who knew about these things thought the Earth dead and gone."

"How did you manage?" asked Demeter

"Shhh," Chloe said. Copret continued,

"The woman's name was Emily and she lived many years with us, and her son grew up in our midst. He was strong, funny and quick on his feet. The bears took from him the genes which cloned you. We knew that at the appropriate time a human being would do better here than any of us for a human being would have the sensitivity to understand and use Trecrogo, grown from his own planet. From knowledge of Emily's son's abilities we built the fortress the way we did, and here Trecrogo has stood building up her strength, ready for Zaqui and the battles to be fought against Crilodach. Every year that has passed the fortress has grown higher and stronger. You could throw planets at us now and Trecrogo would be unshaken. She is the second greatest weapon in the universe. Trecrogo will draw down the enemy as sure as light attracts moths."

"That I'm a clone of the last human being I knew but I never guessed he was so ... powerful." Demeter whispered under his breath.

"There were other humans in the universe who were far away from Earth when we arrived. A few communities and a few people but you are the clone of the first to grow up with the laws and knowledge of the Sangyma. He lived many years. He died at the age of hundred and eighty seven. You're all he was and more." Copret walked to the eighth step down. He stopped and pointed.

"From this stairwell you will derive your strength. Come." Demeter stood by him.

"Now touch the walls on either side of you with the tips of your fingers, only the tips. As if you were touching butterfly wings." Demeter did so.

"The stone tingles," the boy said.

"Press gently," guided the bear.

"The tingle is a throb. The walls are moving."

"Don't let go, let the pulse of your heart steady the pulse of Trecrogo."

"I'm scared."

"Of course you are, now slowly, feel the warmth on your fingers. Your hands. Feel the muscles in your arm. Feel that power."

"They feel heavy," said Demeter.

"And your feet?"

"My feet?" He looked down, he was floating.

"Now press hard against the stone. Let the stone mould in to your palms. Feel the depth of Trecrogo's heart. The magic will enter your muscles and flow with your blood. You can feel your bones."

As Demeter did as Copret told him the walls gave way instead of pressing against his hands and suddenly his whole body was aglow. He was floating above the steps. Copret was on the top of the stairs with Chloe but they were different. He saw them differently. He saw an aura around them. Bright orange, and he saw their faces but somehow they were their faces throughout their lives, at every age. He saw the babyhood of Copret and Chloe. He read the lines in skin and fur. The scars from his battles. Her insecurity and determination. Their eyes were bright. He looked around them and suddenly he realized why Chloe's mouth was open.

He was hovering high above the stairs now, looking around the room. He saw through the stones as if they had been glass and through them he could see the whole plain around them and across that, he saw through the mountains as if they had not been there. Wherever he looked he could see in a straight line of vision and his body felt light. He rose higher and he saw below him nearly all the rooms of Trecrogo. He started to laugh. The Xandyc water Copret had given him to drink calmed him. He saw rooms he had not seen before. He saw the corridors and arches were like sinews. Then he saw the foundations, like stars, bright and lustrous. A sea of light. Beneath the foundations he saw the living roots of the fortress He saw through everything and round everything. He felt happy. Unbelievably happy.

The same part of the ceiling as before opened up above him. He rose into the air while below him Copret and Chloe raced up the steps to stand on the parapet as all the stairs on the parapet disappeared leaving only the single flight down to the lower floor. Where they had been slabs of stone slid into place that would become flying platforms for the army that would defend the fortress.

He lifted a finger and both of them rose upwards to him.

Chloe felt herself off balance and reached out to grip Copret's arm to steady herself.

"Careful," called Copret, "we can't fly. We're here because you want us to be. If you forget us we'll fall to our deaths."

"I won't let you fall," he smiled. "I feel so free, so light," he laughed again, whirling round.

"Now Demeter there is one more thing you must do. Look up at the sky. See the stars. See one looks brighter to you now than all of the others?"

"Yes. I can see clearly. The star burns with an orange glow, the same as your auras."

"Call to the glow," ordered Copret.

"How?" asked Demeter.

"Just call. Feel you want the star to hear you. Feel you have something to say."

"How do I put that into words?"

"Say whatever's in your heart."

Demeter looked at the star, so beautiful and distant. As he stared the music of Trecrogo filled his ears and he lifted his hands. Suddenly from his left hand, came out a pure beam of light. His arm began to feel unbearably heavy. He called out. He was fearful. No not fearful, he was dizzy.

"Demeter!" cried Chloe.

Demeter had to think of her again as he had been distracted by the light and she was falling. He put them both down to be on the safe side.

"What's happening?" he asked.

"You're calling the next to come," said Copret.

"Who?" he asked.

"You shall see when they get here."

"How do I stop this?" he asked the bear.

"You don't. Let Trecrogo do her work. Once the fortress is satisfied the signals will stop of their own accord. You have authority here Demeter, but not all the power. Sometimes Trecrogo will think for herself. We made her to be that way."

"Why?" he asked.

"Because Tegriel thought we would be unwise to give all the power to one person. Or even to a few. Each and every person must have some power. Coming together makes us very powerful."

"What if Crilodach stops some of them getting here?" asked Chloe.

"We all have our individual battles to fight along the way. I have faith in the strategy of the Sangyma."

"Because we need each other we care for each other," said Chloe. "People who have power over others cease to care about them."

"Beings like Crilodach," said Copret.

"That name again. Who is It?" asked Demeter.

"I would have thought Wei K'un would have told you. Maybe not, maybe Its something you have to meet face to face, to truly understand such depravity, such heartlessness, such cruelty."

Gradually the energy lessened and the hold on Demeter lightened. He sank down to the ground until he stood before them, his skin still shining. But now Demeter no longer looked unsure. He was flushed with excitement and a little more than pleased with himself.

"Will this go?" he asked, looking at his shining arms and legs.

"No, you've made the link, you and Trecrogo are almost one now."

"Look!" shouted Chloe. "I think they're coming."

Above them right across the entire sky bright lights blazed in profusion. Burning balls of fire fell to the Earth like a rain of hectic red flames, gleaming in long arching columns. First a few and then tens of thousands and then hundreds of thousands. Speeding towards the ground they burst through the sky from space, twirling and streaming like the remains of fireworks being drawn by the first of all forces, gravity, to the ground. Tumbling and crashing deeply into stone and soil. Copret scratched his chin. They shot down like sparkling fragments of shooting stars and his eyes followed them and watched where they landed.

"Is that who I called?" Demeter was open mouthed at the spectacle.

"Well, they'd have come sooner or later, though later would've been better," growled the bear.

"You sound worried?" Chloe said, watching the display. Copret licked his claws,

"They're Crilodach's creatures." The children gasped in sudden horror. "They always move swiftly but this is fast even for them. They moved instantly even though they were unaware we'd saved the Earth or where we were hiding. Still they have ever been, everywhere. If we have to face them alone, we will."

Chloe's heart sank at Copret's words. Demeter's throat tightened, forcing him to cough. They watched the columns of fire falling everywhere in front and around them, thousands, upon thousands of them; then millions. As each landed the burning stopped and turned to feet, bodies, hands and heads. The grass beneath their feet withered. Heads that were bent down, slowly raised themselves to look ahead with deep set, blank blue eyes. Then the skin was covered with grey armour and their hands reached out for weapons. Weapons that grew from their fingers. Like spears. Like swords. But not the same. These burned with the blood of millions already slain and were part of the creatures, extensions of their many arms. These weapons were hungry for death. The multitude formed into ranks without a single order being given whilst behind them the firework display increased their numbers by the second.

An endless army began to assemble before them. Tall men. Their blonde hair frosted and sleek. Their blue eyes narrow and piercing. Their mouths set and straight. Even as they fell those who had already landed let out a cry. A burning, harsh cry of defiance and hate aimed at Trecrogo. A few landed against the walls and burned up, one landed on the roof and vaporized in front of them, startling Chloe.

"Steady," reassured Copret as she jumped in fright, "they may be many but Trecrogo is a match for them. We will see what fighters It has sent in good time. Their first task is to build up their strength."

"And their second?" asked Demeter.

"Do you need to ask?" Chloe asked, wrinkling her nose up as the stench from their foul smelling sweat reached her.

Demeter stared at the host that spread out before them. The aura around them was blinding white. Their faces were deep set and had no age. No childhood. They lined up in their multitude and still the burning lights fell. Though Chloe could not count them all she knew they were in their hundreds of millions before an hour had passed. Not a piece of land was free of their feet. The ground in front of the fortress turned from a green wide plain to a vast crowd of tall bodies. Masses and masses of bodies. And the fire above lit them up, so their blond hair glowed. The hills in the distance were crowded with standing men. The trees had been felled and crushed into the ground by their weight.

"They're so beautiful!" said Chloe.

"More beautiful than I?" asked Copret.

"I didn't mean ..." began Chloe.

"I know what you mean," he smiled, scratching his stomach and growling deep inside his throat. "They look beautiful because we naturally think lovely things aren't dangerous. Crilodach has resorted to an old trick. It has been taken by surprise after all and not had time to plan deeply. Tell us what do they look like inside, Demeter?" Demeter, who had not taken his eyes from them for a second, replied,

"They have nothing inside. They have an emptiness both of colour and feeling. They don't even carry with them a life–history of birth and parents. They seem to me to be steel. Whatever was living in them has been broken and remade into an absolute resolve to destroy everything they touch."

"You can see inside them?" Chloe asked.

"Since I touched the power of Trecrogo I can see aura's around people and their inner light. There's no inner light in these people. An emptiness is in their eyes. The colour of their brains is strange. Almost without any colour at all but a feint glow all in the same place, all the same size, a vague greyish tint edged with crimson. And there seem to be no thoughts. I sense nothing coming from them. As if they were dead."

"They're not dead but they may seem so for their life force is not their own. They are Crilodach's through and through. Trained by Its second in command, Frin–Ghirzan. Dedicated to Its cause. They'll attack us as soon as It gives the order."

"But we're only three," Chloe said.

"Trecrogo was built for one to defend if needs be and that one we have here."

He ruffled Demeter's hair with his huge paw. Demeter stared at him and then back at the army in front of them. He was able to defeat them? He wondered if he could. Surely that was impossible. But somehow with Copret by his side and standing on Trecrogo, everything seemed possible for him. He looked at Chloe and he realized why she had been chosen to teach him. The teachings of the mind did not make a resilient warrior, as much as the fidelity of the heart. A mighty warrior is made by their loves, not their orders. Just as the creatures besieging them were made by their lack of love.

Demeter knew that his ancestors had been amongst those who had killed a Sangyma. The Sangyma's name had been Kowler, a far-sighted and intense Sangyma, quiet and studious, who had loved animals and was torn to pieces in a great battle on Earth. Some of those who fought him may even have come from Demeter's own family. In all the aeons of fighting before, only Crilodach's magic had ever brought down a Sangyma but these humans found a new way. The Sangyma decided humans were too dangerous and wayward.

In choosing a human to unlock the fortress, one of the possibilities they took into account was that Demeter might turn and try to use Trecrogo for Crilodach instead of against It. The Sangyma planned for this. They chose his teacher with great care. They chose a Terika woman who was near his age. If he should ever think of betraying them he would be betraying her. That should be impossible for him if he were truly human.

Of course they were right. Demeter would defend Chloe to the death. He had no doubts about the side he would fight on. Love too, in these days, was a weapon as potent as hate. Just as sharp as a sword, just as deep as any other magic.

They waited. The three of them. They waited for the beginning of the end of the oldest war of all.

"Do you see anyone different amongst them?" asked Copret.

"They all look the same," replied Demeter.

"Then Crilodach isn't there yet. Maybe Its too angry to come Itself."

"Why's It angry?"

"Because It didn't know the Earth was here. Because you live. Because It cannot break Trecrogo unless It comes in person."

The bear smiled and let out a great roar that seemed to spring from all around him. The roar sounded like a battle cry to the enemy. The enemy looked on without flinching.

"Because we fooled It!" roared Copret.

The first of the horde before them suddenly formed into denser ranks and in their upraised hands appeared shields, long and sharp which they wrapped into long barb-like hollow spears and with a mighty shout millions of them were thrown towards the stones. Like a flying wall of arrows they arched at various heights, a solid wall of metal seeking out

186

the stone. They lodged deep into Trecrogo and as they slid into the stone Demeter let out a cry and fell forward, clutching his legs. Copret leant forward as the men began to use the barbs as hand and footholds and climbed upwards without touching the stone which would kill them. As they climbed the metal on the shields rubbed off on to the soles of their boots, preparing to protect them when they breached the top. Looking down Chloe saw this sea of blonde hair rising swiftly like a tide bubbling upwards.

Copret tore one of the spears out of a stone that lay wedged just beneath him and letting out a fearful roar that filled the whole plain he tore off the point with his teeth, throwing away the rest. The remnant danced in the air falling towards the men waiting to start their climb. They shook their fists and roared back. He then turned and lifted Demeter's head and spat into his mouth. Spit now mixed with the poisons in the spears. Demeter coughed.

"Now you're one with Trecrogo you will feel everything the fortress feels. My spittle will attack the poison in your system and drain the pain away."

Demeter managed a weak smile and sat on his knees. He could feel the men climbing up the walls. His eyes widened. They felt like millions of ants crawling up his skin. He wanted to scratch. As their hands pulled on the barbs he felt the barbs pull on his skin like thorns. He wanted them gone from him. He shivered and stood up,

"I must prepare," he told them.

"What do I do?" asked Chloe, going up to him. Copret held her back by the arm.

"Let him do this alone."

"Copret we're all in danger, we could be killed. You must guide him."

"I have. I've given him freedom to know he may fight or he may not. He chooses to fight. He will find his own way now."

"And if he chooses badly?" she asked.

"Then the Sangyma have chosen badly before him in making him the key for Trecrogo and not someone like you."

"Me. I don't think I'd be much good."

"We're in the hands of forces you don't understand yet Chloe. Not everything will be won because of our plans. Some things will happen only because we make them happen. Some things won't happen not only because they're not meant to happen but also because we don't make them happen. Most dangerous of all, some things that we would want to happen if at all possible, may not."

"I don't like that much uncertainty."

"That is the way in war," the bear told her.

Demeter disappeared inside and almost at once he was above the stairwell and the whole of Trecrogo began to move. The men climbing the walls were thrown back on to the ground and their barbs were pried out as the walls of the whole fortress shifted, stairs turned and slotted into stairs, the curve of the walls slid inwards and along. The sea behind them lapped hungrily and the central part of Trecrogo slid upward. Then from Demeter's hands light blazed into the sky and there, where the magic of the enemy still lingered creating their weapons and more of their number, Demeter took their spells and turned the sky into a sheet of glass that shattered, cascading down on their heads shards and spears of their own making. A surge of panic shook the enemy, sending the army running for higher ground with their shields above their heads. Copret smiled under his shaggy hair.

"You've won us a respite. They'll come again." He folded his arms and took a deep breath, then he unfolded his arms and clenched his claws, "We're all ready now."

He lifted his arm and out of the walls shot a long wide lance which he caught in his left paw and Copret reared up and threw the heavy weapon into the enemy with all his mighty strength. Exploding beneath the ground debris was thrown up in huge waves of dirt and stone that crashed over the high ground, spilling men across the plain and churning them around. Demeter brought down the thick clouds that had built up in the air and the clouds moved amongst them curling around and choking anyone they touched.

"Such a pity they will not all die so easily," Copret shouted.

"Why did you throw that spear when there are so many?" she asked.

"To keep them off guard," replied the bear.

"How are we going to defeat so many?"

"Demeter has the feel for Trecrogo. He'll do wondrous things in the days remaining to us," he told her.

"When will the others get here?" asked Chloe, afraid to leave his side. He scratched his chin,

"When they get here."

"I don't like the fact that the enemy can get here in seconds and our side takes ages."

"We're here little one. If no one else comes we must manage. If others come we may manage better. Rely upon yourself and what you have to hand. Remember what I said to you, not all victories are won through planning."

"What can I do, I'm the weakest of the three of us?"

"Once you've walked upon Trecrogo you can no longer define your power or that of others. This place changes people. Look for a weapon that makes use of your rare eyes."

"Look out!" she warned.

The men were wading through the fog belt. Hacking at the clouds that swarmed around their feet up to their ankles but no higher. They clawed their way through but even as they clung to each other against the shock-waves, they heard Demeter roar. Spouts of mud threw themselves up, lifting men as they did so, smashing them against the walls of the fortress where they burned to ashes. The spells in the clouds smashed the enemy against each other. They crawled up the stones using the fallen barbs like pickaxes and Demeter felt them and writhed in discomfort. They were digging into his skin. He had to wash them off. Copret roared. Mud caked their hair. Still they tried to crawl. Then Demeter heated up the walls and they burned red hot and the clouds boiled until a sea of steam filled the air and the men fell into the cauldron of heat. They roasted. The skin burned from their bodies.

Those on higher ground trawled amongst their dead and dug into their bodies with their hands. They tore the bones from their fallen. Many of them regrouped and came back sailing on the clouds in large boats of bone built from the dead in moments. Long boats like skeletons come to life. Even as they sailed back towards Trecrogo, more fell from the skies to replace those who had been slaughtered. Demeter counted them.

Part of the parapet floor of Trecrogo detached from the surrounding stones and moved across the stones to the bear. Copret jumped upon the floating stone and flew above the heads of those on this muddied sea. The Onäis, built to take the weight and size of a Trecrogo fighter in flight, was one of the gifts of the fortress giving aerial combat to the bear. Men tried to land on the Onäis, many vaporizing as they fell because the bejal acted like a net sweeping them up from the air. Those that survived, Copret, with his mighty arms and claws, tore to pieces. This was a bear's work. And as he moved anyone watching him could be forgiven for disbelieving this bear could ever be gentle. The children did not know that Copret had been quiet for many years, waiting to avenge Breseut. He was not going to waste this chance.

Still more soldiers came and still the magic mixed in the clouds raged. They turned the grass and mud hard to make the ground brick–like, so Demeter immediately sharpened the blades of grass so they cut into the bones as they landed. The sky burned red with falling fires. New men arrived. Their skins harder against the sharpened grass. They clung to the stones as they fell and started to climb from many different levels. These men did not need the protection of metal. The enemy was reacting to every move Demeter made.

Copret knelt on the Onäis which moved to the shifts in his weight, tilting and turning in a short arc skimming the walls like a razor, cutting the men down as if they had been no more than hairs, their bodies flying away from Trecrogo their faces contorted and angry. Still there was a terrible scream from them not of pain but hate. But they were too many for Copret. Even as his mighty arms began to tire many of them mounted the parapet and stood atop the fortress.

There, where there had been many entrances to the rest of Trecrogo, there remained only one, by which stood Chloe. Above her, looking at the swarming mass of the enemy was Demeter, his eyes elsewhere for the moment as Copret, being engulfed by men on his Onäis, was fighting for his life. She was alone.

With a sudden movement Demeter loosed bolts of silver and blue that sliced into Copret's assailants immobilizing them and allowing the bear to throw them down. Copret turned and started to come back and he caught sight of the men surrounding Chloe. Demeter felt his sudden anger and fear.

Ten of the men were closing in around Chloe. She had no weapons. She did not run. She stood by the top of the stairs facing them. They towered above her. Then out of the blue from Trecrogo there came music she could finally hear. Demeter lowered himself to their shoulder height, lifted them all at once with a wave of his fingers and hurled them from the parapet. He held them above the ground for a few seconds and dropped them on to the ground where a million blades and burning fog awaited them. Then with a voice of defiance, stronger than his years, deeper and louder than his lungs could have made alone, Demeter let out a cry heard by the entire host before them,

"Crilodach will not win here this day!" he shouted, as knowledge of It had filled his mind from the music in the fortress and he was filled with disbelief something so vile could exist.

As he spoke the clouds churned and turned blood red. Weeds choked the soldiers and salt burnt their skin. From the depths the mud began to boil and rumble, shooting into spouts around the millions in their skeleton–bone boats, reaching up to those still falling to the ground. Above them more clouds gathered and in the rain that fell, bright flashes of yellow fell like stars. The men struck out with their weapons at the thundering light. Their ships crashed against the stone walls or were driven down beneath the ground never to be seen again.

The falling lights bounced off the foggy surface and mingled together. The magic brought calm. Across the surface of the clouds a golden light danced. In the calmness the army regrouped. Crilodach's armies did not like the calm. They always left in their wake a deadly silence, but they hated facing silence.

Demeter felt them at his feet. Copret arrived back and Chloe ran up to him. Demeter breathed in and let the music rise sweeping across the plain, and the yellow rain burst out into light and from the depths of the clouds there came a sigh. As if the whole planet were breathing out. As if the plain was sighing at the sweetness of the music. Swiftly the boats and the men vanished before the defenders' eyes as the huge sigh crossed from one end of the plain to another in a passing second, with barely a ripple on the clouds. Chloe and Copret heard their own breathing for the first time since the start of the battle. The men vanished. The barbs vanished. The roar of their voices vanished. The bone ships vanished.

Copret was hot and tired as the Onäis slid back into place and he stepped lightly back on to the parapet. Hidden once more amongst the stonework the Onäis would wait for the next call to arms. Demeter floated down to them. He was almost smiling.

"Another brief respite," he said.

"Brief is all we'll ever have," revealed Copret, easing back his shoulders and masking his wounded arm so as not to alarm them, "not that we need any rest."

"What were they?" asked Chloe.

"The first of the many we'll have to fight to get to Crilodach. I wish I'd some of my friends with me, you would not have been so close to being hurt."

"I should never have screamed like that," she apologized.

"Why not?" asked Demeter.

"I showed fear," she said.

"Nothing wrong with fear," smiled Copret.

"If you hadn't I mightn't have seen you in time," added Demeter.

"Thanks," she said.

"The action was well executed," came a woman's voice.

Startled the children turned in fright and there before them stood a tall woman with eyes deep black and ebony skin. Copret opened up his arms to hug her.

"Not a second too soon," he said.

"I was held up. You seem to have done well without me," she said.

"They're not bad for beginners," laughed Copret.

"I suspect Crilodach was merely testing our defences," Lilah suggested.

"It has had a great surprise finding we'd built Trecrogo behind Its back," said Copret.

"So this is Demeter and you must be Chloe," She looked at the children. Copret brought them forward.

"Who are you?" asked Chloe.

"She's called Lilah. She's a friend," Copret told her, "perhaps the most loyal friend you'll ever have."

"You do me more honour that I deserve Copret," smiled Lilah.

"Not at all, and you know exactly what I mean," argued the bear.

"How did you get here?"

Copret disapproved of Demeter's question.

"You ask how Lilah manages to appear, why she does not walk up the steps as we do, does not announce herself? How Trecrogo allows her to be here? How come you did not feel her presence or sense her coming? Accept her, you'll sleep better at night and be more awake during the day not to question what Lilah does or how."

Demeter looked at her. He couldn't see her aura. If he could, he sensed he would not be able to withstand her immense power. She stared at him as the experienced warrior she had become, summing-up a new soldier beginning to understand what war is all about. The lightning speed of death. The anger that grows in the heart of those without hate. The fear of failing. They understood each other. She then looked at Chloe. She smiled. Chloe smiled back, a weak smile. She was still quaking inside.

"Just in time," said Copret as he saw the blue streak across the sky. "Rataplan is here."

"They were like an unruly mob," said Lilah. "Now they have their general, strategy will rule the field. Come, we have work to do before they attack again."

The Short Goodbye

There was a hollow silence in the eerie streets long before Midrak, still leaning slightly on his sister for support, and Tobia emerged from the ruined building. This building had stood close to the centre of a large city which had once been set to the south of rolling hills beneath spectacular skies but now floated in space, encircled by a russet bejal, filled with shocked Arvernat silenced by the speed and ferocity of the onslaught they had survived.

The silence was so deep they fancied they could hear each other blinking in their proud isolation in space. The loss of their entire planet was mirrored in their inability to fully understand. Unwilling to fully understand. The silence made their rib cages ache. Unspoken in a birdless, breezeless, sleepless silence, disbelief and apprehension emanated from them. They longed for someone to speak. To say anything, no matter how foolish. To give them all vibrant and worth-while thoughts to divert their attention away from this nothingness. To give them back a sense of their lives in the immense tragedy that with an eyeless calm, stared back at them. To give them back all they knew they had lost forever, before they knew that forever was but two days. To give them back each other.

Midrak, Lilah and Tobia were the only ones moving. Their footfalls sounded like alarm bells and their breathing like sirens. The airlessness that failed to ruffle their hair made the city feel slightly alien. Nothing is alien to magicians. As Filvani points out in his Book of Derivations, a series of thoughts based on the laws of magic,

> '*Magic Is Part Of The Whole Universe And Magicians Are Part Of All Magic So No Part Of The Universe Is Alien To Them*'

Everything made the Arvernat believe this silence was their fate; voices had no place in their existence anymore; speech no strength; thoughts no point; life no direction. Silence created nothing but a listless expectation of ...

nothing more. Only speech could permeate the despair that filled the remnants of this nation. Without that, silence seeped into their skin and lungs, joining them together in sadness. Maddening them with a drowning sense of futility, spreading around them like a veil wrapped perfectly to fit their skins. The silence was painted on to Lilah and her brother with lumpy brush strokes, like a leaden weight making walking harder with each step they took; harder to move; harder to think; harder to live. The silence clung to the Arvernat with claws, dripping with dread. Their faces felt their tears, as if they were being pealed alive. They knew what had happened. What could the three of them possibly say to the eyes that followed them as they walked towards what was left of the city wall?

How could Lilah answer their questions when every one would be begging her for a hope she could not give? She could not give them life. She had been born to live a life of short goodbyes, brief friendships and even briefer joys. Which is why she fought her feelings for Rimfelder. Her feelings had no place in his life. The only words she had to say were so filled with sorrow, she preferred this abyss of silence as she walked to the explanation she knew she had, in all fairness, to give. She shed no tears but she cried with every one of them.

Lilah looked directly ahead momentarily catching a look here or there as she turned her head to check on her brother. Tethval and his people had survived this nightmare. This loss. This emptiness. How would she break this silence? Midrak, looking at the devastation, wondered how any of them were still alive.

"This is an awful silence," Midrak told Lilah, telepathically.

"Shock," replied Lilah. "They have seen their world shattered. They know whatever lies ahead we have to lead them. If we do not, no one can. That will be the end for them."

"Their eyes are almost pleading with us?" thought Midrak.

"They are waiting for us to speak. They have lost all their words. What could they say? We have to say something to them. We are the only ones who know enough to explain any of this."

From doorways, on rooftops and along streets, even from those who had run into the city and had never seen Lilah before, silent stares followed her, imploring her to speak.

Midrak cursed his own weakness for bringing this upon them. If he had been faster on Ruz they might have met Lilah here and been gone hours ago. Because she had had to fight for his life she had given Crilodach time to find them. Its claws sank deep. Fulminar, who was only now recovering from his ordeal, was beginning to speak to him. He felt equally to blame. Midrak did not yet know where he was exactly but as is the way with these things the place had a means of telling him. He saw the lights shining nearby and somehow he knew they were not torches but Arvernat eyes. He touched the stone walls of the houses, steadying himself as he walked, and they resonated against his fingers, as if he could feel their atoms quivering still from the attack. He looked at the stars around them, running through the charts that Palik Tomil had scattered all around his library, in his mind. Trying to make out where in the universe he had landed.

Tobia, with that sure knowledge of the blind, mixed with Ruzniel teaching and her inner core of magic that was Tegriel, knew that this ending would have happened anyway. And something else. Tethval's place in this fight was not over. Lilah had come to collect Rimfelder and stayed to fight for Midrak but something else had come for Tethval. Something even Lilah did not know. Tobia was convinced of this though she was uncertain exactly what. The thoughts did not come from Tegriel but from the vibrancy of the magic in the air around her. She knew the sadness in Lilah was real but she did not share her feelings of dread because she could see the Arvernat fighting elsewhere with as much tenacity and strength as they had shown here. Perhaps a touch of Tegriel's prophesying was rubbing off on to her. Or perhaps, having been saved by Bofindle, the bejal had shared a secret plan.

Weighed down by war, aware of the city's thin hold on survival and utterly determined to do all they could until the last moment, they walked through the crowd of parting survivors. As she walked, Lilah thought she knew that this terrible battle, though the beginning for her, was the end for the Arvernat. The Arvernat did not know what the beginning or the end of anything meant any more.

To watch your world pulled to pieces and still be alive afterwards is not something any of them had imagined. The Arvernat for all their anger at the tyrant had never thought about destroying everything, but now the unbelievable had happened. They believed they must be dead in some fashion they did not as yet understand. Or they were in limbo waiting to be told they were dead. Or perhaps this sudden confrontation with the complete silence of the universe left them with absolutely nothing to say. Nothing to do. Confused. Movement and laughter were gone from them, drained like wine from a bottle. All they knew was how to wait, though they no longer had any sense of what they waited for. Until Lilah, Midrak and Tobia came out and walked amongst them.

They saw, as she passed them, that Tobia was blind and Midrak was walking by occasionally leaning against the remnants of walls where the cobbles became particularly irregular. The moment they saw them they knew they had waited for the three of them to explain. To speak. To help them to live or die. The Arvernat did not know which nor cared which, as long as something was offered and as long as the offer came from Lilah.

Shock. Awe. Terror. Lilah looked into their hearts. She saw hand reaching out for hand. People gathering close to each other for comfort. Touching each other. Allowing the realization that they were alive to permeate their thoughts. Their eyes shone out. The light was swallowed by the blackness of space. She looked at the city through their eyes. Familiar places had become strange. Half broken houses, streets that ended after the gates and this endless darkness where once hills and sky had lain, beckoning them to go on journeys and explore places that were no longer there. No more roads. No other cities. Nothing to explore except the sum of all their fears. You cannot rebuild upon nothing.

Bofindle glowed with that warm, dying glow of a bonfire giving out no more heat than an average light bulb. Stars flashed, the last bits of rock from the planet vaporized. Birthplaces, woods, rivers, walks, towns, all the mines, were gone. The land beneath their feet, which they had always taken for granted, seemed brittle. Reality should have depth beneath the feet. Hardness. Surety. This reality was dark, empty, morbid and yet, eternal. The Arvernat could see no future.

Lilah closed her eyes for a brief second as she walked. Far worse was to happen. She was about to bring their end upon them. At the end of a normal life, you have to say goodbye to everything, piece–by–piece, over years. She had no time. She refused to weep but liquid still welled up behind her eyes, her heart overflowing. She had been trained to control this agony of sorrow that exists before Zaqui.

In the certain knowledge of finality, bonds of friendships form very quickly. Feelings flow like waterfalls. Sacrifices would be made for another as if for a friend. Her sorrow was for the loss of all that was so briefly touched. Her task was to try to ensure, in some small part, that all that was worthwhile did not vanish. That somehow their fates would bond with a newness of life. That those who came after would feel the Arvernat had lived even if they did not know them. That they had made choices, fought battles and stood against Crilodach. Tethval and his people were like the unknown children a mother can never know, the thousands who are not born from her womb. Lilah had shared a small time with them but knew them well. Saw their worth. Felt their power. This was so very difficult for her. This was the part of her journey she had railed against so many times and always the answer was the same. As Filvani further writes in the Book of Derivations,

'The Fate Of The Few Determines The Fate Of The Many'

When you have the ability to use great power you lose sight of the everyday challenges of others. Long ago the Sangyma inscribed a set of principles to set alongside the laws of magic. Principles derived from the laws. Their purpose was to teach magicians how to feel as others feel. Helping them keep a sense of balance when dealing with people who are not magical,

Never Betray,	Always Help,
Never Assume,	Always Inspire,
Never Lie,	Always Reason,
Never Demand,	Always Teach,
Never Harm	Always Protect.

"Are you alright?" Midrak's real voice came to her like a soft breeze so still was the remaining air, breaking the silence that had held her like a statue all along their walk through the crowd.

"Perfectly," she whispered, smelling the remnants of the Lazab on his breath.

"You seemed to stop walking for a second as though you did not want to go on," he said, concerned.

"I said I was alright," she replied, firmly.

"Are you alright?" Tobia asked him, touching his sleeve with her hand.

"I am feeling stronger with each passing second," he told the Ruzniel.

"Good." Lilah said smartly, "I cannot take invalids with me."

Midrak thought about the thousand chances that had led him once again to be near his sister after so long. He had often reflected how a magician's fate is not their own, that they connect with forces of nature beyond their freewill which seem to use them with no regard for their safety.

A billion dangers change even the simplest act into a game of chance. Chances that make up a life. Decisions that are forced upon them because they have one goal and one goal only. Each and every spell is a learning experience. Every spell takes place within a unique time and place but equally there are some spells which take place everywhere at the same time. Midrak did not possess the power to handle spells with such cosmic symmetry. Lilah did.

Despite her power, he felt Lilah's sadness like a mantle falling over them, and he understood her. She was in mourning. He saw what was going to happen. What had to happen to all peoples as the fight with Crilodach in the name of the Sangyma moved relentlessly forward. Lilah, looking at him, gripped his hand tightly.

Fulminar was a warm presence in his head. An added strength. An added wisdom. He began to realize how Tobia must feel being able to touch Tegriel's mind at any time she pleased. He was getting used to knowing he no longer had any private thoughts. That they thought together and spoke in turn. Fulminar's voice sounded like a soft bell in his head. Never speaking unless Midrak asked him too. Acting in harmony with Midrak. Two forms of magic layered into each other as if knitted together. The ancient crafts of the Sangyma were now his. Midrak would never have recovered so swiftly on his own. Fulminar was learning everything about him so that his spells would become one with Midrak's mind. There would never be a moment's hesitation between thought and action. They would work as one, they would die as one.

As the three of them walked closer to the remaining city walls, Fulminar let Midrak know why they had taken Lilah away. He told him the story of the meeting of the Sangyma. How they had decided he should be taught. How, even then, they knew they had to plan for Lilah's spell-making, to arrange things so they would all fight to her best advantage. Midrak could see now what she had had to learn. Like a light going on inside his head the rays of understanding filtered their warmth throughout his body. With that knowledge came a deeper realization, as if the feelings of the universe were now his, flooding into him like a rising tide. By the time they arrived at the walls Midrak was no longer the same magician he had been on Ruz or even the same brother Lilah had freed from the Lazab. He walked without her help.

"I was so young when you were taken away," he told her. "I clung to whatever remembrance I could."

"I remember you clearly," she answered, putting her arm in his.

"I did not know if you had been kidnapped or simply gone away. No one spoke about you."

He touched the hand of small girl looking up at him and stopped for a second. The children too, he thought. Why the children?

"I left of my own free will with Zananto. Mother was distraught. She did not want me to leave. Father was more distant." She stopped for a second and then went on, "The worst thing was they were not allowed to communicate with me. That must have been more like my dying than being sent away to learn."

"They talked briefly about you when I finally asked them a few years before I went to Palik Tomil. I think they had hoped I would not follow you. Grandfather Gentle told me to follow my heart."

"They underestimated you."

"I think rather they would have given anything for the times to have been different. For us to have been a normal family," he said.

"We all do."

"Did you know what lay ahead of us?" he asked her.

"Until the learning was over I do not think I understood

200

anything I had been told. When they said my studies were complete and that I was ready, I thought I knew, but what I knew after all those years is nothing compared to this. They can never prepare you for looking into people's eyes. That, you have to learn for yourself. That first fight, when you do not know what the enemy will do next, when everything you have spent years learning comes down to split seconds and sudden inspiration. Your heart is in your mouth and Bofindle flashes in your hands. I understand sadness, I conceive loss, I realize that the only children I will ever give birth to are resilient hope and the conquest of fear. Practice cannot prepare you for that."

"They are great children," said her brother.

"They are death and battle. They are the end and the beginning. They are maybe and perhaps. They are pure chance. Nothing is definite anymore. The universe is a maelstrom and we are here to swim in her; to swim and drown."

She had put off this terrible moment for as long as she could. The three of them turned,

"You?" she asked her brother.

"I would not be here if I had not decided following you was the better way. Though I am glad you are here and I am glad we have two of the Sangyma with us."

"I am not sure having kin fighting together against It is a good idea. If we have to sacrifice the other to succeed we must do so without hesitation."

"Would that be possible even if we were sacrificing a stranger?"

"Hesitation before our enemies will destroy us. There are others yet to gather together. Each of them has a life to offer before Zaqui."

"And after Zaqui?" he asked her.

"Feelings and ideas may die for a little while. New minds will find them and gather them like flowers to enrich their thoughts."

"You know for a moment back on Ruz I was surprised Tobia said she was to take me to you. I knew then that I had learned the laws because in my deepest heart, I wanted to fight by your side."

She took her arm from his, her eyes scanning the faces of the crowd around them.

"Some lives are easy to chart for even in chaos, magic

makes demands. The enemy knows that we are limited in what we can do but some things have been closed to It from the dawn of time. It does not see or know exactly what happens in the first second of creation. That was the time when all the particles of magic were created, when the three Sagitæ came to us from the last universe. The billions of things that happened in that second are unknown to us all. That frightens It. For all Its deviousness, Its plans are really not much more than a wish–list. It has only ever shown one path, that of power and dominance. We stand before It. It thinks It knows our strength, It has played out this battle in a million places on a million days in the past. It has warred against us in every planet where It could find us. Tested our strength in every era. Surprised us in each millennium. And we have tested It in our turn. In the coming war we will see which side has learned to the best advantage."

"Could we make such a devastation as this?" he asked, gesturing to the city scape in front of them.

"We will not willingly kill the innocent. Crilodach will, and far worse, It will put the innocent deliberately in our way. It will strike us from their homes, use them as decoys, dress them up to ambush us and make our battle plans harder. It will dupe people who do not know and cannot understand. That is why we tested It and Its creatures. Defeating a few of them to find out how they think. Their numbers, no matter how vast do not matter if we can out–think It. It is resolved to destroy us. We are determined to stop It."

She looked at him after they finished talking, because she feared to look longer at the Arvernat. Her brother would go on no matter what. He would die with his eyes open. He was her brother. She had to believe that his death would not be a betrayal, but a release. She knew he would not sacrifice her. That part of him was not his weakness but his strength, a strength that Crilodach had learned to use against Its enemies and one she had to guard against. Her heart ached with that sensation of heaviness and pain that only comes when feelings are so deep they momentarily become all you are. And the memory of those precious moments becomes who you are.

Midrak, with Tobia close beside him and Lilah not an inch smaller by his other side, faced outwards to the waiting Arvernat. Tethval and Rimfelder had made their slow way to the front and stood with their comrades. They were pleased to see Midrak standing and knew the rescue had been successful.

Cruelty stared them in the face, the touch of freedom blinking at blackness and myriads of stars but not one home left for any of them. Bofindle now burned like a beacon but like all lighthouses the warning message was, 'stay clear, there is only death here. This is a place of rocks in a clear sea. This place will wreck you. This place is death to travellers.'

Tethval already knew without her saying anything what was in her mind. The dullness in his chest told him the same thing. There are some battles you can survive, some that change your life and one you know you cannot outlive.

The Arvernat had shouted themselves hoarse in the battle and fought to within a second of their lives. They knew Bofindle, solid and quiet, was all that kept them from oblivion. A magic they did not and could not control. Even as they waited they had the feeling that this remarkable ally that had been brought to them out of the blue by strangers, was to be taken away. This was the reason why they had all so intently stared at Lilah as she walked amongst them. Their lives were in her hands and somehow, through that unobserved marriage of intellect and crisis, they felt she could not save them.

In the intense, bare, dry atmosphere the sun was shining from beneath them, one of the many strange effects of floating in space without an orbit. Their world would never see a sunrise or sunset again. Their time to live no longer existed. In another place, amongst another people, there might have been a riot to keep possession of Bofindle, but none of them voiced their opinions or moved against the strangers. Their silence was filled with esteem. They had seen the creatures Crilodach had created and were in no doubt of Its malevolence. They all knew Lilah had stayed to save her brother. They respected that. The tyrant would never have done the same. Lilah was one of their own.

Lilah saw the strength of purpose in the way they held their bodies, their straight backs, the swift turns of the head. They did not all look the same but she knew that everyone alive in that city, in that place, felt the same, would live and die for the same reasons, for the same purpose. Small though they were in number they were an army she wished she could save. Her voice failed her for many, many seconds.

"Midrak, you join us at last." Rimfelder's statement broke the quiet. His was a welcome, friendly voice. How apt, thought Lilah, that a man of words should be the first to speak. She knew he had been driven to speak to support her. He felt her every doubt, her species of sorrow. They were leaves on the same tree, grown from different branches but nurtured by the same energy.

"I do," replied her brother, "A little worse for wear and grateful to my sister and all here who fought for the time to rescue me from my own foolishness."

"You find us amid our ruins."

Tethval's voice was wrought with emotion as he spoke. His green skin still dripped with sweat. His eyes were dimmed as if he had been crying. But the Arvernat could not shed tears. The tyrant had not believed tears were necessary amongst slaves. The light from their eyes also cleaned them. But he had made them a people. A people capable of love. That made them stronger than the tyrant had intended.

"I am truly sorry for this," said Midrak, "I did not choose the time. In the days ahead I shall choose very little. I failed you. If I had been more aware, my stay may not have heaped this turmoil on your heads. We would have been gone and left you alone long before It found us."

"I may be sorry too, but I know the truth," said Tethval, "Our loss is not your fault Midrak. You mustn't blame yourself in any way. Just as the stars vanishing aren't your fault or the tyrant's existence isn't my fault. These things are, that's all. There are powers greater than us and whatever has happened here, now, would have happened, one way or another, anyway."

"You are kind to excuse me," replied Midrak.

"This war is our war as much as yours. As we have discovered, a true war of worlds," said Tethval. "If this is the end of all things that we've known and the beginning of things we'll never know, then we gained our freedom too late and we lost all we fought for too swiftly. That is our tragedy, not yours. You've already seen another world die. You'll see many others disappear. Who knows what horrors you've yet to see. Who knows what's been in the past. You may come and go but the end for us would still have been the same. We would rather be aware of what's going on around us than be ignorant."

"Your words have great strength," said Lilah.

"No one here is sorry you came. No one is sorry we helped you," replied Tethval.

Tobia took Tethval's strong hand in her two small hands, "You would have loved Ruz," she told him.

"You would have loved this world," he replied. "Is this to be the way? All things destroyed? All things and nothing left to say we were here, this was our life, our work. Are we destined only for oblivion?"

"Nothing lives forever, not even a spell," replied Lilah.

"All things must live though," begged Rimfelder, "for in the living is meaning."

"Even bad things Rimfelder," replied Lilah. "Sometimes mostly the bad things."

"But if we fail, the better part of creation, the part that holds compassion higher than all else, that part will never live again."

The poet caught his own words. He had spoken without thinking. He did not know where the ideas came from. They chimed in his head. This could not be their final hour. After all they had been through. Rimfelder looked away. Words were in his brain. Thousands of words. They were teeming in his mind for the first time in many months. As if he had a thousand poems to write and yet he felt he had no time to write so much as one sentence.

The stillness around them closed in. The silence was broken only by the breathing and coughs of the people as they waited for the conversation to start again, occasionally standing up and walking the few hundred yards which now encompassed their entire world. Everything that was said was relayed to the crowd behind, in whispers. People nodded agreement or sighed. A few stood by the sections of broken walling not taking much notice, warming their hands against Bofindle and staring into the blackness, remembering the hills and forests they had walked through but a day before. Remembering the roads and cities they had lived beneath for centuries. This blackness was lifeless. They longed to be able to walk for miles. To move freely. To see shadows play in the evening and rain fall at dawn. To see mist rolling across the valley. They longed for anything that spoke to them of sleeping, waking and a day to live through. And yes, strangest of all, they even longed to see their old prisons. Feeling nostalgic for the mine openings and the twisting caverns and walls that, though unforgiving, were nonetheless a home. For somehow even their suffering had been proof of living. Now their lives were held in the hands of another. For all their fighting, all their struggle they were still not free.

Some of them re–lived the army of rocks, their friends coming to their aid, the ferocity of the battle, in their heads. They felt they should had won something, yet in this victory they had lost everything. All the energy drained from them. Like the condemned they merely waited for a verdict. Tobia and Lilah sat down on fallen, stone blocks on the edge of the courtyard looking into the darkness above them.

"We cannot wait here for long," said Lilah to Tethval.

"Why did you come here?" asked Tethval.

"Crilodach would not be looking at you as long as It thought the tyrant was in control," she said.

"You know who sent for you now?" asked her brother. She looked over at Tobia,

"Oh yes, I know."

Lilah's eyes settled upon Rimfelder. They looked at each other. Then her gaze went to the people and her face hardened for a moment. Her heart felt like stone as she saw them waiting for some guidance and she knew she would give them none. In fact she knew she would confirm for them the worst news of all. She knew her duty was to leave them to die.

"So poet, what do you think you will write about all this?" she asked him.

"Nothing and everything," said Rimfelder, "what could be written about this? I feel numb. Empty of joy, full of fears. Lost. The words in my head are twisted out of shape but they teem. That they are there at all seems incomprehensible to me. Write these feelings all down? No. No I think these words must be spoken aloud. They await their time like the rest of us. Maybe they've even lost their time, like the rest of us."

"We have need of great words at this moment," suggested Tethval.

"I need some reason to lift up my thoughts, to examine my heart. I couldn't be uplifting. If I can't leave them feeling hope, I'd better not say anything."

"Words are the bravest things known in the universe," said Lilah.

"Who told you that?" asked the poet.

"Every spell needs words and if words had not been created with great strength of character they would never come to us and allow us to throw them into the battles against our enemies. They would freeze with fright in our throats and refuse to come out. They would run into our lungs at the sight of blood, quake with fear at the smell of death. They must learn how to be strong. When they are strong so are we. Only we can be weak, scared and voiceless, never the words."

"So true," said Midrak. "There is no magic without words. In every situation ever known to us, war, pestilence, birth, love, death – words have always been our longest and most faithful friends. They are always there. They are our every thought. They move between us enabling us to stay friends. To make new friends. Without words there is no life, even those born dumb find ways to communicate. Magic needs to communicate with us through words. We need to communicate with the universe and we do so through words. Words have become what we are."

"The first lesson we are ever taught is to look for the right words," agreed Lilah, "if you can find the right words you can have anything you want."

"What words could describe this? What was the point of all this?" asked Rimfelder, "We had only just gained our freedom. We were on the verge of creating a new world. A better world. And then this destruction and slaughter. An entire world gone."

"Not only your world," said Midrak, "look above you."

Even as he spoke they raised their eyes and there in the growing night in the dark, in the breathless emptiness that was their island, they saw bright stars bursting and vanishing. Far away. Worlds were dying not because the enemy was destroying them but because the old was giving way to the new. As Filvani taught in the Book of Derivations,

> '*Renewal Is Perpetual*'

"Now is the time for us to move on," said Lilah.

"Where do you go?" asked Tethval.

"To a new battlefield," she replied.

"Can't you stay for a while?" he asked, thinking of his

people.

"Time is pressing. Zaqui is but two days away."

"There's one who must come with us," said Tobia.

"Just one?" Tethval asked.

"Just one," Lilah replied.

"Who?" asked Tethval.

"Rimfelder," Lilah said, turning to the poet.

"Me? Why? I'm no magician. I can't fight. I can't make magic. I was useless against those things Crilodach sent to destroy us."

"If you were listening you would know your words will be vital," she told him.

Lilah lifted her hand until the palm faced his chin staring intently into his face. Then she moved, her palm changed colour and the skin blushed red as small sparks bubbled up from her finger tips. They surrounded his face and lifted the hair on his head.

"There is a meaning you shall discover in due course. In the meantime you will accompany us. We have a long way to go."

Rimfelder took a deep breath. The sparks entered his lungs, he felt light on his feet, strong, and ready for a journey. He suddenly lost all fear. He did not care what happened to him. Then she looked at Tethval and around him at the remnant of his people and said softly,

"I do not have the power to take more than Rimfelder."

"We ask for nothing more than what you see around you, if that is all we are to have for the short time remaining."

"But ..." she hesitated and fought for her voice to remain steady and strong, "I must take Bofindle."

"Do so," urged Tethval, still not wanting to hear what he knew she was going to say. "Such a weapon should never be far from someone who knows how to fight."

"You do not understand," she said slowly, "Bofindle had to destroy your planet in order to overcome the enemy. The enemy did not destroy your world. They would have delighted in seeing us dead but they would have found more delight in torturing hostages. Here, for a while, in this city courtyard we have been unmolested."

"You did what you had to. I've no argument with that," said Tethval.

"What remains here," she explained, staring at him, "remains because Bofindle protects the city."

She stopped. She looked at Tethval steadily. His eyes lit up briefly and then he nodded.

"We all knew that was the way of things. When you fight you learn quickly that battles have their own way of being. Their own tides, their own time keeping, their own sense of purpose that seem at one stage or another to rule the fighters, not vice-versa. Since our world disintegrated I've felt there was one more event still to come," he stopped bit his lip, then asked, "How long?"

"The sooner we go the better," she said.

"Can we do nothing for them?" Midrak's voice was hollow.

"Nothing," his sister answered.

Tobia went and clutched Tethval's hand again. He had sat down feeling utterly defeated and for a moment lost the strength in his legs.

"So much and so many will be lost," she said, "you're not even the first and we, who stand around you now, will go in our time. We don't do this to you on purpose."

"Tell me little blind one," said Tethval, "do you think the small number you take with you will accomplish their aim?"

"They'll try. They'll try to their utmost strength. They'll never stop. And when they die, who knows but what they leave behind might tip the balance. If we lose we lose everything for everyone, for evermore."

"If you lose our deaths would have been for nothing," Tethval said.

"We'll be fighting for you" said Lilah, "Crilodach perverted the programming of the satellite that enslaved you. Somehow It was manipulating time for the tyrant came to this world from the distant past. If we win maybe It will not be there to do such a thing to any other people."

Tethval stroked Tobia's hair with his heavy hand.

"When I was young I fell in love," he said. "She was a beautiful Arvernat. She moved like a gazelle. Her skin was perfumed, her hair long and thick. I loved her more than I can say. But even I didn't know how much I loved her until one day, when we were digging I heard shouts. A rock fall had crushed her. I was like a mad idiot. I wouldn't rest until I'd single-handedly removed all the stone. No one worked with me. There was no need. I flung boulders out of the way three men could not have lifted working together. I found her. I lifted her into my arms. I felt as broken as she. Until today Pashtul, our daughter, has kept me from being a mere shadow. Now I feel the same way again." He looked at Lilah, "Tell me Lilah, tell me if I shall see my wife again."

Lilah was quiet. She dithered between telling the truth and lying to a man about to die. Tethval would have hated her for lying.

"All I can tell you is that if we fail, there will never again be lovers. No man and no woman will ever feel free to care for each other. The enemy has no need of love."

"Will I see her again?" he persisted.

"If our ancestors had not been ready to fight, and had they not be victorious, you and she would never have lived at all. Others who will live in the future need us to go forward now. You are not a sacrifice, you are part of the battle. Part of life. Nothing and no one can take that away from you."

"All love is in the past," Tethval whispered.

"Not all love," murmured Rimfelder so softly only Lilah heard him and her eyes blushed.

"Then," Tethval said, looking at Lilah and Midrak, "I shan't grieve that I wasn't chosen to go with you. Please, let our end be swift."

Lilah got up and walked over to Tethval and kissed his hard skin tenderly on his left cheek.

"When my time comes I hope I shall be as strong as you."

"I hope you will live," said Tethval. "Find this magic you seek. Keep yourselves whole and be the ones to create the new worlds. Bring them up with the laughter in which all children should be raised. Never let them touch the coldness of night or fear the darkness of being hated. Let them be rich with happiness. Do that much in memory of those whom you leave behind. Never allow others to be enslaved. Not for a day. Remember the Arvernat!"

The others took up his cry. Tethval took his daughter's hand. Lilah called softly to Bofindle. Within a twinkling the great girdle around the city vanished and was a metal staff in her hand. No sooner did they see the bejal go, than she vanished with Midrak, Rimfelder and Tobia into the Ossendark. The city that had become an island was swallowed by the blackness of space without a sound. Thousands of Arvernat faded into the dark. There was no great explosion. Almost as if the city had been sucked gently away and nothing existed but the billion, billion atoms that could make a planet. Dust. Yet in the dust the particles of magic flowed. They moved like a river towards the end. Gathering with all the particles ever created. Touching and dancing. Always moving. Thriving, thirsting, longing to be galaxies and planets again stretching in long filaments across the universe like the alveoli of lungs sucking at life. All flowing to one point. One place. Zaqui.

Far away eyes watched, saw and cursed. The travellers were coursing through time and space, even as space and time shrank and seconds became longer. Now a mere two days remained. Not the short days of Earth but nonetheless short enough. The battlefield would shrink to a space where magic would be so rapid the eye could not keep pace with the spells. Outstretched arms would grapple with each other. Backs would be against backs, and each would smell the breath of their enemies as they struggled.

But not yet. The next stage of their journey was to go to the fortress, Trecrogo. As the stars twisted and fell towards each other, as everything still living spiralled and danced towards one place, Trecrogo would become their home. From there the Onäis would take them to wherever they had to go to meet with the enemy. From there they would watch and wait. This was the place they would defend to the last. The heart of the magic of the bears. The centre of a supreme creation embodied by room after room of thinking, detailed planning and aeons of struggling. Crilodach's inner eyes saw the travellers and knew their destination.

It had known about Lilah for so long her name was etched into Its brain with hot irons. Spellmakers were Its curse. They had managed to upset Its plans so many times It had lost count. How could Its armies be armed against a spell no one had ever fought before? It hated Lilah before It ever met her. In many ways Crilodach would have wanted to be a spellmaker. To be able to go above and beyond one's own being, into a realm of imagination that could remodel reality. That Tethval and the Arvernat had defeated Its machine was one thing, that Lilah had appeared and started her campaign against It was quite another. She must be stopped and her followers destroyed.

If Rimfelder's head was spinning from the speed of events in the past days he was completely overthrown by the attack on the Ossendark. He felt decidedly unsteady on his legs as the Ossendark was shaken, though until he looked at Lilah's face he thought this somersaulting might be normal. He could see in one look this was not how the journey was supposed to go and a fear gripped him that made his stomach turn over and his teeth clench until his jaw hurt. He reached out. Lilah's hand missed his and grabbed his shoulder with such a strong grip spasms of pain flooded down his back. She raised Bofindle to act as a bulwark in the Ossendark. Bofindle felt unusually heavy. Sluggish. She held the bejal in her strong arms but because the weapon was slow she did not have time to stop the disappearance of her brother and Tobia, sucked out of the Ossendark in the ambush.

Midrak felt a rush as his body was swayed from side-to-side and he instinctively grabbed Tobia's arm as he felt more pushed, than pulled, away. Fulminar cried out and his last message to Lilah was one of assurance,

"We will get to Trecrogo," he told her. And then Tegriel said to her,

"We will not meet again." Then they were gone.

"What just happened?" Rimfelder shouted, as he felt the roots of his hair being ripped out and witnessed Midrak and Tobia vanishing.

"Stay low," she ordered, fighting to get Bofindle in the right position. He crouched with her and feeling the sides of this strange object bow in and out and twist this way and that. He tumbled over once or twice but all the time her hand gripped his shoulder until he almost wept at the vice-like grip that centred his body against the direction he seemed to want to roll.

"Are the others hurt?"

"I do not know where they are," she told him.

"But you came just to find your brother ..."

"And now he is doing what he needs to do to survive and so are we."

Her voice was firm. That was the end of the discussion about Tobia and Midrak. As the attack continued unabated his mind raced. Tethval was dead. Left behind to vanish into nothingness. The sense of loss cut into him sharply. He found his breathing became laboured. Everything he had known all his life, every inch of his home, was dead and gone. His world of streams, seas, forests and cities, smiling people and children had dissolved into a myth. Only stories would ever be told about them now and even those could only be told for a few more hours. Only he was left to tell them and he did not have the time to tell them and anyway, everyone he met already knew everything he knew. His memories were locked inside himself with nowhere else to go. He felt a crushing heaviness, a fathomless sadness in his mind like a stone that weighed him down and made his neck feel close to snapping. A sadness that all the light around him did not alleviate. He and Lilah were alone. His confusion rose like a nightmare swamping his mind and making him fear every step he took. He did not know these feeling were part of the concerted attack Crilodach was making on the Ossendark. Trying to destroy their resolve before they landed on Trecrogo. Thrusting the poet's natural tendency to worry into a blistering despair.

Lilah, too, was fighting morbid thoughts. Her brother gone into Crilodach's clutches? Or had she felt the disappearance was Fulminar's doing. She was uncertain. Why had Bofindle moved slowly? Why had resisting the attack been so hard? Crilodach was not close to them, Its spells were still far distant, they should be able to weather this attack with relative ease. How strong had Crilodach become that It would attack the Ossendark? Was It closer than she had anticipated?

"Is this the enemy?" Rimfelder called out.

He was now holding her arm with his other hand looking at his certain death. All the time the attack continued she held Bofindle with her free arm and gritted her teeth at the strain. She did not reply.

He could not see things clearly in his mind. A light seemed to have penetrated his thoughts and blinded his memories, clearing out his brain, leaving only room for what was absolutely necessary. His inner nakedness craved some sense of certainty. Words formed. Strange words. In a language he did not know. Calming words in lucid and curled script.

"Can't you stop It?" he called out. Something happened to Rimfelder. His mind was filling with images that were not part of his life.

"You will find out soon enough exactly what It is, and when you do you will wish you had never had to know," she said.

Her words were making straight pathways in his thoughts. Tearing out the thoughts Crilodach had sent to him. The fear was clearing. The uncertainty was lessening. These words all made sense, they came to him with more and more understanding. She was teaching him the laws of magic.

Light Is Energy And Energy Is Magic

The words had a logic, reason and strength. Hope and thought. They gave him a sense of future by explaining how a past was possible.

"Why did It only take Midrak and Tobia?" he asked.

"It hasn't finished yet."

"How can you be so calm?"

"I just had to let thousands of people die. I cannot cry about my brother. He is alive and Fulminar is strong, that is all we know."

She did not tell Rimfelder because she did not need to, that Tegriel had warned her something like this would happen. That their first meeting after many years would have to be brief. That she was not to worry. She trusted Tegriel but she had not expected her brother to vanish in an ambush. Crilodach had tried to kill them all. Bofindle was returning to her.

This worried her. Not the fact that Bofindle had been sluggish, things happen and she was trained to take the unusual in her stride, but the fact of her not knowing exactly why Bofindle had been sluggish, angered her. Magicians always want to know. Their ability to uncover the unknown, find out and learn about the hidden is where their greatest power lies. Worse, for the first time the bejal had not shared with her what was happening. Spells within spells, she thought.

There are many who have written stories about Bofindle in different worlds and times. Bofindle has fought on more worlds than you can see in one glance of the night sky when the stars are packed to the brim. The weapon is drenched in blood as are all the bejals that fight Crilodach. In the beginning Bofindle was a piece of matter thrown clear and remaining intact in the vast explosion that created the universe. Untouched by the heat. Whole. Incredibly strong. So dense there was nothing ever created that could make so much as a scratch upon the bejal's surface. Compared to this bejal the heaviest metal is but air. Found by Kalevala, the first spellmaker, Bofindle was the perfect weapon to use in the fight against Crilodach. Able to gird Tethval's city as tightly as a wedding ring around a newly-wed, Bofindle had once again proven powerful beyond the ability of minds to describe. No one ever saw Bofindle that did not marvel at the weapon's ability to do the right thing at the right time. But right now, Bofindle had acted strangely. Lilah for the first time, was unnerved.

"Certainty no longer exists," she told Rimfelder.

The Ossendark began to quieten. The thumping and twisting slowed to ripples. He could stand again.

"The galaxies are breaking apart. What kept them in place is changing. Our hope is only that the Sangyma have given us enough power, and Filvani understood the laws well enough, for his theories to be right. If they have missed the mark, we will fail."

They both stood up but she did not take her hand off from his shoulder for a while longer. Her eyes looked at the way they had come and the way forward as the Ossendark took them without any more upset now she had righted the course.

"You know for a moment when you chose me," he told her, "in the destruction around me, I was elated that I'd survive, that I'd live for another day, another hour. Scared but breathing." He paused, "Survival is going to be just a fight. There's no end to the danger. No tomorrow when sleep comes and muscles relax. No peace. Just fight, fight, fight until the last moment you can fight, and then nothing."

Her face was caring and open, her eyes deep as she answered,

"Does that frighten you Rimfelder?"

He blew through his lips, feeling his hands shaking and lied,

"I don't think fear is something I can give in to."

"Good."

"I don't see any betrayal in your eyes," he added.

"What does that mean?"

"You wanted to save Tethval and the Arvernat. You wouldn't easily let someone die."

"I wanted the Arvernat because they are good fighters and we have need of good fighters. Need and my ability are two different things."

"You don't regret leaving them behind?"

"Of course. But what is regret to me? I came for you and my brother. If I have to, in the days ahead I will sacrifice you both."

"We shall see," replied Rimfelder.

He saw by the flash of anger in her face she was not used to being doubted. Her lips were pursed tight against her teeth as she looked intently upon him. He faced her. Feeling her mind probing his. He was uncertain of every moment, but he was not afraid any more.

"Take me at my word," she said, letting go of his shoulder.

"I shall take you at your heart," he replied. "Oh I know," he went on putting his hand up in turn as she opened her mouth to speak, "what we have to do is hard and I know none of us is expected to survive, but I watched you. You could have left from the room without seeing us. You didn't have to walk through us and talk to us. I saw the tears in your eyes as you swept away from my home. I saw how much you didn't want to do what you did. I saw you stayed to explain to Tethval before you left. You didn't just desert him and his kith. You had to make him understand. You didn't need to do that for any reason other than you wished him to know you acted against your better instincts for the greater need."

"Understanding sacrifice does not make loss any easier," Lilah replied. "All life is interconnected. Part of our teaching is to feel for others. Sense their life force. These feelings help us in our work. When others die, magical folk feel their deaths. We die a million times before we die. This is what makes us different." She added, "Most people don't argue with me when I tell them how things are."

"I'm not most people. Poets are rare."

"There is more to you than I realized," she replied.

"You've put the more there," he told her, brushing back his hair.

"No the weird, wonderful and deadly times embedded these ideas in you. All that fighting for a cause you did on your home planet. Making friends with those you had feared, struggling for freedom."

"No Lilah. I am filled by your power, your words, your certainty. And you've given me something else, you put things into my mind I've never known before. Ideas that seem to govern how things are. You've made me want to be different."

She was slightly perturbed. His words were stronger than the man. She felt a power in them she had not felt in the words of other men. They had a life of their own. She could see strength in his steady gaze. No one had seen her heart in all the years she had been maturing, in all the time she spent learning. In the training her tutors had been kind, careful, ready to advise and ready to spend days making sure she was alright. They never pushed her if she felt tired. Their training had been from the beginning, designed to make her stand on her own two feet. She had always thought things through carefully, her feelings had to be secondary. In reality they were training her heart from the beginning, for they knew that her greatest strength would emerge from her feelings, like a butterfly from a cocoon. Love had a place after all. She licked the roof of her mouth with her tongue feeling the slight tickle.

"Why do you have need of my words?" he asked.

"Until now you have been a passive observer of the universe," she said.

"Meaning?"

"Things work around you," she explained.

"Whereas with you?"

"Magic is a creative process. You make spells as you go along. My spells are in unexpected places. When you least look for them. Sometimes magic finds you, because magic is alive. Not as you and I, but living nonetheless. I can change some things and move in the universe in ways you cannot imagine. Magic possesses memory and memory is a force of nature. In order to get things done magic has to make use of those who choose to possess her power. Many are capable, but only a very few make the choice."

"You've given me magic?" he asked.

"I have begun a process in you that is making your words into weapons."

"How?"

"How does not matter. The magic will release your potential. You were chosen to be the one who would free the dragon brothers and bring power to our aid at Zaqui, and you could not free them without my gifts."

"I've a task to perform?"

"You do."

"You should've chosen Tethval, he was far stronger than me."

"He did not have the words."

"I couldn't stop Crilodach with words."

"Rimfelder," she said quietly, "there may come a time when little else will stop It."

"You'd be better at that with Bofindle than me. What I saw back on my world taught me words are useless if weapons are fragile."

"Bofindle? Crilodach is made from the same matter. They are evenly matched," he said.

"Have Bofindle and Crilodach fought before?" he asked.

"Once. Crilodach does not leave Its lair in Damkina but It will, and soon. When It does we need weapons that It is not expecting."

"Like me."

Rimfelder inadvertently looked towards her wondering where these thoughts came from and seeing Lilah's eyes upon him he was filled with pleasure. A sense of floating. A desire to cuddle her. To share her life. To understand, if only for a second, that she loved him.

She raised her hand and touched his and he realized she had touched him with the edge of Bofindle. The weapon felt cool, not at all hard, and her smile was one of confidence. She began to shimmer.

"The ambush was meant to kill us but not you," she told him, "we were not as important to It as you."

"What do you mean?" he asked.

"It wanted you alive."

"Why?"

"Because of the power you might possess. Crilodach knows I am a spellmaker, It could not stop me. And It knows Midrak was a magician and Tobia a Ruzniel. These people It knows, and knows well. It did not know why we saved you. It fears you because It knows you are a part of a new and mighty spell."

"But I'm not magical."

"You are far more Rimfelder. I was hoping to take you to the Calvioli mountain range and bathe you in the light from the ten suns to strengthen you but there is no time. I am sending you on your journey."

"Where?

"You will come to Trecrogo in your own time."

"No, I want to stay with you," he said.

"You cannot. You have your own journey to make"

From her hands he was bathed in a magic that seeped into his skin, his mouth felt as if he were eating chocolate. His stomach swelled with good food. For a moment or two the magic blinded him and then remade his eyes, until he no longer spoke words but could see them, melting into the world around him. Emerging from hidden corners, swimming in the sea, rippling along the flanks of animals, sliding down mountains. Words. Millions of words. Curling around light; shadows in the darkness. They were on his skin and tangled in his hair.

And even as he lost sight of her one name rose above everything. Even as she created the spell that made Rimfelder's words magical, her name lifted him up. Her name was written across his mind and deep in his heart. And then she was not there anymore. He was not scared. Until he opened his transformed eyes. Until he knew he was alone.

Crilodach

It did not look like a man. To have called It male would have been to misunderstand everything about everything about Crilodach. Nothing of gender seemed to be part of It. No one who has ever lived could see an inkling of what they were, in It. What was hair to It, or skin, or ears, or legs? It could change them all. Its disguise was complete. Only Tegriel knew what the beast hid. What It had looked like that fateful day when they had first discovered each other and fought.

It moved with primæval certainty covering vast distances only using Its mind. Seemingly attached to everything living Its voracious magic, like an intricate virus with penetrating tendrils stinging people awake, choked people in their own lies, squeezing them until living hurt. Demanding attention. Obedience. It had never been born in the normal sense, It had existed since the beginning. Although It had taken a long time to make Itself known; a delay the Sangyma attribute to some essence of the Sagitæ though they do not know exactly how. When It had finally touched creation with Its putrid essence, everything felt that touch in some way or other.

When you have a nightmare, that's Crilodach calling you.

When you feel life is hopeless that's Crilodach playing you.

When you feel tears for no reason that's Crilodach making you cry.

The sudden feeling of cold on a warm day, of being lost when you know where you are, of wanting to escape when there is nothing to escape from, of anxiety when there is nothing to fear. The invasion of your mind by another's thoughts. A mind with a purpose beyond your own vaulting over your dreams and putrefying your ideals.

The Sangyma were created differently.

All the Sangyma but Tegriel had mothers and fathers. Different men and women from different races. Sometimes they had been born strangely and there are stories of their births that open wide the eyes of the children and have become great myths and inspiring stories. Two of them have been the founding myths of mighty nations. Born from swirling seas, from quakes or volcanoes. From the days of a thousand bejals and the time when thoughts became real the moment they were thought, when battles raged between armies of opposing thoughts and their multi-headed offspring. Battles from which the present day stars were created. For every star is on fire, and fire makes myths, but myths that glorify others make Crilodach jealous.

Sometimes their parents had lived in great danger for the enemy has always known where the power lay that produced great magicians. If you ever meet the woman who will give birth to a magician you will know her immediately. Her eyes are bright; she smiles with the softest hint of melancholy; she speaks with a voice of honey; she laughs with a ready wit. She is already magical herself and you will want to tell her everything you ever knew and everything you ever wished for and everything you can remember and when you have finished the telling, you will weep for having nothing more to say and her smile will be as soft as a kiss and her eyes full of happy tears.

Their parents had each come from different worlds; their cumulative wisdom and teachings inherited from every part of the cosmos. It was as if they had been chosen. But when they were chosen and who chose them no one knew, not even the Sangyma themselves. They simply were who they were. In all the time of the universe there had been two hundred and forty one Sangyma. Tegriel had known each one. But then Tegriel was unique even amongst the Sangyma.

Filvani, thinking about how different the Sangyma are in their approach to life, writes in a strange paragraph in the Book of Derivations that he thinks atoms can hold memories. He believes atoms that have been in living beings retain a feeling of that life even when they are in new beings. Even when these same atoms end up in inert things like rocks. If you are sensitive you can feel the ancient life force of these atoms resonate in your mind. Filvani suggests that everything contains an atom or two of someone who has lived, and for that reason everything should be respected. These memories connect all nature. That is what makes the Sangyma so powerful. They tap into an entire universe of thought.

When asked if one atom contained one thought Filvani said no. He believed many atoms came together to create a single thought. A point on which several other Sangyma disagreed.

Crilodach owned no allegiance to any peoples, flags, communities or planet. The atoms in It had never shared themselves with anything else. They were dense, dark and slow to move. This gave It a hard skin, and made Crilodach unable to understand anything about other living beings. Requiring no air It did not see why anything else needed to breathe. Requiring no food It did not see why others needed to eat. No water had ever touched It. Crilodach did not possess a tongue but Its mind could talk more loudly than a supernova with a deep, rich voice that seems to change the words of the languages the listeners understood until they sounded sinister, desperate and frightening.

When It talks you have to listen for you would not hear anything else, like lightning flashes an inch from your ears. Its roar flattens armies, passes through solid planets and reverberates across solar systems.

No, It was not male, nor yet was It female. No softness of nature, no inborn desire to create ever touched It. What It created It created because It needed the creatures for some purpose. What It created was always as twisted as Its twisted purpose.

It was Crilodach.

The being known to every people who have ever evolved, but not always called by the same name. Yet whatever name It was given was spoken in hushed, dread whispers. Making one think of harm, torture, loss, fear and all things foul. Some talked of It in the night, some talked of It in the depths of the sea, some talked of It and death in the same breath; some talked of It and fire in the same breath. Whatever they feared most they associated with Crilodach. The being from whom those on Earth got the word 'evil', not knowing the proper name, they never used the word correctly for evil is more than a word to describe badness. Using words describes nothing about Crilodach, and yet to understand It, Crilodach must be described.

The only living thing never to have understood that life can be shared. The only being to seek endlessly for death by killing whatever It could, so that It would alone continue to exist, continue to think, continue to loathe. That is all It wanted to do. All It knew. To destroy all other feeling was Its purpose. Not to have to share existence, space or time with anyone It did not wish to.

It feels that It is the entire cosmos. That there should be nothing else. It is resentful of any and every other living thing which lays claims to any part of the universe and calls a planet their home, a sun their centre. Resentful of any and all other life. Disbelieving anything has a right to life which does not serve Its purpose; which is not a servant to Its vanity and Its wishes. Its will is paramount. Its way of being the only one that matters. It does not believe in difference, or accept that everything living should make the effort to live in harmony with everything else. It believes in dissent, disunity and war, as long as they serve Its purpose. Everything should serve Its purpose. This incredible selfishness is one part of the key to Its character.

Crilodach never sleeps for Its eyes are Its heart. What It sees gives Its life purpose. It would rather die than close Its eyes. It has never let another being rob It of a second of knowing. Sleep is Its enemy. Its eyes are crystal cold. No one could say how many eyes It has or how deeply It sees. It lives on an unending tide of desire, a feverish call to action against all life. It never rests. It is unable to rest for even with Its immense, ageless energy, to try to rule the universe takes all Its time and power. Everywhere It sees enemies. The Sangyma and their allies testing It, overturning Its wishes, disturbing Its schemes.

Its armies never stay still for staying in one place would deny It the right to be everywhere and watch everything. It never built anywhere but on Its home planet, Damkina, upon which It first changed Its appearance. It has no need of buildings when there is a universe to inhabit. It seeps into the pores of everything. Hides behind, and in, every thought, waits to show Itself in every action, every decision, every belief. Waits to be newly created in every living creature as soon as that creature turns to It and reaches out wanting a share of Its power. Many turn towards Crilodach. It welcomes them all, promising to share. The most deadly deceit of the most selfish being ever known. Yet selfishness and deceit are not the whole key to knowing Crilodach.

Crilodach has no friends for It sees no need of friends and accepts no equal nor cares if those around It live or die. Those that do live near, It uses. Nothing other than a bejal could come close to Its power. It has no wife or love of any being, for being utterly selfish It shares Its thoughts with no one. Once you have heard Crilodach's name or seen Its works, you know how It thinks. It sees love as a weakness to be exploited in Its enemies. Something only to be used as a weapon. Crilodach could not make or inspire love and It does not actually understand how others do. It has no brothers. No sisters. It does not know what kinship or closeness are, so It has become unfeeling towards others, indifferent to all feeling. Yet selfishness, deceit and indifference are not all the keys to knowing Crilodach.

What Crilodach has in plenty are armies. Armies of things that do not even know they serve It. Every being that lives and dies feels the sway of desire, the attraction of Crilodach. Because It exists they too must choose between the same things It did. Between sharing and selfishness. Truth and deceit. Love and disinterest. Many choose to do as It does and in so doing they become part of Its army, to lesser or greater degrees. They think they hold power on their worlds but always they only share a portion of what It allows them. A town, a country, a planet to play with, is all they get. They have no idea of the true extent of Its powers but like those who follow rainbows, they believe they can see them, but they are always just out of their reach. Each and every planet that falls to It, is one less place where Its enemies can find a haven. One less place Its enemies can draw upon for help. One more place that adds to Its right to rule. This is the power game It plays with the Sangyma. Selfishness, deceit, indifference and power are not yet all there is to know about Crilodach.

As Bofindle can only be held by Lilah, so the powers of Crilodach can only be held by Crilodach. By the being who created the need for there to be, brave and honourable people. There are those who serve no one and nothing, breathe hate and eat pain. There are those who endlessly search for certainty in victory over others and in gaining that victory feel strength and power. Just so, there are those who are the opposite. Who stand like a mirror, and when Crilodach looks at them and sees their determination It does not see them. It sees Itself as they see It. But in seeing this It does not change, nor alter Its strategy, for in holding up this mirror It sees only one thing; other beings live that are not Its slaves. Crilodach is blind to Itself.

Crilodach has a weakness. It cannot ignore life. It is possessed of a desire to dominate. This desire rules It, gives It Its purpose. If desire were a living being Crilodach would be desire's foremost slave. Crilodach does not understand this, all It knows is It is angry. Frustrated. Time is running short and the Sagitæ have not been found. It knows the universe is shrinking and Zaqui is close. It feels the claustrophobia growing in Its mind. The anger shows It how much It has won and how much It has lost. The shrinking of time shows It how far It is from all that It desires. Selfishness, deceit, indifference, power and desire. Now you know much about Crilodach.

Crilodach growls in a small dungeon which stinks from being unwashed for all the years the prisoners have been held here. Rough–hewn, bare stones show hands have tried in vain to dig through them in places, even eat through them to escape. This small dungeon rings loudly with such intense suffering the air feels troubled by the pain. Crilodach is looking at the bleached bones of a small Ruzniel and It curses them in every language It has ever known.

"Where are they?" It cries.

It raises that voice that comes from nowhere and fills the entire complex of Damkina. The stones seem to shrink in pain as their atoms are compressed by the sound and sparks fly across the room with the bones. The dry bones, withering where they lie, cry out. Cry out in an old pain. Cry out as if they remember flesh and skin. Cry out for the life they once held and the remnants of that life they still cling to. Cry out because Filvani was right, atoms remember.

Crilodach knows how to torture the dead. Pain can have no end in Damkina. The Ruzniel's pained cry croaks at Crilodach and then goes silent. The Ruzniel's bones say no more. Again Crilodach cracks the bones, whips them with fire and breaks the atoms inside in Its temper with strength enough to break every bone of everyone in Damkina. The smell is of burning as the heat in the dungeon drives the air away. Beside these bones lie the remnants of two other Ruzniel. The dungeon is barren and hot. The bones are strewn about; legs, arms, heads and empty eye sockets, ribs and finger bones; skeletons of pain. All the bones quake and rattle at the attack. Wither. Crilodach's thick skin does not feel the heat. Nor do the three Ruzniel anymore. It does not care for their screams. It has no mercy. These Ruzniel hold a secret. A secret that could give It eternal life. A secret It must find. Its only hunger is for this secret. Where are the Sagitæ? Are they the secret to surviving Zaqui?

Aeons ago these three Ruzniel were brought to this place. The three who had seen the Sagitæ that had appeared whole and complete at the birth of the universe. Three cosmic jewels perfectly smooth and oval. Three coloured stones that should not have existed, surviving from the old dying universe into the new. Surviving the cataclysm that took everything else. A cataclysm Crilodach knows It cannot survive in Its present form. But with the Sagitæ, who knows what could be possible? So began Its search and the wars with the Sangyma. Who would be first to find the secret? Who would survive? Crilodach mistakenly thought the Sangyma shared Its desire to survive.

Bound and gagged, these Ruzniel had been brought by Crilodach's servants to this dungeon. The servants had smiled as they dumped the Ruzniel on the ground and they told It what they had found out. They expected rewards. Power. Riches. Life.

Until then It had never known It might be possible to survive the great tide of destruction and birth that was Zaqui. Until then It had confined Its desires to within this universe. But suddenly true eternity opened up before It. Desire ripped through Its mind and eternal life became the only idea It loved, became Its obsession. To be reborn and to rule anew forever. To have power over Its own existence even beyond existence. To be thirstless, hungerless, friendless and all powerful forever. Crilodach fell in love with Itself.

At first It was going to have them killed. It had actually told Its servants to kill everything around the Sangyma. Until the Ruzniel were taken prisoner It had assumed this existence was a struggle between Itself and Sangyma and nothing more. Sometimes It would win and sometimes It would lose but at no time could complete victory belong to either side. That the Sangyma could never defeat It was no compensation for It not being able to gain complete victory. The long war had not gone well. The Sangyma had won far more freedom for other life than It had wished to give. They had proven tough and resilient adversaries and It knew It would have to take them on one by one. That It would have to be subtle. Play hide and seek. Fight when It could, give them leeway when events suited It. This It did. And It did well. Only after the first three Sangyma were dead did It fully realize what It could be fighting for. They found the Ruzniel. It was then Its servants brought It a gift. Then Its selfishness, indifference, desire and power all made sense.

The only things that stood in Its way to eternity were these three Ruzniel. At first It had left Its servants to hit, whip burn and gauge the information out of them. But even broken, blinded, skinned and burnt they said nothing. Then It had taken over. Long, long ago. How It had tortured them to the very pores of their bones, to the edge of their lives and finally into death and still never a word. The servants were sick of the sight of the torture. Several killed themselves rather than spend another day listening to the cries of pain and see the suffering.

Never in Its long existence had Crilodach seen such strength. Even It marvelled at the Ruzniel. What It could do with such a race at Its beck and call did not go unnoticed by It. But Crilodach hated them, knowing their strength came from their hatred of It, from their duty to the Sangyma, from their loyalty to their fellow Ruzniel. It had begun to wonder if the Sangyma would have been an easier target. Surely It could have made them talk. It had watched these three Ruzniel knowing death was their only hope and It had robbed them of even that with Its vile spells, but still they never gave in. Never. Until one day It had crushed one of their souls. That had been a good day. It felt the ripple of dread go through the other two and as It turned to them in Its triumph, one of them at last spoke. As the voice rose It had felt elated. It had sensed victory at last It had won, the only feeling It craved.

"We" said the Ruzniel, slowly from deep within her bones, "know ... nothing ... but this ... you ... must ... never ... have ... the ... power ... to ... survive ... Zaqui."

The Ruzniel woman took three days to speak those few words. As if forming them was a task of great memory. As if giving them sound was almost beyond her strength. After these words were reported to It, Crilodach had screamed like a maniac and cut out the tongues of those who had first brought the Ruzniel to It.

"You bring me things that never speak. You enticed me with your stories. Never speak again!"

The two remaining Ruzniel heard Its roar.

It tortured the minds of the Ruzniel with Its own, but even inside their heads It could not find the information It wanted. Even entering their minds It found nothing but their stubborn determination not to reveal what they knew. It crushed them again and again. Never did one of them give away anything and all the time It knew they knew something. Knew they might be able to lead It to the Sagitæ. The secret of the Sagitæ drove It insane with desire. It was Its dream and Its longing. Everywhere It looked and everywhere It asked the same question, where are the Sagitæ? This one desire seemed forever to be out of Its reach. So It showed Its anger and frustration every day, and when It did not torture them It tortured everything else It touched instead. Frustration and worry that It would eventually die, led It to be more ferocious and unforgiving than ever It had been. Terror that the Sangyma would survive was unbearable to It. And a deep anger. An anger that these Ruzniel could withstand more torture than any in Its armies or any of Its creations.

It kept searching. Wherever there was even a whisper of the Sagitæ It looked. One thing It did when It killed a Sangyma, was to check everything about them It could. It watched their comings and goings. Nowhere did It ever see a hint that they were hiding the Sagitæ or trying to hold on to eternal life for themselves. But were they bluffing? Were Tegriel's prophecies all a lie to goad It?

To get around this wall of silence It had created the Lazab to infect minds, to twist thoughts as Its playthings. Hoping that the three Ruzniel may have spoken to their own people. Left clues. Said something.

Every planet It devastated, every life It took, It was always looking. Always hoping It would find them always dreading someone else finding them. It knew the three Ruzniel must have hidden them well, Its armies tracked back and forth wherever they had been. Its armies ripped planets to pieces looking. Gouged out whole solar systems at Its order. Wondering. Wanting. But never a sign. Never a glimmer. Did Crilodach have enough time to find the Sagitæ, work out what magic they possessed and make Itself as invincible as the Sagitæ? Every defeat made It more angry with the Ruzniel and It tortured them more until the second soul expired.

How terrible a thing to torture a soul to death. The pain

shivers through the cosmos. Stars flicker. If that Ruzniel's Sangyma had been alive he would have felt the loss, but Hulingey had been the first Sangyma to fall at the hands of Crilodach's growing armies. Hulingey the Fond, they had called her for she loved birds. Yet a bird killed her.

Only the bones of this one Ruzniel remained with any chance of saying anything. Only these bones and with all the hate It could muster, with all the foul thoughts and frustration of the ages in Its mind, It ground them to dust without asking anything else. Time was to be Its final ally in Its search and in a strange way time was the Ruzniel's final ally, because Crilodach ended his torture now Zaqui was so close.

It listened to the Ruzniel cries with disgust knowing he would not speak, even now. The Ruzniel do not fear death. Their greatest fears lay in Crilodach winning the war. Understanding that, they would never talk and that made It corrosively bitter. There are some things worse than death and they decided giving It total power was one of them. They had the power to stand up to everything It did. How, It did not know for It never understood this sense of loyalty in others the Sangyma inspired. Being a creature that changed in order to deceive and get what It wanted, It had no understanding of those who do not change because they feel to change themselves would be to betray themselves. Crilodach had purpose but not convictions. You can only have convictions if you believe something can alter your behaviour. Crilodach bowed to nothing and because of that It understood nothing because It never tried to understand, It did not see the point of understanding someone else.

It had spent all of Its time tracing every move of those three Ruzniel trying to find the places their feet had touched. Looking with their eyes. Teasing the air, smelling their life forces. Using every spell and art It knew. It had never got so far into other beings' lives before but instead of learning about the Sagitæ, It only felt Its stinging failure to find them. Nothing. No scent. No sign. Now, with but a few days left, all It had were these piles of dust and bones, no longer crying in agony. No longer sensing they were failing to stand up to It, and struggling to remember where they were and what was causing their pain so they could find the strength from somewhere to keep their silence.

The Ruzniel were dead. Gone. Crilodach suddenly felt

empty. As if It had lost something. It became wary. It had been suspicious that maybe the Sangyma had the secret all this time. Had managed to take the Sagitæ from Its clutches without It knowing. It was nervous now the end was nearing. Maybe the Sangyma would be able to live on. Maybe It could be destroyed by them. The idea of their triumph as It died had never been far from Its nightmares.

So, even as Crilodach tortured the Ruzniel, It had tracked the Sangyma down with evil intent. One by one. Fought them to a standstill over the long ages. Killed them. It could not keep them alive as It did the Ruzniel for their souls were never Its to command. The only beings in all the universe whose souls were greater than Its powers to lengthen death were the Sangyma. It thought long about how they could have been created. What created them. But never in Its wildest dreams did It ever occur to Crilodach that It might have been created. It created Itself. That is what It believed.

And so It had found a Sagitæ by chance. One. Holding the cosmic jewel in Its claws It immediately realized they were powerless unless they were all together. It had locked that Sagitæ away. Locked well away because Crilodach did not fully understand the magic in the Sagitæ. Though It would never have admitted that to anyone. But then the bears had come and in a devious and vile plot they had stolen the Sagitæ back. That had been the beginning of Its hatred for the bears and for one bear above all others. The extraordinary Hiesia. The one prisoner who had escaped from the very heart of Crilodach's empire.

It had been surprised to find Fulminar still alive. It had not expected that. It made It think the others may have eluded It too. Made It think all the others may still be alive, in one form or another, despite the death of their bodies. Another thought that troubled Its mind. Another worry as events began to take their natural course and the universe began to die. Things It had never thought about seemed to become realities. As if in all this time It had been living in self-deception. Thinking It knew how matter worked but in fact It never had. It spat hate at the dust on the dungeon floor. It did not grieve for Its ignorance. If It was ignorant of anything so were they, for It had many, many eyes and It never slept. It was not possible for the Sangyma to know more than It did. It had to survive.

Crilodach was clever. It knew that there was always chance

to be taken into account. The luck of one person could alter any well made plan. A chance encounter, a fluke, an unexpected occurrence, the unusual, the unlooked for, anything could make the Sangyma victorious. So It hunted with ever increasing care. For Crilodach found, having lived with one desire for so long, It now had one fear.

As the end began to draw near Its own death loomed large. It did not want to die. It did not want to be destroyed. Even if the laws were true and It could be created again in the new universe It did not want to die in this one. It did not want this sleeplessness to end. It did not want to have to crawl up the hill of birth again. It remembered how it had been. For then, for once, Crilodach had been in pain. It had been vile and hot. Not a heat you feel, a heat you are. Not a fire that burns you but a fire with which you burn. First had come Its mind. Bursting with power forged in the stars. A mind filled with self. A mind simmering with light and dreams. A mind fused with passion. There had been such pain. In the pain had been the idea of Itself alone. Nothing else. No other thinking presence in the whole cosmos. It loved the idea. It was supreme.

Crilodach's pain had subsided in time. Its senses joined Its mind, suddenly there were stars to see. Millions of them. Kindled in the same fire, mixed with the same passion shining with the same light. Only different. They were not as It was. They were thoughtless. They were there to host life. To give life. To sustain life. The little lives of other beings. It could not stop them. Something held It back. It had to struggle to free Itself. It had wrongly assumed that struggle was called birth. Whatever the power was that held It back, It finally overcame after billions of years.

Its purpose now was to take life. To enslave and impoverish, to belittle and destroy. Now It suspected that the Sagitæ might be alive. Living beings. Cosmic jewels more powerful that It. Now It suspected as Filvani had done, that the Sagitæ held Its birth back to allow other life to evolve.

Crilodach thought It owned the stars. It had hated other living things but every time It attacked them or disregarded them, the Sangyma appeared. For the first time Crilodach saw men and women. Had to see them for It could not destroy them when they acted together. Then It had found It needed Its own allies. It searched the worlds and tried to find them but It could not make friends. So It offered power and freedom and spells from a distance. In secret ceremonies and through half understood books. It never left Damkina but sent Its spells to do Its work. Then many joined It and with them It fought the Sangyma. Through them It fought the universe and all the laws of magic.

Filvani died over his precious books. Even as he read to himself in that glade, preparing the paragraph on Lilah that proved cells could host such immense power, Crilodach's winged creatures slew him. Buried him in their steel barbs. Another enemy dead. But Crilodach was not one step closer to finding the power the survive Zaqui.

Magicians had set up Academies on Ruz for the study of the laws, the same to which Lilah had been taken as a young child and where she had learned the fathomless learning. There she had been taught how to die a hundred times and live a hundred more. How to divide herself in many parts, how to travel the Ossendark between the worlds, use Bofindle, perform wonders and create new magic spells if she needed them. Later she had taken that knowledge to other places, and in them the power within her had been forged upon the anvil of learning, and made into the greatest spellmaker of them all. Greater even than the first spellmaker, Kalevala the dog, who in the battle of the eight worlds had thrown the enemy off guard by leaping from one world to the next without using the Ossendark.

Fulminar had fallen in the same battle as Filvani. How Crilodach had soared at that, two Sangyma on the same day! But Lilah had escaped Its clutches. Who could have known Fulminar's spirit sped to Ruz and rested their secure and untouched. Only the Lazab could have crawled unseen to await their chance to kill him. Lazab acting without telling It they had found a Sangyma. That made It suspicious of their motives.

Zananto fell last of all. Crilodach was particularly fond of the trap It had set for her. By then, already nearing the end, It knew, at last, the Sangyma knew all about the Sagitæ. And one thing more It had managed to find out. The remaining two Sagitæ It had not seen were turquoise and amethyst. It had tested Zananto about them. Told her about them but as with all the others Zananto said nothing as she died. As she died Crilodach realized her soul was intact. That the reason It had not been able to defeat her entirely. Someone else, Fulminar, already possessed a part of her through his love for her. It screamed in rage at this for It saw their plan. Their plan to defeat It. It searched for that plan. It tried to think as they thought. But since in all the ages It had never tried to think as other people think, It did not succeed. It was not a skill It possessed. It was left reliant upon Its own powers. Its confidence in Itself and Its final victory, had always been unending.

None of the Sangyma ever revealed that they were aware that three Sagitæ, three small insignificant pieces of jewels no bigger than a human hand, came through the cataclysm untouched. They did not want It to live forever, only It wanted that, and silence in captivity is a soldier's final weapon. Crilodach believed they wanted the Sagitæ so they could live forever. That was Its greatest mistake.

For Crilodach this was all a game of sorts. A way to pass time as time passed. It knew in all the skirmishes and fights there was always this one question, this one aim hidden behind all the fighting. It wanted to survive Zaqui and the Sangyma wanted to prevent It. Though It had defeated them, killed them, and rid Itself of their interference It felt no better, no more free, no more secure. It had all taken so much time. Almost all the time there was and now It saw as the space in which to fight shrank, that they were not as dead as It had wished or thought. It had watched people fruitlessly die before Its armies knowing they could not win, and It had never occurred to It, that this heroism displayed something greater than their stupidity.

It occurred to It that the three Ruzniel, through some art, might have communicated with the Sangyma long ago, maybe that was the true source of their strength. That some magic helped them all withstand Its torture. It cursed. Nothing could have found those three Ruzniel in Damkina. Nothing of which It was aware. It was aware of everything, was It not? Doubts began to plague It now they were dead. Doubts had never plagued It before. It had wasted too much time trying to make the Ruzniel talk. Their suffering had been a weapon they had used against It.

Now matters had come to the end. The Ruzniel bones were ash. The third soul was dead. The worlds of living beings were being swept away. Its time was coming and for the first time in an age, It felt uncertainty. It cursed Its armies and Its luck. But Its vigilance was still strong and even as the universe began to collapse It sensed that this was also the time of Its greatest chance of success. The Sagitæ would be travelling to their fate too. At some stage they, or the people who held them, had to show themselves. As all matter sped into one place they had to appear. They had no choice.

All It had to do was to be ready. It would have to act swiftly. Decisively. Alone. It was strong, clever, a brilliant magical being cradled by death and swaddled in hate. Its mind was focussed. It knew the laws. It knew that all 'magic is energy'. It knew that death and life shared existence. And It was sure that 'in the end, all things shall be one' was the purpose of separating them in the first place. It was this law It hated the most. It did not want to boil in the cauldron with the atoms that were the Sangyma. It wanted to be free of any unity with them.

The greatest sadness for the universe was that Crilodach had no heart. Nor in all the worlds and all the age of time was there ever a being that could have loved It. Tegriel was loved by Yu'te, Fulminar by Zananto and even Lilah was going to find the great passion of her life as she fought alongside the others, but Crilodach knew nothing of love. Nothing at all. Nor did It ever think It lost anything by Its ignorance. For there is an unwritten law, one that Filvani did not put in his book. 'We live our ignorance' is not a law of magic but an overriding truth of all life. Spoken by Filvani as a warning to all magicians. The difference between the Sangyma and Crilodach was that they did not want to live their ignorance but in Its ignorance Crilodach felt It had everything worth living for.

Let the end come. Let the stars dissolve and nature roll herself up and create herself refreshed and new, potent and promising. Let her breathe upon countless atoms and swirl in soups of fire. Let her manipulate, twist, thirst and mould, strengthen and give birth. Let her bellow with her rages across the void of emptiness and hurl herself with every force she possesses into a maelstrom; Crilodach did not care what she did, just as long as It lived forever.

And if It did live on It would not let her create as she wished and in her fashion. Not this time. This time It would create as It saw fit. If It created at all. The molten hate of Its being It would pour into every nerve and sinew of every creature It made. It would twist the laws to make the universe cold. For in coldness It would never feel the pain of fire. In Its mind at this moment, were the worst fears of the Sangyma. The nightmares that had kept Lilah awake long into the night. Crilodach had plans. Its own universe. A million planets. All Its own. Everything Its own. Nothing that was not in Its image. And then there would be pain. Then It would teach nature for making It feel such pain. Then It would pay back the Sangyma. It would collect their atoms. It could do that. It would make them live again just to cripple them and make them powerless. Give them the same minds so they would know why they were tortured. Wring them into impossible shapes. Watch them burn over and over again. But first It had to have those three illusive Sagitæ. Those three small pieces of incorruptible turquoise, jade and amethyst. These cosmic jewels that promised so much.

At last It left the dungeon and propelled Itself to a long and deep room where silver lined walls shimmered in the pale light. As It passed they lit up and images appeared upon them of places and people, but whether they were near or far, memories or the present, only Crilodach knew. At this moment It was not interested in what they showed or had to say. It only put them there as a show for the minions who came to Its presence. For some reason lesser minds were always in awe at seeing events unfold before their eyes, as if they were watching TV. They were mesmerized — delighting in not being seen as they stared at other people.

It had already seen the destruction of Tethval's planet and inhabitants. It had seen the attempt by Its Lazab to defeat Midrak. It knew that Fulminar and Midrak were now one. It saw Lilah and knew her for what she was. It sensed a gathering of might. Its enemies were also aware there would be a time and place where they would all face each other. Where there would be a final battle of wills. It reached out as they moved. Its spells coursed through the fabric of time and space hitting out at the Ossendark in which the travellers flew. Lilah felt the tug of Its power and lifting Bofindle in her firm hands she swept sideways rippling the atmosphere around them. Sparks flew. Midrak shouted out. Bofindle raced around them as Crilodach's clutch opened to grab one of them. It reach out, Midrak called, again Bofindle flashed breaking the spell as the bejal manifested magical teeth, dissipating Its spell into the void. Crilodach was unable to take Rimfelder prisoner. All It had managed to do was send Midrak and Tobia far off their expected course. It did not have time to look for them. A fact that would come back to haunt It. For It had not felt the spell that helped them and brought them to Damkina.

Crilodach seethed. It had lost sight of them, blinded by Lilah. It felt anger. She had to be killed. It felt Fulminar inside Midrak and knew Tegriel's mind was inside the mind of the Ruzniel but Lilah moved with the swiftness of thought. In the instant of time they would have at the end, she would be Its most dangerous adversary. Her speed was not natural. Crilodach sensed she was changing Rimfelder. Rimfelder had no magic. Yet. Of all of them he was the most dangerous to It just as Lilah explained to the poet. Rimfelder was the unknown. It would have to find him and deal with him.

"Hagouti," It called.

Its call reverberated throughout the planet. When Crilodach calls you do not wait. You go. From the ground at Its feet wisps of smoke arose, and an acrid smell that would make normal eyes water, filled the place. The smoke rose high and fell to the floor. The grey smoke congealed and shone red as Hagouti appeared.

Hagouti was the only creature in Crilodach's life that did not grovel. Many years ago as a test Crilodach had thought about creating something. About fashioning Its own living, breathing creatures. It had dreamed of an army of such creatures able to do Its bidding without It having to command. Set on their course by Its magic It had wanted them to be extensions of Itself. Like sensors constantly sending back information. It thought It could master creation and make them look like ordinary beings and have them as spies everywhere. It was a brilliant idea. They would have been a formidable, secret army.

But when you have no heart for creation, what is made cannot but be perverted and ill. Crilodach's thoughts were not of life but of death, and death was altered by It to become alive. Hagouti was death twisted by the mind that made him live. His blood was acid, he could not maintain his body form for long as doing so hurt him, so he had to vanish in smoke and be borne along by the air. Walking crippled his muscles and bones. His bones were made from too much metal and his muscles had little give in them. In bodily form he was unable to function well. His mind burned with longings but he never knew what they were. His thoughts ached with questions he could not answer. His tongue swelled in his mouth but he had few words to express anything. Hagouti was sick, mean and vile, but he was also a creature of Crilodach. That made him dangerous.

He could not be touched. The skin burned off the hands that touched him when he was not mist. His spittle scarred flesh. In his smoke form he choked people to death filling their lungs with toxic vapour. His ability to kill in every way possible was unmatched. He had never failed his creator. So great was his desire to know what he was he went anywhere, everywhere, wishing to know and never finding out.

Crilodach never told him he was a creature of Its creation. Hagouti knew others had fathers and mothers and so he looked for anything that was like him. But nothing was. Everything he saw was alien to him. Always he thought maybe one day Crilodach would tell him. But It never did and never did he know his creator had no reason at all for creating him except to prove It could create something. A something. A helpmate in the endless search for eternal life. A helpmate that assured death. A helpmate who was a servant. A being It would have killed in an instant if Hagouti failed to serve. Hagouti never failed.

"I've seen," he said to Crilodach, "the stars falling. The worlds dying without your touch." Crilodach growled as Hagouti spoke. "I felt Bofindle." Crilodach growled deeper and said one name,

"Lilah."

Hagouti nodded and as he did so his face creased up with the pain in his neck. He evaporated to ease the agony. The name was a command. Hagouti vanished from Crilodach's side and with his great master's eyes upon him he wafted over the silver panels on the walls to begin his search for Lilah. He did not know yet where she would be found. There were many possibilities. But when he did find her he would fly there.

He knew how to kill her.

The End of Earth

After being apart for a long time, the worst place for friends to meet again is on a great battle field. A place where chance plays with lives; where festive thoughts cannot survive. When there is no time to play catch–up, to enjoy each other's company or share news.

As Lilah approached Copret with all the friendly desire to share a joke and a smile, talk, laugh and exchange stories, they both knew there was not the time and this was not the place. All they could do was be happy they were together, take some comfort in the fact they faced the dangers ahead together, then concentrate on their unfinished task forgetting everything else. For everything else had forgotten them. Neither of them asked questions of the other, or did anything that would have suggested they had not seen each other since Lilah had been a child when Copret, as he always did, had brought the new found spellmaker a present. He would throw her into the air and catch her as she fell into his heavy, scarred paws. In those days she had traced her fingers over those scars and Copret had told her how he came by each one. She had shivered, hating to think of her friend hurt and bleeding in the midst of the enemy.

Even their hug hello was light because affection would take time away from watching the enemy's next move; from gauging the enemy's state of mind. They had to scan the sky against an aerial attack. Breathe in the heavy, wakeful air which, like an expectant audience, waited for the army's onslaught with surreal fascination. Lilah had to listen to the silence that enshrouded Trecrogo and the few defenders until she became aware of every time their eyelids blinked, every change in temperature that touched skin, ever variance in colour among the shadows that crisscrossed the parapet. She could feel their flesh creep and the hairs rise on their necks when so much as a head turned in the ranks of the enemy. She became aware there were children here and she looked at them, noting how grown up they appeared, how stern in their faces, then she looked once again at the enemy ranks. There was no future for them unless they could defeat this army. This army could not defeat them without killing them. Whatever brought them all here, how many were the chances, the twists and turns of fate, they had found absolute certainty in one fact and one fact alone; these millions wanted to pillage Trecrogo and kill the few defenders.

Still, she remembered the promises she and Copret had made to each other when they played, when they leapt from tall trees as she trained, rolled on the ground and found themselves back-to-back, so close they could feel the heat from each others' bodies as they circled her teachers who had trapped them. How they learned to anticipate each other, to fight as a team, to act as if in a dream, to change and shift their bodies until those who trapped them were tripped up, left lagging behind and beaten. Then they promised they would always be there for each other. They swore an oath. How many years ago? They had been through all that so that today, they would have no need to talk. No need to smile in welcome. Lilah counted the new scars she could see in Copret's fur. No time to ask where he received them, all that was left was to keep their shared promise.

She felt encased in an invisible armour. An armour that spread out from her mind, covered her skin in a crust making her numb to everything. She was no longer on Earth, no longer breathing, no longer waiting. The battle had already commenced before she had landed a single blow. For her friends around her this was just a respite after the first attack. For her all battles merged into one. All she wanted to do was to get her friends out of this battle alive. After a few minutes even that small wish disappeared. She looked deep into the enemy and peered into their hatred of all things, and then all she wanted to do was kill them. Kill them all. Because after they were dead she could rest. In rest she could finally say hello to her friends. But this war would give no rest. All rest was over.

Copret's hairs rose down the entire length of his back. His spine tingled. His muscles tensed. He growled deeply. The defenders could see that enemy reinforcements had arrived even as Lilah stepped from the Ossendark, transfigured with the light that blazed from Demeter. She stood on the edge of the parapet of Trecrogo, looked across the enemy army with her steady, black eyes. She hummed to herself. She held Bofindle in her left hand and beat the bejal slowly against the palm of her right hand keeping time. Chloe stood by her, grateful in a way that another woman was there. Demeter, too, felt stronger. Trecrogo and he were no longer strangers. He had faced a storm. He would never be unsure of himself again. So swiftly, in the space between life and death, between one nano–second and another, does a boy become a kind of adult.

Behind the reinforced army that spread like a plague across the plains and swept up the hills, they saw the Earth saturated with men ready to battle, with a passion for killing, eager for any blood. Pressing in on the men in front to get a glimpse of their enemy. The defenders felt that their first success had had no impact at all. As if their tired muscles ached because of all the work that lay ahead of them not because of all the effort they had just gone through.

Lilah had no doubt that in Its anger and bitterness, Crilodach would fill every square inch of land with Its men sending them all against Trecrogo like a tsunami. Battalions turning the ground to mud with their boots. Battalions that ground their teeth until the air was filled with the grating sound, as if they were trying to eat into Trecrogo to get at their prey. As if the venom that sizzled in their saliva when they spat, could burn through stone.

Battalions of men pressed against each other in the very moment of war. The very breath of defiance. The very hope of death. They would strike again soon. Unleashing their power against Trecrogo. Craving the same things Crilodach craved. Filled with the promises Crilodach had made to them. Ignorant of all else. Battalions dedicated to one aim filled with one passion. To kill. To see blood on their hands. To survive the butchery.

These soldiers ran towards death with the same joy hunters on horses feel hunting animals. With no feelings at all but their own elation, their own prowess, their own sense of supremacy. They would not even stop to help their wounded, so intense was their frenzy for blood.

Faced with this unending mass of soldiers, Chloe thought herself helpless. Of all those here she felt she was the least equipped to fight in any way. She feared the start of this new battle. She wanted to be able to play her part but she felt she was no more than a feather in the path of a hurricane.

And with them a new warrior walked followed by Copret's watchful gaze. The men around him made room for him.

They did not press upon him. They showed him respect. He took a clump of the muddy soil in his left hand and tasted, making sure this was the Earth. A planet he had last seen when he had been a foot soldier. A planet that should not exist, a fortress built without him knowing. Was this the Sangyma's grand strategy, to hide behind a magic wall?

General Rataplan, a powerful man whose thin legs didn't seem enough to hold him upright, looked at the task ahead of him through his narrow green eyes, with all the skill of his centuries as a general in Crilodach's army. He had fought for Crilodach on scores of worlds, with various armies, losing only three battles in his long career. For each one he lost, he lost a child. Crilodach's retribution for his failure. His eldest son, Wiyan, his youngest daughter Koolan and his second son Badew all died because he failed. He did not consider the complete destruction of a planet as a loss. He did not consider the loss of entire armies much of a loss. Crilodach always had more. Always more. Always battles. He would not accept any loss in efficiency.

He stood upon a mound looking towards Trecrogo. This was not a new battle. This was not a new target. This was not a new enemy. Like Lilah he knew this war was always bigger than any single battle. This war was larger than the battles on any single planet. Larger than the petty wars between races. A million planets fighting each other was but a skirmish. Rataplan's war, Crilodach's war, was the only war. He had crisscrossed the universe bringing the artfulness of his mind and astuteness of his military planning to places and peoples that did not even know Crilodach existed. He had washed himself in blood. He had left behind him utter destitution but at least his three surviving children had lived. They would all live. Crilodach had promised them life to come. He never questioned Crilodach. This war was everything to him because victory gave life to his children.

Here, though, Crilodach had been taken by surprise. They had not known Trecrogo had been built or that Earth had not been destroyed. Under cover of a pretend implosion the Sangyma had spirited Earth away. Scattering the Losek soil upon the surface and in this valley they had half-grown and half-built a mighty fortress. Crilodach was sure they had trapped themselves. Their magic counted for nothing if they had to resort to secrets. It did not suspect the dual nature of the fortress.

Rage was the first thing Its general and lieutenants had felt. That on Earth behind their backs, at this crucial time, their enemies had stolen a march on them. Its rage in turn burned a fresh anger into their hatred and steeled their resolution. Of course they knew only the bears could have done such a thing with the Earth and built Trecrogo so quietly. Only they had access to the power needed. The army would settle with them afterwards. They would settle with them all. They would crush them, even if they had to take their hatred to new levels of frenzy, so completely did they hate. They had no room left for any other feeling.

But through his eyes and his armour, Rataplan could sense the awesome power facing him. He saw Lilah. He had heard about this spellmaker. He had been told what they said about her power. He had asked for every man available to Crilodach. He had asked for every free siege engine and every weapon. He had been given them. Never had he commanded everything before. They had been thrown back from the first assault because he had not been here. This would not be swift. This would not be easy but the army had their backbone. They had their general.

The walls did not look the same to him as they had to Demeter and Chloe. How they looked depended upon how you think and who you are. Like all things touched by magic, bejals see you even if they have no eyes and Trecrogo was an almighty bejal. They see into your heart and deep into your mind. What you see in them is your own reflection. Not of your face and body but of your inner self. A mirror to everything you have become and every dream you want fulfilled. The texture and colours of your appetites.

To Rataplan the walls appeared cold as ice. A bulwark against his army. A shield protecting his prey. This was not a home. Not a place of wonders. This was a thinking enemy with roots that went deep into the ground and spread out through the world around him. A part-grown, part-built edifice that reeked of the Sangyma. He hated this place. This scab. This disease. This violation of his desires. The sight of the walls offended him. He wanted to level the fortress. To ground the stone down and spit on the ruins. He longed to bring down the defenders and crack them open. His claws ached to snap their bones.

He surveyed his army. He knew the countless millions before and behind him could all be sacrificed and they would still not be able to take Trecrogo without cunning. He breathed through his mouth with a rasp. He saw Demeter suspended above Trecrogo captured in that sinister light that surrounded the boy. That light seemed threatening even to the general. The boy was on display. Every soldier could see him. Demeter was like the flag Crilodach's enemies had often flown above their emplacements in battle. They had a strange love for flags. A rallying point. The boy was a challenge to Rataplan and his men as important as any weapon. He knew Demeter was central to the fortress. He was the power. Somehow he had to get to the boy. But what army could get through Lilah and Bofindle?

"Well?" asked Hagouti.

Rataplan turned away from the sight of Trecrogo and looked at the half formed head floating in a misty body by his shoulder. Hagouti was anxious to begin. He was always eager to get on with the killing. Some said this was because he was eager to satisfy Crilodach's orders, others that he was just a good killer. But you cannot fool a general whose life a thousand times had already rested on his ability to read his soldiers' minds. Hagouti, Rataplan knew, was apprehensive of failing and wanted to get things over with as quickly as he could to quell his one fear. The fear that never left any of them. The fear of failing and facing Crilodach's anger.

Rataplan answered him slowly with the air of a man not used to being rushed but used to being obeyed. He weighed his battle strategy taking in Hagouti's sinister stare as if he had been glancing at a moth. His voice was steady as he sharpened his claws on the whetstone he carried by his side at all times.

"How long d'you need?"

"How long can sustain the fight?"

Rataplan bridled and looked at Hagouti as if the question were a challenge. He scratched his armour so quickly and fiercely, sparks flew.

"Copret's good, savage, powerful and the Onäis is an efficient weapon of war extending his reach across my entire army. The boy Demeter grasps fistfuls of the power at his disposal even as I speak. Lilah's joined them. I'll need every man I can get, and more. We'll fight the whole night and day if we have to but don't expect any to survive."

"I'll need the night to find a way in, once inside my work

will be swift. A whole night and day is more than enough time. But you must press them hard. They'll sense my presence if you don't occupy all their thoughts. Your assault mustn't falter for a solitary second."

Rataplan spat. The soil burned where his spit landed sending up a foul smelling wisp of smoke.

"We'll give you the time you need with our blood, but," he added slowly, "if Copret comes out to meet us again you'll not be able to kill him if you're inside Trecrogo."

"He's my secondary target," Hagouti said, moving around the general, "I'm here to kill Lilah."

"I'll keep him busy but none of my men will be able to get near him. The team I've assembled for that is still with Frin–Ghirzan."

"Why isn't Frin–Ghirzan here?"

"He's his orders just as I. If all goes to your plan we'll not have need of him."

"I don't see why his specialist troops aren't here. He spent years training them, they should be here," said Hagouti. "I thought you'd asked for everyone."

"A good general always keeps men in reserve. I assure you we'll give you the time you need. Can you handle your part of the plan?"

"Do your part and I will."

Rataplan did not move his head but his claws came close to tearing into Hagouti. They never got along, they had argued ever since Hagouti had been created. Rataplan had wanted to murder him on several occasions but neither of them wanted to feel Its anger, so they always stopped short of fighting.

"Copret mayn't be a Sangyma but they trained him. The Onäis is small and limits the number of men I can get close to him. I've seen Copret many times. That confounded magic protects him as securely as armour protects me," cursed Rataplan.

"I don't care for the problems you face. Your orders are simple. So are mine. Once I've dealt with Lilah I can go for the bear, not before."

"He's got tricks that would surprise even you."

Hagouti looked Rataplan in the eyes, something he could only do when floating as the general stood two feet taller than he did in his bodily form. He rasped between his teeth in his half mist, half solid form.

"All that surprises me are your cowardly excuses over the handling of a bear."

"I'm no coward," Rataplan shouted, truly angry.

"Prove yourself by covering for my attack," demanded Hagouti, his eyes flashing. "Stop telling me of their strength like some recruit in their first battle blubbering that the enemy is unexpectedly armed."

"I don't have to prove myself to you."

"Oh but you do general, you most certainly do. I'm your death as much as anyone's. Remember, Crilodach gave the orders but I killed your children."

"I remember," said Rataplan, coldly.

"I can wipe out this entire army if I was so ordered. I need the night to get into Trecrogo and you will give me that time whatever the cost."

"And after?"

"After?"

"What other battles do we need men for?" asked Rataplan.

"There'll be no more battles once Trecrogo falls," said Hagouti.

"There's always battles," scoffed Rataplan, "Kill Lilah you still have to deal with Demeter. We can't penetrate his light."

"The child will be useless without Lilah and Copret."

"I disagree."

"Then you know more than I do."

"I always have," said the general.

"But are you ever right?"

"I'm always right in matters of war," Rataplan replied.

"They kept Trecrogo secret from us for generations. They may even have the Sagitæ inside and we'd never know. We must find out. When this is over if Copret still stands, so what? He'll not survive Zaqui but if we have the Sagitæ we will."

"Will we?" asked Rataplan, seeing Hagouti was thinking only of himself.

"You mistrust Crilodach's word?"

"I mistrust you, but you're the only one who can get us into the fortress so I'm stuck with you."

"You underestimate your army."

"I underestimate nothing and, in matters of strategy, no one. I know this enemy. Bofindle isn't a toy, and who knows what this Chloe is capable of, I've yet to see her fight.

Besides all that, who else are they keeping in reserve?"

"I never thought to see the day General Rataplan worried about reserves," Hagouti's head was becoming mist as he spoke. "I think you'd stand here all night talking rather than fight."

"I'm a realist," shouted the general to the empty air. "How come we know of them now, how come you were unaware this place existed until today?" He thumped at the air with his fist, "You with all your knowledge, all your planning, all those battles, what were they for if this place was being built under our very noses?" Hagouti appeared behind him,

"We knew they were planning something but even we don't know everything about them. We only saw them here when they sent out their beacon. Perhaps they're over confident and didn't care to remain secret. Perhaps they're ready for you. So what if they are."

"You criticize others for just being careful but you're practiced at finding excuses for yourself," said Rataplan.

"We all have an art," he vanished and on the air came his last words. "Killing is mine."

Rataplan looked at his servant, a thin, ancient man who had been with him for many years. He waited. This man was a rare being able to sense Crilodach's creatures without seeing them. Rataplan had found him as a child after a brutal civil war Frin–Ghirzan had instigated. Frin–Ghirzan was a good commander, he had shown Rataplan the child. 'Keep him with you,' he had told him, 'you'll find him useful.'

Rataplan had argued with him but he had insisted so the general had kept the child and soon found how useful he was. Telling him when he was being spied upon. The child became a man and saved Rataplan's life on more than one occasion with no more than a raised eyebrow or a soft word. The general waited until his servant nodded.

"He's gone sir," he said, in a high voice that sounded more like a girl's than a man's.

"We don't creep in mists, kill in sleep, climb vertical walls without ropes or travel across galaxies unaided. We don't cast spells or wave wands," said Rataplan.

"The soldier is always given the heavier burden in the fighting," his servant told him.

"We're duty bound to fight as only those who can die, fight. I don't doubt Hagouti's power over us but she's up there. Raw power is up there. A spellmaker and a bear.

They'll be like a scythe through grass to my men."

"She's powerful," agreed the servant.

"She's lungs. Lungs can be broken. That's what Hagouti said. Lets get ready to buy him the time he needs. Get my lieutenants, we'll launch the attack within the hour."

His servant left him and sent out orders to his lieutenants in the field to attend their general. They came to Rataplan hard faced, armoured, ready. There were none here who would not willingly lay down their lives to protect their general but even they were wondering what he would say to them, for they had seen Trecrogo. They had seen Lilah arrive. Copret pacing the parapet and seeing off the first assault. The child in the light. Magic changes the odds in a battle. And though they knew Crilodach's presence was always with them they had heard the old stories. They had been told that Bofindle could hurt Crilodach. That once, when all was beginning, this bejal turned the tide of battle, saved Tegriel and imprisoned Crilodach in Damkina. There had not been a spellmaker with the power to wield Bofindle in their lifetimes, so they came to their general hoping to be given special orders. Rataplan, for his part, before he told them what they had to do, already imagined the look of horror in their eyes.

Chloe looked at Lilah for a long time with all the fascination a young child has for someone who instantly becomes their hero. The woman looked so strong and tall. Her eyes were steady, black pearls. Her black skin shone. Her long red hair wrapped around her head like a hat. Her teeth brilliant, flashing white as she smiled a smile that could melt your heart. Copret stood beside her and she got the impression that they were talking even though their mouths didn't move. They were like two statues, only they were not statues. The movement of their eyes as they gazed upon the enemy, gave away the fact that they were very much alive. Strength emanated from them like heat from a fire. She did not want to stand far away from her. Everyone who met Lilah felt the same, the need to be close to her, stay with her, because somehow that made them feel more alive.

That, and the way the light spreading out from Demeter lit up half the plain before them, softened Chloe's fear.

Demeter had lowered himself down, but he stayed elevated a few feet above them looking over Rataplan's deployment of forces. Lilah did not fear numbers. In any army there were always those few who had the real power. They were her primary targets.

"I can smell Rataplan though I don't see him yet," said Copret as he curled his claws.

"Crilodach honours us with all Its bile, dressed up in metal and served with hate," replied Lilah.

"They drop from the sky again in endless battalions," said Demeter.

"They're like grains of sand kicked up by a storm," growled Copret, "They wear you down. They never stop coming."

"How does Crilodach recruit so many?" Chloe asked.

"He's the entire universe to pluck them from," replied Copret. "This is one army. See how they're all the same? One army. One purpose. Its got thousands of armies. Sometimes It fights with germs, sometimes with bombs but most often It uses men like these. From breeding farms on a thousand planets all trained on Ghirzanben by the master of arms Frin–Ghirzan. A place you'll never have to see. Thankfully."

"They're like a plague," whispered Chloe.

"Do not hate them Chloe, hate will limit you." Lilah's face was unsmiling as she spoke. "Think of them as prisoners of Crilodach's mind. They are without hope, they are here, like all soldiers, because they do not know how to be free."

She let Bofindle rest on her shoulder and wrapped one arm around Chloe's shoulders without taking her eyes off the army below them.

"Really?" asked Chloe.

"Really. They were made to die. That is all they can look forward to. Crilodach uses life for Its own purposes. It does not care for the individuals in Its armies. It has never cared. It lures them by promising them all they desire if they are victorious."

"We're going to die too. I know we are, I read the charts. I know why Trecrogo is here," whispered Chloe.

"That does not mean we will die tonight. Nor at any time other than the time of Zaqui," said Lilah.

"Or that in dying we lose anything," suggested Copret.

"Some people think there is more to death than nothingness," explained Lilah.

"My people don't," said Chloe.

"Yet the atoms in you feel your life force. They will remember being you. Being part of you. Every atom that has been part of a living being remembers. They seek out the chance to be part of the living again. To be part of the wonder of thoughts. Atoms breathe thoughts from universe to universe," said Lilah.

"Especially mine," smiled Copret.

His fur ruffled. He felt that old ache in his limbs to be up-and-fighting, to be hacking into the enemy. He flicked his claws together to make sure of their readiness.

Chloe was mesmerized by the army that sprawled over the hills and deep into the valley miles away. She thought she could see more of them moving against the horizon. Crowding into each other. She could almost feel them overrunning her. She shivered. They were more than before. She could smell them. Their fetid breath was a constant breeze against the walls. She felt wafer thin. See-through. Like a drop of water vanishing into an ocean. She asked them,

"Why don't we have an army?"

"Because sometimes power can be wielded better by a few in the right place, then by the many," explained Copret, licking his teeth, "tactics vary but the wisdom of the Sangyma at this time is not to be disputed."

"The more people we had prepared for this day the greater the danger Crilodach would have discovered the fortress," Lilah added.

"Wouldn't we have more chance if we had an army as big as theirs?"

"We shall see, Chloe. We shall see," said Lilah.

"We four are an army," added Demeter.

"She speaks out of fear," thought the bear to Lilah.

"You should have given her some of the water too, then she would feel less alone. She is only a child yet," thought Lilah.

"I've children, they know how to fight," replied Copret.

"She will never grow into a woman," Lilah reminded him.

"Such is the fate of our time. Perhaps we could give her something to make the fear less?"

In this off-hand manner he showing his own fear. He had been close to death many times but that is not something you ever get used to. His manner was a touch expectant, because a part of him was longing to see how Trecrogo performed and another part was apprehensive in case any part of the design proved defective.

"Why don't they attack us?" asked Chloe.

"They're waiting for the command from general Rataplan," Copret told her.

"What's stopping him?" she asked.

"He's meeting with his lieutenants right now," Demeter revealed, looking through the shadows and hills.

"They will come soon enough," Lilah warned them.

Rataplan looked at the three men standing to attention before him with one eye. The other eye never left Trecrogo or the figures who stood on the parapet, barely moving. High as a mountain side, the fortress sheered away from the soldiers taking up positions immediately below. Once more he was going to test his ability against Copret. Twice the bear had forced him to retreat. Three times they had fought each other to standstill. If there was one thing Rataplan wanted before Zaqui, more than anything else, he wanted to kill Copret.

The three men were dressed in dark blue, their boots muddy and worn. They had been with him a long time. When Crilodach had imprisoned their fathers, the three dragon brothers. The lieutenants had all been wounded many times in various battles. Entrusted with their own commands as their experience grew. They were loyal to him through–and–through. They stood looking straight ahead, their arms by their sides, their weapons secure with their battalions. The breeze created by the millions breathing, caught at wisps of their hair beneath their tight helmets. None of them blinked. None of them remembered their fathers. Rataplan was their father. The army their home. Killing their family. Their faces were raw with never being indoors. Their skins hard from being out in all weathers. Their eyes drained of softness. These men had worn out metal armour in Rataplan's service.

"At ease," Rataplan commanded, momentarily waving his hand.

They relaxed. Their hard faces turned to Hagouti who now sat on the ground, pained by his human form, already weary of waiting. Rataplan took delight in making Hagouti repeat himself to his lieutenants. He liked to see him suffer. Rataplan looked at his servant and asked,

"Are we secure?"

"Yes," the man replied. "Only the one you invited"

"Our aim's to keep the enemy occupied while Hagouti gains entry into Trecrogo. We've to fight them hard. They mustn't have any time to think of anything but where our next blow'll land. They mustn't probe their defences and find Hagouti creeping up them from the sea. I want constant effort, no slackening, no wavering."

"Do we send a contingent with Hagouti?" asked Ferveiss, one of the lieutenants.

"I go alone," said Hagouti, "that way they're less likely to see me. They'll have eyes looking for any and all of your troop movements. Alone I will slip through."

"I see since the first assault they've been joined by Lilah," said Arnveiss, another of the lieutenants.

"I know," replied Rataplan. "She's Hagouti's primary target once he gets inside."

"Think you can take her?" Ferveiss asked, turning to Hagouti.

"Is there anyone I can't take?" replied Hagouti.

"She's as powerful as any Sangyma," pointed out Arnveiss.

"More, she's Bofindle by her side," snapped Jurveiss, the third cousin.

Rataplan looked at his three lieutenants. These cousins had worked their way up the ranks like one man in three bodies. Their loyalty to Crilodach was cast iron. Their loyalty to Rataplan was unshakable. They did not fight for name or fortune, they fought for the joy of killing, and because of that, they had been granted extended lives by Crilodach. Crilodach had hoped that gift would make them willing to tell It Rataplan's secrets, but they never did. The cousins did not betray their adoptive father. What they did not know, and what Crilodach had never told them, was that as the sons of dragons they would have lived a long, long time anyway. But they believed they were like Rataplan and since their dragon bodies had been hidden from them they never thought to question him. Yet, now they were arguing. Questioning his battle plan. They had never done such a thing before. They had been badly shaken to be beaten off by two children, one of whom did not even fight, Copret and the fortress. He had to make sure their uncertainties vanished.

"Whatever else happens here we must fight until we hear Hagouti give us the all clear. Our effort is purely in regard to his mission. He's our secret weapon. Losses mean nothing."

The men nodded. This was their battle order. Nothing else mattered. Whatever doubts they harboured were now silenced. But they were still thinking about how Hagouti would get into the fortress. They knew as well as anyone else Crilodach had promised them all eternal life once the Sagitæ were in Its grasp yet here It was willing to sacrifice a huge army for one or two lives of the enemy. They did not trust this strategy. Was Crilodach, the most fearsome of all commanders, scared?

"Ferveiss, you'll lead the left flank," ordered Rataplan, "Arnveiss you'll take the right flank, I'll lead the centre and Jurveiss you'll command the flow of troops from the rear. Keep them coming. However many are lost at the front keep them coming at a run. I want no let up."

"You'll have 'em if I've to whip 'em there myself," promised Jurveiss.

"I'm not up to full strength yet," said Arnveiss, wiping his mouth with the back of his gloved hand, "We took the brunt of the first attack. That child has more tricks in him than I expected."

"How long before you'll be ready?" asked Rataplan.

"When do you want to start?"

"In less than an hour."

"We'll be ready in less than an hour."

Rataplan nodded to himself. That was the answer he had wanted his lieutenants to give. He was satisfied they were up to the mark. The men saluted and left for their command posts. Hagouti began to become mist again saying,

"Tonight is going to particularly dark."

Hagouti vanished. Rataplan eased his hand over his neck. He felt tired. He always did just before a battle. All tiredness left him once the fighting started. Then he felt the hunger to win. He thirsted for victory as other people thirst for water. He looked on Trecrogo once more. Already he felt he had been here too long. He had looked out on those stones until they were imprinted on to his memory. He had begun to count them and see in his imagination the bears building their fortress. This was the beginning of the final battle.

The final confrontation. The gaining of the Sagitæ. He sharpened his claws. Made sure his leg armour was secure. He took a deep breath. In his mind was one thought. To win. To kill to win. To overcome the enemy. To save his remaining children.

"You may go," he said to his servant. His servant rose, stretched his tired body and looked around,

"The war does not end here," he said as he bowed.

Rataplan looked at him, then at Trecrogo and then to his servant again. His servant was gone.

"The war does not end here," Rataplan whispered under his breath making fists and resting them on his knees. "I'll paint those walls red before the morning," he swore.

"The general's angry," Ferveiss said to Arnveiss, walking away hurriedly after they had left and before they took up their positions.

"So'd you be if you had Hagouti breathing down your neck," replied his cousin.

"I remember when the general was last like that. We were at Juralana, remember?"

"I'd hardly be likely to forget," replied Arnveiss, holding up his hand revealing the loss of two fingers. "He lost his son because of that defeat."

"We've never had as huge an army to control as this," reminded his cousin and brother in arms. "I prefer when the general isn't angry. Anger clouds his judgment. Only when he's calm do I think we'll do well in the assault."

"You and your omens," Arnveiss mocked. "When will you learn naked power wins, not the alignment of stars or the general's good humour."

"I know what I know," replied Ferveiss, "I've seen things that shouldn't have been. I've felt this hidden power, like water running beneath everything."

"Which you think's what?" asked Arnveiss.

"I don't know."

"Then why worry?"

"Because all powers need placating. I don't know exactly how to get this power on my side. Have you never sensed anything?" asked Ferveiss

"Nope."

"Has Jurveiss ever mentioned anything?"

"Not to me. We've more important things to think about. The men have been restless these past months. All this waiting around for a fight. They need strong control. Forget mysteries," cajoled Arnveiss, "you're the power others need to be scared of cousin."

Arnveiss slapped him on the back and went to join his troops. Ferveiss did the same, throwing off thoughts that made him uncomfortable. Thoughts that there was something about himself he did not understand. As if something or someone was coming to find him and he did not know why, or who, or when.

The left flank, under the watchful command of Ferveiss floating above their heads, moved up to the boundaries of Trecrogo and stopped. The right flank mirroring the left, step for step, showing their support across the plain and then they too stopped. Lights lit up the sky as flares were sent up giving commands to various battalions. The whole parapet of the fortress was ablaze with light emanating from Demeter, flowing like a carpet across the stones and wafting downward, painting the walls a ghostly white. This second army was not the indisciplined rabble of the first attack. They had possessed more courage than sense. This army could not be stopped, only destroyed.

Copret's wounded arm, which he had tried to hide, was tied with a thin bandage now that Lilah had noticed the gash. His claws ached and were still stained with spots of blood as he surveyed the enemy army manoeuvre into attack formation. His bright eyes widened when he saw Ferveiss floating above his men. He had a score to settle with him. A village on a distant shore and the fisher family who had lived there. Friends he had known. A family he had seen grow for twelve generations. A great love of animals and nature pervaded all their thoughts. Honest people with no wish to upset the universe. He had had to bury the pieces Ferveiss had left him to bury. He swallowed down a deep, long growl. His teeth flashed. Ferveiss knew he had been seen.

"Here," offered Chloe by his side, "Lilah said I was to dye your bandage with this to lessen the whiteness. She says she can see the white shining like a torch from one end of the parapet to the other."

"I don't really need the bandage," admitted Copret, bending down and allowing her to take his thick arm.

"But then you'll bleed again," she argued "and I don't think you want to argue with Lilah."

She daubed the thick, brown paint on. There was something in the paint which blended so well you would have thought he was all undamaged fur. The ache in the wound also vanished. He looked down sniffing. The bandage did not smell of paint but of balm.

"I'll bleed from other cuts before morning."

He smiled. He let Chloe finish painting over the bandage with easy, swift brush strokes. He looked at her work, growling some appreciation.

"I didn't feel a thing," he lied.

"What's that smell?" she asked.

"That's Crilodach's army."

"What a stench," she said, putting the brush into the small pot of paint.

"The smell of this army is sweat and determination. Fear and knowing," he sniffed deeply, "and a strange hope. They want this to be the last battle."

"You can smell all that?"

"You can't hide anything from a bear," he replied.

Lilah stood on the very edge of Trecrogo, her feet balanced half way on and half way off the wall like a diver on a diving board. Bofindle tingled at the closeness of the enemy formations. Copret sniffed the air. Chloe peered down, seeing the army almost touching Trecrogo's foundation. She hoped there were no hidden doors down there.

"They'll flow like a torrent upon us," explained Demeter. "See in the distance, they try to hide but I can see through the hills. They've been building ships, against the possibility of a sea attack upon them. They're thinking ahead. They also have someone directing the supply of men and machines with great precision."

"Probably Jurveiss as I don't see him at the front," said Copret.

"You know who they all are?" asked Chloe. Copret laughed and said,

"Not every soldier. See Ferveiss," he pointed, "he's the one floating above the flank there, and over there the tall man floating above the army's shoulders on the right flank's Arnveiss, his first cousin. With those two in the front their other cousin, Jurveiss, is there somewhere. The three of them are ever together. Their fathers were brothers but they are not fit to lick their fathers' claws."

"Are brothers," corrected Lilah.

"Could they still be alive after all this time?" asked Copret.

"They are. I have sent someone to bring them here."

"Oh that I'd love to see. Rataplan facing the three dragon brothers he imprisoned."

"Their fathers are dragons," Chloe said with awe.

"A worse trio of sons you couldn't hope to find. They've nothing of their fathers in them," Copret told her. "I've hoped many times they would die together, rather than continue to shame their fathers' memories."

"Perhaps today you'll get your wish," suggested Demeter, exercising his fingers into fists and out again as he prepared the weaponry that was coursing through his veins. His clothes seemed to have changed now. His hair was longer. His body was changing the more he fused with Trecrogo. He could see things that up to now only Lilah could see. His true transformation was beginning. More than just the information Trecrogo was designed to give him, the fortress was arming his brain. He was in touch with the magic of the bears. He saw so many rooms in the fortress. He could hear the discussion of Sangyma long dead. He was in touch with everything that had touched Trecrogo. As long a history of magic as has ever existed.

"Those cousins are an army of their own," growled Copret, "They've a lot of blood to answer for. A lot of suffering. They've been made lieutenants in Crilodach's army because of their coldness. I'd a chance to kill them once. I should have."

"What happened?" asked Chloe.

"I mistakenly let them live."

"No," said Lilah, "compassion is not a mistake. They had surrendered."

"Their kind never surrender. They used my leniency to live on. Instead of changing their ways, they planned their battles better. They used peace as a weapon and all talk of peace as a lull in which to build up their strength. They're an eternal enemy who abuse treaties and abuse goodwill.

Frin-Ghirzan's trained killers are never to be trusted. If they'd ever defeated us they would have taken to fighting among themselves just for something to kill. That's how far down the well of hate they've fallen."

He growled deeper as he saw the cousins float closer. A tempting target for an angry bear but Copret was too canny to be drawn. His claws ached but his mind was clear. He knew he was high on Rataplan's target list.

"They know I'm here and they know I'll not give them the chance to surrender again. I swear this day I'm their nemesis."

"Movement on the hill to the middle-right," said Lilah, her eyes fixed in the dark distance.

"Got them," replied Copret.

"He was there with his lieutenants just now," said Demeter.

"Who? Crilodach?" asked Copret.

"No general Rataplan, and there was another with him," replied Demeter.

Copret looked at Chloe then he whispered to Lilah,

"One other? Who do you think he is?"

"One of Crilodach's creations," she replied.

"I'm glad we've eyes in the back of our heads," he growled.

"Here they come." The call was from Demeter.

He had not left his position suspended in a cylinder of light, overlooking the enemy. This was his post. Being here was his duty. He knew his place gave him immense power at his finger-tips. Watching Copret as he fought and watching over Chloe, he had been filled with a feeling of wonder as he moved his hands and saw the army mowed down. He had sensed the tremors coursing across the plains from his actions. He no longer had any doubts about who he was or what he had to do. A depth of history flowed through his mind longer and greater than any human had ever known. His knowledge spanned vast distances, grasped incredible ideas, delved the wonders of magic and all of this had flowed into him in the past hours.

He had taken no food nor asked for any water. He looked at the enemy moving like some multi-headed beast spewing out venom from endless mouths. Millions of men divided into battalions, and the battalions into legions, moving in co-ordinated ranks. They had practiced all the years of their lives so that they could move with not a single one out of step. Transparent clouds from their body heat billowed over the parapet as if from an open furnace, melting hope away. If discipline alone could intimidate they had already won. Except the defenders here were no ordinary people to be intimidated by any manoeuvres or numbers.

There were no war cries. No shouts of triumph or calls for victory and blood. No horns blaring, no shields hammered with swords. Just millions of men on the move. They took up their positions and waited. With the ground shaking as they moved. With the ground groaning as they stamped. The air ached with anticipation. This time there was no residue of magic in the sky for Demeter to weave into a weapon with his light. You don't catch Rataplan out with such tricks. But Demeter had more magic at his finger-tips than Rataplan had ever seen.

A tidal-wave stretching out as far as the eye could see, bearing down on Trecrogo, threatening to crash over them with a hatred more intense than the force in exploding stars. Rataplan's armies always instilled fear, but he knew these troops, for all their training, were useless for anything other than a diversion whilst the bear and spellmaker commanded Trecrogo. A good general always knows where he can be beaten. Rataplan knew his weaknesses. That was his strength.

Chloe however was still feeling powerless and out of place. She wanted to be able to do something. No one had time to talk to her in the first battle in which everything happened so fast she barely had time to think, and no one was looking at her now. She moved close to Demeter and he looked down at her for a second. He seemed to understand. To know. He nodded his head and behind her she saw a section of the roof give way and there below her was an armoury. She walked to the edge and a beam of light settled beneath her feet and lowered her down as if she had been a feather gently falling to the ground from an eagle high in the clouds.

Floating felt like being bathed in cream. She could not feel her body at all until the last foot when Demeter, seeing the army begin the attack in earnest, turned away dropping her and above her, where there had been an open roof there was nothing but solid stone. The darkness quickly gave way to a dim light. Around her the weapons on the walls and floor flashed and burned. She looked stunned. There seemed enough here to arm thousands. Did Trecrogo expect reinforcements, or were they already supposed to be here?

Had something gone terribly wrong? Terror gripped her for an instant. Then she pulled herself together.

"I wonder where any reinforcements are going to come from?" she thought.

She went around the armoury and as she came close to the doorway the heavy doors silently opened. She peeped out and the darkness of the corridors greeted her. She had no idea where in Trecrogo she was.

So focussed was Demeter on the enemy that he did not see the small boat bobbing on the water rowing quietly towards Trecrogo from behind. A sea mist closed over Hagouti now and then, as the boat's prow never faltered from a straight course, borne forwards not by any currents but by Hagouti's own malevolent power. The sea-mist clung to the stones mingling with another mist that wafted from the boat and sought for a way into the fortress with his tenacious grip. The boat sank out of sight and this mist cast about the walls looking for a weakness, seeking cracks or holes but of course there were none. Like a snake he slithered and wafted over the stone, this way and that way, clinging, stopping every so often like a safe cracker listening. Once his head materialized and his ear touched the stone only to have his skin burned at the touch. Trecrogo did not permit him to listen. He shrank from the wall scared in case he had given the game away. Indeed the touch did register with Demeter but his hands were full and the touch was so slight he decided to deal with whatever had caused the alert later. A mistake he would curse himself for and never repeat in the hours of fighting ahead.

Finally, Hagouti found the window on which Demeter had sat and from which Chloe had looked out on to the sea. The now empty chart room. Drifting into the room he saw the places where the charts had been taken down from the walls. He allowed himself to take his solid form again. The pain in his body made him grimace. He did not form his legs and feet. He did not want to tread upon the floor. He knew this place would send out an alarm loud enough for Lilah to hear if he did. He looked around like a finger-itching thief. He darted to the door which did not automatically open to him. He became mist again and wafted through the lock.

His pale hands appeared on the other side of the door. He drifted down the corridors, his sinister eyes searching like a carnivorous beast's for easy or wounded prey. Spittle in his mouth bubbled with every hot breath. He did not like the feel of this place. The aching strength of the stones. The fortress reeked to him. He had been so long with his own thoughts to have his mind filled with those of the bears made him feel sick. Trecrogo wanted to know who he was. He heard the same music Demeter heard, questioning him. He felt a presence testing him. The fortress decided to dispatch someone to find out what this strange feeling in the mist was for even though Hagouti's movements were slight, the bears would not have allowed their fortress to let the smallest thing go unidentified.

He could not risk Trecrogo probing his mind. Unable to bear the pain in his hands he became wholly a mist again wafting slowly around trying to get his bearings. He felt the army attacking. He felt the men dying. His mind could feel them because he was linked to their fate. Their deaths made him stronger. Their spilled blood filled him with energy, took away his pain and gave him pleasure. He was torn between delighting in this feeling and the need to move as swiftly as Crilodach ordered, to kill Lilah. He felt Demeter, whose actions throbbed through the stone like muscles tensing and relaxing as if Trecrogo was an extension of the boy's body. Everything seemed bound to everything else and everything living was sensing everything else that lived. Such was the shrinkage of space in the encroaching closeness of Zaqui.

He was unsettled. His violent thoughts were no longer allowed to be his only thoughts. For the first time in his existence as people died he not only felt their deaths, but he heard their last thoughts, felt their last feelings. Even as mist, this unexpected discomfort did not dissipate. Demeter may not know he was inside the fortress, Lilah and Copret may not be aware of his presence, but Trecrogo knew something. He didn't have much time, Demeter would be alerted soon.

Chloe had to make her choice. She looked at the ranks of weapons and knew most of them were useless because they were far too big for her hands or short arms. Shields she could never lift, spears as tall as the room. Then, propped against the wall besides an emerald studded mirror, she saw a bow and quiver. She picked up the bow and tested the string. The twang echoed throughout the room like a warning knell that sent shivers down her spine. If she had looked closely she would have seen every bit of metal in the room glitter brightly as she tested the string but she couldn't take her eyes off the bow. She bent down and picked up the quiver. She wrinkled her nose.

"Typical, only got seven arrows." She was going to put the bow down again but something stopped her. She looked at the arrows. She pursed her lips and took a deep breath.

"Oh well I'm not that good a shot anyway so missing with seven isn't much different from missing with twenty."

She fitted one to the string and her sharp eyes focussed instantly even in the dim light. As if the arrow was helping her. Her arms were rock steady. She knew that she had never been able to aim anything so accurately. She did not stop to look for a helmet, somehow she felt the bow and arrows would suit her perfectly. How could she know that they had been made for her and her sharp eyes?

She walked to the door which let her into the corridor again. Her eyes could see nothing in the darkness for a few seconds, then at the end of the corridor Hagouti wafted down. She saw the mist clearly and in the mist she saw that Hagouti possessed two forms. Trecrogo was showing her the stranger so that they could find out who he was.

She bit her lip. For a second she thought maybe the enemy had breached the walls but then she dismissed that idea. Surely there would have been a lot of them sneaking around. She did not know who Hagouti was but she ran down the corridor on soft feet and followed him, the bow in one hand, an arrow in the other. She stopped at each corner, peering carefully around, half wondering if whatever he was would be peering right back at her, nose–to–nose. Wondering if she would have to kill him.

Rataplan came towards his men, passing them with a roar, running at Trecrogo. This was the signal they had waited for. Lilah standing tall, lashed at the army of men using Bofindle like a massive pendulum ploughing through their ranks massed at the base of Trecrogo.

Many new enemy girdled the Earth. Not all faced the defenders. Many faced the sea knowing on the far shore lay the fortress. Once Hagouti was inside they prepared an assault but the conversations between the sea and the bears had been long. The roots of the fortress spread out beneath the water a strange, unknown kind of seaweed with tendrils hundreds of miles long and the sea changed as only the sea may. Demeter heard them and turned to fight them but the water swirled, bubbled and boiled so that nothing could float upon the sea's surface. The far shore was battered with violent storms no spell could calm. No attack would come from that direction.

The sky was devoid of stars. Had Rataplan thought to distract the defenders by pretending to start a frontal assault whilst his plan had been to attack from above? She swept them away like flies bringing Bofindle up at each pendulum stroke and whirling the bejal around her head before flattening more of the troops below. She used the might of Bofindle as some would use a simple piece of hazel stick to disperse a plague of flies.

Copret, on the Onäis from which he could not be thrown, ripped into the right flank, roaring like a beast as his claws connected straight into their bones. He flung them over his head like some demented reaping machine. Demeter blazed light across the plains blinding them and sweeping them from the top of the hills, burning them up and making them trip over each other in such numbers – thousands of them at a time – they had difficulty lifting their weapons. He turned their weapons against them as those that slipped were crushed by the weight of the men pushing from behind. He sent wave after wave of tremors tearing across the ground to throw them off balance, causing many of the soldiers to kill each other by treading on the fallen and breaking their necks.

The tides of battle are many, and different for each person. Those who hear the noise about them and are caught up in the fear–filled force that is survival. They join their cries to the cries of their comrades, and the cries of the enemy. The noise of their weapons is as great as any shouting. The front line, as they fall, impart their strength to the second line which walks over their dead and dying bodies. The wounded fall and accept the crushing feet of their comrades taking heart that they always go forward, that upon them their comrades have stepped up a little way towards their objective. Then the second line falls upon the first, face to face, armour sticking to armour. Torn. Bound in blood and death. And others step upon them and fall. All the time the dead make a wall. A mound upon which those behind climb to continue the assault.

The dying themselves know the battle is lost for them. The universe is lost for them. There is nothing more to their story. Their atoms already buzz with release, their dreams as empty as their veins. In every war where countless millions fight over land, water, food or gold, dreams have always died with the dead. Dreams that filter into the atoms that break free from the rotting corpses and become part of other living things, in which the dreams can become nightmares.

Wars change as weapons change. Battles deserted swords for guns. Stealth became more important than numbers. Surprise more important than agreeing a time to fight. No more men lining up and charging on horses and elephants. First they crawled forward and observed the enemy from afar, planned their best way forward, aimed their artillery then fired from a distance. They flew over the enemy, they watched them from mountains, caves, skies and nearby planets. They spied on the enemy generals. They spied on the enemy leaders. They learned all about the battles their enemies had fought, and steeped themselves in their strategy. They estimated their strength, if they couldn't find spies to tell them exactly, and judged their ability to respond. They asked about their training, they made assumptions about their willingness to fight and die. Then they played mind games before a single soldier was ordered into position. They tried to create weaknesses in communication and supply lines. Battles became things fought in other places than on fields with flags waving. Politicians fought with words, parliaments fought with threats, watching became a weapon. Secret messages, codes and spying became as important as anything an army could do. More important than the number of men prepared to die. More important than single battles. To know became the way of winning.

Then the armies changed. As weapons grew more powerful, the powerful leaders grew more armies because armies could be wiped out with the press of a button. Robots came to be used which were expendable. Robots could be made in large numbers and could withstand damage and still fight, even with arms detached from their bodies they could still kill. They were strong but such robots could take a long time to make.

Genetically modified beings were used who were considered of use for the purpose for which they had been bred and educated. Soon battles were fought on different planets to those who waged the war. They did not care what lived upon those planets. They only cared about how many of those left living were their own soldiers. Victory at any cost. This was the only thing that never changed in all the wars since time began. Everyone wanted victory. Only the Sangyma seemed to know that victory never lay in defeating the enemy. If you can change your enemy into a friend you can save lives. They had subtle minds. More subtle than Crilodach's. Crilodach could never be changed so they made Its obstinacy, Its weakness.

Magic plays a greater part in the ending of the universe than at any other time. As the stars collapse events meet over smaller distances. Energy was being unleashed all around them. Gravities switched in seconds. Yesterday and today became one. A spell and a bomb could create the same havoc in this diminishing space. A spell and a whisper could contain the same power. Enemies, being forced into a smaller and smaller area, found that there was no time to think through a problem. If the plans had not already been laid, now was too late to generate them. To instantly react and fight was all that was left. The combatants could no longer use proxy wars. They had to face each other.

Crilodach's forces, schooled in the finest training fields on Ghirzanben, were more than men. They were unstoppable. They flowed down to Trecrogo like a sea, and for all Copret, Demeter and Lilah could do they never ceased to flow. Pushed on by their own determination and their limitless number as if they were being birthed, grown and thrown into battle in seconds. Fierce and loyal to nothing outside of their own numbers they piled up in masses on the ground. Broken and dead they lay upon each other. The dying crawled to be part of the heap so their dead bodies would help lift up their living comrades and they would still become part of their victory. And above the dead more dead. More bodies.

Copret's claws were red. Bofindle was dripping in their blood, Demeter's hands wearied with the power of his slaughter and still they came on. Still they came and still they died as if dying was their object. As the hours passed their bodies became a rampart for others to walk over. A rampart climbing as high as Trecrogo. They crept higher and higher towards the top. If he had been given time to think, Demeter would have understood why there were no windows in Trecrogo facing the land. As if the builders knew this was what the enemy would do. As things were their single window placed at the back for a crucial purpose, almost lost them their spellmaker. As the battle progressed the bodies piled dangerously high. Until the fresh men who took the place of the latest ranks were able to throw stones and hurl spears on to the parapet. They clattered around the defenders feet and vanished in sparks of blue fire.

Then Ferveiss and Copret met floating high about the battle, and Arnveiss joined in as they tried to kill the wounded Copret. Tired and almost overrun, Copret pulled hairs from his body and threw them into the air and suddenly twenty Coprets appeared. All identical. All raging and blazing and clawing. They fought the troops and some were killed and each time one fell the enemy gleefully laughed but the others remained, and that meant the real Copret still lived. They fought on screaming and cursing, angered by the deception.

Arnveiss saw the brown painted bandage on Copret's arm loosen first. In the encroaching dawn light he saw and he knew who the real Copret was and he attacked with his bodyguard.

Chloe stopped by an archway and walked into a room of yellow light. She saw Hagouti floating out and opened her mouth to challenge this strange being whose head kept appearing and disappearing. She stopped herself. He did not know she was following him. Whoever he was she had a chance of surprising him. She knew that was important. The bow in her hand felt warm and mighty. The arrow in her other hand felt as if the shaft and arrow-head had no weight at all. She realized the bow and arrow would tell her when to fight. She understood the weapons in Trecrogo looked like other weapons but were not as other weapons. She was about to discover just how well she had chosen.

She ran on. Hagouti wafted down the steps and stopped. He turned. He saw nothing, he sniffed the air. He hissed to himself softly. His eyes looked around then he went up a set of stairs and in the near–distance he heard the clamour of battle. He was close to the parapet. Chloe slipped out from behind a pillar and softly followed him. Now the arrow notch was resting on the bow string and she held them downward ready to bring the bow straight and shoot at her target in a second. She heard the noise of battle. She knew he was heading for the parapet. She knew now he was trying to attack them from behind. Then she stopped. In her mind she saw Copret. She saw Arnveiss. She saw the great bear struggling. Lilah occupied. Demeter had not noticed. She straightened her back. She looked around but nowhere could she see a way out. She raised the arrow. This was ludicrous, not making any sense but in the darkness, and down a corridor she fired. She felt she had to. She felt called to.

She was amazed. She saw the flight of her single arrow curve round the corridors avoiding being noticed by Hagouti, up the steps and flew out on to the parapet then headed directly towards where Copret was fighting. The arrow did not fly to kill one man but flew to do the work the images in her mind wanted done. She had shot the arrow hoping to clear all the men from around Copret and the arrow flew through them and around them. Copret saw them fall and saw the arrow do great work and gave a roar. He knew Chloe had found the weapon they had made for her.

The arrow flew back to her. Even though she had moved position. Silent as a butterfly landing, unbloodied, in the quiver. She had another in her bow, ready for the creature which was stalking the corridors. She looked at her bow. She did not feel so helpless anymore. She had saved Copret's life. She could see him revitalized and winning. Her arrows were dangerous.

Hagouti wafted over the floor. A door stood in front of him. He looked around and taking shape opened the door. The room on the other side was empty. He walked through, and into a corridor and up more steps. Then more steps and as a mist, turned right searching for his prey. He heard voices above him. He was almost there.

"Who are you?" demanded Chloe.

He was shocked at the challenge because the voice came from behind him. He turned round, his eye materializing with surprise. Chloe stood in the centre of the corridor her arrow aimed at him. He assumed she had been hiding near where she stood. He would have been surprised to know she had been following almost from the moment he sneaked into Trecrogo.

"Child, you can't harm a mist." His voice was full of threat and pain.

"You don't know what I can do."

The arrow never wavered. These weapons in Trecrogo knew how to be handled. They made sure those who used them instantly had the skills required to make effective use of their magic.

"You don't know what I can do," he sneered back.

But he was wary. He did not know this enemy. He had heard of the children who taught the clones. They were fearless. Never given to rash acts, they were teachers, playmates, thinkers and fighters. This girl had been chosen to teach Demeter, cloned from a human being no less, so Hagouti reasoned, she must be the greatest of her race.

"You can change from man to mist. Identify yourself," she demanded. He realized she had been watching him for a while to know that. Had she alerted the others? Was his ambush uncovered?

"You've been spying on me."

His hands appeared and touched the walls lightly, the mist swirled around him. The hands vanished as the walls burned them. She kept the tension on the bow and the arrow straight to her line of sight. As he moved towards her she moved slightly back.

"We defend Trecrogo. Who are you?" Her mouth was set. "I will not ask again."

"I'm a messenger," he replied. He became a man again, "A mere ... messenger."

He raised his hands almost in surrender as he spoke. He eyed the bow. He could sense the bow was magical. He did not trust her. He needed to get close to kill her. He took a step towards her.

"Stay where you are. Who sent you?"

"My master," he replied bending his head slightly, "I was sent to give a message to Lilah. An important message. Urgent."

"Then why are you creeping around Trecrogo. Stay there, I'll shoot if you try to take another step."

"I was trying to find my way through this place. I've not been here before. Everything is unknown to me. I was lost. I heard the noise of battle. I followed my ears, so to speak.

I don't mean you any harm. Put the bow down. We're wasting time here. Your friends are in danger. They need my message. I could save all your lives."

"Why didn't she know you were coming?"

"How could we tell her without alerting the enemy?" He smiled, "You know whom I mean." He stepped closer. She stepped back.

"There's a front entrance for our friends."

"I couldn't get through all those troops. I came in from the sea, I found a little window but this fortress is so confusing. I've only been trying to find Lilah, child, that's all."

"Your next step towards me will be your last." He stopped moving. "What is your message?" she asked him.

"Do you need to point that thing at me I'm only a messenger. Your arms must be getting tired."

"My arms are fine. What's your message?"

"I must tell only Lilah," he replied, "before morning," he added.

"Then she's never going to get your message," Chloe told him. He stared at her, struggling hard to hide his anger.

"You're only a child, why are you fighting in this terrible place?" he asked, losing patience.

"That's my business."

They stood looking at each other. Moments passed like hours. She did not trust him. She did not believe him. The bow stayed steady. The arrow stayed pointing at him. Being hindered was the one thing Hagouti hated more than being defeated. He was furious.

"I can't deliver my message from here," he whined.

"We don't leave this place until you tell me what you came to tell her, and who sent you."

"I told you."

"I want names," she snapped. He was breathing hard.

"Child this shape is difficult for me to maintain."

"So?"

"So I need to become mist again," he told her.

She watched him transform and as he did so she saw something new she had not seen before. Its greenish hue still had a certain shape. There was still the outline and a smell she recognized, the same stench came off the army outside.

Then Hagouti swept down upon her and she fired the

arrow which ripped through the mist and he felt real pain. Felt the arrow's coldness. He screamed. How could he feel her attack? Weapons passed through mist. Nothing can cut a mist. He stopped. He swirled in upon himself and formed himself again. He was lying on the floor. On his back. His shoulder was shattered. The arrow was back in the quiver. Another was in the bow.

She had only wounded him. He cursed. She could have killed him. How was that possible? What weapons had ever been created that could harm or could stop him? For the first time in his existence, Hagouti was scared. He looked at her. She looked at him. He rolled and became a mist and fled from her. His screams echoed across the walls. She raced after him.

The ramp of the dead was as high as Trecrogo. Rataplan was on the mountain. He looked behind him, more men were coming as Jurveiss hurried them on. He looked at the defenders. Where was Hagouti? He spat on the dead men beneath his feet. He had never trusted anyone but his own men. His own lieutenants. Everyone else always failed in the end.

He drew his arm up and waved on the men. They continued forward. The horde still had no ending and still came at the defenders. Lilah, Demeter and Copret churned them like a three-headed machine eating people. Still they came on. Hungry to die. Unaware that the fortress was not merely defending them but actively, magically, fighting Rataplan's forces.

"We can't go on like this," said Copret, feeling his arms ache as he flew past Lilah to attack a knot of the enemy.

"We have no choice," replied Lilah, still wielding Bofindle like a mace swirling about her the length of Trecrogo and obliterating the men as they strove to keep their footholds.

Demeter tore into their lines with greater and greater power but no matter how deep he cleared a path, the lieutenants filled the gash again with endless reinforcements, their very number deadening all hope, as if they were sucking at their hearts like parasites, willing them to give in. The defenders fought on. The enemy came on. The darkness grew. Until the air was oppressive and heavy with them. Until they could smell their sweaty and dying bodies. Until the fumes from the ramp filled their nostrils and their eyes were tired of the sight of them. Still the enemy increased. Still they pressed home. They looked for advantage. They died looking. Now the bodies began to rise above the parapet. As if the whole universe were sending armies to drown Trecrogo in bodies. But the men who climbed this pile of bodies were tired. As tired as the defenders.

Copret growled, ripping into half a dozen more of them with one sweep of his arm as the Onäis tipped and banked skimming hundreds off the advancing climbers.

"Our fight gets more bitter Copret," snarled Ferveiss, facing his oldest enemy.

"I gave you quarter once, I'll not again," warned the bear.

"I want only your head," snapped Ferveiss, attacking him.

He struck out at Copret who met his clawed hand with his own and held him there in mid air. The enemies looked into each others' eyes, struggling with each other to throw the other to the ground. Though neither of them could see the ground. They held each other at bay, their eyes filled with anger.

"Still you fight on the losing side," Ferveiss grunted.

Copret felt a new power in Ferveiss's arm. He had wondered if the enemy would grow stronger towards Zaqui. He had his answer.

"At least I have a side," growled the bear.

"The wrong one," Ferveiss told him.

"I'll always be opposed to you," he replied.

"You're strong enough to be a winner … why give your strength to the weak?" Copret loathed being this close to this dragon's son. This killer of children.

"My strength is a strength you'll never understand."

"Your strength is about to be broken."

"Never!"

"We're numberless. You can't win this battle." Ferveiss struggled. His breath was laboured as they tussled.

"I'll die trying," Copret told him.

"Death for you would be too easy," snarled Ferveiss, "I've better sport planned."

He broke free bringing down his left hand to strike, but Copret caught him with his injured arm. Despite his pain he held Ferveiss again in his iron grip. Again they struggled.

Copret saw amongst the dying soldiers Ferveiss's bodyguard closing in to help their commander. This time there may not be a magical arrow to save him. He did not have a free hand to pull hairs from his fur a second time.

Chloe had lost Hagouti for a second but as she swept on to the parapet the arrow was still in her bow. She was almost flying her feet were so fast. She looked up in time to see Arnveiss with twenty men by his side, swooping down to the pinned Copret. He would never be able to take them all on. Looking at Arnveiss's head, she let go the arrow and quickly fitted another sure that her quarry, that strange creature, was here somewhere.

Just as his hand reached to strike Copret from behind the arrow sliced through Arnveiss's head and he fell dead, almost at the bear's feet. Ferveiss screamed in disbelief and anger,

"Cousin ..." he wailed.

He broke away from Copret. Copret turned and with two sweeps of his claws felled the twenty men who were stunned by their leader falling. Copret was panting hard as he saw the arrow flying back to Chloe who was almost kneeling as she hunted for Hagouti using her arrow like a night-sight.

"More," roared Copret.

She turned and saw the army almost for the first time. Forgetting Hagouti for a moment she ran forward and fired three arrows looking at the ranks of men. The arrows flew through them, cutting down dozens in seconds. Her hands kept shooting, the arrows kept coming back to her. Copret growled and looked for Ferveiss.

Lilah lifted Bofindle to strike yet again. This time she wanted to strike harder, to flatten down the ramp and stop the teams of men mounting the parapet. She let the bejal roll over the men like a steamroller, crushing the dead deeper together and lowering the ramp. Rolling up and down. Then a few thousand of the enemy formed and waited for Bofindle to roll down, as the bejal reached them they leapt. High. Fleet-footed, on to the top and over. Suddenly there they were facing the defenders. Chloe had one arrow ready. Demeter was trying to stop the army behind Bofindle, Copret was tearing through men trying to get to Ferveiss, and Lilah stood with her hands raised.

Bofindle leapt from the ground. She was startled as the weapon shook in the air, floated above them all. Rolled. Almost writhed. The men, sensing tiredness, rounded on her and hundreds of them poured towards her screaming in anticipation of killing her. She set them on fire. They burnt up as they tried to reach her and on their burning corpses more came oblivious to the fire at their feet. Hundreds of hands were reaching to grab her. Chloe shot and her arrow flew through a hundred of them. Her other arrows came back. She loosed them as soon as they returned.

Bofindle began to glow and along the bejal's entire length a line of blue light shimmered like a straight, thin laser light. The light intensified. Bofindle split in two. Lilah had never seen this before. Ferveiss, who was holding his cousin's head under his arm cursing Chloe, bit and scratched and clawed at Copret who reached for him. Then Copret was engulfed by Ferveiss's bodyguard.

Demeter tore into them and freed Copret as the light from Bofindle widened and then something else happened that had never happened before. There was a silence in the tide of a battle with Crilodach's army. An awe. An unforeseen spectacle. Everyone was panting as they looked in wonder at the depth of the blue light. Old enemies knew each other's weapons and what they could do but this was unique. From the depths of the magic and the depths of the unknown, came the unexpected.

Rising out of Bofindle, tall and strong with lights in their eyes more intense than ever before, came Tethval and thousands of Arvernat. All those who had been in the city when Lilah departed. All those who had waited in silence when she and her brother walked out into the remains of their city. All those who had sat in silence and fear as Lilah and Tethval talked and Tethval had nodded his head sadly and turned to look at his people with a face full of agony. All those who had seen their world die and lost their friends and families, had tasted freedom and lost the reason to live. All those who had understood what Tethval could not say to them. All those whom Lilah had thought dead.

They had been prepared to die before their time because they saw this fight was greater than their own desires. That this fight was taking in every living creature and every planet and their sacrifice would be one amongst countless sacrifices. Tethval the warrior and his specially bred people who had freed themselves because they so wanted to live. The people who had been silent and prepared to die were here, their skins still green but they had been inside the heart of a bejal. Inside the heart of Bofindle. They were changed.

Lilah felt amazement, which was a big thing for her. She was surrounded by an army of unlooked-for reinforcements. Chloe stood open mouthed not sure, to begin with, if they were enemies or friends but soon realizing why Trecrogo had so many weapons stored in the armoury. Demeter felt the power Bofindle gave out. Like two fires meeting, the power of Trecrogo and Bofindle combined for an instant and the enemy outside faltered. Hearts raced. Copret, who knew by instinct who was friend or foe, roared so loudly the living shook as they heard him. His roar was one of victory.

Now Lilah knew why, as they were attacked in the Ossendark, Bofindle had been slow to react. The bejal had not left Tethval and his people behind but hidden them, preparing them to fight when needed. When Crilodach attacked them Bofindle was still rescuing them and could not react quickly enough to keep the four of them together. She knew why the bejal had kept the move a secret. She saw and understood that by not sharing this with her, Bofindle had ensured Crilodach, during his attack on the Ossendark, would not suspect what had been done. She gained new respect for the bejal that had been by her side since childhood.

Tethval and his people, men and women, poured down landing on their feet, their eyes blazing. Now the light from their eyes was not just to see in the dark but had become a weapon. Their feet touched the top of the mound of the enemy, cracked through the burning bodies as they leapt up to the parapet and stood in a long line, three lines deep. Their eyes blazed out. The light from their eyes pushed back the army and held them at bay far down the rampart of flesh, an impenetrable light. Nothing reached the rampart as they stood guard.

Demeter, able at last to breathe, used his power to sweep away the bodies that had been used as a ramp. Millions of them became dust. The tireless attack finally faltered. The enemy shivered. Chloe stood with an arrow in her hand but no targets. Above them Ferveiss looked at them shaking his fists in anger.

"Damn you Hagouti," he hissed between his teeth, "damn you."

Rataplan watched in awe at what he saw. He too wondered

where Hagouti could be. Had the enemy captured him?

"We'll hold them off," Tethval assured Lilah.

Lilah allowed herself a smile as Bofindle returned to her hand unblemished from the magical dissection. The continuous effort of the fight had tired her but she kissed Bofindle.

"I did not know," she told Tethval.

"I think there's much yet to learn for all of us," replied Tethval. He put his arm around her shoulder, something she never let anyone do,

"The very atoms of the universe are taking sides. Energy is flowing towards you and towards the enemy," he said.

"You have learned much in the last hours," she responded.

"I've aged years," he said.

"What happened to you?" He dropped his arm and shook his head,

"I can't tell you everything because I simply don't know. All I can tell you is we never died. We never felt pain, we were just wrapped in this amazing space. We were clothed in warmth, we breathed without coughing up dust for the first time in days. We felt invigorated, as if we could build our world again from scratch. Nothing felt impossible. You disappeared and we were still alive, bewildered but not worried. Pashtul said we must have died and been reborn somewhere else. We felt changed. In the distance we heard faint words. Snippets of words." Tethval waved his hands in the air, "We knew what they were yet we couldn't repeat them. Then we heard noise, thunderous noise and a way out opened up before us and we ran, falling into this place. I saw you standing there. Above me I saw Bofindle. I think then for the first time I knew what had happened."

"I am so ..." she began.

"No need to say anything," he said finally looking at her with his eyes dimmed, "Our lives happened the way they had to, to win this war. We're stronger. We're alive. You made the right decision."

"I'm glad you survived," cried Copret who had heard everything and flew down next to them. "The fight was getting so a bear couldn't roar loud enough anymore."

"No!" warned Chloe.

All this time she had been watching for Hagouti, certain the creature was around somewhere. Her skin prickled thinking about him. They turned to her to see her staring at Lilah as Hagouti leapt up the final stair where he had been lurking. Lilah turned in time to see Hagouti flying with the speed of death disregarding the weaker targets. He enveloped her where she stood before she could raise Bofindle to protect herself. She managed to push Tethval to one side saving his life.

"Stop!" cried Demeter, but he was prevented from doing anything by Copret's paw.

"If you tried to kill him with your power, he'll simply move out the way and Lilah mayn't have time to defend herself against you. You wouldn't kill her but you could injure her." Demeter stopped.

"What is he?" asked Chloe.

"Hagouti's his only name. A creation of Crilodach's. Now we know why the army was relentless. They wanted to blind us to his presence," the bear told them.

"What's he doing?" asked Tethval.

"Trying to suffocate her," said Copret.

"No, I won't let him," cried Chloe. "My arrows can hurt him."

"How do you know?" asked Copret.

"I hit him once as I followed him here. In his shoulder."

"You knew he was here?" asked Copret.

"I saw him, he wouldn't tell me who he was. Said he'd an urgent message for Lilah. His master had sent him. He tried to get close to me so I shot an arrow but he escaped."

"You should never have faced him by yourself," said Copret, putting a huge paw on her head, "You're a brave young girl."

"I wish I'd killed him."

Chloe stood crying tears as she stared at Lilah. Lilah was surrounded by mist but she had stopped breathing instantly. Hagouti could not enter her lungs. So he clung to her face and body. She could not move. She looked through him to her friends. For the moment she was all right.

"He can't kill her yet," said Copret, "we've some time."

Tethval and his people stood their ground aware of the new threat. They kept the army at bay by themselves as the others gathered round Lilah.

"Hagouti you shan't take her," snapped Copret. The mist swirled and Hagouti's face appeared near Lilah's face smirking.

"You can't stop me," he said. "You're unable to stop me.

I only need to wait. Just wait. She has to breathe. When she does I'll break her lungs."

"Look at your army. Rataplan is beaten. Unable to take a few, a small few of the many who'll fight you here. Trecrogo is too strong a fortress. Give up now and I'll go easy on you," Copret offered.

"Your people built Trecrogo well Copret, but even this fortress will fall in due time. As you'll all fall one by one. Wait a while. Watch. She'll have to breathe. She needs to breathe." His grin widened, "You can watch as I choke the blood in her veins. You can watch your esteemed spellmaker die."

He took delight in prolonging the agony of her plight. Lilah's eyes did not blink.

"Can he?" whispered Demeter.

"Hagouti can kill anything and anyone," replied Copret quietly. Out loud he shouted, "You shan't kill her."

"Spare me your whining, bear. Look to yourself. Your time is at hand. I'm your death too. And you child," he turned to Chloe, "I saw what you did. I'll avenge Arnveiss. Your arrows can't harm me again."

"Is he telling the truth?" asked Chloe.

"Shhh," said Copret.

"Tethval?" Chloe pulled at his arm.

"Yes?"

"Can you do anything?"

"I can always try," replied Tethval, "but I might not succeed."

Demeter's heart ached. He saw Lilah suffering. He heard the seconds passing like drums in his ears. How long can she hold her breath? An hour? A day? Ten minutes? Lilah looked through the mist surrounding her and saw them standing there. She knew Tethval and his people had the enemy secured. She looked deep into Hagouti and the creature felt her eyes searching him.

"What do you expect to see?" he asked her. She did not reply. "Answer me," he demanded.

Nothing makes Hagouti madder than being ignored. Then the second strangest thing happened in the long battle they had fought that night. As if time and magic were becoming one and place had no meaning.

"How close is your own death?" asked a new voice. A male voice. A Tsarbo.

Hagouti swirled. None of the others had spoken. Lilah knew the voice. A sense of contentment filled her limbs. He was there. He had arrived safely.

"Don't come any closer," snapped Hagouti.

The others wondered to whom he was talking, none of them had moved. Though three of Tethval's people had left their post and moved behind and to the left and right of Lilah. They were going to charge as a last resort and pull her free even though the move was suicide for them if they succeeded.

"I'm as close as I need ever be," replied the voice.

"Stay back!" screamed Hagouti, twisting this way and that to see this new enemy. The defenders looked at each other.

"The creature's finally been driven mad," said Copret.

"How can I back away from Hagouti," said the voice. "Only those who fear you back away."

"Who are you?" screamed Hagouti.

"I'm Rimfelder."

"Who's Rimfelder?" Hagouti's eyes darted from place to place trying to see him.

"A poet," Rimfelder replied.

"You don't fear death?"

"Who's he talking to?" asked Chloe.

"I've no idea," replied Demeter shrugging.

"I faced you once before" Rimfelder's voice replied, "I saw many friends die. I didn't think you were of much worth then, and I don't think you're of much worth now. Less even. You battle for the joy of killing. You serve rather than lead. You threaten my love."

"There's only one kind of death for everyone," growled Hagouti, unnerved by this voice. He could feel nothing, see nothing. Yet Rimfelder was a presence. A living being. Hagouti wondered if this is how people felt when he was close to them. Or if this was a ghost come to try to haunt him. Ridiculous. A ghost cannot haunt death.

"There are many kinds of death," argued Rimfelder, "I'm surprised at you for not knowing that."

"Death is death," snapped Hagouti.

"Your kind is the knife in the back, the dark swift betrayal. Your kind is the child suffocated, the broken bodies of your own army stretched out in their millions without you even caring, the nameless grave, the forgotten hero, the deprived talent, the lost pet. The child never allowed to grow up, the young girl beaten and burned by a murderer, the dog hammered to death, the elephant shot to clear the land. Your kind is torture and injustice. Your death has no name but shame. You've no place on Trecrogo which is a fortress of honour and friendship."

"Come closer. Feel my death," said Hagouti.

"You can't see me, you can't touch me. I've a book here. Your death is written here," Rimfelder told him.

"Never," cried Hagouti swirling.

Copret looked at Bofindle. The whole time the bejal had been there, waiting for a chance to fly to Lilah's hand. The others stood watching Lilah.

"Your death is signed and sealed," said Rimfelder, "Death has no friends and yet his rooms are full." Then Rimfelder spoke these words,

> "If passion heals then make me passionate;
> If salt–water soothes then make me the sea,
> And do it now before it is too late
> To soothe and heal the wounds from Hagouti.
> If laughter pleases make me comedy;
> If dancing delights teach me every step;
> If medicines cure make me the remedy
> If ideas build, make me their concept.
> And if a word can be a magic spell
> Blunting the claws of death where they bite most
> Then let these words come now so I may yell
> Crilodach shall not rule, nor all Its host!
>
> Release your chains and change from mist to man
> And beg us to forgive you, if we can."

Hagouti screamed as the words Rimfelder spoke echoed across Trecrogo. All those standing on the Parapet heard Rimfelder's poem. The words filled them with hope and renewed energy. Tethval smiled.

"You recognize that voice?" asked Copret.

"That my friend bear," smiled Tethval, "is a very special man."

Hagouti was no longer able to keep his shapeless form as the words seared through him. He became the misshapen person he had been created to be. Standing by them his fingers biting into his palms, his back twisted. The pain was etched on to his face. Lilah stepped back taking deep breaths. Bofindle flew to her. She lowered Bofindle to Hagouti's head, the words of the magic spell ringing in her head. Copret came to her side and held her arm gently. She did not look at him.

"He was close," she said,

"But he failed," said Copret.

"No, not Hagouti, one of the ones I saved. Rimfelder. I sent him to Vingura."

"He's in good hands then," Copret told her.

"That was his voice. That poem was a spell," she said.

"You look worried?" Copret said.

"I know where Vingura will be sending Rimfelder. So much rests in his shoulders. He does not know how important he is to us."

She looked at her friend and his great bear eyes looked deep into hers.

"We've other worries," he told her, "He must take care of himself."

She looked at Hagouti. Her face was angry. Not so much for his attack as at her weakness in having been trapped.

"He knows Crilodach better than anyone else. We could use him," suggested Copret, resting his paw on her hand as she clutched Bofindle.

"You are right," she answered, putting Bofindle into her hair. She looked around.

"I heard Rimfelder," Tethval said, half asking, half telling.

"The poet has found the power of his words." Lilah smiled because she had never thought to look into Tethval's strong face again and was more than happy the Arvernat were here not because they would fight, but simply because they were alive.

"You saved the right man," Tethval repeated.

"As did Bofindle," she smiled.

Lilah breathed in a long, sighing breath. She had held her breath for longer but never for such a good reason. Hagouti moved but Demeter held out his hand,

"You'll not leave here," the boy told him.

He snapped his fingers. The stone opened up beneath Hagouti's feet and he fell into a prison crying both in anger and fear.

"He'll have to keep his flesh and blood form," said Demeter. "That will make him suffer a while."

"I want to talk to him later," Lilah replied.

"What's happening down there?" shouted Tethval, his voice was apprehensive. They all felt the quake.

"Demeter secure the area," shouted Lilah.

Demeter raised a transparent barrier like a fence around them to which they held on to as they were all buffeted by the shaking of the Earth.

General Rataplan saw the emergence of the Arvernat almost at the same time as messengers told him Arnveiss was dead. With victory almost theirs, with his men having done more than he could ever have ordered them to do, he felt crushed. Worse, the new weapon held them at bay and he began to feel he was being pulled away. As if gravity were losing hold of the planet. Ferveiss moved his cousin's body from the front line and some of his men thought he was retreating. The line closest to Trecrogo broke in half. Then the rampart was hammered down and he could see the bones turned to dust and the mud mixed into a red clay.

His eyes were seared with sweat and the physical pain of seeing defeat, once again, facing him with all that that foretold. The terror his children might be executed flooded his body. He shouted for more men to advance. He strode forward. But he did not move. He could not get closer. The pull upon him was becoming too great. Was Crilodach recalling him? What magic was this that forbade his advance?

Around him his bodyguard were also feeling the power and soon he realized the entire army were being pulled back. Then he heard Hagouti. For a few seconds his heart soared even as he knew he could not mount the parapet and stand lording over his enemies he knew they had done what they had been asked to do. He could not be held responsible. Surely his children were safe.

The defenders looked out over the parapet on to the vast scene before them as dawn broke. The winds began to swirl around and the light from Tethval's people became unnecessary as the Earth started shrinking. They all crouched down and held on to the parapet and each other. Demeter stood immobile, his arms by his sides, Trecrogo slowly rotating as if unscrewing her deep foundations from the dying planet. The roots of Trecrogo were sliding away from the planet as the Earth started to close in. Rataplan's army was being withdrawn.

The stars seemed to be swimming. There was a dizzy feeling in Chloe's head. Things speeded up. She reached out and felt Copret by her side. She clung to his arm forgetting he was wounded. Soon no one could be seen outside Trecrogo. They were not fool enough to believe they had seen the last of Rataplan but they knew for now he was gone. The attempt to take Lilah's life had failed. Just. Crilodach had recalled Its army.

Smaller and smaller the planet became, rock becoming harder and harder, compacting. Particles compressing until there was no space between them. All life vanished. Everything became dust. Emptiness plundered their horizon. The sun still shone. The moon flew along into a new orbit. The sea momentarily lapped and then vanished. Everything vanished. Darkness. Silence. The swirling finally stopped. Trecrogo was alone amongst the stars. No longer turning. The stones burnished with the battle. The first part of Trecrogo's design was fulfilled. The strong roots grown in the magic of Losek soil were tapering downwards. They curled up and hid beneath the foundations, waiting for their next use, which would not be long.

"What was that?" said Chloe softly, almost disbelieving what she had seen.

"Can you see anything?" Lilah asked Demeter as she looked up at him.

"Nothing, he replied. "Trecrogo is secure."

They all stood on the parapet looking, wondering. Waiting.

"I see something," said Tethval.

The lights from his people pierced the dark and their sensitivity showed them a small, cosmic jewel. They drew the jewel to them through the darkness, falling lightly into Lilah's hand glowing in her palm. She turned the priceless jewel over. She recognized the Sagitæ from Zananto's descriptions. For all the Sagitæ's lightness there was a good weight in her hand and some of the light was mottled with what looked like dust and imperfections. Turquoise and smooth to hold. Tethval shone his light through the Sagitæ and they all watched the twinkling light. There was a depression small enough to feel as she rubbed her fingers along one side. There was a deep silence.

"One of Sagitæ," said Tethval. Copret whistled to himself.

281

Lilah looked at Tethval.

"You know of them?" she asked.

"Bofindle told us," the Arvernat said.

"One of them was hidden on the Earth?" gasped Copret, "No wonder we went to such lengths to save the planet."

"Not hidden on the planet," revealed Tethval, turning to Copret, "this jewel was the Earth. They inflated the Sagitæ to allow life to live here. They believed that was the best hiding place. Now the jewel is preparing for a new and final journey. The lights in our eyes have been modified by Bofindle to show us the other Sagitæ when and if we meet with them."

"No one would ever have known the Earth was one of the Sagitæ," Copret said, shaking his head. "Brilliant."

"Tethval," called Demeter, walking over to him. Tethval looked down at the child whose face looked determined and slightly tired.

"Your people have need of more weapons."

Demeter touched the floor and once again the armoury appeared to them. "You will find many things down there but I think the helmets that protect your eyes and allow you to control them will be of most use at the moment."

"Thank you little one," said Tethval.

"Trecrogo will be barely able to go anywhere without being noticed but blazing with your light we'll never hide from anything."

Tethval laughed at Demeter's practical outlook. His people started to go down to look for weapons.

"Where is Pashtul?" asked Lilah.

"She did not leave with us," Tethval replied.

"Perhaps Bofindle has other work for her to do," suggested Lilah.

"I'll see her again," said Tethval.

"You sound sure," Lilah said.

"I am. I'm more content than I've been in many years. As if all that is really important suddenly appears to me so obvious I should always have felt like this. I feel at last I can do things too. The Arvernat have been to the heart of all that you know, and now I know something you could not answer when I asked you."

"About the woman you loved?" she asked.

"Yes."

"What?"

"I have never ceased to see her. Every day. She is as real to me as she ever was when I could hold her close in my arms. I have held her closer in my mind."

"I am glad you find comfort in that."

"You have seen me again though you had thought me dead. We were designed to mine ores for a tyrant but all along we were being designed to be your allies in this great battle, something Rimfelder understood. Something I know you understand."

"I do."

"Come on you two," called Copret, "we've work to do."

"Does he ever sleep?" Chloe asked Lilah.

"Not that I have ever noticed," Lilah replied, smiling for a long time over Tethval trying to teach her something about magic.

As A Cockroach

Midrak stood like a statue. His feet, instinctively, rooted to the spot. As if the pores in his skin had suddenly become links in a heavy chain that refused to allow him to so much as shiver. He was still in shock after the attack in the Ossendark.

In the blinding dark his eyes stared straight ahead, straining with every photo-sensitive cell to see anything he might recognize. To see anyone he may know. Longing to see the shadow of something living in the impenetrable blackness that saturated the labyrinth around them.

Every nerve under his skin crept with foreboding. He could feel through the hairs on the back of his hands and head, the piercing frost which, mist-like, rolled down the icy walls and curled around the tunnels like a lazy sea-worm. The freezing atmosphere acid-like, etched into his face, trying to make him react to the painful discomfort over his skin. Trying to make him move, to betray himself with a shudder, a sudden breath, the flick of a finger, a blink, the parting of lips to speak, exhaling the last breath he had taken in the Ossendark. This labyrinth was not for the living but the condemned. With each and every second that passed the cold seemed to shroud them with ghastly omens. He had to think of something quickly because he sensed this place was sensitive enough to feel the hair on his head growing. He knew exactly where they were. Although he had never been here before, the stories of this place left him with no doubt because to hear of this labyrinthine prison is enough. There is nowhere in the universe like Hâgon.

By others sometimes just called 'the darkness' and 'the death beneath Damkina'. The foundation sewer below Its stronghold. A name used to describe the underworld in many other worlds because of the stories that abound about Hâgon. Of all Its prisons this was the most dreaded. This was the first labyrinth ever to be built in the universe. Crilodach had built upon a once-beautiful, massive planet twisting the beauty, transforming every rock into primal fear. After

Bofindle had imprisoned It here, after Its first set-back by Tegriel, It had eaten out these tunnels in Its frenzy and freed Itself. Looking back It found It had made a labyrinth, so then It built Damkina above to hide Hâgon away from all eyes. Not long afterwards It started to send Its enemies to die here.

Hâgon is riven with tunnels called the Pângil. Pângil that lead everywhere in an endless sameness, yet nowhere you would want to go, for even if you could walk the Pângil for hours, the journey would drive you insane. Have no fear, you cannot walk the Pângil for even one hour.

That Crilodach's first thoughts were to build a prison which killed everything was typical of It. Then not being content for them to die of starvation, loneliness or commit suicide, It speeded up the process. Midrak knew if he made any movement Hâgon would know; they would die.

There are times, in places where fear rules with an iron hand, where a greater fear with a greater danger lurks ready to pounce and suck out your life, when not making any attempt to fight is the wisest thing to do. When hiding and running is not cowardly. A magician must know that there are also times when you must stay still, not breathe, not hide, not run. When you avoid the danger that hunts you by not-being-there. When you know what a spell is looking for you may have a sliver of a chance of buying yourself some time. Like dodging a bullet. Most of a magician's life is spent seeking out such slivers. People who don't know about such things call these slivers 'chances', 'luck', 'fate'. They are, of course, nothing of the sort. Chance is a spell you do not know, fate an incantation spreading out from the atoms around you and luck a helping hand from a deeper magic underpinning our very existence that you simply do not know.

Midrak's finger tips were already frozen with the dampness. His fingernails ached with the chill that ran up his arms and around his neck. His bones felt like icicles from which his leaden blood dripped into his soul almost like a tocsin. He was sure Hâgon must be able to hear him. He held his breath, for even a breath here could give away their position to the searing presence that seemed to pervade everything. Not daring to breathe he heard Fulminar call inside his head, so loud his voice seemed to echo in the darkness that enfolded them making the blood in his temples pound with the Sangyma's warning, sounding from the moment they had materialized.

"Move so much as a inch and It will know you are here."

Fulminar confirmed what Midrak suspected, so awful a truth he had not wanted to believe. Even though the evidence was everywhere. Hâgon. There was no way for a person to accidentally find this awful place. Crilodach banished Its enemies here with a flick of a claw, It drew them here as if Hâgon were a magnet grasping at all things yet to bend their knee to It. Here they were lashed by the fierce hurricane called Gâmor, that stormed down the chambers seeking skin to flail with utter indifference. Gâmor was the reason why no one lived more than an hour down here.

The ultimate prison, the place from which no one escaped, as much death to magicians as to ordinary races. Sucking out blood with an unquenchable ease. A belly inside a great beast swallowing everything that came along, churning them through the bowels of a devouring magic. To Crilodach, Gâmor cleansed the labyrinth. Rid It of Its enemies, made the Pângil safe from intruders who did not deserve any life. This wasn't murder in Crilodach's mind because these beings, Its enemies, were no more than a waste of atoms. It did not fool Itself that this was any form of justice. This was not a real prison, for no one who came here was ever put on trial. Crilodach had no sense of justice or punishment. If you were taken prisoner in Its vast, unrelenting march to rule all life, Hâgon was your destination. A place of immense foreboding few people had the courage to even name. The Sangyma Zananto had given the prison the name 'Hâgon' which in her language meant 'hopeless'.

"How do we get out of here?" Midrak asked Fulminar.

"How did we get here in the first place?" he replied, fearful that even their thoughts would be overheard. "Did It bring us here?" Fulminar wondered.

"If It did why are we still alive?" asked Midrak.

"Maybe It is playing a game with us," suggested Fulminar.

"A day and a half before Zaqui if It gets Its hands on any of us It will just kill us."

"Unless It wants information," Fulminar said.

"Then why place us where we will die in a few seconds? We should be in Its claws being tortured unless ..."

"It does not know we are here?" ended Fulminar,

"How can that be? The very heart of Hâgon is Its own

heart. Nothing is here that It does not send here," Midrak said.

"Something else sent or brought us here?" Fulminar concluded.

"Such a thing does not exist ... nothing but Crilodach rules Hâgon."

"Up to now, but as you just pointed out, we are a day and a half from Zaqui. A unique time," said Fulminar.

"The only power to do this would come from Lilah."

"She would not send us into such danger without planning beforehand. Even if she was taken as much by surprise at the attack as we were, she would have said something to us however brief."

"Maybe she had a plan but no time to tell us?" Midrak said.

"Or maybe someone else had a plan and they could not tell us."

"Such as?"

"I am thinking, Bofindle."

"Bofindle," Midrak was astonished.

"Why not? So many secrets surround Bofindle's creation, they say the weapon's magic is older than Tegriel's."

Tobia leaned sideways to step nearer Midrak and stopped instantly at his telepathic command and Tegriel's firm refusal to move inside her. No one had ever been here who was not Crilodach's prisoner. No one had ever felt this cold that had not died soon after. No one had ever been lost in this darkness without going insane or being eaten by the insects that lived on their dying flesh.

They were two statues in the dark.

They were alone.

They were cold.

They were in mortal danger.

They had both stopped breathing. Stopped blinking. Knowing they had to move to get away they did nothing. Nothing was all they could do. And yet in the darkness there was movement. Imperceptible. Coming from behind the stones. Scratching. Millions of tiny feet. Shuffling. Moving. Alive. A dusty, stony, musical march of millions of insects.

Far away down the Pângil, Midrak felt the Gâmor rushing towards them. The flaying hurricane of Hâgon. Gâmor did not know for certain they were here but they had materialized in the Pângil and Gâmor would know something had changed.

He knew that Gâmor would find them, touch them and in so doing reveal they were here. Throwing them off their feet with unseen hands they would be blown all the way through the Pângil. Gâmor would strip them to the bone but keep them from being smashed to pieces on the stone walls. Created by Crilodach, Gâmor also liked to play with the condemned. Once Crilodach knew they were here It might stop Gâmor before they died, to torture them Itself. What awaited them was horror and pain. They could not afford to be caught by the Gâmor. They could not be caught by Crilodach's minions. Capture would mean the end of their plans before they had even begun to be put into action.

Midrak was desperate. How could they escape? The air was changing from the fearful cold, to a hot, burning blast. The rumble of Gâmor began to make the stones at their feet move as if they were uncomfortable. Unsettled. Uneasy. Undigested. He imagined the deep scored lines in the stones near the bottom of the walls were made by the fingers and claws of those being dragged away by the ravenous Gâmor, desperately clawing at anything to save themselves. Losing their fingers in the effort, broken off like immature twigs from a branch. Fingers that the insects dragged away for food. Each and every hour Gâmor made a bitter journey along the intricate and seemingly infinite Pângil. An endless tour. Crilodach did not want this nightmare of hopelessness becoming a back-way into Its the upper halls of Damkina.

Yet Crilodach did not know they were here. How could that be?

Maybe It did know. Maybe It did not think they were worth any more personal effort to kill than to toss them into Hâgon. No that was not Its way. Information was always useful. Midrak was a magician. She was a Ruzniel. Both were travelling with a spellmaker. There was no way Crilodach would not have interrogated them if It was responsible for bringing them here. It would use Midrak against Lilah any way It could. It could even scoop Fulminar and Tegriel out from their bodies.

But why would a friend send them here of all places? What was here that was important? Something strange was going on. Another hand. Another magic. Who could fool Crilodach and attack a group of travellers lead by Lilah in the Ossendark? No, Crilodach must have attacked them but It would never have brought them here.

There was no answer to the puzzle.

Perhaps whatever had brought them here had misjudged and sent them to the wrong place, where they were to die without a fight.

Tobia, who had not heard them first, saw them first with Tegriel's guidance. The black and yellow striped backs were invisible in the dark. A few crawled over her foot, scuttling out of the path of Gâmor that was coming upon them with all Its rage. Large cockroaches were making their way into the crevices of the walls, holes they had built leading to safety, and from which they could come out in their thousands as if from nowhere. The darkness was all one to them as they felt their way with their antennae. These were the insects making the noises behind the walls. Behind the walls where the searing, seeking hurricane Gâmor could not get to them. Creatures suited to Hâgon: long–living, hard backed, foot–slogging wanderers capable of going without much water for weeks, night sighted, small and careful. Even as Midrak immediately saw in them their salvation, he had no idea at all that they were also the incredible answer to the questions in his mind. Not all of them were what they seemed to be.

"Cockroaches live here," she said in her head. That was the last thing she said as a Ruzniel for a long time.

Before the thought had fully died away in their heads, Midrak and Tobia were on the floor, scuttling over the other cockroaches and through mounds of dirt, making for a convenient hole in the wall. They had changed into cockroaches. Thick dust stuck to their feet as their antennae twisted and turned in time to the other cockroaches. They could hear the chatter from the other cockroaches very well now. Millions of them were in the stone. A whole nation of insects making a cacophony of noise that was so loud neither Midrak nor Tobia could hear Fulminar or Tegriel very well as the Sangyma urged them to get to the relative safety of the crevices.

There was no more silence, only the rushing tide of urgent messages to get out of the way, and chemical trails leading to different places. Chirps between friends and relatives calling them all to find shelter behind the walls which were buzzing with activity, movement, hellos and reminders. Hâgon was filled with more sounds than the rage of Gâmor but you had to be small to hear them all and you had to be a cockroach to make sense of them. Here was a world within a world. They had built a labyrinth of their own every bit as intricate as Crilodach's, extensive as Hâgon but much smaller. Following the filaments between the stonework. Making long, interconnecting tunnels, worn smooth by the hardness of their bodies passing by in countless numbers for generations, maybe for as long as Hâgon had existed. Cockroaches that climbed out of the rubble of their once beautiful world to survive in Its buildings. The scrapers, diggers and tunnellers that, unknown to the wider universe, survived in the bitterest part of the cosmos.

The two of them followed the scurrying cockroaches. Their new companions crawled over each other seeming to spew from nowhere into every crack. Some carrying burdens, food or bits of rags for bedding. Dust clung to their feet. They all wanted to get to safety for they too would be killed by Gâmor, smashed against the stone to leave blood stained marks on the labyrinth walls and nothing else. Within another hour even that blood would be blown away to the last cell.

"Here," suggested Midrak, as he found a hole close to their heads with his antennae.

"What's that strange smell?" she asked.

"Chemical signals, that's the way these cockroaches tell each other where to go."

They both crept into the opening, pulling with their front legs and pushing with their back legs, as their encased bodies just managed to get into the entrance by turning slightly sideways and jiggling about. Tobia unceremoniously pushed Midrak as she was pushed from behind by others desperately vying to get out of the Pângil.

Midrak's six legs, covered with thick dust from the floor, looked like they were wrapped in thick, heavy socks. His specially shaped feet pulled him forward with surprising strength. Tobia was pushed sideways once inside, by the others rushing in but she regained her balance easily. The extra numbers of legs acted as braces in all directions. She spun herself upright, her antennae twitching.

"Listen to that wind," she said, raising her head, her legs spread out to either side of her, her head tilted to listen.

"Its much louder to us now we have the sensitive hearing of cockroaches," noted Midrak.

"And the other sounds?"

"The language of the cockroaches. They are all babbling at once."

"Do you understand what they are saying?"

"Not a word. You?"

"No, but Tegriel does," she revealed.

"Good, then he can be our interpreter."

She braced herself and pushed herself back into the thick dust behind them.

Midrak squeezed himself smaller, and their antennae felt around the entrance to the crevice just as another cockroach found them and pushed desperately to get inside. Midrak grabbed at his head and pulled, helping him to get out of danger just in time. The cockroach seemed to understand that they had saved his life and he showed this understanding by staying close to them, not blindly walking over them in the cramped space. Midrak found that strange. He did not know these insects were so intelligent. For a moment he wondered if they were some new creation of Crilodach's but he sensed nothing of It in the cockroaches around him. Quite the opposite, in some of them he sensed friendly warmth.

Gâmor blasted down the tunnel like a train. Hot, roaring power, sucking the cockroach nearest to the entrance backwards until he was wedged into the crevice, his legs struggling against the empty air. Had the opening been a little wider he would have been sucked out and them along with him. Dust flew everywhere and everything became covered with filth as the wind roared past. The darkness became airless for frightening seconds. The fall in air pressure thumped like a hammer in their heads forcing them to grip the stone and lower their bodies to the ground. Bracing their legs with every muscle they had. All the cockroaches clasped to each other. Their armoured bodies protecting them from the worst. Even out of the Pângil you could feel Gâmor bow the stone walls outward. The hurricane seemed to take forever to pass, sucking at time as well as the air.

The storm had eyes. Feelings. As the cockroaches had antennae, Gâmor could sense living beings in the three dimensional view Crilodach's spells created in the Pângil. Gâmor retained the memory of every inch of the Pângil, always knowing when someone moved. Crilodach made sure of that. And even after passing by them their heads still thumped with the pulsating noise and their hearts beat fit to burst, to be replaced by the mournful certainty of Gâmor's speedy return.

They waited as the terrifying storm blew past. The cockroaches caught out, stuck hard to the walls and the dusty floor for as long as they could and then they were torn from their holds and squashed against the stones. If Crilodach had wanted them all dead they would have been, but insects did not worry It. Its indifference to the cockroaches was their salvation. More than he knew for Midrak was about to find out, as he was beginning to suspect, many of these were no ordinary cockroaches and they were at the centre of the spells that had brought them here from the Ossendark.

Tobia's antennae felt the walls and other cockroaches as they clambered over her shell hard body to go home. Moving with renewed energy to bring their scraps to the rest of the community. Midrak scraped at the wall with his front feet and sniffed the air.

"That's over for a while."

"Here anyway," she said.

"We should move along with the others. We will find nothing of use in the Pângil but maybe these chambers will take us out of here. The sooner we get going the better."

"Do you know why we're here?" she asked, feeling her way along behind him.

"We must have work to do here."

"But," she answered, moving her front feet carefully over another cockroach that had stopped to turn and go down a different tunnel, "where are Lilah and Rimfelder?"

"They did not journey here with us," Tegriel told her. "Whatever attacked us in the Ossendark, whatever brought us here, did not bring the others."

He did not tell her then he knew the Ossendark would be attacked or that he had told Bofindle to link with another and send them to Hâgon. He would tell Tobia in time when she would understand his prophecies, but no one else would ever know. A few, like Fulminar, would guess the truth. Though right now he did not ask Tegriel and if he knew that Tegriel had known he was going to be killed all those years ago, he did not question his silence. When you trust a Sangyma not all questions need to be answered for you know you are in safe hands and the truth about Tegriel was so incredible, so huge and so important, silence about his ancestry was the safest strategy.

"Are they safe?" asked Midrak, making way for a group of cockroaches going in the opposite direction to go out into the Pângil to pick through the dust and see what Gâmor had brought them.

"None of us are safe, but I imagine Lilah to be more safe because of her powers than anyone else," answered Fulminar.

"We cannot worry about them," Tegriel told them, "we are in the heart of Damkina. This may present us with a great opportunity in the day ahead."

"How?" Tobia asked, dubiously.

"While we are here we may be able to find a way to listen to Its plans. It does not know we are here, so we have the advantage. We got here the only way we could, by not knowing we were coming, now we must make that play in our favour," replied Tegriel.

Two cockroaches beside them nodded slightly in agreement. Midrak noticed this and wondered how they understood what they were saying. He knew they could communicate in the same way because he heard them in his own head, but he was interested that they could understand the ancient language of the Sangyma.

"Not a bad plan but if we find out anything how do we tell the others?" asked Tobia.

Midrak lifted a front foot, which had been his hand, to his face and rubbed off some of the dust. He felt another antennae touching him and he looked around at the cockroaches beside him. They seemed agitated. As if they were deliberately making room for him and Tobia. Tobia thought they sensed something kindred in the two of them, maybe because Tegriel knew something in them was not cockroach.

"We will cross that bridge later," said Tegriel, "whatever else we do, once we stop being cockroaches It will discover us. For now this is our best way forward."

"Are they deep," Tobia asked of the cockroach tunnels. She fended off a cockroach which pushed her sideways trying to get passed her in a hurry to get to go home with two feet rolling some food along the floor.

"Careful," Tegriel's voice commanded her in her head. "Even as cockroaches you must be careful," he told her.

"Move as they move. If you do not It will know."

She crawled over two inquiring animals and past the two who seemed to be showing them the tunnels to go down almost as if their front legs were arms. They moved off after Midrak who was creeping along the side of the wall feeling his way with a growing sense of mystery. They had survived Gâmor. The incredible was possible.

"Walking sideways stuck to a wall feels strange," she told him.

"But very useful," he replied. "They have obviously been here a long time."

"Why do these insects collect dirt?" Tobia asked.

"Dirt? Those are the remnants of Crilodach's victims. Who do you think cleans up?" asked Midrak, "I can smell the skin and flesh from here."

He stopped crawling for a moment and looked ahead. There were different eyes peering at them from the dark. Kindly but small eyes.

"That's ghastly," she said, turning her antennae on to the dirt and feeling a piece of cloth. A dress. A tunic. A shirt. Who knew? The owner was long dead. She was flooded with a deep sense of sadness, thankful that she was with Midrak

"Who are you?" Midrak waved his front feet and moved his head from left to right as he spoke.

The cockroach came out of the darker recess and looked from Midrak to Tobia and back again. This one was not the same colour as the others, and was larger with a purple line across his entire back and yellow around his eyes. The sense Tobia had had that they were not all cockroaches was very strong in this one.

"I saw," he said to them. There was silence. "I saw you change," he added.

"You can talk to us," Tobia said, surprised.

"There was a time when most people would tell me to shut up all day long I talked so much. My name is Balvieure. I've not seen so fast a change before."

"So?"

Midrak checked behind them to see if the other cockroaches were massing to attack them or something sinister but they were not. They were all scrambling to get back into Pângil and find something to eat before Gâmor came back.

"I thought he had to be closer to make the change you see. I thought you'd be fresh scraps within a few minutes."

"He?" asked Midrak. Tobia felt queasy at the thought of being eaten up by hundreds of cockroaches.

"Of course you don't know, stupid me. We're all in the dark at first," he laughed nervously, "the one who changed us and so saved all our lives."

"We changed ourselves," said Tobia.

The cockroach took a step sideways as she said this and shook his head slightly. What she said was a revelation to him.

"Then ... you are also magicians."

"We may be," replied Midrak.

"There's no maybe," said Balvieure.

The cockroach came further forward unafraid. Midrak could see one of his back legs was missing. Balvieure caught the look and lifted his head slightly,

"Wasn't quick enough one day. The leg got caught in a crevice. Broken clean off. If I'm ever changed back I may have to limp." He lowered his head and looked down at Tobia. She felt like patting him on the shoulder but of course as a cockroach this was impossible. She had nothing to pat with and he had no shoulder.

"You're not an ordinary cockroach," Midrak said, "the others feel us with their antennae to find out who we are, they understand us but do not talk to us. What is your story?"

"None of us with the purple streak on our backs is ordinary. We all have our own stories of our journey to Hâgon. Every one of us thought he or she was lost, forgotten, dead until he came. He changed everything. Until you, he was the only magician with the power to change. He made the real cockroaches able to understand us so we could all live in harmony. Who are you?"

"Why do you want to know?" asked Midrak

"The enemy has many ways of trying to find us. You may be spies sent to trap us," replied Balvieure.

"If that's so, you're already caught," Tobia told him.

There was a scrapping sound from different directions and they looked around. As they had been talking many more cockroaches similar to this new one had surrounded them. Some upside down above them ready to drop. Tegriel asked Tobia if he might speak through her.

"My friends I sense in you, people who have found a way to cheat Crilodach's death sentences, is that true?"

"Perhaps," replied the Balvieure, knowing this was a different person. Two people inside the cockroach, these were impressive magicians and he should know he had seen a magician long ago. Several of the cockroaches muttered to each other. Having two magical strangers turn up was surprise enough, finding out one of them contained yet another magical person was amazing. Especially at this time for though they were hidden away in the dark of the labyrinth they knew Zaqui was close.

"Midrak, introduce us," suggested Tegriel.

Midrak told them who they were. There was a silence and then Balvieure moved forward and touched them both with his antennae. Tobia felt as if dozens of tiny feathers were stroking her head.

"Many of them have been here so long they've forgotten their names," he told them, "If they ever had one. We were all sent here to die but there's one here who changed us, kept us alive. We've lived alongside our quieter cockroaches, waiting for the day we'd be free. A day he tells us is nearly here." One of the others moved forward and whispered to the first.

"Of course," he nodded at them, "you're right. Come along, he'll know what to say to a Sangyma far better than I."

"I wonder who 'he' is," thought Tobia.

"So do I," said Midrak to her, "so do I."

Tegriel smiled to himself. For he knew very well who they were going to meet. They were about to meet the one responsible for bringing them here, to the last place in the universe any magician would have thought safe. One who had rarely listened to Tegriel's advice but nonetheless one much admired and loved.

Within the crevices they found these larger cockroaches had tunnelled new byways and plastered the walls with metal shards that shone as they passed filtering light from high above them down into their homes. For the first time dimness lessened the impenetrable dark. This labyrinth within the labyrinth was a home. Winding a course along the narrow corridors. Their chambers followed the stone walls of Hâgon around, up and down, widening and narrowing all the time where the digging had been easier or harder. Crossroads formed at the joints of the stones, dips and burrows in their millions, many dead–ends that were in fact sleeping quarters for whole families. Several larger chambers

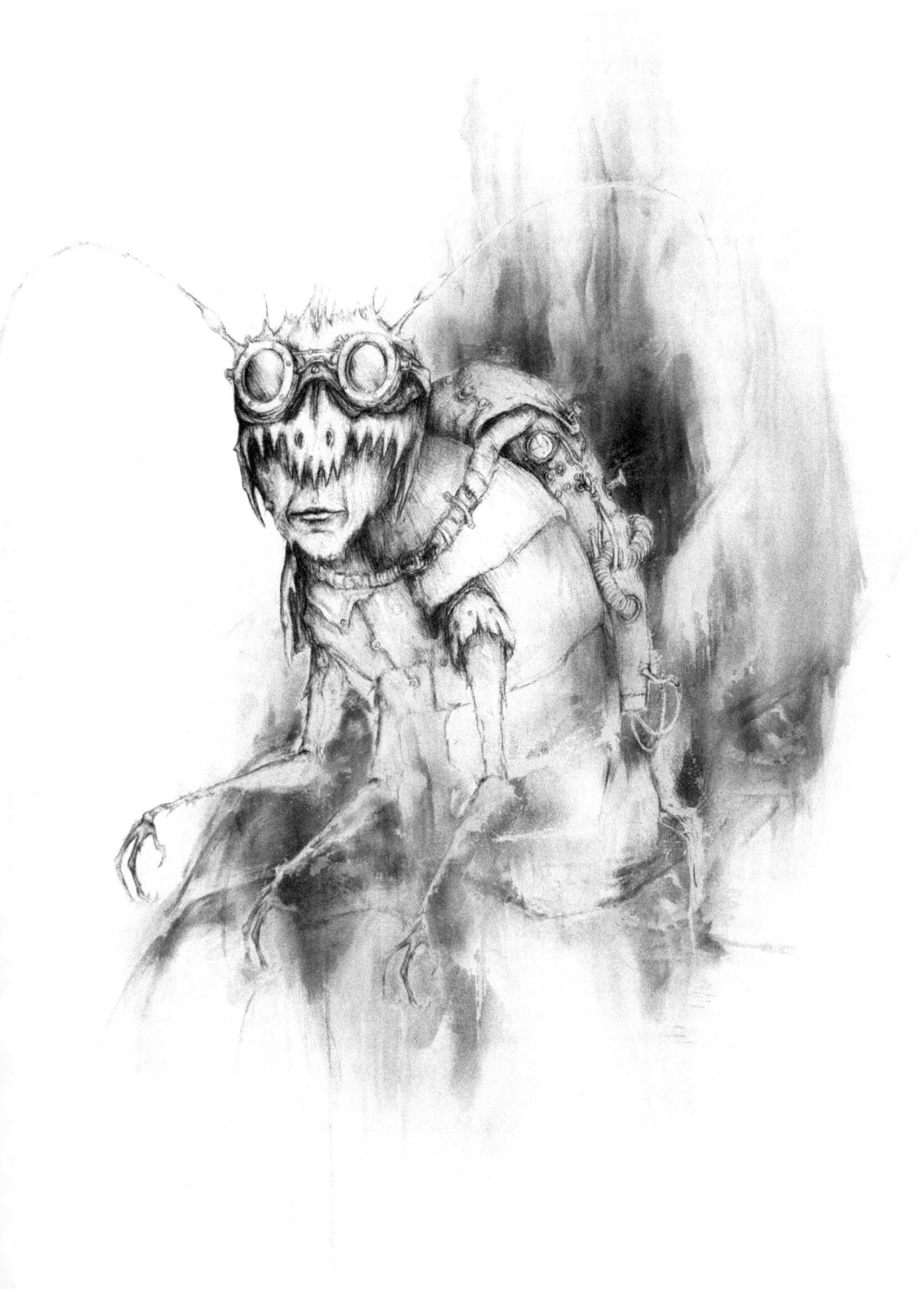

Cockroach

were set at intervals that were used as meeting places. And a few more special tunnels that moved almost straight upwards and from which the smells were different. These tunnels went into Crilodach's main complex above ground. Damkina. There was only one thing that spoke of a strangeness about these insects. One thing that would have come as a huge surprise. For some parts of the stone had been burrowed away completely and to keep the stone from collapsing pillars of diamond had been inserted and all around these low, wide chambers, were remembrances usually only found in burial grounds. Here, and nowhere else, hot rocks from deeper in the planet burned. Small rocks that gave out heat, no smoke, and never went out. Warmth. At that moment Midrak realized the cockroaches crawling over Tobia giving him the idea to change into two cockroaches in order to escape had not been an accident. Of course not. There are no chance occurrences with magic.

Almost too small to be noticed, ancient and colourful along the walls, were etchings and drawings done by creatures using anything they could to make marks. Midrak looked at them. Languages of people, names, maps anything that linked them to what they had lost. Millions of names, places, times. All from Crilodach's victims. As endless as the tunnels themselves these murals gave the walls a homely feel, a permanence, if only by their number. In them were memories. The history of the universe depicted in paintings of suffering belying in their artistry the stiff, awkward movement of cockroach legs. Midrak shook his head as he saw more and more. He recognized the names of some of the places – great worlds where terrible battles had been fought. Then he realized that each and every one of them had been a defeat for the Sangyma. In his mind he saw the millions of cockroaches as possibly millions of those they had long thought dead and gone. With a blinding flash Midrak knew whatever or whoever had brought them here, had brought them to a hidden army sitting right beneath Damkina. The thrill of realizing this was mirrored by Fulminar's warning to him to stay calm and stay quiet.

They crawled along. There was only a little dirt along these tunnels and every–so–often a small opening in which he could see a cubicle. A place for individual cockroaches to rest and think. In them were little pieces of wood used as tables, or pieces of rag draped over the entrance for use as a door. A remnant of the creatures these insects once were. People who liked privacy once–in–a–while. People who needed to get away and be alone. People just like them locked up in a body that was not theirs, simply to survive.

They moved along with added speed. Tobia kept up with ease, as she could see with her antennae without needing Tegriel's help. There was a lot of activity around them. Word had gone out to the cockroach community that new magicians were amongst them. Or as many of the cockroaches said to each other, there were more Sangyma amongst them.

Then they came to a low round room and were led right into the centre. Those behind them did not enter but waited expectantly. All around they knew hundreds were listening. Either at the entrance to the tunnels that speckled the room, or in lines behind them, pushing forwards, hoping to catch a glimpse or hear a word that was spoken. News of the magicians who had changed themselves had cascaded through their homes and brought them all out like spectators.

He had told them things were moving. He had told them things were changing. Zaqui was coming. Their imprisonment would soon be over. They all wondered if the day when they would be themselves again had arrived.

"Strangers have come to us," said Balvieure.

There was a silence and a cockroach moved forward and came close to Midrak. He touched him with his clawed front foot, his antennae gently fluttering. He moved back a step, his head moving left and right.

"Fulminar old friend," he said.

"You can sense Fulminar," gasped Midrak

"I should hope so. He and I were friends long enough not to forget each other."

Fulminar smiled inside Midrak. The smile of an old, old man suddenly remembering a voice and in that voice came memories in a torrent; memories of laughter, danger and friendship. Of a friendly face and magical encounters but most of all of a friend he had long thought dead.

"Gertis? You are here," Fulminar said.

"And if I am not mistaken you host Tegriel," said Gertis touching Tobia. "Wonder of wonders to have you both with me again."

"Gertis," said Tegriel, "how did you manage to get here? I am delighted."

Tegriel had to appear not to know everything. He could

not risk the problems that would arise if they learned his greatest secret.

"That story is not so long," Gertis scratched his head with his antennae, "though the idea to become a cockroach was not the best one I ever had. Cannot be anything else here without It knowing. In fact your prophecy gave me the idea, remember when you said 'in endless dark the tunnels within tunnels will hold your friends.' Remember me laughing when you told me that, Tegriel? Though how you knew I would get here I have no idea but this is what you were talking about, right?

"I think so, yes," said Tegriel.

"At least I managed to save a few others," Gertis said modestly.

"More than few I am guessing," said Fulminar.

"Well more than a few then," agreed Gertis.

"How did you get here?" asked Midrak who had heard of Gertis (quite a bit in fact as Gertis being the youngest of all the Sangyma was very often the favourite with young magicians.)

"I surprised Crilodach," he replied.

"Be honest," argued Midrak who did not believe anyone could surprise It.

"I did. I was up top and I sort of saved my friend."

"What exactly happened? Because you do not just find your way into Hâgon without Crilodach sending you," asked Midrak.

"Well I found out that Timberel, my best friend from my old village, had stopped his people going over to Its army. You are never wise to stand against It when you do not command any magic. They came one night. Kidnapped him. His family and mine go back a long way. Several of his ancestors have worked alongside the Sangyma and one was a trained magician."

"Indeed he was. A very fine young magician. In many ways you remind me of him Midrak," said Tegriel.

"At first they were going to cut him to pieces but in the fight before they took him they saw a gift I had given him. Well of course I might just as well have written my name in the sky, they knew the gift was from me and they hauled him away to find out what he knew about me. They took my gift, which was a feather from the wing of a snowbird. I knew the feather was on a journey as soon as they kidnapped him.

There is just something about those feathers, once you have been with the snowbirds they seem to become a part of you. Anyway I knew my friend was in trouble."

"How did you get a snowbird feather?" asked Midrak

"That is another story," Gertis told him, "and far longer than this one. I set off immediately to rescue Timberel before they sent him to prison. I knew if I asked you, you would forbid me, so I went ahead on my own pretending to be you."

"Which is typical of you," Tegriel told him.

"I thought that would draw them out faster. I was right of course. Have you been inside Damkina? Nasty, cold, huge, oppressive place. I have seen some animals taken into there that just dissolve the moment they touch the stone floor. Not a place for honest folk to go."

"I always said there was a streak of craziness in you," complained Fulminar.

"I was hardly going to involve anyone else in what I knew would be the most dangerous thing I had ever done. I was very glad I had refused the offer of help from Timberel's family. I was safer only worrying about my own skin and my friend."

"So you thought Hâgon was the best place to hide?" asked Fulminar.

"Not on your life. I thought Damkina was. Gave me the shivers, all that dodging and hiding. Funny thing is It does not have a great many soldiers inside, they are mostly deployed outside. It did not know I was here. I heard It banish Timberel to Hâgon, saying if I came to find him or not they did not need him alive anymore. That was when I leapt."

"You what?" Midrak supposed for a second Gertis had attacked Crilodach.

"I leapt to his side just as It banished him. The spell caught us both and we found ourselves here. It never caught me. When I got here I heard Gâmor coming so I ran thinking I had more trouble than I could handle. I fell and in front of my eyes was this cockroach disappearing into the wall. Quick as a flash I changed us and dragged myself into the same hole. Had to do a lot of pushing I can tell you there were about twenty of them in a small space. After that I realized Crilodach probably took me for dead so I set about making the tunnels and paths inside the walls a bit larger, hoping to find a way out. Took forever of course. Whenever I heard crying or weeping I knew new people were here so I went out to save them. I take my hat off to the cockroaches who were here because they helped. They used to come to get me. I think they liked having us around. Crilodach never comes down here so for a few hundred years now not everyone It has sent has died down here."

"We saw the rags and food," pointed out Midrak.

"Oh yes, every time I save someone I make some food for the cockroaches here. That's why they like me, I make gourmet stuff. Some very good recipes. Flick of the wing stuff really. I spread the offerings around a bit, enough to ensure no one suspects what is going on."

"Have you ever found a way out?" asked Fulminar.

"We have burrowed up into Damkina proper, high above us. I go there rarely. We have scouts who watch and report back. We are very up-to-date with the comings and goings up there. Apparently I am thought of as rather precious by the people down here." He scratched the ground with his front feet. "That's probably why they obey the strict rules. I mean I would not want people to get upset and stuff like that but if It ever suspected, well, that would be the end for all of us."

"What rules?" asked Fulminar

"No changing back even for a second. I can tell you some of them nag a lot about that but once a cockroach, always a cockroach. No going into Damkina looking for a front door. No doing anything 'not cockroach.' So no music making. I cannot tell you how much that annoys them. The food I make is the only magic allowed."

"You were very brave to rescue Timberel in this manner, but you were foolhardy to do so alone," reprimanded Tegriel.

"If you say so," apologized Gertis. "Though I did not save him for long. He hated being a cockroach. He missed his family. He hated the smell down here. He just withered and died of depression."

"I am sorry to hear that," said Midrak.

"Do you know how you got here?"

"Your doing?" asked Tegriel.

"The best I could manage under the circumstances though Bofindle helped me. Bofindle contacted me. Crilodach was attacking you in the Ossendark. All a bit of a rush. I did not know how many of you there would be and got you here as fast as I could but I lost track of you in the Pângil. Scouts were on their way to find you, I was very worried I can tell you. I am just very glad you worked the secret out for yourselves. I am told you had seconds to go back there."

"Do you know what happened?" asked Tegriel.

"I sensed Lilah was in the Ossendark and many thousands of others."

"Thousands? No Just Lilah and Rimfelder," said Midrak.

"I am sure there were more than two. I do not make mistakes like that. When I realized there were so many I just made a grab for those Bofindle was putting in my way, knowing that Lilah can take care of herself."

"Strange," said Tegriel, "I had the same feeling that there were more amongst us than I could count, but could not put my finger on why."

"Maybe that's because you were using my finger," suggested Tobia.

"Hah, The lady has a sense of humour," said Gertis.

"You have kept yourself busy down here," observed Tegriel.

"I have managed to build an army down here even though I could probably get away if I tried. In fact my being here has made Damkina our front line."

"We thought you had died," moaned Fulminar, "and you were building an army under Crilodach's nose, doing better than any of us."

"Very courageous," agreed Tobia.

"It has never come looking for me so I can hardly say what I did was courageous," argued Gertis.

"I think you have done everything I expected of you when I first invited you to be a Sangyma," Tegriel told him.

"You might have let us know," grumbled Fulminar.

"It would have known if I had tried to send messages out from here. Took every ounce of magic I could muster just to get you out of the Ossendark without It knowing but I have learned a few tricks in the time I have been hiding here. It made a fatal error in thinking Itself impregnable. Hâgon is not secure," said Gertis, excitedly. "Its soldiers are always gossiping amongst themselves and there are endless messengers coming and going in Damkina. I can bring you up to speed with what It is up to."

"What's the layout here?" asked Fulminar

"The labyrinth is not patrolled except by Gâmor. Our

303

tunnels mirror just about the whole complex now, they extend a thousand miles down and about a thousand miles across. We have scoured around for years but found nothing more than dank chambers and long tunnels. However the main complex of Damkina is huge, three or four times larger than the labyrinth at least."

"You must know the complex well," said Midrak.

"Despite all the time we have had since, we have barely explored half of what's to be found there. We are in much greater danger up there than down here and have to be ten times more careful. It has store rooms filled to bursting with stolen items and when you think who It has stolen from there are probably many bejals in Damkina any of which might be useful."

The idea flashed through Tegriel's mind that Gertis did not know how useful. But the time was close now they would know. When the whole of Tegriel's life would make sense to them all and most especially to Tobia, as she finished the first part of her travels with the Sangyma.

"We need to know where Crilodach is right now and what It is doing," said Tegriel.

"Cockroach communications are excellent. We know what It does within seconds. Right now It is ripping into Rataplan and his lieutenants. Some battle has been lost. In recent weeks It has spent a lot of time in Its favourite room."

"I wonder if that was us," whispered Tobia.

"You were in the battle?" asked Gertis.

"In one, yes, with Lilah. She was making her way to Earth," replied Midrak, "when we were attacked."

"Ah, Trecrogo. I was always impressed by the plans for that place," said Gertis.

"The fortress still stands though the Earth has finally gone," replied Tegriel. Gertis scratched at the wall with one foot.

"Gone," he repeated. "Quite a loss." He turned away for a moment and Tegriel spoke softly.

"Down here I suppose you have not been able to keep a close watch on the stars. Zaqui is close."

"I must admit I have lost track of time. It was very angry to have missed killing her. A few heads were lost when that happened," Gertis congratulated himself, "I blind-sided It completely. It has no idea what happened. I have been perfecting the technique of piggy-backing on Its own spells.

As they go out I send out one of my own, much smaller, and by the time my spell goes to work Crilodach does not sense a thing. Although I have to say putting a snatch spell into his attack spell on the Ossendark was not a small thing to do and I would never have managed without the help of Bofindle."

"If It got wind we were here we would all be dead," pointed out Fulminar.

"Since when did that fear ever stop any of us in the past?" asked Gertis.

"Never once," admitted Fulminar.

"It is ranting fit to burst up there," Gertis told them, gleefully.

"We should push the advantage this situation gives us," suggested Tobia, "or risk just being prisoners who happen to be alive."

"Indeed we must," said Tegriel. "And we must be swift."

"We should take to the tunnels that go up to Damkina," suggested Midrak. "We will have a clearer picture of our choices once there."

"Its soldiers never let an insect go by without crushing us. You will have to do as you are told if you want to survive," warned Gertis.

"We would not be Sangyma if we were not determined to take the fight to It," said Fulminar.

"And you would not be who you are if you ever did what you are told," Tegriel told Gertis.

"I stayed because staying fitted in with your own prophecy. I just knew this was the right place for me." He backed away from them revealing an opening in the wall, "But I guess if this is Zaqui we should not shrink from the last battle. I know many here who long for another chance to fight It."

"Would they be more successful this time?" asked Midrak. "They were all beaten before."

"In ones and twos they lost, yes," said Gertis, leading the way. "But we are an army now."

Others moved slowly behind them as they left the chamber and entered the tunnels.

"By the way, there is another person here," he added, as they readied themselves for the long climb upwards, "Manfray. He said to me you had told him when he was a child he would one day have many more legs and fight at a great battle."

"I remember him," said Tegriel. "And I remember telling him that."

"Your prophecies are often very accurate," observed Gertis.

"But the time of my prophecies is now at an end. I cannot see what will happen to anyone any longer."

"No matter," replied Gertis, taking the first steps on a steeply sloped tunnel, "they have always held us in good stead and not a few people here feel you knew they would be here. That fills them with a sense of purpose. Not many have wanted to commit suicide in all the years we have been waiting. I cannot tell you how every victory you had, filled us with pleasure. To have that revolting creature spitting fury, because of the Sangyma, has given us hope down here. No longer feeling like insects in the dark but more like avenging spirits waiting their chance to prick at Its feet."

Tobia felt Tegriel almost smiling inside her. There was a contentment in him. She did not understand why as they were in such a dangerous place but she had sensed things about Tegriel no one else knew. How could she not, as she was sharing his mind? His knowledge was vast. A large part of his power rested upon what he knew about events before anyone else, and she realized the Sangyma has chosen well to have him as their leader. Yet, as is the way with those with his knowledge, he followed an exacting and exact path.

The tunnels that went upwards were very steep, inset with many steps that were more like ladders. To take even a small step as they hauled their surprisingly bulky bodies upward they needed all their legs and active antennae to keep balanced. Manœuvring was not easy but they soon learned that the reason the leg–holds were so close together was because they doubled as body support, to lean against when one wanted to take a brief rest.

At times the stone was too hard to cut out any steps, and then became the insect equivalent of climbing a smooth, vertical pipe from the inside without ropes. To begin with they rested by pressing their hard backs against the tunnel wall and wedging themselves at an angle. Gertis and the others were more used to the climb and made the first section in one go. But even they needed rest and at points along their climb they had dug out flat chambers, with very low roof space, where cockroaches could rest for a few moments between stones. There were not many of these and everyone took advantage of them when they found them.

As well as the narrowness, Tobia also noticed there were no drawings or paintings in these tunnels and chambers. They were bare and cold, very cold. She had thought the labyrinth out of Gâmor cold enough but the higher they climbed the colder the tunnels became. Not just the chill you feel on a bright, cold winter's morning. Her outer shell was not cold at all, but a cold that seeped into her, intent upon freezing her blood. Every step up she took, her whole being wanted to turn back. Until she had to fight the impulse to run away with every new step. There was nowhere to run. Taking steps became an agony as if she were wading through quicksand. Her nerves clamoured to turn back, but she could see Midrak was facing the same problem and above him even Gertis was walking in silence. A silence that was needed so they could concentrate upon walking upwards and not give in to running away.

"We have had to keep the tunnels narrow," Gertis told them, as they rested on the third level, "when we first started this and made a wider set, the guards set traps for us. This way they cannot go hitting the stones to try to hear where our tunnels are located. They are too narrow to sound hollow, so we can move around with impunity as long as we stay in our tunnels. You'll find we can still hear a great deal because cockroach hearing is acute. Our narrowest tunnels go right up the paint work and help us hear even more … not that there is any paint work but we get that close. You can smell the helmet oil on their hair sometimes."

"What's making this cold?" she asked.

"Fîdech. A spell of some power," he told her. "I did not know what was happening at first. The closer we got the fewer would stay to dig. I realized Crilodach was using Fîdech to ward off enemies. I am sorry I dare not make you warmer, if I had ever tried It would have known and It would have come looking for me. You have to fight the cold on your own. Just keep telling yourself there is nothing to fear. Focus only upon walking. The spell will not leave you if we enter Damkina proper but only grow stronger. I have no way of knowing if the cold will become stronger than your ability to cope."

"There's a lot to fear up there without a spell," she pointed out.

"Yes there is but not as much as the spell makes you

think."

"The spell tries to stop me thinking," pointed out Midrak. "Draining one of any sense of place. But then this whole, horrid complex drains one of all emotions but for fear."

"Imagine what this would feel like if you had your own body. Fîdech is not cast to keep cockroaches away," said Fulminar.

"You recognized this spell?" asked Midrak.

"We know of all Crilodach's spells," replied Tegriel. "Across many worlds Crilodach conquered It cast this spell to keep them from ever fostering life again. Do as Gertis says, concentrate only upon walking. We will deal with anything else when we get to the top."

They kept up their climb and behind them she could hear many others climbing up. The quiet scrapping of their shell hard bodies against the tunnels' walls and their breathing was picked up by her antennae. Midrak hauled himself up and stopped. He sensed they were close to the areas of Damkina Gertis had mentioned. Gertis had told them all to be very quiet for the last few hundred feet. He took them over a small rise in the tunnels and then heavy stones barred their way. Gertis led them all on a long, weaving pathway between the stones until he came to a small hole between the stones. This was only big enough for one cockroach at a time. The stone felt like ice. They all crept into the hole one behind the other as they had been all the way. In here they could not stand fully on all their legs so they had to pull themselves along on their stomachs.

Using all their legs when they could, they pulled and were pushed from behind until Gertis stopped. Behind him Midrak stopped. Gertis was listening. Would they hear Crilodach? After all Tobia had heard about It, would she finally hear Its voice? Feel It close?

No one would move until Gertis gave the order so they all stayed where they were, crammed into a small space. The minutes went by slowly. Behind them more cockroaches were arriving and as their lines grew longer the chances that some would have to maintain themselves in the tunnels by wedging their bodies became higher. Several feet slipped but though the army was struggling, they all kept quiet. Determination swept the ranks. Patience was a weapon too. If any fell or slipped too far those below braced themselves and those above lowered their back legs to give their friends something to haul themselves back up with. Gertis knew the difficulties of moving the whole army at once but he could not stop them following. He felt their time of waiting was over, but he could not get out yet. Over the years Gertis had learned a little caution. He knew their strength was in the fact Crilodach did not know they were there. As they were, they were no match for It. The only reason Gertis had moved at all was to show Tegriel, Damkina. He had not given any order for the others to follow them. They had decided to do that on their own.

And then for all the slowness and stress of getting there, he moved forward and Midrak quickly followed and so did Tobia. Her front feet felt nothing but air and she flipped over losing her balance, trying hard to force herself ever forward. She bounced off Gertis' back and landed on her feet.

Behind them the other cockroaches were moving upwards. The line was easing and everyone at the back sensed they were moving into Damkina.

And one of them called Leoprin, who had been a wolf, remembered something Tegriel had told him by the camp fires when he had been a cub. That an army would emerge from nowhere into Crilodach's own lair. Leoprin had told this prophecy to those closest to him.

Antennae twitched in the dark and from all over their ancient home, cockroaches emptied their sleeping quarters and crawled upwards towards their enemy. Fîdech was overcome in them by their conviction that their time for revenge was close.

Rimfelder Meets Vingura

Rimfelder landed on his feet with a thump. His eyes were out of focus. He heard something chink against glass, then roll over something else like a hard ball over wood and somewhere else something hit the floor, didn't bounce, and rolled away. He took several moments to get his bearings. He felt as if he had been violently pushed from behind, turned upside down, stretched and eventually dropped on his head. That was certainly no way to travel. His hands rested on an oak tabletop which was all that had stopped him from being sprawled out on the floor.

As his sight adjusted to his surroundings he found himself staring into two steady, almost shimmering, grey eyes that looked back at him without blinking. The blue–haired man they belonged to did not move a single muscle or even appear to see him at all as they found themselves suddenly looking at each other in the gloom. They were very close, almost nose to nose, yet Rimfelder could not hear him breathing. His flowing robes, encrusted with rubies, did not rustle in the warm breeze that Rimfelder felt flowing past his own face. The man's mouth did not move in either a smile of welcome or a grimace of disgust, nor open to speak.

The hairs on the back of Rimfelder's neck rose as he looked steadily at the stranger's unresponsive eyes and stony face slowly realizing that this man was as still as a statue could be, yet looked like he was made of skin and bone. The poet was sure he was a man but was too scared to reach out and touch his face. He thought he could hardly be real because he showed not the slightest sign of life. Unless he was recently dead. Rimfelder shivered. The last place he wanted to find himself in was a crypt or worse, a place where the dead were being used for some reason. Slowly he began to take in more of the things in the room around him. The sudden fear that she had sent him to the wrong place gripped at his chest. He was scared to look around too much but he was more scared not to. He was scared to find that he was alone. He was scared to find he could not look into Lilah's beautiful face and eyes to imbibe her confidence.

He turned his head. He immediately saw, sitting next to the man, an elderly woman in a crushed-green velvet dress, stitched by hand with peacocks displaying in all their magnificence right across the folds and arms. The dress flowed down hiding her arms but showed her small wrists, circled with bracelets in diamond and emerald. She wore a strange ivory-coloured headdress that looked endless, curling round and round her head travelling upwards adding two feet to her height.

She, too, was motionless. Both of them had colour in their cheeks, yet for all that, they appeared to be dead. Even if they were not, they certainly did not display the most important, normal sign of life; movement. They were not breathing. Their eyes did not focus. They did not respond to his sudden appearance. Somehow before they 'died' they had dressed in their finest clothes, sat down and then ... what?

He was about to say something like 'hello,' until he felt the presence of many others. Nothing had moved, no one had moved, but he felt them looking at him. He looked around the room which was becoming lighter as his eyes adjusted to the weak translucence of the walls and ceiling. He was in the middle of a huge, silent, motionless feast. A lifeless feast of beautifully dressed people, their ornate clothing bathing the table with muted colours. They gave all the signs of a celebration though any festivity was hidden way down in some forgotten part of themselves. He felt as if he were captured inside a painting, where a changeless moment had been described by a brush. People painted as they had been in life. He wondered if this was some terrible punishment, or some vile imprisonment concocted by their enemies. That Lilah or anyone she knew would have done this to these people seemed impossible to him. In a way he was right, and in a way he was wrong. For Crilodach this would not have been a punishment harsh enough, for statues cannot feel and It enjoyed giving pain, but then again the laws of magic would not have made people into statues unless they had chosen to be. If in that choice there was benefit in the struggle, the Sangyma would not have stopped them. Choice is always a straight line. You either have one or you don't.

He counted these diners who were not dining. He was crouching on top of a large, round wooden table at which sat the thirty-five people. The table could have accommodated thirty-six but one seat just beside him was empty. All the other seats were taken up by people who neither moved, nor breathed but stared ahead of them as if they were all mesmerized by something invisible. None of them reacted to his landing, as he had, in the middle of their table on a pyramid-pile of fruit, which he upset all over the place until apples rolled off on to the floor and even into the lap of one of the diners. That was the noise he heard when he arrived, a ripe apple rolling into a glass and one rolling on to the floor. For one brief, terrifying instant he thought the empty seat was meant for him. More apples rolled off as Rimfelder hastily moved and slid to the floor from the table between the two people he was closest to, the man with the grey eyes and the woman with the weird headdress. The fruit rolled across the floor and bounced casually off the wall. His heart was pounding. The room was morbid in the way rooms are in which you are the only thing living. A smell rising that fills your nostrils and grabs at your throat, choking your responses and clutching at your nerves saying, 'Run, death is calling for you!'

He stared wide-eyed, his back to the wall. The people were of all ages. There were eighteen women and seventeen men transfixed around a table of sumptuous food and silver goblets filled with wine. Yet the wine did not move to the slight vibration he made getting off the table. One of the oranges rolled into a glass. The force was hard enough to upset the glass on to the floor but nothing happened. He could not smell the food he saw. Nor the wine. He got up the courage to touch the huge sugar fountain and licked his finger. No sweetness. The food was as real and unreal as the people. Without great knowledge of such things, even Rimfelder knew magic was at work, but he did not know whose. He feared at any moment the enemy would appear but he feared to stand still in case he, too, turned into a statue. Was this perfume magic too? Perhaps he was already turning into one of them.

Their clothing, new, clean linens and silks, gave off the warmed smell of freshly prepared garments. He had no idea who they were. He listened intently for the lightest sound but heard nothing. He stood there slightly behind some of the diners wondering if their clothes hid weapons or if at some sudden signal they would all jump up and add him to the feast as a diner or as a dish.

He wished Lilah were here. She would know what this was all about. Even if she did not she soon would. She would know where to look for answers. She would have a dozen ideas of what this all meant, if anything. Or even Tethval. His old friend now lost, would shine his eyes and tell him he had known more scary things. He rubbed his chin and looked away from the frozen diners to the room as a whole.

The low ceiling was decorated with paintings of the night sky. Hundreds of stars. By each one a piece of writing he could not read but he guessed maybe they were names for other worlds. Names of planets, suns, solar systems and galaxies. He wondered where the servants were to wait on these wealthy people, with their fine clothes speckled with jewels. Maybe something they ate had frozen them giving the servants a chance to get away. Had they been poisoned? Magicked into statues during a rebellion? Was he here to break the spell? Could he, even if he knew what the spell was? If they came back to life would they fight with him or against him? He could not stand still. He was too unnerved to stay in this room, torn between the fear of running and the fear of staying.

He began to walk around the deathly quiet room treading with great care over the tiled floor. He felt as if he would fall over at any moment he was so dizzy with fear. After twenty minutes he found a pair of doors behind a pair of black, heavy curtains that touched the dustless tile-floor. The warm air he had felt on the table came from behind this door. He tested the worn iron handle shaped like three horse-shoes. He pulled them down. The doors opened with well-oiled ease and like the rest of the room were so quiet he almost began to doubt his hearing was working.

As the doors easily swung open, he was surprised to find himself outdoors. Then he realized he was not outdoors but under a huge glass dome through which shone a warm light from a fading sun that took up half the sky. He looked around at all the glorious flowers that were kept in large beds, tall ferns and bushes with bright red, yellow, black and blue flowers. As many colours as were on the clothes of the

313

motionless feasters behind the door. He stepped forward. The doors silently closed behind him. He turned in time to see them shut. He stood unable to take his eyes off the doors for several minutes. The ironwork and wooden inserts on the panels were of strange animals. Around the outside ran the same language he had seen on the ceiling. He breathed out in exasperation. How was he ever going to make sense of any of this? He wiped his forehead. He was sweating but the fear he had felt was subsiding. The sunshine was welcome.

"How d'you feel?"

A face appeared from behind the bush on his left. He jumped and peered at what seemed like eyes and a smile but could easily have been berries nestling amongst small, waxy-green leaves.

"Who are you?" he asked.

"Why don't you know?" asked the man, upset at the question. That was not the response Rimfelder had expected.

"I just don't."

"That's more than a bit worrying I'd say," said the man.

"And I feel, in fact I know, I'm lost," the poet told him.

"Yes, well, if you don't know who I am, in all likelihood you won't know where you are. That you feel lost, or at least not sure what to feel, makes perfect sense to me."

The man's narrow eyebrows went up and Rimfelder shrugged his agreement.

"I can quite see feeling lost would be the thing. Very difficult though. Very poor timing on your part."

"Actually, I know exactly why I feel lost," said Rimfelder, "I just found myself in that room back there with a lot of very life-like statues out of the blue."

"Did you now. How much out-of-the-blue would that be?"

"One minute I was with my friends somewhere else, the next I was on that table inside, upsetting apples everywhere."

"Upsetting apples," repeated the man, quizzically.

"I'm sorry about that. Wasn't something I could control under the circumstances."

"Ignorant people usually knock things over," said the man, wryly.

"I'm not ignorant."

"That's a matter of opinion, no? You not knowing anything about where you are or who I am says 'ignorant' to me."

"Well, I suppose I'm slightly in the dark."

"Just slightly?"

"Look, what's the crime in not knowing where I am or who you are?"

"A crime? Never at all. A shame, definitely. This is hardly the time to have people around who're ignorant. Not after all the years of planning and waiting."

"Planning?"

"For your arrival," said the man.

"Me?" said the poet, very surprised.

"Well no, but for sure someone like you."

"I'm not the you, you were expecting?"

"Not so far."

"Should I be here at all then?"

"Well when I saw you come through the door I was relieved, even thankful, given you're late. Now I admit to being rather curious, somewhat let down and not a little miffed."

Rimfelder stepped back so as to see who the man was as he came out from behind the bushes in his garden clothes. He was as tall as Rimfelder, broad shouldered with long blue–black hair and a tireless smile. His face was heavily lined as if he were very old but his voice was that of a young man. His work–clothes were dirty with soil and drops of water where he had been watering the flowers in the huge dome for the last time. Yet even as they talked Rimfelder noticed his clothes began to change. Slowly at first. The dirt just fell off them. As they talked more, his hands became clean. In fact his whole demeanour changed and softened until Rimfelder thought to himself,

'Definitely magic,' adding out loud, "I can't help how you feel, I didn't plan to be here."

"And that's the point because everything that's happening was planned. Minutely. To the last point. To the final moment. And you're not in those plans at all so you say. Mystifying. Upsetting. A little bit odd."

"I hope upsetting the apples didn't upset your plans."

The man blinked as Rimfelder spoke and then laughed,

"Oh, very good. Very nice turn of phrase. I like that. Here drink this," the man suggested, passing a glass in front of his nose held on the ends of long, brown fingers, sniffing, smiling and passing the drink on to the poet. "Apples upset my plans, yes very amusing."

Rimfelder took the glass which had appeared out of nowhere, thinking the man's direct manner was odd as they

315

were strangers. He smelled the delicious fragrance of the warm liquid in the glass. He did not sip any. He thought of the statues and wondered if this was how they had been drugged. He lowered the glass and began to look at the man suspiciously. The man nodded and explained,

"I made that with the berries of the blue bush over there. Nurala Hortaxis. The merry bush. Helps you relax when you're going to be doing the things you're going to be doing. Drink up, the mixture isn't efficacious when cold. In fact the fats thicken and don't help the cholesterol at all. One of the side-effects. Everything has side effects, one of life's problems."

"What I'm going to be doing?" queried Rimfelder, still not drinking.

"You sound spaced-out," said the man. "Surely you know just a little bit? They didn't tell you, did they? Along with not telling you my name. Curious. Annoying. I expected you to be prepared in some way. I do hate last minute briefings."

"Who are you?"

"Vingura's the name. But the nature ... well that's an altogether different kind of story." He smiled at the poet and the poet managed a weak smile back. "Well we're all a bit confused by nature one way or another. If you don't mind me saying you seem very distracted. Not at all in sync with the spirit of the times. Half-witted."

"I was with some friends, we were in the Ossendark, two of them were lost, then my other friend sent me here and you seem to have been expecting me, though no one told me I was coming here. I don't know where my friends are or who those people are in there or who you are, Vingura. And though this garden is very pretty and pleasant to be in, this last few days I seem to have been in a constant state of agitation so now I can't appreciate such tranquillity or beauty."

Vingura looked at him and furrowed his forehead. He made something of a grunting noise in his throat and scratched his eyebrows, annoyed. He pursed his lips together and said,

"I'm guessing your name isn't Gwedling?

"No."

"That explains a good deal. Since you're not the one I was expecting I cannot expect you to know who I am or anything about what's going on. The drink isn't actually for you but

316

as you're the one who's here and time is pressing I suggest you drink up and then we can get on with things. I've always found in these matters that I'm best advised to go with what I've got even if he wasn't what I wanted and seven times out of ten to go with the unexpected if the expected don't turn up."

"What about the other three times?"

"Knowing when you're in the three-out-of-ten, young man, is what distinguishes the great magicians from the merely modest ones."

"I don't understand."

"Anything I've said or something in particular?"

"Well I don't understand anything or how you could calmly accept I'm the wrong person and tell me to use something not meant for me? I could be your enemy."

"Oh, 'meant' isn't a word I've learned to use. In this life you go with the flow and if you're using the Ossendark you're the kind of chap I was expecting even if you're not the exact person. Fact is our enemies don't know much about this garden except that we exist. They never bothered much with us. No armies come to this place, no conquerors. Only those in need of healing."

"Don't I worry you?"

"Why should you?"

"I'm not this Gwedling person you were expecting."

"And not pretending to be him either."

"I never pretend to be something I'm not."

"But my enemies would," pointed out Vingura.

"You're a judge of character."

"And a good one even if I say so myself."

"What was Gwedling expected to do?"

"Ah, he was going to receive a gift."

"Of what?"

"A book actually."

"A book actually?" repeated the poet.

"Having that drink will help you immensely right now, so drink. I haven't time to make another, they expect me at my seat within the hour."

"Your seat?"

"In the room you came from."

Rimfelder thought about the room and recalled the empty seat. By now Vingura's clothes had definitely changed from work clothes. A new silk cravat was round his throat and opals neatly sewn on to his sleeves. Realization dawned on the poet.

"You're going to be sitting with them?"

"Indeed."

"And ... be like them?"

"I should hope so. Won't work if I'm not."

"Are they dead?"

"Not yet."

"But they're not moving."

"I see you noticed. Very observant." Vingura was almost enjoying the poet's disbelief.

"They're not eating."

"No, well they'd have to move to eat wouldn't they?"

"What's wrong with them?"

"Nothing. They're just already in the book."

Rimfelder looked at the flowers, the red sun no longer providing sustenance for the garden and sipped some of the warm drink without thinking. He was going to stop but somehow when he started he had to finish. He faintly heard Tethval in the back of his mind warning that was the dumbest thing he could do but he gave the empty glass back to Vingura as the warm liquid entered his system. Rather than make him light headed or poison him, he found himself calmer, somehow stronger and much more alert.

"You're no coward," said Vingura.

"Why do you say that?"

"I could've been poisoning you."

"You don't look like a poisoner."

"If you can discern that much about character you're not the wrong person even if your name isn't Gwedling. What is your name by the way?"

"Rimfelder."

"Well Rimfelder tell me, do you care about dying?"

"We're all dying aren't we?"

"In many different ways," agreed Vingura.

"From what I've heard over the last few hours none of us have much longer to live."

"There you go, you do know something about what's going on."

"You can't have been through what I've been through and not know something about what's going on. All that planning you've been doing though. All for nothing."

"Why?

"I wasn't part of them, this Gwedling man was."

"You assume Gwedling's a man."

"I'm sorry … yes."

"Assume nothing and you may live a while longer. Anyway, you're part of the plans now because you're here. Even if Gwedling was here I'd be minded to send you off together."

"I really want to get back to my friends," he replied, "they've need of me."

"I can assist you to help them from here."

"Much as that sounds charming Vingura, this place is a place of peace, tranquillity – and strangeness I would add. A garden is not a place from which to wage a war. Right now I believe that's what we're supposed to be doing. In fact I'm probably only here because we were attacked. Maybe Lilah got the address wrong."

Vingura's eyes widened at the mention of her name.

"What d'you know of war?" he asked.

"I was just in one."

"Yet learned nothing I see."

"What is that supposed to mean?"

"I told you to assume nothing. This may be a place from which to wage part of a war, maybe even your part. After all armies are conscripted as much from people living in small villages and quiet homes as anywhere else. A gardener is as much a soldier as a boxer or a hunter once they enlist."

"I haven't time to discuss the philosophy of war with you Vingura, I really, really must return to my friends. If I can."

"As should I. You've travelled a long way. Your body needs to adjust. You can never rush these things, indeed you can't, but now you'll be ready. Now the magic has begun to work. Those cobwebs of uncertainty are being brushed away."

There were smells in the air none of which Rimfelder could quite place. A sense of pleasure, like a warm cuddle, that seemed to make movement superfluous. He was as rested as if he had been sleeping for hours yet wide awake. More awake than he had ever been. Not a muscle was straining. When he walked he could not feel the ground. For the first time he felt every muscle in his body as if he was aware of all his nerves and every bone in his skeleton all at the same time. Signals reached his conscious mind he had never heard before. How his heart was pumping, how his liver was working away and what all his organs were doing, the gurgle of his blood flowing around his veins. Part of his brain was sharing this information with him and as time passed his brain shared more and more as if the neurons were making connections they had never made before. He could almost feel the air passing the hairs on his skin. He was himself, and yet somehow a stranger to himself.

"Where exactly am I again?" he asked.

"Exactly where you need to be I think."

"That tells me nothing, and yet strangely all I need to know."

Rimfelder breathed in, feeling his shoulders rise as his lungs filled with the scented air and then slowly float back as he breathed out.

Such air. Such feelings. Such quietness. There was great strength in this place. Hiding behind the flowers, the glass dome and the jewels that were now appearing on Vingura's silk clothes along with the slippers that threaded around his feet, made of the finest silk with silver beading. Rimfelder felt he was more than just a man. He felt he could reach up and touch the dying stars. That he could stay awake for a thousand years and never feel tiredness. That he could walk upon the air without falling. No pathway was beyond him, no mountain too high to climb, no sea too broad to swim. Vingura's voice broke into his thoughts,

"On the contrary, being here tells you everything you need to know, everything else is merely your personal interpretation," said Vingura.

"I don't know enough to interpret these events," he told Vingura, clenching and unclenching his hands as he counted the bones in his fingers.

"Then educate yourself."

There was a second of silence between them and then Rimfelder began to ask him all the questions that had been piling into his mind since he arrived.

"Why are you going to become one of those people inside?"

"Is that your main worry? What's going to become of me."

"I would've thought that would be anyone's main worry. I mean this whole statue business seems very unnatural."

"That certainly wouldn't be my main question but then obviously you tend to think of others. A good sign."

"A good sign of what?"

"That the Gaddia, that's the name of the book, will be given to the right person."

"What would your main question be?"

"What was Gwedling supposed to be doing?"

"I can guess that."

"You can?"

"Something to do with the book you mentioned. Books are made to be read."

"Very good. I see you have a brain on you. So you'll understand, since you know that, that I've to join my friends in there because that's the way to create the book. I'm the last to give the entirety of my magic to the pages."

"You mean ... they'll all make the book you're going to give to me by ... by becoming like statues?"

"We will."

"How does that work?"

"By giving up our magic and our spirits. That's what'll give the Gaddia power. By giving up the atom of magic in each of us and making them part of the book's pages, the Gaddia will become your secure guide to the way ahead."

"Will you all still be alive?"

"Certainly not what you'd call alive."

"So you'll just sit in there together all doing nothing."

"I wouldn't say helping you out, is nothing," said Vingura, a little offended.

"I wouldn't like to be a statue," shrugged Rimfelder.

"You sound upset about my fate."

"I found that room very spooky."

"Come now, you know very well we won't be there for long."

"That's true."

"We have to make the Gaddia, and the Gaddia is a weapon in this war."

"And this book meant for Gwedling will be mine now?"

"Unless he pops along in the next fifty minutes I'll have no choice but to go with you. If push came to shove, I might choose you over him anyway as long as the choice is mine to make."

"Why?"

"Because he's late. Never a good thing to be when you've an appointment with me."

"Maybe I'm in the right place after all. My friends had a lot of magic about them. A lot of things were left unsaid or merely hinted at that I found hard to understand. Being here I feel I am becoming someone else."

"The drink is working."

"They'd give their lives for the truth, they'd understand you."

"Say no more about your friends," he looked left and right, "to be on the safe side. You never know who's listening. We're assembled to give our power to the fight. Gwedling was the man we'd expected, a strong warrior but I've waited a week now and he's still not here. Perhaps his world's already gone, perhaps It found him first."

"He may still arrive," pointed out the poet.

"I'd say you're a last minute replacement, not perfect perhaps but suited and more to the point, here. In my opinion, and in my experience, being here is nine-tenths of all the luck you're entitled to in this life."

"What if he comes and I'm gone with the Gaddia?"

"He'll remain here until the end."

"What will he do?"

"He'll have a day to wander the garden and kick himself for being late. He won't be able to ask me any questions the way you have done. But then I don't think he needs to ask so many." He sighed and rubbed his hands together. "You know, I'm not going to worry about him. We won't get anywhere trying to worry about someone else's fate. Time's short we must carry on as fast as we may."

"I feel sorry for him."

"So do I but if he ever turns up he'll feel more sorry about you."

"That's not very encouraging."

"Not that you're unready to face dangers. I can see you are. But you seem reticent for the task ahead yet have no choice but to go where I send you. I wish you were more courageous or even a little more inquisitive, curiosity never hurt anyone."

"Well if I'm to help and be 'courageous', I'll need to know a few things."

"Such as?"

"Who exactly is Vingura?"

"My father was exactly a king, though I dislike the title Prince Vingura especially as I've nothing to be prince of anymore. Especially as princes are pretty poor examples of anything except indulgence and selfishness. I'm myself; part healer, part mystic, part soldier, part magician, part dragon."

"You're part of many things."

"You're not?"

"Since this all started I've been fairly insecure. I've no magic in me. I'm not a warrior because I've no strength or skill with weapons. I'm not part prince for certain sure. I write. When I used to have the time. Now time seems to be unravelling very quickly and just as I feel I've something to say something else comes along that wants me to speak so swiftly I lose myself, and nothing gets written. Words are difficult for me. Almost strangers."

"Events flood upon you, you mean. Giving you hardly any time to think and no time at all to plan. As if your feet were not your own and your brain is playing catch–up and everyone else knows much more than you'll ever find out?"

"Like nothing I've ever experienced before," Rimfelder agreed.

"You know, do you not, some of the greatest fighters we've ever had, have never wielded so much as a knife?"

"How can that be? When armies race against us armed to the teeth. When unimaginable forces are gathered to destroy us. I've seen what they can do."

"Strength is in one's character as well as in one's muscles. You have character."

"Character isn't a shield."

"My dear Rimfelder character's better than a shield."

"Oh come now I've been told many things but never that an unarmed poet can fight an army."

"Not all enemies carry weapons. As my father would have said, all weapons begin in the imagination. There are many weapons in that armoury that the worlds have yet to see."

"Too late to make any of them now."

"You think we've no surprises for the enemy?"

"I'm sure you do."

"You think you may be one of them?"

"I'd be very surprised to be. Though she said my words would become weapons."

"Well as my father also said, be prepared to be surprised."

"Is your father dead?"

"A long time ago. He didn't have much strength of character. Too spoiled."

"You're a king then."

"No, now I'm something far more important."

"What?"

"A teacher. I've prepared your body for what you're about to see with that drink I gave you, now I must prepare your mind for the Gaddia."

"I wish I knew where my friends were right now."

"I know of the spellmaker. I felt her presence all about you from the moment you arrived and was delighted when you confirmed her name. She obviously has had her hands full or you'd have been better prepared to meet me, but no matter."

"She's an amazing woman."

Vingura looked back at him,

"You're not the first to fall in love with her."

"Why do you say that?

"No cause to get defensive. Truth be told I'm probably a little in love with her myself. Spellmakers of her calibre have an aura about them men can't resist. Even old men like me. Added to which she has natural beauty."

"Do you think she knows?" asked Rimfelder.

"About your love for her?"

"Yes."

"I'm sure she does."

"She sent me here to get rid of me."

"I doubt that very much. If she sent you here she knew Gwedling wasn't coming and you'd make an excellent replacement. She was certainly thinking clearly for next to a warrior I'd choose a poet to give a book to any day."

"I'm a fool for loving a woman such as her," said Rimfelder, who was letting the drink talk for him a little too much.

"You'd be a fool not to."

"To find love at this time. When all love is impossible."

"My dear poet, this is the time when love, above all things, will be our most potent weapon. Who knows but your love for her may be the cleverest magic of all."

"Magic is clever?"

"Magic is brilliant," Vingura told him.

"Brilliant enough to defeat Crilodach?"

Vingura stood stock still for the merest moment and then said,

"You know Its name has not been spoken here in many ages." Rimfelder felt he had spoken out of turn and was about to apologize when Vingura added, "So time someone did, I suppose."

Vingura nodded his head and a table appeared on which were the ingredients to the drink he had made. He tidied them up letting them float away behind him and vanish into unseen cupboards. Within a few seconds the table vanished too.

"I wouldn't like to leave things out for anyone else to have to clean up. I'm a bit of a tidy freak."

Rimfelder looked at the large gardens and the perfect cut of every bush and almost perfect plants beds. This garden all seemed a million light years away from war. And Vingura knew as well as he did, no one else would be coming here to tidy up. Perhaps trying to pretend to be normal helped Vingura get through the difficulties of his last hours. He replied,

"Will It come here now?"

Vingura brushed down his sleeves.

"Nowhere is safe from It," he went on, "but some places are harder for It to find than others. Its never attacked me but the universe is shrinking. Many things that have been hidden will become known. Which is why we thought Gaddia would help. The thirty-six of us are the Gaddia, the secondary defence of the Sangyma, as Filvani liked to say. We were all born in the same year, on the same day on thirty-six different planets. We were all touched by the same cosmic event, a bright star on the edge of the universe broke into pieces and sent showers of light to the very edge of the universe. To the place where time ceases to exist, right there, where the universe is still creating space. For as you know time and the universe are one and the same thing." Rimfelder didn't know but he nodded anyway, and Vingura went on, "As the light came close to our planets the pieces gradually slowed down and a few photons, thirty-six of all the billions that were there, entered into our minds at the exact same second we took our first breaths."

"Giving you all magical powers."

"Giving us all knowledge of each other. For with the light came vision. We all saw that star, we all saw the edge of the universe and Zaqui. You can't be normal after that experience as a baby, or settle for being a prince."

"I can understand palaces wouldn't hold much attraction to you after that," agreed the poet.

"Of course we didn't know what to make of our feelings and thoughts until we'd grown to be eight and the Sangyma visited us."

"This Gwedling, has he been taught about Gaddia?"

"Certainly."

"He knows what to expect? How to handle various weapons and what have you?"

"Certainly."

"And with no time at all to learn anything I come along and you give the book to me. You're taking a huge risk when so many lives are in the balance."

"You lay no claim to art or office, that makes you honest. You appear here after being attacked in the Ossendark, that makes you an ally. You come to me at just the right moment, that makes you important. You speak of things only the Sangyma know, that makes you special. The more I think about you, the less the risk I am taking becomes."

"If you know about Li ... the spellmaker you certainly know her work but I only agreed to go with her because my own world was destroyed. I was just thinking of myself."

"What d'you feel you've learned about her?"

"She's the kind of person you'd do anything you can for. She has a strength that calls to you. She makes you ashamed of your petty weaknesses and makes you want to achieve great things just by looking at you. She seems to be power and wonder all wrapped into one. She's at once a woman and yet an unstoppable force. Certainty and yet danger. Knowledge and yet the unknown. She would die for us all and yet ... she demands we also die for her cause."

"Are you sure your name isn't Gwedling?"

"Rimfelder, I assure you."

"Well you speak like a seasoned warrior. What's the last thing you remember clearly before you arrived here?"

"After everything went haywire in the Ossendark I talked to her. I wanted to know where the others were. She wouldn't tell me. She said she was sending me away. She gave my words power, although I don't feel any different. Maybe I'm a mistake on her part."

"That's the first really silly thing you've said since you got here."

"Surely that's possible?"

"Of all the things that are possible, and there are many of them, that'll be the one that's impossible. I realize you don't entirely know the Sangyma and their ways and so I'll grant you some latitude, but you being here is definitely what she intended."

"I'm glad you're so sure."

"She has Bofindle with her?"

"Yes, she does."

"Bofindle would have known we were close to creating Gaddia. Now there's a pretty wondrous bejal. Imbued with a lot of Tegriel's special knowledge, dug up from beneath a mountain complete and whole by the spellmaker Kalevala. There are those who say Bofindle's a Sagitæ in disguise. I don't hold with that because I was always told the Sagitæ stand for peace and Bofindle is the mightiest weapon known. Though, of course, Bofindle always chooses our side making us assume that maybe the bejal is peaceful by nature."

"Chooses?"

"Oh yes. Bofindle can't be wielded by anyone unless the bejal allows them permission. Even Crilodach couldn't pick the bejal up if Bofindle didn't want It to."

"I wish a weapon had chosen me."

"My dear Rimfelder where have you been the last half-hour? One has. That's why you're here. That's why we've connected. Gaddia will be yours."

"Are all you magical folk connected? You all seem aware of each other's existence."

"Every magical atom in the universe is connected. Those atoms form a special bond. Not only do they react together they also feed off each other. Knowing what the left hand does strengthens the right hand. The universe can only end you know, once every atom has experienced self-knowledge. Something loosely called life by some species but a better word is awareness."

"Every atom?"

"Every one. Takes a lot of time. Even the ones in Crilodach though unlike everyone else Crilodach never loses any atoms. Do you know It never sheds Its skin? Unlike us, the atoms in It are fixed. Not one has ever moved. Not one has become anything else. Some think that's the reason for Its behaviour. There's no atom of goodness in Its entire body. Not a single one. Think of that."

"It sounds abnormal."

"Not for It. For It we're abnormal. Allowing new atoms to bond with us. Sharing ourselves with the universe. It finds that repulsive. They say magicians lucky enough to be made with just a single atom of another magician are ten times stronger and more powerful because of the memories that atom retains."

"That's quite an increase."

"Now you can see why memories are particularly important. Memories are a face of nature. As you'll learn in the coming day, as Gaddia helps you, others will know where you are, and take strength from what you do?"

"Do they know I'm here?" he asked.

"If not yet, in a very short time I'm sure they will."

"Are the people inside," he pointed to the door, "aware of me?"

"Very much so. I can tell you they're impressed so far even if you aren't Gwedling."

"Still, when all's said and done, I wish my friends were here."

"You must stop worrying over them. Wherever they are, like you, I'm sure they're where they should be. Their fight is their fight, not yours. We're all part of one war for every battle leads to every other battle. You'll play your part and believe me, your part will not be a small one. Now come along here."

Rimfelder liked Vingura. Maybe the drink or the fragrance of the garden was messing with his brain but there was no threat here. He followed Vingura through the garden beginning to believe that he did have a task to perform and the power to win through, whatever the task was and wherever the Gaddia took him. He believed that the Gaddia would lead him through immense danger and to amazing places. Vingura brushed his shoulder and picked out two hairs.

"These aren't yours." He held up the two strands of hair. "Let's see who they belong to, shall we?"

Vingura placed them on thin discs of silver that appeared in his hand and rubbed some oil into them and placed his nose close to the silver and sniffed. He took a small match and lit the oil on his hand, which immediately caught fire with a yellow flame. The silver heated up when he touched them. The hairs and dust vaporised. The fire on his hand rose with the vapour and swirled in the air. Vingura looked deeply into the burning smoke. Rimfelder thought he could see shadows forming but he would not make anything else out. Vingura nodded seeing everything.

"You were travelling with a Ruzniel," he said.

"Yes. Tobia."

"Well, well, you do keep high and mighty company. Since the spellmaker has no need of a companion I assume a magician was there with you, this Midrak perhaps?"

"Her brother."

"This one I don't recognize. Tethval, there is a light within him, deep, piercing,strong. He's a friend of yours, your name burns brightly in his heart."

"He's dead."

"This light isn't dead."

"Believe me we left him behind. All the Arvernat died. She couldn't save them. She said that I alone was all she could save. The best she could do. Our world was destroyed after a struggle with Its army. They ripped everything to shreds. Everything I've ever known turned to dust."

"She chose you and all this time you've been saying you're not the right man."

"That's different."

"How so? Because a woman was asking you and I am far less pretty?"

"Because my choices were to go with her or face death. Anyone would've chosen as I did."

"The magic doesn't lie. Of course errors creep in as matter continues to compress at this incredible speed but Tethval is alive as far as I see."

"I would be happy to think so. He was my closest friend. We fought together to liberate my ... our world. He'd been a slave all his life so he knew more about freedom than I've ever known."

"Despite what you think I don't believe this Tethval is dead. If he were I wouldn't have sensed him amongst your companions in the Ossendark."

"Well I don't know how he was there. He certainly wasn't visible."

"Your not knowing or seeing doesn't mean he wasn't."

"Look, I don't want to be rude but if this Gaddia can help me get back to them, I'd very much like to get a move on. If not I'm not sure I should take the book at all."

Vingura scratched his ear with one hand and washed his hands under the running water of a fountain Rimfelder had not noticed before. Rimfelder reminded Vingura of a dog he had once lived with. He never wanted to go out preferring to sit curled in front of a fire or wrapped up on a chair; but pick him up and put him outside and he was off like a whirlwind running over every field and racing round the woods as if he were possessed. Rimfelder was unsure of himself but give him the slightest encouragement and there was no stopping him.

Vingura was now dressed in truly splendid clothes and around his long hair gold threads were winding their way stand by strand, making his head glitter as if lit by a hundred small lights continuously moving up and down the strands.

"Well, we have to finish up here. I don't know that your path will be the same as theirs. The Gaddia will choose your way and that's that."

"I must be with them," Rimfelder told him.

"Oh, I'm sure you'll be with them one way or another but I'm not sure you'll be going back right away. At least not to her. D'you know where she is right now?"

"No."

"Well you soon will. Then the Gaddia will know what to do with you."

He laughed to himself and his eyes twinkled. Rimfelder furrowed his brow and sighed. This whole 'everything is connected' thing was difficult to understand. He realized Vingura meant everyone else knew what was going on but he did not, which was not so easy to accept or so comforting to find out. Vingura took Rimfelder back into the room from which he had come and walked behind several of the seated magicians to the centre of the far wall.

"The stories of these people and their exploits are great and numerous. Why you could fill a library with the works of Hindrel," he patted the head of the woman with the turbaned headdress, "and that would be but the start."

"But ..." Vingura held up a hand and interrupted the poet.

"The time for telling you is over Rimfelder. Now you must learn as you go. I think you'll do well. I really do. The Gaddia will be with you. The work of thirty-six magicians isn't a small book. Each page will contain their wisdom, their hearts and above all their power. When what you see here's gone, when these bodies and this room vanish, the Gaddia will remain with you until Zaqui. Guard us well and use us to guide your steps. Above all always listen to what we tell you. The Gaddia will never be wrong."

"I hope I live up to the faith you place in me," replied the poet.

"I'm sure you'll do your best. As much as I'm sure your best is magnificent." He picked up the fallen apples and placed them back on the pyramid of fruit.

"You think highly of me for someone who just met me."

"If you carry on trying until the moment you die, you'd have done all that could be expected of anyone," said Vingura.

"If your book doesn't help me find Lilah and the others I'm not sure the Gaddia will be of much use to me. I'm not a magician. My best hope of helping in this war is to stand with those who are."

"Gwedling's not a magician. That's why we chose him. Magic can't cure everything or fight everyone. Crilodach expects Its enemies to be great magicians. You'll come as a surprise to It. An ordinary man with two extraordinary gifts."

"But magic is the only thing in our favour. I saw the fight in my own city. I saw the unbelievable power."

"And maybe, my friend, where you're going and what you'll do, will be even more important that what everyone or anyone else is doing, or has done. Ever."

"You know where I'm going?"

"If you accept the book I know where you'll start."

"Where?"

"Will you accept the Gaddia?"

"Will I understand all this better?"

"We'll try to help you though we do not know everything."

"I accept."

"For your own self or for hers?"

"Does that matter?"

"Personal bonds will be broken. They can't survive. Your pain may be greater than others because of your love for her."

"This is no time for cowards who don't accept their own feelings." Vingura was impressed by his answer and said,

"The more I learn about you the more I know you're the right person for this task and that's that."

"Will you tell me where the Gaddia is supposed to be taking me now?"

"To the place found by the three, lost Ruzniel. Through hidden places. To the hiding place of a Sagitæ."

"By myself!"

"You've the book, which means you'll not be alone, and here will be three others."

Vingura sat down. In front of him, a glass appeared with a different drink, red and smelling of raspberries. He drank the liquid in one go, licked his lips and said,

"In the old days they said the drinks made here were the finest in all the worlds. People would come from many places to be given drinks of different natures. We were quite popular. Drinks that made you forget, drinks that made you remember, drinks that made you happy, brought you laughter, cleared your mind. So many kinds. We used to grow whole fields of bushes just to make one kind. Whole fields. Think of that. Thousands and thousands of berries. All the juices made by hand and magicians would send their friends here ... such a busy place ... a place of healing ... sunshine ...."

Vingura had stopped talking. Now the man was as still as the others. Rimfelder realized he had spent so much time fighting against being chosen he had not asked him half the questions he had wanted answered. He touched the old man on his shoulder as if saying goodbye.

Vingura's eyes were shining. Across the table the breeze picked up. The food vanished. A huge book took form and shape. The pages floating into the binding from all around the room. The life forces of the seated people flowing into the stitches and pages. The pages folding themselves. Stitch work being done by invisible fingers to keep them together. The binding forming around them, inlaid with designs of fruits and animals, the end papers crisp with the designs of the palms of the hands of the thirty–six magicians, holding the binding to the book stronger than glue. On the cover a gold and blue ornate picture of a dragon appeared across the top and down the spine runes of a language he did not know. Done. The Gaddia lay closed on the table. Rimfelder went over. He touched the cover with his finger tips. The embossing felt warm. He let his hand run over the cover which smelled of the domed garden and then he opened the book with a crack as the spine stretched open for the first time.

As he did so the room vanished. He was in the Ossendark again, only this time he was alone. He saw the parapet on the fortress. The blinding light from the Arvernat and he grew angry seeing Lilah in difficulty. He heard Hagouti gloat. He spoke out. Hagouti reacted but the others did not hear him, did not see him. He felt the creature writhe uncomfortably. Rimfelder's voice was angry. The Gaddia was in his hands and the first page contained lines in his own language. He read them aloud. They were strange. He had no idea what they meant but his voice was firm and never faltered as he read. He read the whole verse. His voice carried across the Ossendark without him knowing and they passed over Trecrogo. He felt more alive than he had ever been before. Surging up from somewhere deep inside himself he sensed that immense power that made him want to touch the stars. He was amazed. He was renewed.

When he looked at the page again the verse was written in his own handwriting. As if the Gaddia had taken the words from his brain. As if his brain was aware of things going on that his conscious mind could not grasp. Rimfelder felt connected to the universe in a new way. He had found a window on to existence and by looking he could see further, deeper and more clearly than all other people. As if he stood on top of a tall building and he could see the whole city beneath him and every individual living there and what they were doing through the brick work and beneath the ground. Only the building was a book and the city was as large as the universe.

He felt Hagouti. The smell of the creature and how he writhed in his brain. He felt his deathly coldness but he also felt his own strength for he had contained the creature within his words. He heard his voice and spoke without opening his mouth. No matter how Hagouti twisted he could not escape the poet. Rimfelder pulled at him until his grasp on Lilah broke and he yelled in pain but Rimfelder held him tightly. The poet felt he could crush the creature there and then. He sensed he should not. That there were things he should do and things he should not do. Hagouti's death was not for him. He knew Hagouti was real. Somewhere. Some place where Lilah was fighting. He knew he had had a hand in defeating him.

At the time he read these first words, he had no idea what they meant or what they had achieved. Nor would he, but many times he would open the Gaddia and many times he would read, looking for some direction or idea of where he was and where his friends were and how he might find the Sagitæ Vingura had told him he was to find.

The might of thirty-six magicians who were known to the Sangyma and wise and powerful in their own right had become Rimfelder's weapon, striking into the field of the immediate battle from outside the range of Crilodach's foot soldiers. Not from a left or right flank, but from a flank of pure being, made possible by the laws of magic. As the sixth law says,

अ हम्जिल हालल अलयाअन हरानिल २A अ
हतरानिलहत कैTd नुकीलल ॥दिचतलॶ
अचतिद नुमञA डॵ अॵञहहिर लझिलल

'*A Spell Will Always Travel In A Straight Line Unless Directly Acted Upon By Another Spell*'

"Be wary poet," came Vingura's voice, "be wary and careful. You'll need more than your words for all their power. You're going to the heart of things. You know how you lived for words and for those words that uncovered the truth. You're going to the secret of the universe. To the reason for words. The cause of worlds."

"Shouldn't Lilah be doing this?"

"Lilah has her own song to sing. Her own part to play. You've another. Don't worry too much about what other people know. The magic is rising like the bones of the cosmos lifted from slumber. Their atoms are calling out. They're seeking you out Rimfelder. When you find them, know them. The Gaddia will be your guide but the more you see, the harder decisions will become."

Then the voice went silent. The Ossendark vanished. He was no longer near a garden. For the second time in just over an hour Rimfelder was alone, on a world he did not know. This one was hot. A great storm of noise came from a mile or so in front of him where the land looked red as if a volcano were erupting but this was no volcano but a river of magma, flowing like a great sea. The ground beneath his feet trembled. He held the Gaddia to his chest like armour.

He took a step forward expecting the ground to swallow him up but the rock held firm under his shoes crunching beneath them. On the rocks around him he saw real flame. High above him the atmosphere swirled in chaos as vast clouds madly raced to find black rain. He shivered.

"If this is the mind of the universe," he muttered under his breath, "I now know why everything seems so wrong."

He walked forwards, towards the raging red that looked like fire floating above fire. He struggled up a few hard slopes. He wondered how he did not slip because he would not let the book out of his arms and he was sure he lost his balance once or twice. Somehow he felt the book protected him as Vingura had promised. He was still lost and could not quite grasp what was happening to him. He came close to the top of a slope and sat for a moment. Taking the Gaddia on to his lap he opened the first page again. The words he had read were still there. He went to turn the next page but the book would not let him. He looked at the pages. There were hundreds yet but he could not browse through any of them. He sighed. Obviously, they would open for him only when he had need of reading something. Something the thirty–six magicians would give or create for him as need dictated. He closed the Gaddia, stood up and looked over the rise in the land.

The bright red, he now saw, was a sail. A large, brilliant sail on a long ship that was floating on a burning sea of volcanic lava spewing from some unseen place and flowing so far into the distance he could not see the end. As he watched, the vessel saw him and a wide gangplank was lowered by invisible hands.

"You have to be kidding me," he muttered.

But in his heart he knew, so he walked forward intending to embark. As he did so he silently cursed Gwedling for being late, blessed Lilah with success and thanked Vingura for a drink he was sure was the only thing giving him the courage to continue.

Rataplan Trembles

The room reeked of their sweat. Hardened soldiers, used to hiding their feelings, were dripping with fear. The kind of fear that races from one person to another without words. The kind of fear that will stampede. A rare kind of fear. Men who have seen death, up close, watched their enemies' eyes bulge as they killed them, do not easily frighten. Something special, something with a unique foreboding makes such men scared. An acute understanding of extraordinary pain will make them quake, will make their hearts pound, will make them wish the ground would swallow them whole just so they could be free of this room. This hot, stifling room towards which Gertis was crawling with his cockroach army. This lair. This prison where hope is chained and tomorrow buried in the dust.

The men, in their saturated, dirty armour still hot from the battle against Trecrogo, stood in front of Crilodach as if waiting to be brought to life. As if they wanted to change what had happened enough to sacrifice a leg or an arm to make the escape of Trecrogo impossible. All their training, all their effort had been swept away by their enemies. They wanted to be anywhere but where they were. They would have faced death a hundred times more to postpone this summons. Being dragged off the battlefield by their commander as soon as Hagouti had failed. And where was he? Captured. A prisoner. Possibly Dead.

Their breathing was slow despite the heavy beating of their hearts. They feared to cough or to wipe away the sweat that hanged copiously from their eyebrows and dripped into their eyes. They held themselves as men already dead. They did not even dare to think, for It read their thoughts. They feared to show the slightest nervousness. They feared to draw attention to themselves with the smallest movement.

Its anger was palpable as It flicked Its claws together and went over all they had told It. It was thinking deeply.

Was It preparing a new plan?

Was It going to kill them?

Was It going to fly into a rage?

They felt like flies who had had their wings pulled off, waiting to be squashed. Worse, they felt like soldiers who had failed. Men who had lost some of their confidence and lost the confidence of their commander. Their minds were utterly numb. There were no excuses they could blurt out.

Their eyes searched Its face looking for a clue to how It was thinking about them as It slowly paced all around the room, sometimes moving behind them, which was most terrifying for them as they could not see what It was doing, and then walking in front of them It growled to Itself. They did not know which was worse, to see It or not to see It. Their skins itched. Their eyes ached. Their tongues were dry. They lived through a thousand imagined wounds from Its claws.

They longed to know what It was going to do with them. Their hands hanged stiffly by their sides as if they would never have strength enough to hold a weapon again. Their knees ached, their stomachs tightened as they longed to run away from Its presence. This was worse than assaulting Trecrogo. They felt they had some chance against Its enemies but against Crilodach they knew they had no chance.

They had seen Its orders through to the bitter end on a thousand battlefields. They had carried out Its commands against the Sangyma with ruthless efficiency. They never wondered who would mourn their enemies' losses. They never dug a grave out of respect. They drove their soldiers like cattle. Now they were facing the possibility of their own execution. For all their bravery in battle they felt like children. Vulnerable. Scared. Absorbed only in their own wish to survive. At this moment they knew true fear. Silently, each one of them cursed Hagouti and mourned Arnveiss though, standing in Its presence, Ferveiss and Jurveiss half wished they had been killed and not Arnveiss, just so that they would not be facing Crilodach's anger.

Trying to understand what Crilodach was going to do was futile for talents such as theirs. None can peer into the mind of Crilodach and fathom Its thoughts but the Sangyma. But then, after generations of watching Its actions who needed to fathom Its wishes and thoughts. Crilodach only wanted power and if they did not give that to It, they would be replaced. Sliced into pieces as a warning to others. Their bloodied and broken bodies a sign to others never to fail.

They felt like men who had climbed a huge mountain expecting to see the view of the whole world before them, and instead found only hard, sheer ice. There were no rewards here.

They were not even worried about each other, locked into their own world filled with their own needs, their own wants. Their thoughts as selfish as Its, just not as powerful. Their weapons as vicious as Its claws but not as skillful. Their intent as murderous but not as deep. Their minds as callous but nowhere near as devious. In all things they lacked Crilodach's intensity and perhaps now, as they stood there, they vaguely realized they even lacked Its ability to survive. For Crilodach was the embodiment of life, because Crilodach had always been. If, for one moment, for one precious second they could have awakened enough imagination within their blood–thirsty brains to see clearly, they would have realized that Crilodach could die once. Then they would have seen It feared that more than they feared It and they would have understood everything, from the first battle to the last and seen themselves for the puppets they had become.

For these soldiers death had been a way of life. These soldiers were expected to kill. For Crilodach the effort would have been in not killing. An effort It was displaying now in the heavy minutes that passed after It had been told of the battle, of the discovery of a Sagitæ, of Trecrogo and the new magic in Bofindle.

Crilodach sneezed. Or maybe the sneeze was actually a muffled growl that came out of Its nose. The sound sent shivers down their spines. It looked with withering eyes at the vastness of space. It observed the stars as they continued to vanish. Plucked like Christmas lights in series going out in long strands and leaving behind darkness, which is but the memory of light. An almost untouchable idea that once there had been life where now there was nothing. Spiral galaxies ripped to shreds in seconds. A universe denuded of the central function to create life. And now Crilodach's fiery eyes imagined the end of the celebrations. All coldness. Deep shadows. Looking eternity in the face. Crilodach was cursed with too many memories.

The singing and feasting had ended for so many even as It looked on but this destruction was not a display of Its power. It could not stop the universe ending. Against Zaqui even It was powerless, and that too made It angry; as if events at Trecrogo had not made It angry enough. It had fooled Itself for generations that It had power over life and death but here was something that had power over It. Here was something that threatened It, as equally without a moment's thought as It had given to all Its victims. As effortlessly as It had dealt out death. As It half looked at Its commanders It could see their fear in each and every drop of sweat. It knew why they were fearful. Somewhere in Its mighty brain It felt a hint of empathy for the first time in Its long life. Crilodach knew It should blame them for the failure to take Trecrogo over immediately but It also knew that part of that blame lay with It. There was something after all that only It could do, that could not be left to others. There was a time for armies, and a place for wars, but there was also a time for It to wage battle in person.

All life had been Its plaything. The energy from which all things grew, all things lived, was Its knowledge. Until now there had always been time but even with all the time in the Universe Its patience was non-existent. Blood for the sake of blood had never been a strategy, but a mission. Now It felt an ache in Its muscles as if they were tired. Tired? It groaned inside Itself (the sounds they thought were a growl) and sniffed the hot, thick air again. Its eyes bled hatred. Curling Its claws took ages. Walking around them was like walking in a maze because It never reached the end of walking. As if trying to guess at Lilah's plans, at the Sangyma's plans, was like trying to use tracing paper to outline the clouds. They kept shifting. Again the sound from Its throat made Its men uncomfortable. It scraped at the walls.

Sometimes they had been sent to kill for no more reason than to keep in practice. They had had their share of victories. The great days of reporting Sangyma deaths one-after-another. The swelling of prisons with those who might know where the Sagitæ were hidden. The sense of today's failure ground into Its skin, scarring It as no weapons ever could.

The men around It waited for It to tear their skin off their backs but Crilodach still had a use for them. As time fused with energy It did not feel the need to kill to make them obedient. Zaqui would do that in a very short while. What It needed was efficiency. Resolute action. Why, when It had always been able to rely upon Its armies did they fail It now? Was the universe working against It when winning was more vital than ever before? Crilodach sensed Its own doubt, and rejected the feeling as if It had been asked to rip off Its arm to save the rest of Its body. No doubts. It sensed that a new knowledge was going to come to It, a new idea of why things were the way they were. For even It had not been there at the exact beginning. Even It did not know if there was more meaning to Its existence than It knew. Even It did not know if dying was necessary. Maybe that was why It had been a killer all Its life, to fill up this huge unknown in Itself. Worse, maybe Its nature was a plaything of the universe. Maybe the great and mighty Crilodach was merely a piece on a cosmic chessboard.

A long few minutes ago they had been telling It of the battle on Earth. It had heard every detail, thought through every move they made and every counter-strike the enemy had enacted. The cunning. The audacity. Hagouti failing. Lilah had lived through the first round. It looked away from the stars and without looking at them It slowly said,

"You were unable to regroup after the Arvernat arrived?"

"We couldn't penetrate the light from their eyes. The enemy have gained a momentary advantage," Rataplan told It, flicking his claws together nervously as the silence was finally broken. It growled, clenching Its teeth until silver-coloured blood oozed from Its gums.

"The bears built an entire fortress right under your noses, on a planet you said was destroyed." It roared with Its claws clenched and corrected Itself, "I should have known. I should have understood. The cunning of the Sangyma knows no bounds. I'd the Earth in my grasp once, many of her people were mine to do with as I wanted. None had ever been more willing to serve. My armies from them would have been vast." Crilodach spat at the wall and the acrid smell of burning filled their nostrils. "The old has risen, what was thought dead is not dead. What else lives that should not? What else will come to haunt my plans? This strategy of theirs has been a long time in the planning yet not a hint did I have, not a smell. What could have hidden this from me?"

It closed Its eyes at the thought that the Sagitæ might possess enough power to do this and that Lilah and her rag-tag army might have found them all. What defeats could all three bring down upon It? The idea filled Its mind with a sudden rush. It heard Rataplan saying,

"We can attack again ... "

"Not yet," It said dismissively.

Crilodach kept Its eyes closed and turned Its huge head away from them. Its thoughts flashing like an electric storm in Its brain. It was reaching out beyond Itself. Into the growing darkness. Remembering all It knew of the Sangyma. Feeling for their energy. Looking for their thoughts. It rested Its claw on the huge table, thick with dirt, in the centre of the room. The ideas were flowing inside Its head, tumbling over each other like acrobats seeking applause. Lilah. Who had trained her? What had the bears been doing? What special child could wield the power from the core of the fortress? Had the magic of the Sangyma gone into the stones of Trecrogo? Why the planet Earth? Why save that one from all those that had been destroyed? How magical had the Earth really been? It half suspected the truth. What else had they managed to hide from It? What else? From the torrent of ideas It began to pluck out single thoughts.

"Did you see what happened to Hagouti?"

"They took him prisoner," Rataplan told It. Its eyes flashed beneath the heavy lids and sparks flew from Its skin.

"Not possible ... not possible ..."

"One minute he was around her the next he was in his bodily form cringing beneath her fist. We were almost there, if Hagouti had stayed the course we'd have gained the upper hand."

Rataplan had emphasized Hagouti's failure. It was a ploy he thought would save their lives. It had been Hagouti's plan not his. Hagouti was Crilodach's creation. If Hagouti could fail they were less to blame. They had fought well, they had given him time to do his work but he had fallen. Crilodach could not entirely blame them but Crilodach did not make decisions based on Rataplan's understanding of fairness.

Rataplan waited for Crilodach's decision. He still remembered what had happened to Zibanda his predecessor as Crilodach's general. There was not so much as a piece of bone left of him or anyone who remembered him, not family, race or planet. A name not even written upon water.

"Not possible," repeated Crilodach in a growling whisper, putting his nose close to Rataplan's and breathing heavily, studying the general's eyes,

341

Rataplan

"Unless," It stopped and moved away. "Ha!" It cried and turned on Its heel with the alacrity of a dancer. Putting a claw on Rataplan's shoulder, with the weight nearly crushing him It said,

"Could that be the answer? Come."

Crilodach marched forward and a large section of the floor levitated towards Its claw. Beneath Its claw two crystals shone, illuminated from the light in Its claws and a dim light within them meeting halfway. The light formed into an oval surrounding Its whole body,

"Show me," It ordered.

The crystals, bejals It had captured and chained to Its desire, showed the picture of Hagouti and the struggles with the others, It saw Chloe and recognized her bow from an ancient world long gone, It saw Copret and Bofindle, It saw all the warriors and the fighting and how well Demeter was learning about the fortress and then with victory in their clutches, Crilodach heard the poet's words. A voice Its army did not hear. They were deaf to the poet's words because the words were not meant for them. But the magic in Crilodach's power stored every little thing, like a huge video library It accessed time-and-again to make sure It understood how Its enemies thought, moved and felt. Everyone in the room could listen to the words now. They saw Hagouti move away from Lilah as the words took hold but none of them saw Copret as he stared right at Crilodach almost as if he could see It through the magic It was using.

"Vingura," snarled Crilodach.

"Impossible, I killed him myself," gasped Rataplan.

"You killed the father. You never found the baby boy."

"But the throne has remained empty. The old servants said he was lost."

"The old hypocrite hiding away in a garden too scared to be a king. I should've known. I should've guessed. In that precious garden I wonder what else he did. Who else came there. He could not act alone, he doesn't have the power. That was not his voice but the perfume of his juices was on the speaker's breath."

"Do you want me to find out?"

"There's no point. Vingura's garden. A perfect place to make trouble. He was not born with enough magic in him to fill a thimble. He's extended his reach but the effort killed him. But he's had help. There are more of them. How'd he do this? He needs a channel. A trained person, strong enough to take me on? No, not possible. No, wait, an innocent person. Someone who does not know and isn't afraid? Yes! Yes, there's a new player here whose name I don't yet know. I don't yet see on Trecrogo. But I hear him. The one in the Ossendark. I hear the voice. But how's he finding the words?"

The men had known Crilodach for too long to ever believe It could be wrong about anything. It snarled and then It laughed and punched one of Its clawed hands into the stone which crumbled at the hit.

"Where did this poet come from? Of what is his voice made? Why can't I see his face?"

Rataplan didn't know what he was talking about and did not answer. Thankfully Crilodach was not seeking his answer.

"They're all there on that fortress," It continued, "They've played out their waiting game. The enemy's revealed to us. All tumbling into Trecrogo from different places. New faces with old powers. They must've buried themselves under mountains of stars to escape my spies. Their plans have been long–laid, but mine are deeper. You wait Tegriel, I've plots aplenty for you and mine span the whole of time just like yours."

"What should we do now?" Rataplan asked, steering Crilodach away from their past failure and on to new battles hoping to put their failure behind them and lessen the risk It would exact a revenge upon the lives of his children.

"We?" It snapped, "We? I left this critical battle to you and your lieutenants. You failed. What makes you think you'd succeed against them now?"

"We can't fail," said Rataplan.

"Of course you can. Do you think every victory was the victory I needed? Do you think every battle was a battle I chose? Do you think when you came to me for more men and more weapons and more power I didn't know you couldn't achieve a thing as you are?"

"No but ..."

"There are no 'buts', Rataplan. You've led my armies and for what you are, you've done pityingly well, but armies are nothing now. Pawns to be used for the blood they can shed. This is a battle of giants. Of minds. Of magic older than you know. Not all your cunning is enough to defeat one of them. Even I wasn't cunning enough to see how their plans have come together. They've played me. They've been clever. I longed for their deaths so much they gave them to me. Who knows how many of my enemies live at this moment? Maybe all of them. But where d'you hide the spirit of a Sangyma? And how d'you conceal such mighty magic from me?"

"What do we ... you do?" asked his general.

"What I always planned to do."

Crilodach despised Rataplan and Its other lieutenants. It knew they thought It was going to leave them behind to die. After all they had done for It, they really were as miserable as all other life.

"The time has come for me to lead my own armada," It said.

"You," said Rataplan.

"So surprised? I never fight but in the secret ways known to me. I've never needed to, but this place," It gestured around them, "this home from home for me is doomed. Just as the stars are vanishing so Damkina has come to the end. No better time for me to go out than at the end. Besides my enemies expect me. Do you think Trecrogo is there to stop you? Do you think they muster their might to stop you? Do you think Vingura sacrificed his life to stop you? Do you think Lilah was trained as the last of the spellmakers to stop you? What are you ... any of you and the all of all your armies? I've spewed you out of a thousand worlds as befits my will and feeds my hatred. All your efforts, all your powers you get from me. Before you ever lift a weapon your enemies quake at their knees because you go in my name. Even the fear in your hearts is from me. You see with my eyes, feel with my anger, kill with my arm. Do you think when they stand and fight you, they're fighting you? Who are you Rataplan? Fuevil. A species that continues to evolve while alive growing to be the very image of how you live. Is that terrifying? Do you think they don't see who their enemy is? I ... I am the all of you and more. I'm above you and beyond you. I'm the circle that encompasses everything."

It turned to Rataplan's lieutenants. It looked at them. If It could smile, It smiled now.

"I've new weapons for you. They've fought you all this time because that's what I expected them to do. Down the ages they chose battles and I've sent you. Don't be so surprised if my use of you has not been that which you expected. They've faked their deaths, giving me a semblance of victory. They've given up their bodies to keep me occupied, keep me believing I was making headway. Making them suffer blinded me to what they were up to. They suffered. They saw real death but the sacrifice was all worthwhile to them because the real enemy, me, was being fought on a level above the battles and the blood. Even the myths they let peoples create concentrated on our war. They saw in eventual peace, a hoped-for victory over me. Even those myths I now suspect were there to fool me. Peace was no victory. I carried on the war to give them something to think about. I'm not a creature of peace."

"Tegriel and I have always known everything would end in our lifetimes. We always played our war above those we fought with and even those that fought for us; especially those. How we've played. We've treated worlds like ping-pong balls, races like fetid ponds to be drained. Galaxies as no more important than a brief place to stay. Advancement and riches are nothing to us. Inducements for those with no magic in them." It turned on them with Its teeth showing, "I'm master of every atom in your bodies, I'm the observer of every thought in your heads and when I walk, eternal roads are created. So yes, Rataplan, now is the time for me to leave. Just as I came here and bent this world to my needs so now I leave. For now I've seen they expect me, I'll not allow them to wait. Come."

The general and lieutenants followed Crilodach, who now moved with some speed leaving behind the large, enclosed room that smelled so much of It. A smell of sleeplessness and loathing. A smell that would make you feel sick to the stomach. A smell that stopped you eating or thinking until you had cleansed everything you wore, scratching the smell from your skin. A smell that seeped beneath your skin and yes, there are those who have ripped their skin away trying to free themselves of the smell of Crilodach. Somehow this smell digs deep into your being. More like an experience than a smell. More like a being that wraps around you like a python and refuses to budge, gorging on your terror. Squeezing out your life. A diabolic energy breeding unwanted ideas in your head. Once you have met It, you live with that smell, that feeling, that sense of being a prisoner, forever, with everything you touch, feel and see being covered with Its stench. You can live with the odour, or let Its lingering presence kill you. You have to be strong whichever you choose. Like many things to do with Crilodach, Its greatest desire other than killing you, is to make you suffer.

The room shuddered as Crilodach left. The walls were sucked inwards as It vanished. The ceiling bowed downward as if Crilodach had been a pillar keeping the room balanced. As if the disappearance of Its presence could not be ignored by the walls. Like an unclouded sun in the daytime or the full moon on a clear night, which stand above and beyond, overlooking every action, watching every move, Crilodach's presence orbited Damkina. Without Crilodach the room had no purpose, like a night that would never be followed by day. The threats and commands Crilodach had given here, dripped off these walls, encrusted themselves on the large table covering everything with a layer of rich, thick dust made of dirt and fear. Commands that had etched themselves into the stone changing their purpose from walls to witnesses. Threats that squeezed pleadings from lost voices that still echoed in the departing footsteps of Its soldiers, begging for a mercy that never came.

As they left a small creature slid out from behind one of the pillars and walked slowly over to the table, obedient to the silent command given by Crilodach. Qolcrift was a secret Crilodach kept from everyone. A messenger It used to ferry information and orders to people and places Crilodach allowed no one, outside of Qolcrift, to even dream existed. Qolcrift walked to the table and there, in the air as he arrived, a bangle appeared. This contained the information Crilodach wanted delivered and ordinarily Qolcrift would have grabbed the bangle with his knotted fingers and taken flight to deliver the summons but he heard scratching and went to the wall, absent-mindedly putting the bangle in the dust on the table for a moment. Gertis, behind the walls, heard him and went stiff with quiet. Qolcrift shrugged, picked up the bangle and went his way leaving behind a small circular indent in the dust. From such things empires crumble for that indent in the dust would warn Tegriel that not all was well, not all was going to plan.

In the cavernous silence that was left after Qolcrift walked out of the room following Crilodach with Its general and lieutenants, there came again the slight scratching noise from behind a stone about a foot above the floor at the far end of the room opposite the archways leading out into the rest of the complex. Imperceptible but to the acutest ears, the scratching became a scrapping and grew louder until the dirt that was stuck between the crevice of two stones that had never moved, moved. Pushed out by tiny, eager legs. The dirt fell to the floor in a big clump, giving rise to small motes of dust dancing upwards in short–lived wisps, floating past the antennae of a cockroach that appeared at the entrance to this newly dug hole. The antennae kept coming out of the hole until Gertis heaved himself into mid air. His back legs kept pushing away, his front feet trying to grasp at something in the emptiness until they grasped the wall, bent over and pulled his hard shelled body sideways. His feet held his body to the wall and he turned to face downwards. The cockroach that came after him fell on to the floor as Midrak was not yet adept at vertical walking and his back legs came out before his front legs found anything to hold on to. Tobia immediately came behind him and she also fell, bouncing off his shell and finding herself some distance from the wall, she rolled upright and walked back towards him. The others all appeared in a multitude, twitched their antennae, then fanned out in all directions. They made a colourful mural against the wall and along the floor. As each one emerged they did the same thing, that briefest of moments when they stopped and twitched their antennae almost as if they could not believe where they were, and then they crawled out into Damkina.

Midrak and Tobia watched the others marching over all the walls. Many came down to the floor, passing them without a nod, heading for the corners. Everyone's antennae was moving rapidly. The dust burnt into the floor by years of Crilodach's heavy treading, was hard and prickly but was soon heaving with the torrent of crawling cockroaches. Some as they came out aimed for the ceiling. Others headed off to the table or the few other pieces of furniture that were standing in the room, holding various, mysterious bejals only a Sangyma would recognize even without the covering of dust. Some stood on their back legs and felt the air with their antennae trying to feel for any enemy who might be closing in on them. Scouts hanged from the archway looking further down into the complex. Gertis sent more of them deeper to find out what was going on, and importantly where

Crilodach was because he was sure It would be coming back not having heard the whole of Its conversation with Rataplan. Soon Its lair was heaving with alert cockroaches.

"Where are we?" Tobia asked, feeling the air with her antennae.

"A large, empty room," replied Midrak "keep close to the walls and do what the others are doing."

"That won't help if It or Its guards see us," she pointed out.

"Do so just the same, until we know better what's going on in this stinking warren."

"This was Its lair," Manfray told them, "The vile heart of Damkina. Where has It got to, that's the puzzle? That beast don't move without cause. Not ever. It has lived in this room longer than any of use have been prisoners in Hâgon."

The cockroaches walked along the floor as fast as they could, climbing over others who were stationery for the moment having found an interesting piece of dust or caught sight of a strange shape on a table, or a scent on the air that seemed strangely familiar. Or even just been staggered for a second that they were actually out in the open. Around Midrak and Tobia several other cockroaches stayed close, acting like bodyguards. These cockroaches, who had come out of the hole first after them, had been on these forays before. They knew just how dangerous to be anywhere in Damkina was yet would have given their meagre lives to protect their new friends. They also relished this rare chance to spy more closely upon Crilodach. Midrak knew they were protecting them, an idea that brought a smile into Midrak's mind though he would never have told them as much. Good intentions are always welcome.

In fact all of them were showing great bravery. He began to wonder how they were able to walk this room without being attacked. If he had not been here to see for himself he would not have believed such a thing possible. Thousands of cockroaches in the open with the spirits of three Sangyma at the very heart of Damkina and not so much as a shout or a stomp from the enemy. Crilodach must be as confident as they said It was.

"This place really does stink," Tobia told Midrak.

"The smell is overpowering," said Midrak.

"Gets to you doesn't it?" said Manfray, "This room's empty. No one's reporting a thing. No sign of It nor Its henchmen." He twitched his antennae, "They're saying there's something going down at the front gates."

"The room is not quite empty," corrected Tegriel, "Crilodach may not be here but this place is full. Quickly Midrak we need to get to that table."

"What do you want?" asked Midrak, setting off at a run.

"I want to check something," said Tegriel.

"I would feel safer if I knew where It was," Tobia said.

"Events have forced It to move out. Lilah is doing her work. Let's see if we can be of assistance to her," said Tegriel.

"Crilodach's leaving Damkina?"

Midrak spoke the words and they fell like deep bells upon the ears of all who heard him, sonorous with foreboding. He was saying something unbelievable. Unknown. Crilodach was on the move. The stunned feeling this generated was one that both he and Rataplan shared. The only thing they had ever shared. A feeling of amazement and impending catastrophe. Gertis ordered more scouts to send signals back to those still in the tunnels to reinforce the group at the front gates. Everyone had a standing order to report everything they could see, feel and hear.

In the darkness the cockroach army made their way across ceilings and floors. Scouts were everywhere now. Far behind them word had gone down the tunnels that It had gone. Messages were being sent hastily along their walkways. Many of those queuing up to follow Gertis now broke off and instead went to other places to help the search. Never had their world seen so much activity. Some picked up Its trail and sent word they were following. Others walked higher and further into Damkina than any cockroach had ever thought they could. They grew close to the noise that had drawn them to dark corridors, over cold, damp walls and finally to glassless windows outside of which the stars were shrinking. Here many watched in awe not only at an armada on the move but also the stars vanishing one by one. Not only did they try to count the armada before them, but they tried to work out, from what was left of the stars, where their homes were in relation to Damkina. How far away from their families had they been all these years? Yet, in all this they were also blissfully aware that for the first time there were no soldiers inside the complex.

The silence of the stars did not hold their attention as much as the cacophony from the armada. The noise of

Crilodach's armada preparing to leave was a mass of metal, of orders barked from already tired men, of marching and drilling, of huge engines being pulled into position along the entire front until they could not see anything else but the armada for as far as their antennae could tell. A heaving mass of men and machines preparing to embark for a siege. Battalions of men with different skills and tasks to perform, different weapons and hundreds of marshals. All moving as one. Everything the cockroaches saw was relayed to all the others. Even as Crilodach Itself marched out with Its general and lieutenant. Even as Rataplan peeled off to take command of his section while Frin-Ghirzan, Ferveiss and Jurveiss went to their sections.

Back in the lair the airwaves from Crilodach's movement still hummed around them. They could track where It had left through the set of archway doors. Word was brought to them from the scouting parties and all the while they searched the room, news flowed to them of armouries being emptied, caverns beneath the ground being opened, huge engines being rolled out, and everyone heading for the open ground outside the complex. Then they saw the armada in their heads as cockroaches can transmit images to each other. Crilodach, like a black mountain, snapping Its claws together as the encrusted dust shed from Its skin like vapour from a steaming volcano.

"Eventually we must follow It," said Midrak.

"Tell as many as possible to get here and start feeling around every crevice and hollow. We may find something here that will help us. Be careful, this place will hold many magical surprises and we are not immune from attack because we are small," said Tegriel.

What would attack us in an empty room? Has It set traps?" asked Manfray.

"There are bejals here. They will know which of us were once people and which were born cockroaches. You cannot fool them by appearances," said Tegriel.

"They may send warning alarms back to It if It has broken them," added Fulminar.

"We cannot help that," replied Tegriel. They moved up the table legs feeling their way carefully as they went and stopping every so often to feel the air with their antennae.

"What are we looking for?" Tobia asked.

"Anything that opens Its mind to us. Collect whatever you

find, we must investigate anything we can uncover," added Tegriel. "Gertis, you go to the door and scout outside but do not worry too much about other rooms. This is the hub of Damkina. This is where the most precious things will be found."

"Let's get on," replied Gertis, signally to a few to follow him.

The small army of cockroaches were over every stone, along the wrinkled ceiling, falling into piles of dust and digging out the hidden bejals. Feeling. Searching. Probing. Strangest of all for everyone of them who kept memories from their childhoods of the strength of Crilodach, of the power of Crilodach, of the depths of Its crimes and of all the deadly things of which It is capable, was to find this place, Its room, the centre of Its world – sparsely furnished. Simple stone. Only those whose own centre is magical, could have told you that each stone had a story to tell, that each shadow had a tragic history. That the blood–history of this place was concealed in every atom.

There was an energy here. An energy that Midrak could sense. Feel. Communicate with as if Crilodach had left a bit of Itself behind. A malevolent touch of Its claws. A tread of Its feet. A cough. Even the cockroaches felt there was a vibrating remnant of the life of Crilodach held within the stones. Tobia, if she had been asked, would have said the room needed to be healed. Fulminar would have said the complex needed to be destroyed. Tegriel would have said the lair needed to be analyzed. Had Rimfelder been here he would have opened up the Gaddia and looked for guidance from the thirty–six star touched magicians. He would have found some surprising ideas.

They all knew that Damkina was heavy with sadness. Up to now, being behind the stones had protected them from feeling too much. This room was connected to everything Crilodach had ever touched with Its mind. As if suffering had been used to glue the stonework instead of cement, and bound the stones together with tighter bonds than mere cement is capable of doing. As if this room belonged to the dead more than to Crilodach. As if Crilodach could only be understood by what It had done to others, and never be seen in any other light. Crilodach's endless list of victories were never marked with celebrations but here the cockroach army found they were remembered. The longer they stayed in this room the deeper these memories sank into them. As if memory were a weapon used by Crilodach to weaken Its opponents. They all began to feel devastated. Drained. Homeless. Depressed. Surrounded by the victories of their greatest enemy.

"Try not to listen to the stones," suggested Midrak to them all, "they will only make you miss something more important. Whatever they say happened long ago. Is gone. Is done. We must concentrate on what we can prevent."

"My thoughts exactly," said Fulminar to Midrak.

"They were your thoughts," Midrak reminded him.

They finally pulled themselves on to the table top. They crawled across a table more iron than wood, scurrying over the bejals strewn across the surface. Things that had never moved in millenniums. As if Crilodach were the worst of grasping collectors wanting only to own, never to show. Nothing was recognizable in this dust and muck, just a host of shapes suggestive of curves, flat sides and circles. You would have to have seen them placed on the table or at least have been here before the dust built up, to even know what you were looking at, or looking for. The cockroaches with each step they took with their many small legs gripping the stone like limpets gripping wet rocks on the seashore, were getting slower. Even as they tried to follow Midrak's advice the awfulness of this place was slowly driving them mad.

"We need to move on, the others are suffering," warned Tegriel, looking eagerly over the large table. Tobia could sense he was trying to stop himself letting her hear his thoughts. She wondered what could be so important, or so dangerous, that she should not be told.

Feeling, looking, wondering, the groups of cockroaches became more and more slow. At this time, with this room empty for the first time in history, there may be a chance to defeat Crilodach by attacking It from behind. To find out more about Its plans and so overturn them. But the spells that lived here were stronger than Sangyma magic. Like soldiers succumbing to gas they were being overwhelmed and the thoughts of success were turning to despair. Could they really defeat It?

Only Tegriel knew the answer. Tegriel who had always known the answers. The most far-sighted of all the Sangyma. He knew and yet he said nothing. Nothing about how he knew he would be here; how he knew Gertis would be here;

how he knew what Gertis had done; how he knew Crilodach
would be leaving to go and besiege Trecrogo leaving Its lair
open just as they arrived; how important the defeat of Its
army in front of Trecrogo had been in forcing Crilodach away
from Its lair; how important one of the bejals on that table
was to their entire existence.

He said nothing to them. How could he tell them that even
he did not know how the siege of Trecrogo ended. That even
he, after all the planning and trials ... that even he was in
the dark. For this was the moment that ended all his
knowledge. That knowledge had been an unswerving ally in
their fight but his life ended here. The time was close when
he would leave them all and the certainty, the courage, the
bravery he inspired could not go with him. He had to let
them believe in his unseen powers. He remembered how his
life would be. He waited for what he knew was coming. Inside
himself he feared what he did not know. He had known
everything to this point, but he would never know the
outcome. Never actually see Zaqui, fight beside Lilah or
stand upon the parapet with Copret. His story ended in
Damkina as completely as life had ended for all those who
ended up in Its labyrinth.

Tobia, crawling, feeling the air, looking left and right saw
on the table the smallest glint as one of the cockroaches
opened delicate wings and fluttered making the dust curl
upwards. She twisted propelled by Tegriel's sudden wish to
move and took flight, landing with a slight thump, all her
legs spreading to take the force of the fall. She felt around
her front feet and the small jewel that had shone and caught
her eyes had an unexpected warmth in the chill room. She
flew over the bejal in a tight circle, getting rid of more of
the dust, slipping slightly even with her sticky feet as the
jewels were so perfectly smooth and did not like being
walked over. Midrak joined her.

"What do you think this is?" asked Fulminar.

"I cannot believe I'm seeing this." said Midrak in a
whisper.

"Brush off more of the dust. Let's have a closer look."

Midrak, Tobia, Manfray and Balvieure carefully scraped
away the dust and the dirt on a triangular jewel that looked,
in this dim light, to be very beautiful. Glittering away
completely out of place in his dark and dank place where
there was little light. Leoprin, who had been walking across

the floor with about twenty others flew up on to the table and immediately came over. Even the look–outs looked from the archway. Gertis stared in wonder for a second and then moved everyone on to their tasks. Tegriel exuded an excitement even Tobia could feel. And something else. She felt a pang of apprehension. She wondered why. Then he suddenly changed as he noticed through her eyes, the imprint of the bangle in the dust on the far corner of the table. How had that gotten there? And his thoughts came so swiftly, Tobia picked them up and for several minutes she shared his state of utter confusion.

'Did I miss that,' he thought, 'the last time? How could I have forgotten? No this is new. How could anything be new? How can things change after so much time? It knows. It must suspect. Something is planned.'

Then realizing she was listening to him and how little sense he must be making he said,

"Hurry let me see."

Many of the cockroaches congregated upon the table, and all of them became busy with their wings to reveal four triangular opals set into a lattice–work of scented wood inlaid with gold thread. Each opal had an internal glow and they were set so that there was a small opening in the centre. In the scented wood were ancient letters, carved spirals, images of extinct animals many of which Rimfelder would have now recognized.

"Amazing," said Midrak, "you know I thought this was a myth."

"If we use this," said Fulminar, "Crilodach will definitely sense what we are doing."

"How did It get this? The Upala vanished so far in the distant past," said Midrak.

"Of all things It feared, the Upala fascinated It the most," revealed Tegriel, "owning this was essential. It expended much energy to grasp hold of this mighty bejal, and found It was unable to destroy such power."

"Can the Upala resist Crilodach?" asked Midrak.

"No, It could have destroyed the bejal, but It wanted to see if It could ever use the magic. I am sure It tried to many times, but they say the only ones who will ever be able to use the Upala are the Ruzniel," said Fulminar.

"How did we ever let such a wonder fall into Its hands," asked Manfray.

"I had too," replied Tegriel. "The Upala had to be here at this time for this was our time to open up her magic."

"You had too?" asked Leoprin, stunned.

"The Sangyma are never simple, I'll give them that," Manfray told him.

"Could we use this to go back in time to find the Sagitæ and work out where to go today to gather them together and defeat It?" Midrak asked him.

"What are you talking about," Tobia asked.

"The Sagitæ are bonded to a stream of magic and energy from the place of their birth, from a time close to that when Crilodach and the Sagitæ first came into history," Fulminar explained. "Finding their place at any time would give you the power to trace them throughout all time."

"That is a poor use of the Upala's potential," said Tegriel.

"Why?" asked Midrak.

"Because the Sagitæ are coming to us anyway. The universe is shrinking, none of us will have anywhere else to go but the space that is left to us."

"This is a wonder. Upala, the seeing stones," revealed Balvieure, "the only known magic that can take a person into the past. A Ruzniel at that. I'm guessing Tegriel chose you, Tobia, for a reason."

"Me! I've enough to do here without going back into the past."

"You have only just begun your life," Tegriel told her.

Tobia did not answer him. She was filled with apprehension and a sudden realization that this might be the very thing she had been meant to do. Carrying the spirit of Tegriel with her; the first to be chosen from all her family; staying behind to meet Midrak; all made a strange sense if her fate was meant to bring her here carrying a Sangyma into Damkina. The only way Tegriel would ever be able to get here, disguised and after Crilodach had been forced to leave by the works of those Tegriel had taught.

"Why was the Upala left here?" she asked.

"Not being able to use the Upala until this day, the next best thing I needed to do was to secure the bejal away from those who could," said Tegriel.

"You may never return once you go back. That's a limitation Crilodach would dislike. Besides without knowing from Hiesia herself who made the Upala, no one actually knows what happens. Do you choose where you go, are you actually there or just looking? Are you real or some kind of ghost? At least that's what we were told when we were young and first taught about bejals," said Balvieure.

"Any Ruzniel or do they have to be magical because I was told an ordinary Ruzniel would be killed by the journey," added Manfray.

"Could we change past events by going back in time?" Midrak asked Fulminar.

"There is no way of knowing if you go back with your existing memories intact," lied Tegriel.

"Where would we go anyway?" Tobia asked.

"To the beginning," said Fulminar. "Definitely to the beginning I have a few unanswered questions about Crilodach and the Sagitæ."

"What's so special about the beginning?" she asked.

"We can tell them there, what is happening now. How else can we help them plan for this moment. They will not be working in the dark if they know what's coming," said Fulminar.

"The only one here who can attempt do anything is Tobia," suggested Manfray.

"That's just a story," she argued.

"No, they are right. A Ruzniel must go," said Tegriel.

"We've no way of knowing if she'll succeed," said Balvieure. "Can we take the risk?"

"I have a good idea," Tegriel replied.

"We risk your life as well," Midrak pointed out.

"Then we must," said Tegriel.

"But going means losing you to this fight," went on Midrak.

"I know but actually I might be more effective in the past to aid your fight than anything I could do here, now," said Tegriel.

The idea was not lost on Midrak that if only one person can use the Upala the best way to increase the odds is to be inside that person in some magical way. He also noticed how Tegriel was forcing the pace of their discussion. He realized that Tegriel had planned this all along. He did not say anything. Nor did Fulminar. One thing he knew for certain was that Tegriel's plans were always sound.

"The rest of you can help Gertis when we are gone," went on Tegriel, "There may be more things here than we have time to uncover but we will never find anything as precious or as useful to us as the Upala. Come along Tobia."

They all nodded their agreement at this and then Midrak and Fulminar touched one of the opals of the Upala. Tobia touched another and slowly the jewels all shone and vibrated. The centre of the wood gave out a beautiful perfume. Unlike any they had ever smelled. The scent of life. Spicy and inviting. The Upadim spell covered them all. The terrible, heavy smell of Crilodach evaporated in an instant.

They all felt relieved. Manfray twitched his antennae in approval. In all the years of their captivity they had never been able to make one foray against Crilodach and now, out-of-the-blue, they seemed to be taking giant steps in their war. More cockroaches poured out of the tunnel bathing in the sweet scent. No longer did any of them fear anything. No longer did any of them find difficulty in placing one leg in front of the other.

Outside the cockroaches watching the armada noticed Crilodach looked back. At first the beast moved as if to go back inside but then It stopped. A satisfied look on Its face betrayed Its thoughts. Then It turned back and urged Its armada to get a move on.

Midrak was touching the Upala which still glowed. Tobia was gone. Gertis stroked his head with his front legs. So much became clear to him. And the majesty and brilliance of Tegriel which had always been a beacon to him, now transformed in his mind to a deep sense of awe.

"I will miss her," Midrak said to himself.

"She has a great task ahead of her and the best of friends in Tegriel to help her," said Fulminar.

"You ... knew this was going to happen?" asked Midrak.

"Because Tegriel told me he could transfer himself into another being, I learned how. When I saw him in Tobia I suspected. Besides, I am his oldest friend that should come with a few privileges."

"You almost got us both killed!"

"Yes, well Tegriel is a bit scant sometimes on the exact dangers of the Saldin merging spell and he was helped by Tobia being so young and having an open mind. As we grow older the mind closes up so merging becomes far more dangerous if not impossible."

"Do you know what her task is?" asked Midrak.

"Tegriel said Tobia had great work to complete. He never told us what. Nor did he ever suggest he knew; although I think he did. I think he knew everything there was to know give or take a few incidentals. The Upala is worth her weight in spells for she has given us our greatest weapon, knowledge."

"That's why Tegriel always knew a good deal about so much," said Midrak, "He knew he'd go back. He had all our futures in his head because he'd lived with us before."

"That is the truth," agreed Fulminar.

"So he can change things. Make them better. Save lives."

"He will change nothing," said Fulminar,

"Why would he change nothing?" questioned Gertis, from outside, his mind giving thousands of orders and keeping up with their conversation at the same time.

"There are great dangers in changing what you know will happen. If you do, you no longer have control of the outcomes. Everything you knew will become useless to you the second you change one event."

"But he could stop Crilodach being created."

"If he could, I am sure he would, Gertis. But I doubt any of us or all of us together could do that. I do not think he was able to go back that far anyway though I do not know for sure."

The light faded, Gertis looked across and down at the Upala. Midrak looked around half hoping to be somewhere else too.

"This was all planned" said Midrak. "Finding Tobia was the spark. He knew he would journey with her. That she would bring him here with us."

"This is his life, to go back from Damkina now, to bring us all safely to this point," agreed Fulminar.

"That is how he knew to find us," said Gertis. "And how so many times he was right about his prophecies. He wrapped up as predictions what he knew with certainty."

"I am happy knowing he has gone back to do his good work," said Fulminar, "Everything is as he wanted."

"Why did no one tell me?" asked Midrak.

"Why should they?" asked Balvieure.

"You feel he did not trust you enough to tell you," said Fulminar.

"Does my sister know?" asked Midrak.

"Lilah knows without being told," replied Fulminar.

"I felt so lost when I met Tobia, I would have liked to have known what was really going on," Midrak said.

"You would always have been asking questions about things being as they should be," said Gertis, "We all would. Tegriel did as he had to, he guided people without them knowing. Can you imagine if Crilodach found out we all looked to Tegriel for certainty? It would have known for sure how Tegriel knew." Midrak immediately realized that Gertis was right.

"You imagine how many missed heartbeats he must have had when people did things ever so slightly differently," said Manfray.

"All part of Tegriel's genius," said Fulminar.

"Sometimes being lost is a very good place to be Midrak," added Gertis, "Though I too would have enjoyed knowing more, Tegriel being less cryptic in his predictions would not have been better for us."

"Well, he certainly looked upset when we heard you had vanished," Fulminar pointed out. "Not at all as he would have had he known where you were."

"In every great magician there is something of the great actor," smiled Gertis. "Wherever he is, we are not there, we are here. You two might want to come and see this. Look."

They looked with their cockroach senses and saw Crilodach marshalling his vast armada. Like ants getting on to leaves to cross a river in flood, they were forming themselves into ranks on ground that split from the planet into Rounds, huge upturned coned sections of the planet underpinned by miles of rock, sailing into the distance in a long unbroken line. Sailing into the darkness of the universe. Thousands were already sailing off and more were going. Long lines of tapering rock all different shapes and sizes, all holding men and machines. All going to one place. Trecrogo. Strange weapons were being loaded as Crilodach oversaw the embarkation. As each battalion was ready It thumped the ground and another piece of the planet floated away. A constant stream. A constant din. It roared Its approval.

"Taking everything with It, It can," observed Midrak.

"Crilodach will lead for the first time in person," said Fulminar.

"This is an armada preparing to break a fortress without a doubt," said Leoprin.

"It wants everything the fortress holds," said Gertis.

"That's the only place that interests It right now," agreed Fulminar.

"We do not have Tegriel to tell us what is going to happen any longer," cursed Midrak.

"No we are on our own," agreed Fulminar.

"We must warn them," suggested Gertis.

"They have Lilah. She will know what is coming. I also think Sanjava left a surprise for It in the fortress and we must not forget, although he did not build the fortress, Filvani's magic is in the roots of Trecrogo. We must make sure in leaving Damkina, that It has nothing to return to," Fulminar told them. "Then follow It."

"We cannot destroy Damkina," said Midrak.

"That is exactly what we must do. We should set charges everywhere, meanwhile the cockroaches should assemble in ranks and get on to those Rounds. We must go wherever the armada goes."

"We might be of some use in a battle, maybe even take out a battalion or two if we transform back to our real selves," suggested Gertis.

"We would have the element of surprise," agreed Midrak.

"We might not do much but we could do something. So many of us are itching to have another chance. They have been quiet so long. They didn't find maintaining their tempers while watching Crilodach every day easy," added Gertis.

"Very well you get your army together and I will set the charges with Midrak. Just one last look in case we have missed something vital here. I would hate to miss something of importance," Fulminar said.

"What you say is true enough Fulminar but if anything else had been here would Tegriel not have told us?"

"He would not have known," pointed out Midrak, "after all, if he has done this before, he does not know anything about what happens after he leaves us if he just left us at same moment when he left us before."

The long age of prophecy was truly over. Even though the scented smell of magic hanged around them they felt a deep sense of loss. The brilliance with which Tegriel had guided them to this moment, had to be matched by their own devotion to finishing the war. Everything depended on them. They had climbed this mountain using Tegriel's knowledge like strong guide-ropes but only their own skills could haul them to the summit.

"Do you think he succeeded in all he had to do?" asked

Midrak.

"How would we know. If anything changes we are still living with the results with no memory of how things were."

"We will not achieve a thing standing here looking," said Midrak shaking his head.

"I will leave the scouts with you," agreed Gertis, "they know their business and the more antennae you have the better. Do not be long, the rate that armada is going they will have all embarked in an hour."

"Hurry up, we don't have much time," urged Balvieure, making to go back to the lair.

Midrak went back to the lair. Fulminar noticed one more thing on a shelf high up near the ceiling. Midrak flew up and walked over to a bottle holding a bright blue liquid. The bottle was twice their size.

"There you see, we might have lost this for good," he said.

"Smells weird," said Midrak.

"Did you ever do any alchemy?" asked Fulminar.

"A little."

"This bottle is worth more than all the gold in the universe. Here, I'll make this small enough to take in your mouth."

"As you wish."

The bottle shrank and Midrak held the cordial with his mandibles and kept it steady with his maxillae.

"The glass tingles," he told Fulminar, with his mouth full.

"So would you if you were as potent a magic as that."

"What about the next bottle?"

"That can cure all wounds. That's not a bejal we will need in the short time left to us."

They flew off the shelf. Midrak and Fulminar ordered the scouts out of the room. Threads fell from behind Midrak as he flew out, sinking into the dust and stones until the whole room was covered. As they flew he covered every room until some twenty were primed to explode. Then with the help of the scouts they laced the corridors until they ran out of threads. Their hour was almost up. Gertis anxiously came to find them

"Hurry or you will miss your place, the last Rounds are leaving."

As they hurriedly flew out they saw cockroaches already filing into tunnels hidden beneath the Rounds, as pieces were torn away and floated off to join the rest of the army individual cockroaches scrambled into them from below their small legs kicking in empty space as their comrades pulled them in.

Midrak, Gertis and the last few, flew into one Round and raced down, cramming themselves into the cavities where many others had gone before them. Here they waited. The ground shook and the rocks beneath them split. Suddenly they were moving. Floating. Fulminar looked behind them through the open end of the tunnel and saw Damkina vanishing into the distance at a frightening speed. More than half the planet was ripped open and gone. The rest was tipping over like a deflating balloon.

"I hope we have done the right thing," whispered Midrak.

"We cannot do anything else but stay close to Crilodach and watch Its every move," replied Gertis.

"What is that?" asked Midrak, as he traced a light in the distance with his front leg, heading towards the planet crossing their line of vision. "Certainly not a star."

"That is the Ossendark. Someone or other is travelling to Damkina," said Gertis.

"Who?" asked Midrak.

"No matter who," said Fulminar, "all of our allies should be at Trecrogo."

"I hope you are right," replied Midrak.

"Maybe someone should've stayed behind to double check no one else can use the Upala," said Balvieure.

"Only another Ruzniel could and they do not work for Crilodach," said Fulminar.

With that comforting thought they decided not to worry about who was arriving on the remnants of Crilodach's world. The traps would set off explosions which would kill them and destroy everything including the Upala. They had their own battle before them. Gertis shifted slightly on his legs as if getting comfortable.

"I always seem to have to be underneath Crilodach," he complained.

"We endure a lot for our cause," replied Midrak with the bottle still in his mouth. "I will be glad when I am not breathing though my sides and have a nose again. Who would choose to be a cockroach."

Land of Exiles

Despite the searing heat billowing from the laval ocean, Rimfelder felt a sharp chill in his bones. The last few days he had felt lost, abandoned, confused, afraid and finally empowered. The loneliness of someone watching cosmic chaos. The sense of being detached from everyone else, like an arrow without a bow, an empty bullet cartridge, or a dead battery unable to energize anything.

The pressure in the universe was rising as matter contracted towards Zaqui. The intensity of the pressure was sending ripples throughout space, joining things together that had never been joined. Hot and cold were coming together in one, inescapable moment. All memories and all times were becoming one. Matter was changing, reacting with time in a new and different way. No longer content merely to be the foundation to everything, time elongated some reactions and contracted others. In some spots time dipped, stopped and vanished with no warning. Time was interacting with space. As Filvani proved in his now famous equation the energy at Zaqui would equal the mass of all the magical particles in the universe multiplied by all the time there had ever in the universe, squared,

$$e = mt^2$$

Out of the dark wastes of deforested space, there came an energy like a huge breath drawing in. Motion mutated matter into senses that were in open rebellion to Zaqui as everything tried to survive. The residue of the heat from spells no longer dissipated into empty space for space was no longer empty. Everywhere was oppressive to a living being. Sharp. Cruel. Ending. Like a huge ballet without dancers, a book without words, a sentence conveying no meaning.

Evolution was over.

Rimfelder knew the impossible, the indefinable was everywhere. If he had seen icebergs floating in the laval ocean that stretched out in front of him as far as his eyes could see, he would not have raised an eyebrow in surprise.

He wondered how Lilah was and his stomach trembled at the idea she might be hurt.

The invisible crew piloted the äis, one of only two such craft ever created, this one shaped like a boat, with calm skill, or perhaps the boat was piloted by magic and no crew. He wasn't sure. The heat billowing up from the surface of the lava served for a breeze filling the single, large, red mainsail. The tiller moved without a hand's guide cutting through the laval ocean but leaving no wake. He had no idea where he was going, but he could see a landless ocean of fire ahead of him stretching way into the dim horizon, burning with a malice that ate into his skin and tried to dry out his blood.

He felt alone. He had to face whatever was to be faced with nothing more than the Gaddia. He clutched the book to his chest wishing he had armour. His fingers gripped the cover tightly, hoping that the power of the magicians was enough to see him through. He watched as everything evaporated into one long, rolling laval–flow. Bubbling. Slow. Searing. He did not move a muscle for a long time. Scared he might tread in the wrong place, or as one does when watching someone on stage, suddenly fearing to watch them in case one becomes them, and how that would ruin the performance because one does not possess their talent. He stood as a statue would stand, on the prow of the boat. He curled his toes in fear that the boat could vanish in an instant and he would be burned to less than ash in no time at all. Once again he wished Lilah were there with him. Once again he missed Tethval.

He only had to see the face of Lilah in his head and her steady gaze and inner strength gave him the will to face the unknown. Her voice filled his mind so completely the unbidden warnings in his head simmered down, then slept. His breathing became soft and steady. Despite the fact that flames shot into the air licking at the sail from the bow, he placed his faith and his life in the Gaddia and in Lilah.

He looked over the side. The heat was so intense he felt his eyes begin to dry out instantly and his hair singe. He ducked back. He did not try to look again. In that instant he was sure he had seen living things in the laval ocean, but then again he was sure he must be dreaming. He did not want to even imagine what could live in such a place or what torture they endured, or worse, what torments they could inflict. He was covered in sweat from the moment he had stepped on to the gangplank wondering if he was doing the right thing and deciding he had forgotten what the right thing was long ago. He sat with his back to the bulwark, eyes shut, and tried to imagine green fields, fresh water streams, long, cool drinks and icicles hanging over snow. The odd minnow darting amongst the rocks, the odd frog croaking, the odd dragonfly dipping and hovering. He was two people at once. A poet who only wanted to write and an adventurer doing his part. In what? A fight that did not lead to anything but defeat, yet in that defeat seemed to give meaning to the whole of history. Perhaps, in truth, all he had become was a man struggling to get back to Lilah.

He began to hear a rhythm in the bubbling and hissing of the laval ocean beneath him. Not quite music but not quite unpleasant. How strange was this experience for him, to be on an ocean that was not a real ocean, in a boat that should not be able to float on lava, holding a book that had many empty pages that he was supposed to fill without having any idea of what to write, or even what to write with. That first poem had appeared as if he had been no more than the catalyst for the words. Maybe he did not have to write down anything, maybe his part was simply to be here. To be there. Wherever there or here happened to be. Not as a pawn in a greater game, but a living purpose.

The ship sailed on. The heat rising and forming a thick vapour that made his clothes crisp and hot, drying out his nose until his nostrils itched. He scratched his back and neck with fingernails that ached they were so overheated. He went into the cabin. Inside there were a few chairs and a table. Marble. Cool to his touch. He laid the book down and pulled off the cover of the barrel on the floor to find sweet water. Whether the barrel had been put there for him or had appeared because of his need, he did not much care. He drank. But no matter how much he drank there never seemed enough. He was sweating more. His hair was dank. His scalp itched more than his nose. He bathed his face and hands. Water dripped on to his sleeves which he watched turn to steam.

How was he surviving this journey?

He opened the book.

The page with the sonnet was still there. He turned a page. He was fearful for a second as his eye fell upon the empty page. The Gaddia had let him turn a page, that must mean he was to do something. A drop of water from his wet lips fell on to the page. The water soaked into the page and spread out. The paper moved like a tide up and down the book, back and forth as if being prepared for a water colour and slowly words materialized in the dampness. Crisping the paper. Flowing letters in blue and gold script but Rimfelder could not understand them. He had no clue as to their language or sound. He waited, looking at the book for guidance. Nothing more happened. He tried to turn another page but was not allowed to. He tried to turn a page back, but the book was fixed. He bit his lip.

"This is ridiculous," he muttered under his breath. "How am I supposed to know what to do?"

He coughed, his throat was dry. His lips were dry and cracking. He could taste his own blood on them. His eyes wanted to close in sleep but every time he moved his hot clothes made him feel very uncomfortable. He had cast off his coat. He paced up and down the room glancing continuously at the Gaddia in case things changed but the page never altered and the language remained indecipherable. He closed his eyes and held the images on the page in his mind hoping for some revelation. Nothing came.

"Maybe this isn't meant for me," he thought.

He splashed some more water on his face and hands. He ran out on to the deck and he felt his hot clothes against the back of his legs. They hurt. He called out,

"Hello ... Anyone ... Is anyone here ... Hello?" He was greeted with silence. Aggravated he tried again. "I need help reading something. If anyone could help me?"

No one answered. He doubted there was anyone here to answer. Besides if anyone was here why should they answer him? Like the others they would know what was going on, he was the only one in the dark. Dark. He smiled a cracked-lip smile. The laval ocean lit up everything. He would never see so much as a shadow here. He went back into the cabin and dipped his head into the water throwing back his hair and letting the water run down his back under his clothes. The steam rolled away from his head and towards the ceiling. He felt his ears tingle.

The ship sailed on, flames tasting the hull. A strange nightfall descended when the lava gave off such a burning light the night sky was almost invisible and what he could see was only through the heat haze that enveloped the ship without enveloping him. There were no stars. In fact for all he knew he was not even above ground. He walked to and from the open book all the time, and even looked closely around the ship, seeing if there were any clues to the words and their meaning. But from top deck to bottom the whole ship was empty. He was beginning to worry he would not find any food until a small plate of dry beans appeared in the cabin, on the table next to the book, they tasted sweet and peppery. Probably something from Vingura's garden, he thought. He half hoped, as he ate, they would magically teach him to read the language on the page. They did not. He scratched the growth of beard on his face. Hairs broke off they were so dry.

His agitation grew like a gnawing hunger getting worse and worse, giving him a headache. He found no rest. Why did they not arrive somewhere? When would something – anything – happen? Lilah had told them all time was pressing. How much longer would he be here, a trapped mariner, imprisoned on an empty ship, seconds from certain death? He did not even know what sustained the ship. He began to imagine the ship evaporating again and the grisly death he would have and what would happen to the book? So much seemed to rest on his doing well and all he could see were the flaws and cracks that would spoil his every effort. Somewhere inside himself he heard his voice saying, 'no one said you would find things straightforward,' to which he answered himself, 'and no one said I would be faced by the impossible.' His bones clicked when he walked. He sat down with his back to the cabin drifting off in his mind to better days and happier times. The heat was driving him mad.

In this mood, fretful and not paying attention, he had not noticed the ship had stopped for a full three minutes. Only when he looked up and saw a unique shadow over the deck that made him jump up, did he see the land. A long, thin, tapering rock rising from the sea like a tower, steaming along a shoreline against which the laval ocean lapped without ever ebbing. A rock shoreline holding out against the lava. A magic island. Accessible only by sailing on an äis. Only now.

As if the unseen crew knew what he was thinking before he did, a long plank slid across from the ship to the shore above the steam landing on two wide, flat, black boulders. Rimfelder went into the cabin and picked up the Gaddia and cradling the open book in both arms, stepped on to the plank, got his balance, and quickly walked on to the outcrop of rock that should never have survived in the laval ocean. Up to that moment he considered that walk the bravest thing he had ever done. Before long he would be doing far braver things.

The lowest rocks were blackened by fire as he scrambled along the only narrow path. He could see his hands covered with the fallout of the burning stone, a fine-powdered, greyish dust. Soon his hair was matted and his clothes seemed to become heavier and heavier. He brushed them down but no sooner had the heavy dust gone than fresh returned. When he reached the top of the path he looked to all intents-and-purposes as if someone had emptied a ton of powder over him. He shook the dust from the book and looked around through eyes burning with the hot dust. He wished he had left the book behind and come with the barrel of water.

Three naked men sat in different parts of the flat, bare area in front of him. Their skin blistered, their hair unkempt, their large, six digit feet almost black with dirt, their tough blackened toenails like claws. Their suffering features would have warned anyone that they were strangely affected but Rimfelder was so glad to see other living beings, he ignored his first impressions.

"Hello," he said, knowing he was going to get an answer because these men had to be magical too but they did not even look up. He wiped the sweat and matted dust from his forehead and said louder,

"Hello."

His throat was dry and in this hot atmosphere he sounded different. More choked and rasping, as if he were speaking over the low continuous beat of drums coming from far away.

Then he noticed the odd things about these men. One was rocking back-and-forth as he sat muttering to himself and shooting glances at the other two as if he were certain they were conspiring against him. Another was playing a game of chess but every time he made a move he would laugh and sometimes he would get angry and point at the empty player in front of him and shout,

"Can't do that move. Can't do that move. Not allowed.

Cheat. Cheat."

The third man sat with his hands wrapped around his knees, his eyes staring blankly in front of him. Streaks of dust encrusted his cheeks where he had been crying but the tears had flowed generations ago. They were all showing signs of mental distraction. None of them moved very far from a small area around them. None of them talked to the others. Almost as if they were deliberately ignoring each other, though they were no more than a few feet away from each other. As this third man, even in his miserable hunched state, seemed to Rimfelder to at least be thinking about something, he approached him first, standing directly in front of his staring eyes.

"I'm Rimfelder," he told him slowly.

The man's head turned up and he looked at Rimfelder without seeing him, his cracked lips opened showing a set of sharp, white and yellow teeth that were definitely animal. His eyes were lizard–like slits, yellow and dull. His bones showed through his dust covered, calloused skin.

"I would speak to you," he said in a monotone, his voice deep and sonorous, "but I've no tongue."

"You must have a tongue if you can speak," Rimfelder pointed out, who had seen the deep red tongue moving as the man spoke.

"Yes one must but I can't as I lost mine. I can't shake your hand I've no hands you see. I'd hands once. I'd a tongue once. But no more. I can't walk. I've no legs. I'd legs once. A long time ago. I know I did but I can't see them now. I can't see anything for I've no eyes. I think I must be dead for I've no heart. No beat at all. Chest all empty. I'm sure you have a heart though. And legs. Good for you. Look after your heart."

"But I can see your hands," Rimfelder told him. "And your eyes and legs and you're alive so you must have a heart."

"Of course you can but they aren't there really. I'm not here really. I hear you but you're not speaking. I'm not really hearing."

"Where are you?"

"Here."

"But you just said you weren't here."

"No I said I wasn't here really."

"I don't understand."

"None of us do. You can't understand until you've some

idea of what's going on but how can you have an idea of what's going on if you can't understand? You can't even begin to understand. Here's all you know and what here is or why here is you've no idea. I've no idea either. Ideas are for people who understand. No matter how I try, I never understand." He leaned forward like a conspirator, "You have to be careful of ideas here though. They don't belong here and get very upset at being here. You know there's nothing worse than a mad idea."

"I'm sure you could understand if you tried hard enough," argued the poet.

"I'm not sure of anything. I tried to understand you know. But nothing's there to be understood. Here," he handed Rimfelder a small, flat dusty stone which had been worn smooth by his endless rubbing with his thumb. "This is here. This is all I know. I've many others. I'll leave them to you in my will."

Next to him were thousands of small, worn stones. Rimfelder looked at them. How long had these men been here for him to accumulate so many? Rimfelder took the stone that was so hot he got burned. He blew on his hand but his own breath was very hot. He bit his lip which ripped and bled some more. He wondered if he was going to become like these three. Had the boat brought him to the wrong place? Was he to be imprisoned here in some nightmare? He moved away, to the man who was playing chess and sat in front of him where his invisible opponent was sitting.

"Ah so, here at last," he said. Rimfelder was cheered the man was obviously expecting him.

"I've this book ..." the poet began.

"I hope you stop cheating now."

"I only just got here."

"I saw you try to move the knight one extra square."

"I'm not here to play chess," Rimfelder told him.

"Aren't you?" The man looked at him, "are you a crab?"

"No."

"Thought as much. Was pretty sure they couldn't live in the dust and heat. They need water you know. They can play chess though. Good players too in a pincer–claw kind of way. They can move the pieces faster. But they don't play fair, all that clicking away with their front claws. Puts a player off. But that's what they want to do. Put you off. Psychological, chess playing crabs. Beat the player not play the game. All

games are won in the mind, all minds are lost in the game.
I don't like playing crabs. Now sea horses is another thing
altogether. Wild players. All eyes. They can see you thinking
about your next move. Can't beat a sea horse, no use trying."

"I didn't know."

"Now you do. You can't do that."

"Can't do what?" asked Rimfelder.

"That," said the man, taking a pawn on Rimfelder's side
of the board and moving the piece forward two squares.
Rimfelder felt uncomfortable. These men made even less
sense than the book.

"Water," mumbled the third man, overhearing them.
"That would be something, water. I think water was cool
and ran in huge rivers I could bathe in. Pools of water. No
dust just water."

"There's no water here you know that." snapped the first
man, "Not for us."

"You don't think there's anything," snapped back the
second man from his chessboard, without looking up.

Rimfelder realized the men were all deranged. They were
trapped. Endlessly looping their thoughts around the same
subjects. He saw at last that this island set in a laval ocean
formed some kind of prison. Perhaps they had been
imprisoned long enough to be driven mad. Maybe they were
sent here because of their madness. Without his boat he
realized he would be just like them after a while. Huddled
in his own corner, trying to make sense of nothing and
letting the nothing that hanged all around them become his
only thought. He stood up and took them all in, in one
glance,

"I've a ship waiting," he told them. "We could leave here
if you wanted." His voice was loud and clear so they could
all hear him. None of them looked up. None of them moved.

"There are no ships," said the first man.

"Oh shut up, Clevian," said the man playing chess and
then he turned to Rimfelder, "he never knows what's what
anymore. He used to be good at chess. Relied on the bishop
too much though. I beat him so much he tried to tell me
chess didn't exist any longer. He left off playing. Left me to
face this cheat. Cheat, I saw that!"

"There's no chess," said Clevian.

"See," said the man, without smiling. "There's no Clevian,
that's for starters."

372

"There's no Clevian?" said Clevian, "That's the first sensible thing you've said since we got here."

"How long have you all been here?" asked Rimfelder.

"Xibalba knows," said the chess player.

"Water," said the third man. "Did you bring water?"

He was looking at Rimfelder. Somehow Rimfelder knew there was a part of all of them that knew he was there, but they were all too confused to have a conversation with him. Or maybe they were struggling to tell him what was really happening but could only do so within their limited allowance of words. He had no answers for their problem but the book Vingura had entrusted to him, did. That was when Rimfelder did one of the cleverest things he had ever done.

"Can you read this?" asked Rimfelder, showing them one by one the open page of the Gaddia with the odd writing. He walked to each of them with the book open and they glanced briefly.

"I can't read," Clevian told him. "Eldet can. He enjoys reading." Clevian motioned to Rimfelder to come closer and whispered in his ear, "He's still got his eyes you know."

"None of you seem to be able to read."

"Take the book closer to him. Go on," suggested Clevian.

"Which one is Eldet?"

"He's over there rocking back and forth like a man on a camel. He used to like books when there were books to be liked. Of course he may not be there. I know he went to sit over there oh ... ages ago. Whether he stayed there or just left his shadow I'm not sure. Although how he left a shadow without a body I don't know. There's so much not to know you could fill your mind with all I don't know and still not find everything that needs to be there."

"Eldet," asked Rimfelder, "can you read this?

He set the book down in front of the man who rocked back and forth as always, yet as his eyes saw the words suddenly he stopped rocking. His eyes fixed on the book. For the longest time he did not move.

"Cheat! Cheat!" said the chess player a few times.

Clevian stared blankly at a stone but Eldet's eyes focussed. Rimfelder saw them moving right to left as he read. Light came back into them. He blinked. He raised his tired hands and rubbed the dirt from his forehead. He tried to spit on his hands to clean them but he had no saliva in his dry mouth. He looked up at Rimfelder after a few moments and then down at himself and around the whole area, taking in Clevian and his brother Opiar. He scratched his bald head and beardless face and rubbed at the dust on his skin and on his hands. He rubbed his fingers and flicked underneath his encrusted fingernails. As if he was seeing for the first time. As if remembering. Rimfelder felt a buzz of anticipation as Eldet's lips moved.

"Still a man," he whimpered. "Still alive." And then after a pause he added, "The spell must have worked."

His voice came out soft and strained as he had not spoken properly in a long time. He brushed off his legs and taking Rimfelder's shoulder to steady himself he lifted himself up. His bones clicked and dust blew up all around them until they both coughed fit to burst.

"Hold the book steady my friend," he told Rimfelder.

He read out loud, the words Rimfelder could not understand, written in Ebiric, the language of the laws,

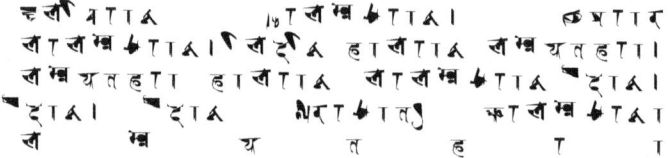

"Clevian Lilomian, Opiar lilomian, Eldet halian lowthia, lowthia halian lilomian. Edan, Edan, Edan frimatu Kilomina lowthia."

After he spoke the Gaddia closed sending the dust that had collected on the pages into the dry air. The three men slowly came to their senses from the depths of a distant place where their minds had walked for many years. They rubbed their tired eyes and stared at each other. Their clothes returned to them as if being painted on to their bodies, heavy with dust and crispy-dry with the heat. They saw Rimfelder from the corners of their eyes and with that instinctive understanding Rimfelder had come to associate with magical folk, they accepted his presence as that of a friend. They all saw the book. He was sure that helped make up their minds about him.

"Friend," said Clevian, getting up and shaking Rimfelder by the hand, "Crilodach said we would be here until Zaqui. Is the time come?"

His eyes were clear. His hand was hot. Rimfelder was glad the book had brought them out of whatever enchantment they had been under.

"I believe so yes," replied the poet. "As far as I know less than two days"

"I need some new clothes," said Opiar, "in fact we all do. These have turned into rags."

"I think there'll be some on the ship that brought me here. The closets were full." Eldet looked at the poet and at his brothers,

"Did Hiesia send you?"

"I've no idea who Hiesia is."

"No? She's a mystic. She was teaching us. We're graduates of her school you might say," said Opiar. "Before we were found and brought here."

"I've come on a ship across a burning sea. I was brought here by the Gaddia. I think I was brought here to find you. I don't know where you fit into the picture."

"The burning sea is Phigata, that's what makes Xibalba the perfect setting to create our prison. Crilodach must be busy not to have stopped you. The Gaddia you say, did you hear that?" Clevian asked his brothers, "Vingura remembered us."

"Yes, yes all very fine but none of us are doing any good standing here. Let's get on to this ship," suggested Opiar.

"Do you have any food," asked Eldet, "I don't seem to have eaten in the longest time."

"We've all lost a little weight," agreed Opiar.

The brothers all laughed and Rimfelder did not understand the in-joke for a while, until they eventually turned back into dragons and he saw just how much weight a dragon loses becoming a man. The three brothers walked back behind Rimfelder leaning on each other as their legs got used to walking again. They looked down at the ship.

"That's an interesting vessel," smiled Clevian, divining the aura of an äis.

"Just what we need," agreed Eldet.

"We are honoured to have safe passage in such a vessel," said Opiar.

They slapped the poet on the back and for the first time he felt relaxed because being in the company of such dragons is always a warm and comforting experience. They all walked down in a procession to the plank and marched aboard with such vigour the plank bounced wildly. Opiar touched the gunwales and pinched himself.

"Just the thing," he said.

"Trust the Gaddia to think of an äis," added Eldet.

Clevian said nothing but looked and scratched his head lost in thought. The ship started to leave the craggy island outpost and they were not a mile away when the island began to sink. The three men watched as their ancient prison vanished into Phigata, aflame, leaving behind a thin wisp of smoke to tell where the island had been. When that dissipated there was nothing to say anything had ever been there.

"Do you think that happened because we'd left," asked Eldet, "or did we leave just in time to escape Crilodach's final execution?"

"I doubt we'll ever know," replied Clevian.

"Unless our new-found saviour can tell us," suggested Opiar.

"There's no use asking me anything. I'm as much in the dark about you, and where we are, to be of much use in explaining things."

"As to that I'm well aware of who I am and where we are," replied Eldet. "We're the three dragon brothers that guarded the Sagitæ entrusted to us by Tegriel ages ago."

"You know about the Sagitæ?" asked Clevian.

"A bit," replied Rimfelder. "Lilah mentioned something about them before sending me here. My friends are even now trying to keep them from Crilodach's claws."

"Well It never got to ours," smiled Clevian, "though It did get to us and imprisoned us in Xibalba."

"I suppose we're going to find that Sagitæ now."

"What makes you think so?" asked Opiar.

"This ship brought me to you, and the Gaddia which was given to me by the thirty-six magicians, contained the words that broke your spell so I assume we're on the way to do more work. Lilah said we've to make sure It never gets Its claws on them. Best way to do that is have them on us."

"What do you think about that?" asked Clevian.

"I never knew the Gaddia possessed the power to free us." replied Opiar, "Vingura found the way. He was always so clever with those drinks and potions. He was ever excited about his 'exotic chemical compounds.' I shouldn't have been so amused by him. He obviously knew a thing or two."

"Took his time," grumbled Eldet.

"Had to," suggested Clevian, "If we were freed before Zaqui then It would have come after us. Our sons are too useful to It to be lost."

"Now I suppose Its too busy with everyone else to bother with us," said Opiar.

"Then we're free at just the right time," said Eldet. "I'll be delighted to see Tegriel again even if we're not to have very long."

"Tegriel's dead," said Rimfelder.

They were thrown into a respectful silence at the news.

"Are you certain?" asked Eldet.

"From what I heard all the Sangyma are dead. Its just Lilah."

"Not heard of her," said Opiar. "Is Bofindle alive?"

"Yes, she has Bofindle. She saved me."

"Well," said Opiar slowly, "could this Lilah have come to get us? Why did she send you instead."

"My point exactly," said Rimfelder, "she went on about some magic that made my words a weapon."

"Ah," said Opiar, "there you have our cause and our reason."

"You do?" asked the poet.

"I see what you're getting at," agreed Clevian, "he was sent to free us because he needs us to join him on his journey."

"I do?" said the poet

"I would say so," agreed Eldet, "makes perfect sense. In which case he could well be right, we may be on the way to finding our Sagitæ."

"Vingura would've known sending someone we didn't know would've made us suspicious," said Opiar.

"Of what?" asked the poet.

"Of you. You could be a trick of Crilodach's sent to make us take you to our Sagitæ."

"So he gave you the Gaddia," smiled Clevian. "To make sure we knew he was involved."

"Only a friend could hold the Gaddia," agreed Opiar.

"You know Vingura that well?" asked Rimfelder.

"As well as anyone can know anyone," replied Eldet.

"I feel good being back again," grinned Clevian. "And in one piece. Even if I appear to be still a mere man."

"This piece is very small," said Eldet patting his legs, "and wingless."

"Nonetheless sufficient," Opiar told them. "In some ways I'm glad we were men in this place and not dragons. This is no place for dragons to live."

"Why not? Think being here would give us a bad name?" Clevian laughed.

"Well at least that unpleasant smell in the air can't be blamed on us," responded Opiar.

"I don't understand if you're dragons ... why are you men?" asked Rimfelder.

"That was Hiesia's idea," explained Eldet.

"And one I didn't like at all," added Opiar. "Odd little bodies that can't twist enough, don't have any claws and as far as I can feel, are incredibly weak. Crack every time you fall over, beats me how anyone could stand being in a body like this."

"When compared to a dragon," ended Clevian, "compared to a fish we're pretty good."

"Not as fast in the water though," pointed out Eldet.

"Oh yes, well most things are weak when compared to a dragon. Even the bears were never as strong as dragons," agreed Opiar.

"She said," went on Eldet explaining, "that we stood out as dragons but as men we'd merge with millions of other people and so be able to hide away."

"And she was right for a while," said Clevian.

"For a while," added Opiar.

"What went wrong?" asked Rimfelder.

"Rataplan. Nasty piece of work. He inherited all the foul techniques of his uncle," Opiar told him.

"Who's Rataplan?" asked Rimfelder.

"If you're fortunate you'll never meet Crilodach's top general. Lasted longer than his predecessor. Does all Its dirty work for It. All Its peeping, spying and warring. Whatever advances Its aims, Rataplan is behind them. Using the soldiers Frin–Ghirzan trains. Another nasty piece of work."

"We have a personal score to settle with Frin–Ghirzan too," Clevian said.

"He took our sons," Opiar told the poet. "As men we were able to take wives and have children. Our sons had a touch of dragon in them. He found us through them."

"When they were born the dragon in them was still strong,

they found us before Tegriel's spells could fully hide their ancestry," said Clevian.

"That was enough for Rataplan. A few minutes, no more, for each son, but his spies were everywhere. They knew," moaned Opiar. "They came for them. Stole them away. We had to try to find them. Rataplan knew that we would try. He watched for us. As soon as he saw us he knew we had to be dragons even though we looked like men. He knew we were their fathers."

"What happened?"

"These bodies let us down," Eldet told him. "I told Hiesia we needed speed and strength to fight Its armies but she told us the bigger we were the more difficult to hide. We were no match for Rataplan's spies."

"No fire or claws," Opiar pointed out.

"No wings," added Clevian.

"And your sons?" asked Rimfelder,

"We never saw them again. But Rataplan told us he would train them to be his lieutenants, that they would wipe out millions of people in Its name. He kept his word. That's just what they are, soldiers in Its army. No way of life for a true dragon."

Eldet, who had washed in a barrel of sweet water and cleaned out his nose, snorted in a satisfying way, spat over the side of the ship but the spittle vaporized in the hot air long before getting close to the lava.

"Come to that we may have to kill them ourselves," said Clevian, drinking his fill and then passing the still full barrel to Opiar.

"Well they didn't get the Sagitæ you hid," Rimfelder said, happily.

"They would've if we hadn't acted quickly," revealed Clevian. "We had to lose our minds."

"You did that to yourselves," gasped the poet.

"An old dragon trick," smiled Opiar. "They tried to torture us but none of their techniques worked because we could only say a few things."

"That and the fact we were still connected to our dragon selves. So though they broke our bodies and made them bleed, we were unhurt." Clevian laughed, "that must have infuriated them."

"So, they finally exiled us to Xibalba, on to that island surrounded by Phigata, there to stay until the end of time,"

Eldet finished. "Hoping the loneliness would get us to talk."

"You couldn't free yourselves," stated Rimfelder.

"How d'you know that?"Opiar asked.

"Because if you could you wouldn't have waited for me but changed into dragons and flown away."

"Far too simple a plan," smiled Eldet.

"True enough we'd trapped ourselves," Clevian told him.

"With a better trap than even It could've devised," said Opiar.

The four of them went silent for a while. Opiar's last words rung out on the ship like a bell. They had lost their children, nothing would bring them back to them. They were travelling they knew not where but they knew eventually they would find Zaqui. There were a few old scores to settle on the way. If they were spared, a few old friends to meet. They were feeling more and more their old selves as the minutes passed.

"Zaqui will not come until the three Sagitæ are all together. They're the key," said Opiar.

"Then we must be travelling towards Lilah," said Rimfelder.

The brothers could not fail to notice how happy Rimfelder was every time he mentioned Lilah's name.

"I need a change of clothes," said Clevian, "In the meantime I'm still hungry and someone said this ship might've food aboard."

"You always did think too much about food," grumbled Opiar.

"Someone has to. My rumbling stomach's about to burst into song," answered Clevian.

Rimfelder had to admit he had not seen any plates on the island or anything one could eat. He had not looked much though, because food was the last thing he had been thinking about. The four of them went into the cabin as the sky ahead of them turned redder and redder. The ship altered course very slightly although the rigging made no sound. As Rimfelder put the book down on the table, plates were taken out and fruits cut up to cleanse their mouths giving them their first meal in many ages. The ship sailed on with the burning waves lapping at the hull and fire flicking up like anxious hands trying to stop them moving. But whatever strength Phigata had, the magic in the Gaddia and the äis was far greater. The ship never faltered or stopped. Nor did Phigata turn wild for the air here was dead and unable to whip up the lava into huge waves. If this ocean ever moved even by a small amount those deep down did the moving. Their constant swimming created any currents that existed in Phigata. The hidden things that Rimfelder had thought he had seen whose burning anger fuelled the sea, already hot, to a white heat. A palpable anger the diners all felt as they sat and ate and talked of places they had been and sights they had seen. Memories. Memories that brought smiles to their faces and tears to their eyes. In that meal they all did a lot of living, which is the best way to spend the day before you die.

The three dragons and the poet ate. The dragons' minds cleared more as the effects of their own magic on themselves lessened and good memories came back to them like old friends, making their hearts warm and their smiles real. Whatever else would happen, whatever and whoever they had lost, however they had suffered, they had been true to themselves. They had survived. Even more importantly, they had been true to Tegriel. He had told them he did not know if they would live or die. Eldet spoke for them all when he said,

"My dear Rimfelder we're dragons. We don't do what we do for glory or a name but for the wonder of the doing. We know what the Sagitæ are and what promise they hold. We know what Crilodach is and the curses It offers. Our choice is clear. We have ever stood beside the Sangyma and tried our best, at all times, to honour our magical heritage."

"We're taught upon the claw and wing that our fight is for justice," added Clevian.

"Anything less makes us less dragon," ended Opiar.

Tegriel always impressed those he met with his intelligence and honestly. Those he asked to do things felt the honour in his asking them. Of course they all knew his prophecies often came true, and he was considered to be specially gifted, but there was no magic in the fact people liked him. People loved him. This was the effect Tegriel had on people, even on dragons. A response Crilodach never cared for and Rataplan never thought about.

Clevian talked softly to Opiar later when Rimfelder was half asleep as they walked out on to the deck, their bellies full, Phigata bubbling away around them. He voiced something both had been thinking.

"You know," he said, "Xibalba isn't your usual kind of

prison. How did the Gaddia find us?" He patted the gunwales as if they helped him think.

"They're not the only magic at work here," replied Opiar.

"Do you remember Tegriel telling us there was magic dust in the universe, like particles, that could not be seen?"

"I do," answered Opiar. "He said they passed through everything without having any effect. Just endlessly swirling around the universe having no reactions or mass but he had often noticed they altered spells in unexpected ways. He said spells attracted them and they would become even more magically charged."

"And the person they were passing through became special because of them," said Clevian.

"Magical folk are a kind of magnet, he said, and around them is the magnetic flux of magic. Did he tell you he had a spell that could show you the magnetic aura around a magician?" asked Opiar.

"Oh yes, a phial of blue liquid could be used, but they said that phial was lost long ago."

"I wonder if our friend over there attracts magic dust," said Opiar.

"He's a wordsmith. The book appears to be all he has."

"But the Gaddia has been given to him by Vingura. I remember Vingura, nothing he did was straightforward. I wouldn't mind betting there's more in that drink he gave Rimfelder than we know."

"You smelled the fruits of the garden on his breath?"

"Didn't you?" asked his brother.

"The moment he touched my hand. Like a lighthouse beacon, one can't mistake those who've drunk from Vingura's garden."

"That might explain the added magic especially if he attracted such particles to himself. But the magic in Xibalba is negative. Our friend's would be positive and somewhere along the line that should mean this place should be exploding in every direction."

"Or vanishing," said Opiar.

"And Xibalba's doing neither."

"So we must be wrong," suggested Opiar.

"Or the äis is preventing Rimfelder and Xibalba from touching each other."

"Physically yes, but not on the level of spells."

"Vingura never knew where Xibalba was or how to get

here. Whatever Vingura told him, his presence here must be his own doing," said Clevian.

"Unless he's being called by that song."

"You hear that music too?"

"So does Eldet. A far off voice calling us along."

"The Gaddia is giving Rimfelder the confidence to use the magic already inside him and the äis is following that song."

"He doesn't know how much magic there is swirling around him," said Opiar. "Nor how much is within him."

"Such a magic cannot be hidden for long," said Clevian.

"Remember Hiesia telling us about Filvani's laws. Isn't there a codicil in them about certain magical thinking not needing a spell to be active?"

"Meaning?"

"Perhaps his magic is in his words and that enables him to escape Xibalba's detection," said Opiar.

"What use is his being ignorant of his real powers?"

"Tegriel's always full of such plots and games. I'll bet you anything this Lilah person knows," Opiar said.

"Maybe the Sagitæ is helping us. Calling us. To get us all to Zaqui."

"Since when did our Sagitæ ever need help getting anywhere?"

"Since Crilodach broke Its ancient chains," said Clevian. "Everything has been in danger since that day."

"Or maybe since Tegriel died," said Opiar.

"Ah, poor Tegriel. I wonder how he died?"

"How can such a great prophet die at all?" mourned Opiar.

"The universe must be a sorry place without Tegriel," said Clevian.

"For all the suffering and wars my best times were when he was around. Always exciting. Always in the middle of things, always up and doing. Like a mighty dynamo keeping the whole war against Crilodach running," grinned Opiar.

"Being hidden away as men was no fun for us," agreed Clevian.

"Maybe before Zaqui we should be dragons again. Just the once. I can feel my power returning with each second."

"Have you decided about the strength of the prevailing winds here?" asked Clevian.

"They weren't strong enough at the island to hold us aloft. The dragon eaters in Phigata would've dragged us down into the fire."

The Dragon Brothers

"Which is how It designed them but what about here?" asked Clevian.

"I sense what you sense. There's a change but I wouldn't trust to our wings just yet."

"I think we'll have to soon though, there's plenty of danger ahead," said Clevian.

"I'd have liked to see Tegriel again. And that little Ruzniel what was his name ... Niteant. He was a great sport flying on my back."

They laughed at the memory and looked out over the searing view, deep in thought. Until they saw the ocean ahead of them lapping up against something that was not land.

"Eldet!" called out Opiar.

Eldet ran up to them at the call and the three of them stood looking ahead. They all growled. Rimfelder hurried up behind them and stopped in his tracks. The three men were still there, at the prow looking intensely ahead at the creatures gathering to attack them. But Rimfelder saw more than that. The men were enveloped in their own shadows, rising against the light from the sea. All around them, tall and large, were their dragon selves. Their front paws holding on to the rigging high in the masts. Around Eldet was a huge black dragon, ebony, shining like polished glass. Along his back were fifteen sharp ridges running down to a tail that was barbed on all sides and the barbs shone with the liquid poison that oozed from them. Clevian was encompassed by a yellow dragon. Taller than the other two his teeth were sharp and pointed along a long jaw. On his wings were added claws and the skin was as sharp as a knife along their edges. He had eighteen ridges running down his back and a short tail, hard and sharp that could cut through carbon steel. Opiar's dragon self was the brown of beech tree leaves in spring. Edged with red his body rippled with muscles. His ears could hear an ant's heartbeat a thousand miles away, his claws were silver and very dextrous, he could turn a key in a miniature lock or braid a child's hair with them. He had two lines of ridges down his back and his tail wrapped around his body.

Rimfelder did not say anything but he saw the dragons strengthen and the human shapes lessen until only the dragons were left. The ship did not tip at their weight nor slow. The creatures of burning fire massing ahead of them gathered in greater and greater numbers. He could see they could fly. They were like a wall waiting for the ship to hit them. Circling in one place as if there were an invisible line preventing them from crossing over. Rimfelder gulped, ran back into the cabin and picked up the Gaddia. He opened the book. There was nothing new there. He took the Gaddia out on to the deck. The dragons saw him this time. Their huge, heavy heads looking down. Opiar lowered his brown head to look at him face to face. The poet had never seen such sad eyes.

"You found us in time, poet," he said. "You wouldn't be able to handle the burning Irghwols of Xibalba."

"We found each other," he replied.

"Good answer," laughed Clevian.

"Why don't they attack?" asked Rimfelder.

"They can't yet," Clevian told him. "First the Irghwols gather. To make their enemies baulk at their number and tremble at what's to come. But these can gather all they like they cannot attack. They are behind glass. Look."

Rimfelder looked and sure enough the ship came to a halt before a pure glass wall against which Phigata bubbled and the burning Irghwols snapped at them without being able to get at them from the other side.

"How like Crilodach," Opiar told them.

"What is this?" asked Rimfelder

"Xibalba proving her worth," replied Clevian. "We know we have to go on and to go on we have to solve how to get through this glass wall. All the while knowing and seeing what awaits us the moment we do."

"Enough to make you want to run back?" asked Eldet.

"Not if that way is the way to Lilah," said Rimfelder.

"We have a fighter with us," Clevian noted. "Be careful of your bravery Rimfelder. Up to a point courage will save you, after that point courage will kill you."

"And that point is where Crilodach begins to use you. Bravery is good in a battle, in a war, on a single planet caught in the moment to save a friend. But when the war is a million years ago and the planet is no more, of what use was the bravery?" asked Eldet.

"If a friend is saved nothing is lost," argued Rimfelder.

"Courage is a short term weapon, you have to learn to fight for the long term," explained Eldet.

"Then we need all we can get because we're on a short

term mission," Opiar defended Rimfelder.

"Be fair to the man," Clevian told Eldet, "he can't take the long view as we can, he hasn't the life energy in him we have. He'll die very young."

"These creatures are not all looking at us," observed Rimfelder.

"I noticed that. I wonder if this glass is as clear on the other side as this," said Eldet.

"A two–way mirror you mean?" asked Rimfelder.

"Maybe. Or maybe they're being shown something they want. After all we're not enough to feed them all so something is keeping so many Irghwols interested."

"Perhaps the äis?" said Opiar.

"Perhaps. This is a mighty vessel of magic," agreed Clevian.

"If they could have gotten round or under that glass they would have by now," suggested Eldet.

"Which means we can't get round or under any more than they can," agreed Opiar.

"Does the Gaddia have anything to say on this?" asked Eldet.

"Nothing," said Rimfelder.

"How about the cover?"

Rimfelder had not thought about the cover and he looked now. With three heavy heads peering over his shoulder and breathing all around him. Dragon breath was actually quite nice after they had eaten fruit.

"That looks like you," Opiar told Clevian, at the dragon inlay on the spine of the book.

"Wouldn't surprise me, Vingura always liked yellow."

"There," said Eldet, "what's that?"

"I've seen that before," said Opiar.

"The figurehead on the ship," Rimfelder said.

Opiar leapt over to the figurehead and with his agile, silver claws he felt around the form of a mermaid and found a lock. The whole figurehead came off in his claws with a twist and he brought the head back to the others.

"A key," he smiled.

"But where, oh where, is the lock," Clevian asked.

"That must be close. The äis wouldn't have stopped far away," suggested Opiar.

"What are you doing?" asked Rimfelder.

"Finding a way forward," replied Clevian.

"But those things ..." he pointed, "they're in our way."

"So?" asked Opiar. "Not quite so brave all of a sudden?"

Rimfelder swallowed. He was sure he was shaking. The wall of Irghwols grew thicker even as he looked. Their swarm thrashing about in a frenzy to eat. The three dragons rose into the air and began to fly up and along the glass looking intently for a lock, taking little notice of the enemy. They found what they were looking for within a short time set just above the bubbling lava.

"Well here goes nothing," said Eldet.

He slid the key into the lock. Opiar gripped with his teeth with the lava lapping at his chin and turned the figurehead. The key turned and the glass shattered into millions of pieces, falling harmlessly into the laval ocean. As the glass shattered even as the brothers took to the air for aerial battle, the creatures that had been rising and falling in vast numbers on the other side, shattered into billions of pieces. There was nothing on the other side but more bubbling ocean. Rimfelder who had been standing like a statue afraid to even admit he was preparing to be eaten, asked

"Where are the burning Irghwols?"

"They were never here," said Opiar.

"Obviously a test," said Clevian.

"A test of what? asked Rimfelder.

"A test to see if we had the courage to go forward into almost certain death," observed Eldet.

"And whoever set the test now knows the answer," ended Clevian.

"Crilodach," said Rimfelder.

"Maybe not. Whoever they are, they know a lot more about us than we know about them at this moment," Clevian said.

"I wonder what will be next," thought Rimfelder out loud.

"I don't think you'll have to wait long to find out," said Clevian, looking at a dark cloud forming in front of them. "I'm going to scout around."

He lifted off from the deck and with a few enormous flaps of his wings he soared high above them and vanished into the darkening cloud ahead of them. The ship sailed on. Opiar and Eldet remaining as dragons, were now unable to go into the cabin, so they stayed permanently on the deck.

"He stood his ground," Opiar said to Eldet.

"He was scared," Eldet observed.

"So was I but he didn't run and dive into the cabin. I've

known some who would have jumped into Phigata rather than be eaten by Irghwols."

"From what I see of the creatures down there that wouldn't have changed his fate."

"There's strength in him," Opiar said.

"Have you looked into his memory?" asked Eldet.

"Briefly."

"And?" asked Eldet.

"He's tall for his people. He's as tall as the Arvernat they made to mine their mines," said Opiar.

"The high respect he holds Tethval in, means those men weren't the kind to be impressed by the height of a man but only his strength of character," said Eldet.

"The Sagitæ is calling to him," said Eldet, "in the song. He isn't just special to the Sangyma he's special to the Sagitæ."

"A man of words and unknown magic?"

"The power to beat Crilodach," suggested Eldet, "has never been known."

Rimfelder sat by himself still shaking. The Gaddia on his lap. So far Vingura's gift had had all the answers. He hoped that would continue to be the case. The darkness ahead turned out to be a huge cave with a golden roof. The ship steered inward and here for the first time a slight breeze caught the sails that was not hot. Clevian was flying with large, sweeping flaps of his wings high above them. After four hours he came down and Opiar took over. They sailed for endless hours. Then Phigata came up against a solid, grey wall of stone above which the cavern carried on.

"The cavern continues for miles yet," said Eldet, coming down with a flap of his wings from his watch.

"Looks like our journey on the äis is over," said Opiar.

"Bother. I always hated walking," moaned Clevian.

Opiar let down his wing and Rimfelder walked off the ship on to the hard stone surface. As he did so the ship changed. Without making a noise the rigging came away, the masts folded down, the sides of the ship folded back and sideways. Everything changed into a more traditional äis and hovered there waiting for them to climb back on.

"That's clever," said Eldet.

"Looks like we'll have transport no matter the terrain," smiled Clevian.

"And we get a place to rest without having to stop moving,"

noted Opiar.

The group continued on their way. Rimfelder sitting with the two dragons who were resting, talking about his life and Lilah and listening to them talk to him about their adventures. They had all lived a long time and seen many things. So much that he would never experience. He sat close to them, unafraid of their huge size but wary of the places on their skins that were razor sharp or poisonous. Far behind them, where the ship had changed to the äis and the land began, Phigata was beginning to flow over the rocks for the first time, like an incoming tide. Following them. Nothing escapes from Xibalba.

The cavern was long, the roof carried the shadow of Eldet as he flew above. The heat they had felt behind them from the lava began to recede.

"Have we left Xibalba?" Rimfelder asked.

"I've never heard of anyone leaving," said Opiar.

"Where are we going if we're not leaving?" asked the poet.

"Where did Vingura say you were going?" asked Eldet, coming down for a rest and letting Opiar take over lookout duty.

"To find a Sagitæ."

"Then I guess that's where we're going," said Eldet.

"In Xibalba? What would a Sagitæ be doing here?" asked Rimfelder.

"Ask us that again when we get there," said Clevian.

"Probably this äis has been used before, to put the Sagitæ here."

"Who would do that?" asked Rimfelder.

"Only the Sangyma use the äis poet," said Opiar.

The sudden bellow from Eldet made them all jump and Opiar was in the air in a second. Clevian followed him and they found their friend being attacked by a group of lesser Irghwols.

"Careful," called out Eldet. "Their arrows are diamond tipped and poisoned."

"They're aiming for Rimfelder," warned Clevian.

Rimfelder saw the arrows coming in his directions. At first one or two and then a whole quiver full, then dozens. He looked around for cover and in his haste stumbled. As he fell the Gaddia opened and he saw a whole page come away in his hand. He grabbed but the page slipped away from his hand and grew upward and outward and curled over him like

390

tent. As the arrows sank into the page the poison soaked into the paper, making strange shapes with the arrow heads forming thick, prominent triangles and squares. Through the page he could see huge wings flying past. The breeze they swept up blew through his shelter and ruffled his hair.

Eldet shook his tail and showers of his own poison rained on the attackers who did not show themselves. Clevian struck at the ceiling above their positions with his tail and rocks tumbled down. But still the arrows came in such profusion that avoiding them became more and more difficult for the dragons. And then one struck Opiar on the neck.

"Go to Rimfelder," he cried, "move the äis out of here!"

Clevian hesitated a second and then Eldet pushed him down with his body. Opiar bellowed and threw his mighty body against the rocks, scattering the attackers and crushing them in the rock fall. His wings gave out and he fell too smashing into the rocks below, breathing his last as the rocks smouldered with his fire. Rimfelder stood looking back for the longest while. He was shaken. Crying.

"They're good tears," comforted Clevian. "He was the best of brothers and the finest of dragons."

Rimfelder could not speak. He walked to the far end of the ship and sat down, shattered. Looking back for an age until his eyes hurt hoping for Opiar to fly out of the darkness and back towards them, where he belonged.

"He mourns Opiar much."

"Rimfelder has much to face," whispered Eldet. "I think he's worthy of our sacrifice,"

"We're only three now, not four, and we've a long way to go," said his brother. Eldet held out his clawed hand to Clevian,

"To the last claw and the last tooth," he swore.

Clevian turned to him and they wrapped their claws around each others arms,

"To the last claw and the last tooth," he repeated.

Mojolo Finds Her Wings

The sky was as high, open and blue as Mojolo could ever remember. The blueness filled her with a wish to fly. To lift her from her dinghy as if she were no heavier than an autumn leaf, buoyed on all sides as she floated back to the ground. To make her want to soar until, from the jet stream, she would see the entire ocean curving from one continent to another. To make her believe she could escape the marriage she did not want the next day. To take her away from the things that tied her down and threatened her freedom. To release her. Unbridle her. The sky was the song she had never written but whose music haunted her, her confidant and friend. Her only ally. At that moment she needed to be a part of the nature around her. To shed her skin as something that belonged to the ground and become something that belonged to sea and sky.

Her wish was about to come true.

The choppy waves glittered where the sunlight caught the crests of the lively wavelets. She let out the mainsail and played her swift, light dinghy over the seawater feeling the brisk air on her face as her strong hands gripped the tiller and played the boom. The sail billowed, the small boat lifted and almost flew across the sea, sharing her feeling of exhilaration. As if sensing this was their final time together, that today everything would change for her; forever. As is the way with boats, the dinghy's knowledge of how things were about to change was radically different from Mojolo's. Sailing boats, throughout the universe, have tapped into the magic of the cosmos. No matter how they are designed or built they all contain a sense of what magic is and what magic can do. For boats and magic are kindred spirits. Sailing boats have the buoyancy to float across water as spells have the buoyancy to float across space.

Salt spattered on her face and dripped from her red hair despite her all-weather hat and cagoule. The sea water stung her eyelids and drenched the dinghy, mainsail and spinnaker. Above the noise of the dinghy on the sea, she heard the self-bailer whirling away sucking the water out of the bottom of the hull. She loved being out on the water, she could almost sense where the breeze was strongest without looking, as if the elements were part of her being. Her feet no longer felt the dinghy, nor her hands the tiller. She lost all thought of her body and became the sea, the air, the wild breeze. Her eyes consumed every nuance of every second. She imbibed everything of nature, even as nature in her wildness was drinking down Mojolo's being. They were becoming one in their glory of the day and the moment. The sense of their own wonder wrapped them together, flew with the sailing dinghy, played with the breeze and soared with the sky. She had been sailing since she was a child but never had she felt this alive. She was amazed by the experience. Her dinghy handled so easily. Everything was perfect. Which is just about how one tends to feel before something magical happens. Because before the magic, you have to be properly prepared otherwise things could go wrong.

Suddenly, as if someone had flicked off a switch, the breeze died. She looked across the water trying to see where the wind made the ripples darker to get her speed back but there were no dark ripples. The mainsail flapped helplessly for a second then stopped billowing. The spinnaker which had been like a large belly bulging from the front of the dinghy, flopped lifelessly across the boat and into the water. Her dinghy was carried forward by a brief momentum and then becalmed, listing as if suddenly caught in treacle. She stood up, balancing herself against the sway of a boat in water but the boat did not sway or tip. The breeze had completely gone, the sea gently lapped against the dinghy one last time as all playfulness vanished. Birds had to flap instead of glide to reach their cliff-side nests. Some splashed into the sea to come ashore on the last of the foamy waves. They made a huge noise. They were scared. The wind had been sucked away in an instant. All movement had evaporated from everything with a terrifying ease. With an unnatural speed that even sucked the energy out of her. Her heartbeat speeded up as she was suddenly gripped by the fear of what was coming next? Something was about to happen. Something that had never happened before.

She looked around, squatting, gripping the side of the boat with her hands for her life. Fear saturating her brain. She had heard that on rare occasions quakes on the seabed

Mojolo

created millions of bubbles that rose upwards taking away all buoyancy from any ships on the surface, sinking them immediately. Drowning the sailors no matter how good they were at swimming. She felt vulnerable. Something new had happened in the place where she had always felt most at home. Something unknown. But for all her fears, all her apprehension and all her confused looking, she could never have dreamed of the storm that was about to be unleashed upon her.

The sky was still blue but she noticed that too had changed. Now the sky seemed to ripple while the sea seemed to calmly curve endlessly into the horizon, as if sea and sky had changed places. She saw the sky billow and blow, rise and fall above her. Waves seemed to flow up and across from the horizon, clouds started rolling like waves and then broke on some unseen shore of the stratosphere. The sun became hidden as the blue became as wild as a hurricane and the sunshine struggled to filter through, as if the sun were deep below the surface lost in the depths of the sky. Clouds plunged into the water around her fizzing as they dissolved. She thought she smelled jasmine and mock-orange. Her heart thumped in her chest. Her mouth open, her fingers gripping the boom as if she were an audience clutching the rails at the base of the stage to get a better look. She was truly terrified.

She fell back as her dinghy moved. Downwards. Not sinking. The entire ocean was moving downwards. As if someone had pulled a plug and the water was draining away in front of her eyes. The coast was two miles away. The coast line was growing upwards at an alarming rate as the receding water revealed the continental shelf. The land became the top of a huge mountain She pulled in the boom, let off the halyards and pulled down the sail. The dinghy bobbed slowly to the weight of her movements. The coast was fast approaching her. As the hull scraped at the rocks she leapt on to what had been the sea bed and gripped hold of the closest rocks, her shoes slipping over mud filled with urchins and struggling sea creatures flapping helplessly. Salt water spattered into her eyes and mouth. Her dinghy slid away behind her and hit a boulder, turning sideways, wedged tight far below her on what was now a steep mountain side. The mast quivered as if the dinghy, too, were scared. The water flushed away around her in dozens of newly made waterfalls.

She was beached. Stranded. Alone.

In a world turned upside down she did not even have the courage to be curious about the sea bed she had never seen. Fish caught out in rock pools, crabs running wild, seaweed draped everywhere and slime that clung to her, which had once been long, gracious plants rooted in the ooze of the seabed and swaying in the currents beneath the waves. The smell of sea–water and mud was all over her clothes. She could only half see. Mixed in with the noise of the sea draining away was another sound. A mysterious sound. She could not quite gauge where this new sound was coming from. She pulled down her wet–weather hood so she could hear more clearly.

She grunted as she struggled to get upright and her soft shoes finally gripped the wet rocks. She clambered upwards trying to get to dry land. She cut her hands several times and tore the cagoule along the knees before she stopped, gave up the effort, sat down and looked around, panting.

The landscape of sea–life encrusted mountains and vast valleys opened up before her. Dying fish gasping in their thousands, large fish flapping their tails in disbelief, old wrecks peeping up from hidden rifts, mud covering everything. Large tracts of land appeared that were once covered with salt water. Exposed, they dripped with water glittering in the light but were already drying out and smelling of decay. As far as her eyes could see a greyish landscape appeared, all colour fading fast from the plant life in the fresh, oxygen–rich air. She shifted her body about to get a better hold and soon was able to stand up by wedging her feet between rocks. She saw the green grass in front of her. Had she been struggling enough to have covered the two miles to the old coast line? Shew knew she hadn't. She started to clamber towards dry land.

A breeze picked up and began to tear up the delicate fabric of the new land, drying the mud in seconds and whipping up masses of dust. Stripping scales from fish. Turning the glitter of the light on the water droplets into nothing. Soon the dust formed a mist at waist height that swirled hungrily around her as if she were in a whirlwind. She turned, shook her head and hurried to get away from the dust storm that threatened to encircle her. She could no longer see where to place her feet. Slipping several times she found herself swallowed up by the dust that stuck to her like fresh paint.

She jumped up gasping for what little fresh air she could take.

Her heart was beating so fast her chest hurt, her mind could not quite take in the disaster she was watching. Fear pervaded her every move. She stumbled often and cursed regularly. Even as she gripped the rocks with her hands to regain her balance she felt her fingers trembling. Or were the rocks trembling? The world had turned insane in an instant. No warning, no explanation. She refused to look behind her from where all the noise seemed to come, she just slipped, slid and half ran. Running had never been such an effort before. She was terrified at what might be behind her. Her only thought was to find other people. To hide until this upheaval was over. Yet in every step she took she began to want to know. To not want to be scared. To want to find out what was happening. To find out if she could do something to make this terrible day go away. She was beginning to get angry with whatever was causing this chaos. With whatever was causing her crushing fear.

The storm shook the granite beneath her feet. Her back was whipped by the hot dry wind as if, whatever had taken all the water in the world, now wanted the water in her. Wanted to dry her out and leave her as withered as the seabed. She was thrown forward on to a bed of dried seaweed. The smell sticking to her like glue. She felt horror sweep over her as her whole body was flung forward. She lost the feeling in her fingers. She could not see clearly. All she wanted to do was get to the grass. Get back to land. The old dry land. Never had she wanted to be home so much. Never before had she felt the sea was her enemy. What sea? She hauled herself to her feet, tearing off her jacket so her arms could work more easily at grabbing hand–holds, and stumbled on, though now there were tears in her eyes. Her muscles ached. Her mouth was caked in dust. She felt as if her teeth were being pulled out one by one in the wind.

Then she slipped, when she was almost there, and slid back between two rocks and for a second, wedged on her back her head facing the sea–like sky, the dust cleared and she saw the lights. Streaks of white, red and green lights blazing in a wild sky. Rainbow lightning. Silent yet awesome. Searing through the bleak clouds and the violent storm. No, they were creating the tempest. Blistering forms streaking from one end of the sky to the other across a continent of black clouds; meeting in the middle; causing turmoil; setting fire to clouds. Or were they clouds? Maybe they were smoke from the lightning bolts which were cutting into the blueness and increasing in number until the whole sky was a dance of colours in fearsome combat.

She stared open mouthed. She knew here was the explanation for the unbelievable revolt of nature that was happening around her. Were they being attacked by some alien force? Was the world ending? Had someone created a vile weapon and attacked her land before anyone could defend themselves? Was she stumbling forward only to find her death? She stared, transfixed by the intense movements above her. There was a system in the lights. The colours seemed to balance, and they met each other no matter from where they emanated. They were drawing closer together too. Until she saw something. Some of the lights came from the hands of a man.

No, not a man.

A being. Floating, flying, dipping and swirling as if he were playing with and in the storm. Bending his body as he moved, rotating, ducking and diving. Then she realized he was not playing — he was fighting. And before him from the shimmering sky she could not quite focus upon, through the dust that had turned to a thick mist was another being. A being whose hair flew about him infused with independence, not like snakes nor hands, but a thousand whips.

Without words these two beings fought each other. Fought and fought. With the wind. With the sea. With the storm. With the stones. With their hands. With anything. They fought and battled down and across the sky. Battled across the world of Mojolo's eyes, battled round and about her, wheeled and fought. She watched, her eyes riveted to their dance, a dance born from the fact that acceleration and gravity are one and the same thing. A fight taking place above the impossible — the loss of an ocean in seconds. And suddenly she heard with a clarity what her fear had denied to her ears since she had scrambled from her dinghy.

So scared had she been she had not realized their battle was also a symphony of sound. They fought in and with the elements. The atoms around them were dancing. Their inner fire released to an orchestra of noise. Fast, breathless, ever changing. These beings above her were talking to each other. Shouting. Calling out in languages she did not know.

She raised herself on her elbows and prised herself out of the cleft in the granite without taking her eyes off them. She was dizzy. Dizzy with fear and noise. The music rose and fell. The battle went on. Moments because hours. The small became great. The great was broken to pieces. The world was in a war in which there would be no truce, only a victor and a loser. She was transfixed. Amazed at what she saw and even more amazed that she seemed to understand. No scream came out of her in her fear. Only wonder. This was magic. She was mesmerized. The ache in her muscles left her. If such a thing were possible in the madness she witnessed, she became calm.

With the instincts she had used all her life to gauge a person's honesty, Mojolo knew the man with the wild hair that moved like fingers was trying to stop the other being. The other one was at once attacking and retreating, luring and trying to beguile the one with the living hair to make a mistake. This was not a battle of equals. She watched. The one with the wild hair was trying to capture the other not kill him. Whilst his adversary was definitely intent upon killing him if he could. She could almost see blood on his hands, though she did not know how, and she had the feeling he was working for someone else for she saw a dark shadow across his heart. As if night were trying to break out from his clothes and engulf them all.

Both their faces were hidden from her. She craned her neck to see what was happening. Then she felt light-headed again and realized the battle was sucking her upwards. The beings had created a maelstrom around themselves. She grabbed at the rocks and clung on but there was no firm hold for her and her fingers lost their grip. Mojolo was pulled into the battle. Up to that moment only her world had changed but now her life changed. She could not fly. The air was not her element. She had no wings. If the battle ended she would fall and be broken to pieces on the waterless seabed. She could do nothing in such a battle. She was drawn upwards against her will, propelled miles high.

Screaming for the first time, she twisted her body round as she was carried by the wind and she managed to face the way she was going ... straight at one of them whose back was to her. She bent backwards and with her feet she tried to guide herself towards him as the wind propelled her forward like an arrow. She hit him in the small of his back with enough force to break the backbone of any living animal. Her knees bent with the impact and she hit his shoulders with the palms of her hands as she tried to steady herself still in mid-air, the breath punched from her body with the impact. She bounced backwards from the blow, her legs in pain. She thought she had broken both her ankles.

Her violent, unexpected kick in the back made the being miss his mark and for a vital moment he lost sight of Sanjava and in that moment Sanjava caught him in his hair, folded him into knots and disposed of him as a fly swatter would a fly. What had taken hours was over in an instant. The wind died down and Mojolo, who was bent double getting her breath back, found herself floating with Sanjava above her world, as the sea swelled up, the clouds rolled back, sunlight broke through and beneath her the planet returned to normality. So much so no one knew anything else. All the people were back in their places going about the daily lives. The other boats were all back on the sea. No one was pointing upwards. There were no crowds gathered to witness the man in the sky. As if they had not seen, heard or felt any of what had happened. But she knew. She knew because she was above them. She had a new knowledge of the world. She was set apart. Her dinghy had disappeared. She was in no pain. Nothing was broken.

She looked up, her eyes gazing at Sanjava who was looking at her with interest. Then she realized two strands of his hair were holding her up having wrapped themselves around her knees and another two were in front of her hands so she could steady herself. She still felt as if she were balancing on springs but she managed. They were two people whose thoughts were those who float above worlds. Looking down upon the creatures who walk and swim and can never float above the clouds. Creatures who can never be free, and yet sometimes can still be mighty in their own way. She had been touched by a Sangyma and though she was not told yet, she had been chosen long before the battle. As a child when she found difficulty fitting in with what others did. As an adult when she preferred her own company to being with other adults. Her instincts had always been different and now she had become that difference. She was with Sanjava, who cannot be seen but sees so much. Her fear had gone. In her head she wondered what nightmare she had been having and wanted a dozen questions answered but

400

somehow she was unable to decide which one to ask first. Yet, with that same strength of character and quest for truth that had marked out her life, she was the first to speak.

"That was terrifying," she told him.

"Forgive me," Sanjava said to her. "I had no choice if I was to stop Agran quickly and save your world."

"Save the world," she swallowed, as if for first time.

Sanjava's voice was mellow. His wild hair now quiet and much shorter. His eyes hazel and full of warmth.

"His magic was using your planet's life force to fight me. I needed to stop him quickly or he would have killed you all."

"I didn't think he looked that mean," Mojolo said.

"An agent of a creature called Crilodach. Agran scouts out potential planets for his master to enslave."

"But you got the jump on him."

"I stopped him in time," agreed Sanjava.

"By using me."

"You were the only person close enough. For some reason the battle was not hidden from you."

Sanjava found Mojolo very interesting. Knowing, as we do, that when one person out of an entire race shows magic that person possesses the entire magic of that race. The events of the past few moments finally began to make some sense even if she could still not quite believe any of the vivid images blazing through her brain had actually happened.

"I could've died!" she said.

"I would not have allowed you to be hurt. That is not the way of a Sangyma."

He was kindly. His clothes flowed about him hiding a hundred spells. The clouds that hid them from the world below still smelled of sweet flowers. His hair was warm to her touch.

"Am I to stay up here?" she asked, gesturing to the empty air and looking around.

"You deserve an explanation," Sanjava told her.

"Hey, I've seen battles before. I know sometimes little people get involved in the wars of giants. This was just a bigger and faster battle than any I've ever seen. You ruined my day's sailing."

"You are not surprised?"

He tilted his head with his outstretched hand holding her chin trying to gauge her mind.

"My father was career military. I've always believed in magic," she told him holding his gaze, "so now I'm over the whole sea–disappearing act I can understand some of what just went on, only some mind you."

"It will know you helped me," he told her, lowering his hand.

"Oh, that sounds ominous."

"I am afraid they will come for you. I cannot erase what has happened from your mind. You are … different. Your passion for nature, your love for all life, is very powerful."

"I thought you beat the guy?" she said.

"There are others. They will smell you out. Magic leaves behind an unmistakable aura. You will not be safe."

"Can you hide me?"

"Yes," he told her, "I have already done so." He waved below them. "No one you know, will know what happened here," he told her. "That way they can continue to evolve without interference from us."

"That's quite a trick," she said, shaking her head.

"I cannot return you."

She sucked in the hot air and blew out through her teeth in a low whistle. She knew he meant more than merely returning to her sailing. She thought he had apologized to her because he had used her to distract his adversary and to win the fight. Now she realized his was a greater apology than she could have imagined. Because he had involved her, he had actually changed her existence. She was now wrapped in his magic. Without him she was prey to Agran's master.

"I can live with that. I'm a pretty sound sleeper when all is said and done," she said, trying to make light of the situation.

"I mean I cannot let you go back. Others would come and that would be certain death for you. Not today maybe, but tomorrow or the next day. You have no knowledge of the enemy and would be vulnerable to their attacks."

"What about everyone else down there?"

"If I take you from here right now, today will be seen by the enemy as just another battle. They may come to this world again but not immediately. We were fighting before we came here. We could have materialized above any of a number of worlds. Agran will be replaced. The enemy will not have reason enough to investigate this world further for a long while."

"Oh," she whispered. "What about those who know me, you know, my family and friends?"

She did not look at him. As if she knew she would never look upon her beloved sea again and she wanted to imprint this magnificent view on her memory. There was so much ocean she had not crossed, so many islands she had never visited. She knew at that second she never would; not on her world.

"They know you no more," he told her.

"You've 'hidden' me from them?"

"I have erased you entirely from the memory of your people."

"To save my life?"

"And theirs. The enemy will find no trace of you if they do appear here. Torturing anyone for information would be fruitless and Crilodach's lieutenants do not waste their time."

"They're safe as long as I don't go back."

"For now."

"All this because you used me as a projectile?" Sanjava laughed at her.

"No." He moved his arms and his cloak wrapped around her, "no, for a reason far more important. Tell me is your name Mojolo?"

"How did you know?"

"A close friend of mine told me once to look out for a woman called Mojolo whom I would meet in the clouds."

"Like a prophecy thing you mean?"

"Exactly like."

"I wouldn't mind a friend like that ... I mean he was right."

"He usually is. Come. I have a place for you where you will be safe from your new enemies. Where I can tell you much you need to know. If you will allow me."

"You're the one helping me fly. I'm not sure I've any choice."

"There is always a choice, but when there are only two choices, and one is death, would you not be crazy to choose death?"

"Never was a truer word said. However if I'm to go with you could you tell me your name?"

"Sanjava."

"Who exactly are you? Or should that be what exactly are you?"

"That I will tell you in due course."

"But you'll tell me?"

"I promise."

"Ok then," she lifted her hands, stretched out her arms, an said, "let's get going."

Mojolo tensed her arms and curled her fingers into a fist, curving her back and easing her feet in the most delicious awakening stretch she could ever remember. She opened her eyes and found she was as much in the dark as she had been with them closed. How long had she been asleep? She went over the events in her head.

She had just finished the same dream she had had many times before. Always the smiling face of Sanjava. Always the fierce storm. When they set off on their adventures together the dream ended. She was left floating in the clouds. Set apart from her world.

Now she could not feel her body. She could not see. Her muscles were drained of strength. She remembered so much, so vividly, and yet she had woken to this darkness. In a darkness she could not penetrate. She had no trouble recalling the faces of her family, the name of her town. Everything was clear and focussed. Even the smell of the sea. She deeply breathed in. With that breath things changed for her again.

This time was different. This time she felt awake. This was not a dream waking to yet another dream. This was not a half–dream wallowing in sleep. She breathed in again, this time rotating her feet. Her muscles were quickly losing their lethargy. She had not moved for a long, long time. She yawned. Such a big yawn she had no idea her mouth could open that wide.

The air smelled sweet as her chest rose and fell, as if her lungs were filling with air for the first time. She felt them almost unwrapping beneath her ribs. She raised her head and her forehead hit something hard. She felt all round her. She seemed to be in a box. For one terrible second she thought she was in a coffin. She pushed and the lid moved upwards and slid down to the slightest pressure of her fingers. She was not in a coffin, but a container. Made to fit her stature with a sliding lid that could only be opened from the inside. The bears knew a thing or two about keeping people hidden and safe while they slept.

She sat up. The room was lit with deep purple lights. Next to her was another shimmering container like hers though much bigger. Huge. She looked around at the stone walls. She looked at herself. The clothes she wore were strange to her. Silk, strong, well tailored and beautifully stitched. She wore two metal bangles of entwined dragons which fitted her wrists to perfection and felt warm and soft on her skin. Her red hair had grown very long. Down to her ankles. Her finger and toe nails had not grown at all. She knew she had been asleep but Sanjava's voice was so fresh in her mind, as if her crazy adventure had all just happened. She brushed back her hair with her hand and to her surprise her hair wrapped around her hands and her face as if cuddling her. She froze and her hair moved down her back and rested. Warm. Quiet. Waiting.

Her hair moved. Like Sanjava's. She flicked her head and her hair remained still. She ran her hand along the strands. Soft. She pinched her arms. She was awake. Was there to be no end to the surprises in her life, she wondered.

Getting up she let herself feel the stone floor with her bare feet for a few moments. Thrilling to the sense of touch after so long. The floor was warm. Warm stone? She looked around. Gazing at the room without any fear. She remembered her terror at the battle in the sky. The terror of having everything she knew turned upside down. The amazement of surviving. Being given an explanation of the colours in the battle. The colours of spells. Understanding through Sanjava the true nature of Agran. And something more. A greater enemy. A vile name. Their adventures together after that first meeting, the great names they had carved as the legends of many peoples. The remembrances tumbled through her brain like autumn leaves kicked up in a sudden breeze, flying all over the place. She struggled to begin to put them in order. Her life with Sanjava had all been real.

She realized her dream had not been a dream but her mind retelling her a key event. That she knew those things had all really happened was essential so she would lose no time when she woke up in asking herself, or others, time-wasting questions. Now all those talks she had had with Sanjava over the years he had taught her, came flooding back. Her heart raced. All they had discussed, all he had said, all they had experienced together. The warrior she had become. Fighting beside Hiesia on Ghirzanben. Retrieving one of the Sagitæ. None of those things were dreams.

Sanjava had told her about the war, about the Sangyma, about Crilodach. He had told her about Tegriel's prophecy concerning her fighting with him. About Zaqui, when the true nature of magic would be revealed. When the true nature of the Sagitæ would be revealed. Her hand steadied her body against the container as she leaned back. She felt the smooth surface of the metal. Near to where she had been lying waiting for Trecrogo to wake her up, was a blue robe. The robe was warm. Her hair twisted into two plaits, one falling down the font of her and one behind her. By the robe she saw two gold pins which her hair picked up and used to tie the plaits. She was calm. Everything happening around her fitted in with her memories.

Done. She stretched her arms and touched her toes ten times. Tegriel's prophecy had said she and Sanjava would meet but that he would die before her. He had discussed Trecrogo with her and she had accepted that he would hide her away to be part of the final battle. Partly because she wanted to know how things turned out and partly because this was the best use she could think of for the last two days of her life. She did not tell Sanjava but she was glad she would never see him die. She was his secret weapon. Lain carefully in the fortress of the bears, watched over by Nulfley, the spell for the hidden yet alive cast by Sanjava and Tegriel together long before Trecrogo was built. Nulfley was one of those rare spells that needs two Sangyma to perform. She would have been surprised if Sanjava had told her just how long she would remain hidden. She had not aged a day.

"There can be no greater task I can think of but this one," he had told her. "You will sleep a long time. You will not see me again but I will always be with you."

He stroked her hair with his kindly hand. The woman who had fought by his side without tiring. Without complaint. Three times she had almost died. Three times he had saved her. Then that last fight in which she had saved his life, but at a terrible price. She stroked her hair as she stood in Trecrogo, remembering his words,

"Always," she whispered.

She was ready. She knew she had Sanjava's magic within

her. Having faced many terrors in battle and learned of the enemy, she would not be scared by what lay ahead.

There was a coiled rope with a brass and silver handle at her feet. She picked that up. The lariat felt light yet strong. She remembered. The lariat made by the island people of Uter, soaked in the oils of the nut trees that only grow in their world. She tied the lariat to her hip and walked to the wooden doorway. The letters twinkled at her. She could not read them because they were not meant for her. She touched the door lightly. The lights came together in the centre and turned and the door opened inwards. She stepped back and let the door swing open past her.

The Arvernat man and woman standing right in front of her stood stock still as if they had been slapped. They had been exploring the corridors but had seen no door on their right. Now they saw the door suddenly appear, open and Mojolo walk out all at the same time. Behind her they saw into the room and the soft purple light but they were so transfixed by her appearance they were unable to recover and peek inside before the door silently closed behind her and vanished.

She was standing between them. Her delicate figure, long hair and the slight smile of welcome on her lips, soothed them. They smiled back. She stared at them as the lights in their eyes illuminated the rest of the corridor, the shields they had been carrying by the sides they brought up to their bodies partly in salute and partly for protection. Embossed with water that seemed to move, Mojolo felt at home. Emblems of the sea were friends to her. Everything of the sea was a friend to her. She bowed her head slightly at these two giants. Like a woman who was used to meeting unknown people and was confident, should they prove hostile, that she could protect herself. She raised a hand in greeting and said,

"Hello, good to meet you."

The man reached out a large, strong hand and shook hers and then the woman stood back and brought her palms together in greeting. This was a traditional greeting amongst the women of the Arvernat. She dimmed the lights in her eyes so as not to blind Mojolo and spoke.

"I'm Lamellen," she said, "and this is my brother Refrit."

"I'm Mojolo. I was given quite a few other names and titles but that's my birth name. I'm glad to know there are people here. I don't want to get lonely."

"You may be expected," Refrit told her.

"You think?" she asked, smiling.

"There are Sangyma here," Lamellen told her, "I'm sure you're meant to see them. They'll know all about you. They know about everything."

"And everyone," added Refrit. The Arvernat had all learned a great deal inside Bofindle.

"Is Sanjava here?" she asked, filled with a sudden joy at the thought of seeing him again. Maybe things had changed; something had happened he did not expect; maybe he had been wrong.

"The name is unknown to us," replied Lamellen, "but those that are here will be able to tell you."

"He has hair like mine. You couldn't miss him in a million years."

The two Arvernat shrugged. Not only had they not seen anyone like that, Mojolo's own hair looked normal.

"Is there a way out of here then?" she asked.

"To the parapet yes, from the fortress no," said Refrit. "This is our last home. There will be no other."

"That sounds about right at any rate," she told them.

She gently stepped past them. Refrit leaned forward, touched the walls where the door had been and wondered to himself at such things as hidden doors. He added this to the amazing things he had seen in the past five days. Sometimes he felt the only certainty he had was his sister, yet even she was changing. They all were, as their minds expanded in knowledge of the universe.

"Our own world is gone," he said, turning to face Mojolo again.

His revelation did not surprise her. She remembered seeing the plans for Trecrogo but she had not been allowed to see the foundations laid as she had wanted. The battle to save Sanjava's life made that impossible. Her own life was ending. She was calm. As she had said to Sanjava at the time,

"Well at least I'll go out with a bang." She smiled at her two Arvernat companions and said,

"All worlds vanish eventually."

"You'll want to talk to Lilah," said Lamellen, "come we'll take you to her. She'll tell you everything you need to know."

"What makes you think I need to know anything?" asked Mojolo.

"I'm sorry I assumed ..." began Lamellen.

"Don't be sorry," smiled Mojolo. "I'm certain sure there are things going on I don't know about."

The corridors they passed through were busy. The closer to the parapet the more crowded they became. Many Arvernat were walking around carrying equipment and messages to various parts of Trecrogo. An organized bustle which contrasted with the empty corridor where Mojolo had met Lamellen and Refrit. But then Trecrogo was a huge fortress and could have swallowed an army a hundred times bigger than the one that was gathered here now. Although anyone who knew the Arvernat would not have laid bets for an army a hundred times bigger being any stronger.

"Your people all seem to be in this part of the fortress. What were you doing in my corridor?"

"We were told to explore."

"By whom?" Mojolo asked.

"The boy called Demeter."

"There you are, someone I don't know."

"He said we were bound to find someone interesting," said Lamellen.

"That takes me back," she smiled.

"What does?" asked Refrit.

"People I don't know, knowing me."

Some Arvernat were armed, some not. They all nodded in greeting as she passed and she nodded back as, slowly, she and her guides made their way up the seemingly endless stairs which never tired her. Her body had rested enough. She remembered Sanjava telling her he was surprised she had seen so much of that first battle. She had told him how scared she was. He told her there was a fixedness in her, part reason – part magic, which he could strengthen. Make her a warrior. How they had talked. How they had travelled. She had learned so much and knew there was so much more to learn. She had run out of time to learn. In that last struggle she had had to give away all the years of her life but for the last two days.

She recalled always being fascinated by Sanjava. She had washed his hair on many occasions with the oils Vingura had given her, and now she found her own hair danced. Sanjava had told her that memory was a face of nature. That everything she would ever know would come to her through her senses and those she would face in battle had more senses than she. She had to compensate by trusting those with more senses who would fight by her side. She knew what he meant about trusting. Their battles had honed her skills. She was more than any woman in her nation had ever been.

She managed to keep pace with the Arvernat until finally Lamellen and Refrit came to a staircase leading out into the parapet. They stopped. They motioned her to go up.

"You're not coming with me?" she asked them.

"We're going back where we found you. We still have work to do. We don't need to introduce you."

There is nothing quite like seeing the brightness and darkness of galaxies and being part of them. To be part of, and yet separate from, them. To see splendour and power and be safe and secure away from the harshness of planets dying and being born before your eyes. Like a rich person looking out on to the world and knowing they are safe for a while. They can enjoy their money for a while. That though the world will try to hurt them, her many weapons would be blunted by their wealth. That somehow they were set apart from all other people.

The galaxies were merging, or slowing down, or dying but nothing mattered to her in that second apart from the view. Trecrogo was Mojolo's richness. She was part of a small band of people drawn together to stand apart. Though she only had five senses they were never more active and alive than right now, right here, with them.

There is almost a smell to the infinity of the universe. A touch more gentle than light that slides through the eyes and sits upon the mind. The endless revolutions of the worlds are an emotion and if you are sensitive enough to feel, you share the emotion. A wonder. A chaos. A certainty. A problem. A knowledge. An unknown. Mojolo was sensitive enough and she stood there taking in her surroundings. He had made her different. Not just because he had taught her but because he had given her his gift. Sanjava's knowledge had given her a wisdom. Inside she was powerful, more powerful than she had ever been. A power that awaited an enemy. Without Crilodach she was nothing. Unusable. Inconsequential. Flawed. Being great is all about who your enemies are. She came up the stairs two at a time feeling her body move with an excitement only an athlete knows.

Lilah saw the blue dress and robe coming up the stairs at

the same time as Copret. Demeter had not sensed her until the hour Sanjava had appointed and alerted Trecrogo to her imminent awakening. None of them expected her and though Demeter waited to see this woman was who felt like Sanjava, there was an air of suspicion on the parapet.

"Who are you?" asked the spellmaker.

Lilah stood with Bofindle in her hand looking at Mojolo perplexed as if she should know the answer immediately but did not. The two women looked at each other, taking in their inner strengths without questions, sizing each up as friends. Mojolo shrugged and introduced herself.

"Mojolo," she replied holding out her hand. "Of the Indoli, the sea people. Friend to Sanjava. You're Lilah right? I was led to believe you'd know me."

"Do you think she's a spy?" Chloe asked Copret. Copret scratched his fur.

"Not impossible. Though very difficult to know how she got here without anyone knowing unless a Sangyma is involved. Mind you I remember Zananto had a helper once. Olwist. Couldn't do enough for her. He was always into everything, was pretty much 'always there', until I caught him sending a secret message by an eel."

"An eel?"

"Oh yes. Clever you see, the eel swims out to sea, gets eaten by an albatross then the albatross gets eaten by a shark and the eel's message is picked up by one of Rataplan's spies, who kills the shark to retrieve Olwist's betrayal."

"And the eel?"

"The eel's dead."

"How did he persuade an eel to take the message?"

"The eel didn't know. The best messengers never know they're messengers. The best spies never know they're being used. That way they're accepted by those they betray. The more ignorant they are of their task, the more honest they are, so the better they spy."

"But how ..."

"How can they spy if they don't know? Spells and dissection mostly," said Copret.

"So she's a spy," concluded Chloe.

"She doesn't look like a spy."

"Did Olwist?"

"Certainly he did. I didn't trust him from the moment I first saw him. And the way he was always 'there'. Just plain shifty. He never put a foot wrong. Never upset anyone. He just tried too hard. Real friends often argue. We mess up but we stay friends."

"Well one minute you say she could be then you say that's unlikely, what changed your mind?"

"Her hair."

Chloe looked at Mojolo's hair and brushed back her own. Maybe she would look good in plaits, she thought. Though how plaits could help Copret know whether or not one was a spy baffled her.

Lilah half overheard their conversation even from a distance. She listened to Mojolo's voice. And her name. A simple name. A name that would convey nothing of character or history to most people, and indeed left Chloe none the wiser, but the name told Lilah a great deal. Mojolo whom Sanjava had protected. No wonder she had not recognized her face. Sanjava had made Mojolo appear differently every time they faced the enemy. Rataplan had never known she was the same person in all the reports he read of her engagements with his forces. Not even Zananto had known what she looked like and Copret had never been told she was still alive. Lilah knew Mojolo's world. She remembered Sanjava telling her he had left a surprise for Crilodach. She knew about his battle with Agran the sorcerer. A being who had played with magic, lied about his powers and misled many people as to his abilities with party tricks and sleight of hand. Then one of Crilodach's spies had met him and Agran had vanished for a year. He had come back arrogant. He caused much mischief and heartache before Sanjava had hunted him down. Lilah could sense the sea in Mojolo. But something else. A dark feeling. This was not the sea she knew but something else far more violent. A weapon.

She was how Sanjava had projected his powers into the final battle. He had kept Mojolo secret even from his fellow Sangyma. No one knew he had chosen her. Lilah thought about him. She had been there when they buried him and she remembered how quiet his hair had become. She could not place Mojolo's face, but she knew that red hair.

Now she knew she was no spy the spellmaker shook Mojolo's hand quickly,

"How did you get here?"

"I woke up here." Mojolo shrugged. "Somewhere below where Lamellen and Refrit found me. Well, we found each other. Well, sort of bumped into each other by the door. Good timing actually."

Demeter came over and as she saw this glowing boy she nodded her head towards him almost in reverence. In her tradition people who glowed were held in high esteem, much the same way some people look at halos though of course, they don't exist in real life.

"There are many rooms here," he told them both, "I've not explored them all but I felt her wake up. She was asleep a long time. She's been gifted by Sanjava."

Lilah picked up Mojolo's plait and as she touched her hair the strands wrapped themselves around her arm in greeting. Lilah smiled,

"So many wonderful things are not lost," she said. "Sanjava was a good friend of mine, and Copret," she pointed to the bear, "has fought by his side many a time. I was not expecting anyone like you. Sanjava only left cryptic suggestions that you would be here."

She liked the look of Lilah. Her stance broached no retreat. Her eyes were shining and clear. Her perfect teeth shone as she talked. Seeing Copret reminded her of her friends the bears and especially Hiesia. She did not know the Arvernat but she knew they were fighting alongside her kind of people, which made them her kind of people too.

"He chose you to be here and become one of us. He has kept his magic alive through you. The Sangyma did not die as readily as It was led to believe," said Lilah.

"He's really dead?"

"We thought he was, but he is not. For you are here and you have his hair," soothed Lilah.

"We're glad you're here," said Chloe.

"Wherever here is," Mojolo replied. "You may get some more help yet, there was another container in the room where I awoke."

"I see nothing," said Demeter.

"Maybe not but one's there, massive too," Mojolo told him firmly. "You could fit a dozen of your Arvernat allies in easy."

"There are some things Trecrogo only allows me to see when they are needed, as with you," said Demeter.

"Whatever is hidden will come if and when called," suggested Lilah, who knew exactly who was in that other container. One part of their plan could only be executed

413

once Crilodach was here.

"Copret do you know anything about that?" asked Demeter.

"I know after we drew up the plans Tegriel made some additions. I assume this room is one of them. My cousin was taken off to do some work but you know me, if a Sangyma is involved I let them get on without question. I couldn't oversee every bit of the building and I wouldn't have been worried by anything Tegriel suggested even if he didn't tell us exactly what he was up to."

"Are you hungry?" Chloe asked Mojolo.

"Sure," she replied. Chloe took her hand and took her down to get something to eat.

"She's the one Sanjava chose," said Copret, scratching his back. "Little thing isn't she."

"You were suspicious of her at first," said Lilah.

"I'm suspicious by nature. That spy cost Zananto her life and I haven't forgotten how that felt. The one message that I didn't intercept."

"Do not blame yourself," said Lilah.

"I was there, I should've stopped him."

"You cannot carry the weight of all our lives on your shoulders."

"I knew he was suspect. I failed her," argued Copret.

"She would not have thought so," Lilah told him.

"She always did forgive me too quickly."

"She told me once, when I was fifteen, that the microscopic world reflected the universe, that particles and atoms were like planets and between them all, were vast stretches of space," said Lilah, "She said the atoms inside magical beings reflect physical reality in the same way. Inside us right now the universe is at war, with all the spells and their power, all the unanswered doubts. Stretches of silence punctuated by unremitting violence."

"You see that in Mojolo?" asked Copret.

"There is something she has I have not seen before. Not her hair or the lariat, something deeper, a flood, a tempest of bitterness. The war in her is more violent than I have ever seen in anyone I have ever known."

"Tegriel never made any mention of this in his prophecies," Copret observed.

"Maybe he told Sanjava and no one else. He was always on about a need–to–know as far as his prophecies for the Sangyma were concerned," Lilah reminded him. "Inside her

Copret, inside her I saw an ocean. Wild and vast. A flood of anger. She has passion, and a desire to win. She will never give up but what is that ocean inside her that is greater than her?"

"You sound almost scared of her," said Demeter.

"I am not certain about anyone having a power in them they themselves do not comprehend," explained Lilah.

"She's an ally, I am more than content to have someone Sanjava trained here," said Demeter.

"I want Crilodach to come in person with blood on Its mind because for certain that's how I'll face It," growled Copret.

"Do not try to face It by yourself," Lilah ordered him.

"Don't worry yourself about me."

"She isn't," suggested Demeter, "she's worried about how many of us will rush to save you." Copret scratched his face and growled.

"I hope Trecrogo isn't going to tell you the wisdom of the universe all in one go."

"If nothing else the fortress showed him how to argue with you," smiled Lilah.

Copret put a paw on Demeter's head and patted him. His paw glowed a deep auburn from the light around Demeter and was still glowing an hour after he took his paw away. His wound also eased a great deal.

"I have the plans drawn out you wanted," announced Tethval coming up the stairs with three large rolls of paper under his arms, "I'm thinking you'll find we're too few to cover everything you wanted done but since we're not going to be needed for long I've been able to extend duty hours."

"Don't make anyone too tired before the battle," warned Copret.

"Back in the mines we could go for forty six hours without sleep," Tethval told them.

"A precious skill to have, in the last day of life" Lilah observed.

"Did you see the girl with Chloe?" asked Copret.

"Downstairs. Refrit and his sister Lamellen claimed her as their find before getting on with their duties. She's chatting to some of the others. Seems a friendly type."

"Even now people try to make friendships," Copret observed.

"People will be people," said Demeter. "Wouldn't you

rather die with friends than with strangers?"

"Death is everyone's friend," replied Copret.

"Let's see those plans. We need to make some modifications, she will be able to hold an entire section by herself with her hair," said Lilah.

"If she knows how to let the strands think for themselves," Copret said.

"I think she knows," Lilah suggested. "Sanjava would have made sure of that, knowing she was going to fight with us. Besides we all know the stories of the one Sanjava protected, even if none of us ever met her. She stood against Zibanda, she fought with Kalevala, she saved Sanjava's life. She is a mighty ally."

"She isn't the kind to stand in front of us and start boasting about what she can do and who she knows. Her mind is focussed on the battle," said Demeter, who had seen her aura. "She is the only one of all of us who chose to be here."

Tethval raised an eyebrow and opened his mouth to say something about one person standing alone to fight, but decided not to say anything. He would see what he would see, he decided. That would be enough. Copret looked around the parapet watching the Arvernat deploy to their positions, running through a hundred strategies in his head for every step they took. For every conceivable battle array of the enemy. For every precious moment of the day left to them.

"Have you thought over my suggestion?" Lilah asked Tethval, as he flattened out the rolled plans with his carefully drawn strategies on them that now had to be modified because Mojolo had appeared.

"I don't like the idea of dividing our forces," Tethval told her. He gestured to the paper, "This plan shows we barely have enough forces to maintain Trecrogo once fully surrounded and using your estimates of the numbers opposing us, which by your own admission may fall short, the siege will be fast, viciously contested and furious. Even with Mojolo, to send some of our forces away would deprive us of the advantage she gives us in numbers, weakens our defences here and loses us valuable fighters."

"What do you think Demeter?" Lilah asked, as Chloe joined them again.

"Crilodach'll be on Its way here with Its entire army. We'll be facing multiple attacks from all sides, above and below.

If we can stall that advance midway, in any way, but not stop them, we'd be showing we're desperate more than that we're strong. It doesn't know the true abilities of Trecrogo and maybe a surprise attack outside the fortress will stop It from guessing. But Tethval is right, if we need all of us and more to defend Trecrogo as is, then how can a few of us stand against It and Its army somewhere else and hope to come out alive?"

"We'll have surprise on our side," pointed out Lilah.

"Even so," said Demeter, "I can't leave Trecrogo at this critical time. I need every minute to make sure I can handle the power of the fortress. Tethval how many men can you spare?"

"I'd ask for volunteers and they'd all stand forward. I'd be loath to send more than a hundred given our chances of harming Crilodach are a million-to-one."

"Will you be one of them?" asked Lilah.

"I wouldn't ask them to be going alone, even with you. From the first time we took up arms, I've fought by their side in every battle. I feel that my duty now more than I ever did."

"I'll go," volunteered Chloe.

"Despite not being sure?" questioned Lilah.

"Better to be in a fight that's going than waiting for one to come my way. Besides I don't like being parted from you, you make me feel a lot braver."

"And you make me feel braver little one," replied Tethval.

"That I don't believe," she scolded him.

"I think you need to stay here Chloe, Copret will need you in case we do not return," Lilah told her.

"That I will," agreed the bear, in a voice that told Chloe they wanted to keep her out of the ambush. Chloe did not argue. They all knew when Lilah had decided something they had best go along with her. Just as they knew she was only asking their opinion. If none of them went with her she would go alone.

"I have to go," she said, "to make It see we are ready for It. I can do some damage." Her voice was stern. "And as you said It may see the ambush as a desperate attempt by those who cannot defeat It. That is to our advantage. If It has too much time to think It will see through our plans and all the planning of generations will be wasted. We must make sure It comes here and fights as puffed up with Its own self-

417

importance and as angry as possible."

"But we know Its coming here," Chloe complained, "and from everything you've said I don't think adding to Its self–importance is possible."

"Is It angry enough? Is It keen enough? Can we make It blind enough to fall into the trap we have set? The only one who knows about the window in the back of the fortress is Hagouti, and we have him imprisoned."

"You're right, It would come on to Trecrogo after a surprise ambush from us with Its blood lust high. Especially if we got close to It," said Tethval.

"Exactly," ended Lilah.

"Is it worth the sacrifice just to make It more angry?" he asked.

"We cannot risk It being less angry," she responded.

"How do we stay in touch with you?" asked Copret.

"Demeter will be powerful enough to hear me if I call," she told them. "I do not think we should be too far away. We will have to give ground quickly. We will not have much time to reach you. Maybe minutes from here at most."

"Between Crilodach and the middle of nowhere," said Copret.

"The best place to be," she told Copret.

"The Sangyma have all planned to be in Trecrogo in one form or another," said Copret, "and Sanjava's hair being here through Mojolo increases the odds heavily in our favour. Do you still need to go?"

"You forget we have lost Midrak and Tobia, and with them Tegriel and Fulminar," said Demeter. "Though I sense we are all still connected in some way across a huge tide of history and that Midrak is making his way here even now."

"I'm as pleased as the next bear the Sangyma are still around but I'm against this expedition. I'd rather It came on us where we know we're strongest," said Copret.

"I'm for the ambush," said Chloe.

"For what reason?" asked Copret.

"Because strength isn't everything, and as Lilah says, we need It in a certain frame of mind. Though I don't know exactly why, I can see that matters."

"The child has spoken," agreed Tethval.

"I suppose surprise is a decent enough weapon against Crilodach's claws," snapped Copret.

"Stop being aggravated by the fact I have decided to ask

you to stay and look to the defences here," said Lilah.

"Is that what this is about Copret?" asked Tethval, "You thinking we're leaving you out of a battle?"

"I don't care to let my friends face dangers without me," snapped the bear, "anymore than you do."

"There'll be enough danger for all of us in a few hours," Demeter told him. "More than enough."

"The Arvernat are ready," Tethval said.

"Let's get started. We have no idea where Crilodach is, so we must hurry to find Its armada. Demeter did you set the forward warning signals?" asked Lilah.

"I did. They're working. I can give you notice of the direction they'll be coming from. I might even be able to estimate numbers. But things will happen quickly so I suggest if you're going to do this you go right now."

"I don't care much about the others, I just want to know where Crilodach is amongst them. The sudden attack directed on It will be the whole point of the ambush," said Lilah.

"The armada will be vast. I can give you maybe as much as thirty seconds if you need an exact position."

"That will be good enough."

Tethval's hundred and four Arvernat came out in threes and fours, armed themselves and formed into corps of fifteen each headed by one of their number who stood to the left of each group. Tethval looked over their weapons.

"I have never seen swords and gloves like these before."

"And never will again," said Copret.

They all walked on to the Onäis which had grown to encompass them. Lilah turned to Demeter,

"I am ready," she said.

He nodded. She raised Bofindle in front of her and the Onäis, carrying a small army, shot out into the darkness. Engulfed in seconds so that even the sharp eyes on Trecrogo could no longer see them.

"We shall return," she told Tethval, as he looked back at the fast receding Trecrogo which vanished before she had finished the sentence.

"I hope you do," he replied. "The fortress will fall without you there."

They moved swiftly on. No walls to protect them. Just men, a few weapons and a spellmaker. Around them was the whole universe. The Onäis was strong under their feet. The

Arvernat were relaxed, as if they had travelled on an Onäis many times before.

Mojolo came out still chewing some bread in time to see them go. Lilah and the Arvernat looked fine soldiers to her so she was surprised when Demeter asked Copret,

"Will they survive?"

"If anyone can do exactly what they said they'd do, Lilah and Tethval will," replied Copret. "I'll not move from this spot until they come back to us."

He set his feet apart, rested his large paws on the parapet and fixed his eyes ahead. He looked at the stars feeling the weight of time in his fur. He hated others going into battles he wanted to fight. He hated waiting. He hated letting others face dangers alone without him. He knew Lilah was more powerful than him but that never changed the way he felt about being out of a fight.

Demeter took his place floating above Trecrogo. Continually talking to the fortress. Continually being fed by a great magical energy. He was awestruck by the wisdom and planning of the bears. His advance signals were counting the stream of Crilodach's armada that never stopped coming. There was no end to the counting. Demeter began to sense true fear. The child in him wanted to quiver but strength flowed into him from a thousand places until he looked as if nothing could phase him. As the Arvernat took their posts the sight of Demeter floating, immovable and bright, above their heads gave them the same feeling they would have had if he had been a flag. No nation ever boasted better or more dedicated soldiers than those who stood together on Trecrogo.

"Numbers count for less than strength of purpose," Copret said to Demeter, as he watched him counting.

Demeter looked down at him. In the bear's eyes he saw much of what he felt in the fortress. That same power.

Chloe took her place with her bow. Refrit and Lamellen came out with the last of the Arvernat. Family members were sent to separate posts as the sight of each other being wounded or dying was thought to affect their ability to fight. All had their appointed positions around the parapet. Mojolo took her lariat and stood on the stone and lashed out. Flames sparked out of the whip and hurled themselves into the distance. Her hand felt warm. Her hair fell loose and free as she took out the pins. She watched the strands move slowly around her as if she were watching something that was not part of herself. She did not feel the hairs moving on her scalp. Some strands gripped the fortress stones and lifted her off her feet so her lariat was easier to use and flew further out. Each strand of hair was stronger than Copret. Copret nodded to himself,

"She'll do," he said.

Once away from Trecrogo Lilah held out her hands and from ahead of them came a wide, flat platform. Perfectly black. The Onäis slid seamlessly into a section along the right side, then turned black as well. From anywhere you looked they seemed to be all standing on nothing. They found, just as on the Onäis, they could move with ease. The clothes and skin on them all turned equally black as did their weapons. This äis, identical to the one Rimfelder was travelling upon, that had been waiting for them, absorbed them into a perfect camouflage.

"This is useful," Tethval said, stamping his foot on the solid metal–like work.

"Tegriel made this, the first, äis, which Crilodach and all Its minions have never found, at the beginning of the war. Wherever Tegriel went this äis would follow him at a safe distance, and on occasions Tegriel loaned the äis to other of the Sangyma when they needed to travel outside the Ossendark. The bears used the design to create the Onäis. We can watch without being seen, go places without being noticed, wait without being caught, appear suddenly as if from nowhere. There are only two and they are a closely guarded secret. Not only is the äis undetectable, but we cannot be seen until we want to be. Once we make our move Crilodach will know we are there and make us known to Its army," explained Lilah.

"Can we hide anything from Crilodach?" asked Tethval.

"Not for long. Our first attack has to be our best. We must strike deep, fast and with all our ferocity."

"How close can we get?"

"Close enough to touch It but I will have to hang back a little with Bofindle. If I were to get too close too fast It would sense me. I am hoping It does not know enough about the Arvernat to sense when you are near."

"It'll know all about us after today's ambush."

"There are no days anymore," she told him.

"Then how shall we mark this battle?" asked Tethval.

"By surviving."

The äis sped them through the rest of their journey with a silent urgency. Until the deep darkness seemed to be not only around them but part of them. Tethval's men kept their eyes unlit by using Trecrogo's helmets, adding to their ghostly passing in the dark of a starless night. They stood with their backs straight, shoulder close to shoulder, each with their own thoughts.

Still they drove forwards, Lilah in intense thought. The Arvernat gripped the weapons Demeter had given them. Besides the heavy swords that meshed together, each of the fighters had mirrors on the back of thick gloves. The glare from these when they shone their eyes at each others' hands would make the enemy think they were many more than they actually were. They were under no illusions. The armada would move with swiftness to defend their master and the surprise of their ambush would be very short lived.

The äis stopped. Demeter had piloted them correctly. Crilodach's armada was moving fast. The noise of their singing came to them in one sudden roar, as if an engine had started up right next to their ears. Like a tidal wave the armada stretched as far as the eye could see. Their tumult reverberated around the small cluster of fighters on the äis.

Far away Demeter felt the armada. He knew Lilah and the others were close to their quarry. Copret watched Demeter closely as he was the only one with the power to tell them how the ambush was going.

Demeter looked for Crilodach amongst the millions. He saw the cockroaches hidden in the Rounds, not as the insects they were but as the men, animals and women they had been. He felt their dissemination through the oncoming armada and counted their number. He was already calculating what they would need to fight with, and how much damage they were likely to cause with the weapons he could give them. The unexpected army the Sangyma had planned for was massing.

He touched Gertis' mind but Trecrogo would not allow him to communicate with the Sangyma, and with good reason. Crilodach would have known. The cockroaches were great in number, but not as large a number as Crilodach's never ending armada. Demeter concentrated. His carefully positioned signal markers gave Lilah her target. Crilodach was not in the centre of the armada. It was on the near flank, close to where Lilah had positioned the äis. She could not believe her luck.

It did not see the need to be surrounded by Its forces. Its general and lieutenants were scattered at points through the armada that swept towards Trecrogo with aggressive efficiency. In an instant Lilah saw everything Demeter saw and more. Tethval caught the taste of battle. Crilodach saw nothing more than the fortress. A bigger prey than It had been used to but one which contained all Its present enemies in one neat box. She knew It was on Its guard against traps. She also knew without Its armada It could still defeat them.

Lilah and the Arvernat were kneeling as they turned and swept across the heads of the armada on the flank, banked around and crossed below hundreds of Rounds until they were beneath the Round Crilodach stood upon. They saw the immense armada pass over them spread out as far as the eye could see flying towards the fortress, making ripples in the vacuum of space.

"Are you ready?" she whispered. Tethval nodded. She looked at his fighters. "Are they all ready?"

She heard them growl a soft reply. She pressed her toes against the platform. They turned and came up on Crilodach's section from behind like a hand grabbing at a moving target. They were right in the midst of the Rounds. There ahead of them stood Crilodach. One second away from realizing they were there. The äis swept up to It as Lilah leaned back with Bofindle in her left hand. She watched as the Arvernat got closer and then she gave Tethval the signal.

Without warning Bofindle grew to a huge size and came up from behind It, a sudden presence that stretched out from one end of the armada to the other, tipping then smashing a dying star into the middle of the Rounds as if playing a game, slicing the dying star into three pieces causing an explosion that threw light and fire into the armada, upsetting many Rounds, destroying a few and causing many men to throw themselves on the ground to keep their balance. The battle song they had been singing on the flank became screams of panic. Rock, machines and men vanished into space.

Crilodach reacted immediately stopping too much damage

and sending fragments of rock careering out into space where they burned up harmlessly. Sweeping round in an arc Bofindle flew like a spear behind the advancing hoard cutting through everything, sending hundreds of men to their deaths and hundreds more leaping on to the closest Rounds as theirs were broken up. Arms grabbed at arms and heads, to help save their comrades. Even as she gripped Bofindle once more a great roar was heard from the armada.

The left flank of Its armada felt the rain from the explosion unsettle their journey. Crilodach sent out ropes to haul the Rounds, which had broken away, back to the safety of the armada. Swiftly the hole made by Lilah's attack was closed. Even as It brought Its armada back together, Lilah was upon Crilodach. Its general saw and for an instant he waited. No enemy had ever come that close to Crilodach and lived. Around her in a blaze of light, there seemed a thousand men, well armed and strong, fighting Frin-Ghirzan's finest trained troops with surprising ease but being pushed back by sheer numbers.

It looked into the dark and Its eyes saw Lilah. As Bofindle flew to her side It threw Its weight against her. Hundreds of men jumped to Its side pushing Tethval and his fighters further back. The meshed swords swung by powerful green arms cut whole land masses into pieces, sliced through armour and heads. They held their gloved hands, facing the enemy with the mirrors blinding light, as Crilodach ripped into the äis and snapped the ancient bejal in three. Thrown upwards, Tethval and his men found themselves fighting on their enemy's ground and Tethval saw Crilodach snap his men in two with swipes of Its claws. Tethval leapt at the creature and grabbed Its head in his strong arms.

Tethval could not say how he knew everyone went silent. He could not have admitted he even realized the ambush was over when he leapt, for he still heard the shouts of his men, the pieces of the dying star raining down and the roar of Crilodach's anger all ringing in his ears. Nor could he have ever said if he would have done what he did if he had known that in all the ages of the worlds such a brave thing had been done but once before. Attempted yes, many times by many brave warriors, but never achieved. And no one wants to be the first to achieve something everyone else would consider stupid, foolhardy and madly brave. Crilodach had been hidden away in Damkina using others for Its wars for so long no one knew of the time, except in myth, when It had faced weapons and magic. When It had, It was against the Sangyma and so many of the things said of them have become myths none of Its men are exactly sure how much is true and how much is made up. But one thing everyone on that Round was sure of, one thing they instinctively knew because none of them had ever seen, heard, thought or believed anyone could get over their fear enough, to actually touch It.

In no one's memory had anyone ever been seen to touch Crilodach with their own hands as Tethval did at that moment to protect his men. Some believed anyone that did would burn instantly to ash. Some said anything that did would turn to stone. Vanish from sight. Suffer a thousand tortures in a hundred worlds. But Tethval did not burn. Tethval did not vanish. Tethval did not turn to stone. And so unbelievable was the sight that everyone felt something new had happened in the universe. Even Tethval's enemies were impressed.

Tethval in his anger and in the heat of battle with mighty arms and his large hands, wrapped his arms around Its head and pulled It sideways to try to unbalance It and so shocked were Its men closest to It, that for a brief moment they stopped in their tracks. Even as It swung Its head violently and lashed out at Tethval sending him sailing into two of his own men's arms with blood streaming down his face, Crilodach's men were too petrified to respond. They had seen a line crossed they did not believe could be crossed. For no sooner did Tethval touch Crilodach than Lilah slashed at Its legs with Bofindle and Crilodach, the mighty, untouchable Crilodach, fell backwards crashing to the ground. Yet even as It did so It rolled back and leapt up. As fierce as ever. It roared at her. Spat at her and caught Lilah a glancing blow with Its claw as It lashed out which sent her sailing into the air to be stopped by Bofindle which at the same time flattened the enemy around the dazed Tethval.

Rataplan was as surprised as Crilodach at the sudden assault. His own Round was distant from his master but he set off at a run, his private bodyguard following him, as he jumped from Round to Round to engage the enemy.

The mirrors on the fifteen surviving Arvernat, intensifying the light of their eyes, blazed into the faces of the nearest men, blinding them long enough for Lilah to grab Tethval by the arm and leap out of the way, just as Rataplan arrived with his claws extended leaping at them, only to fail to grab anyone. The light even burned Crilodach's body as It looked for the man who had dared to touch It. Bofindle hit Crilodach on Its back. It turned to fight but Bofindle was not there. None of them were to be seen. They had come upon the armada like an earthquake and then vanished like a mist. Crilodach roared, a roar Demeter heard. The attack had cost them eighty five men and women fighters and wounded Tethval and Lilah, but the roar showed Lilah that the ambush had worked. Crilodach was maddened with fury.

"Why's It angry?" asked Copret.

"It was thrown to the ground by Bofindle and wrestled by Tethval," replied Demeter.

"He wrestled It! I knew that Arvernat was mad. Is he alive?"

"Lilah took him off the Round in time."

"Then she lives," said the bear, thankfully.

"Were you scared It would come upon us holding her dead body aloft?" asked Demeter.

"The thought did cross my mind."

"Not only yours," revealed Chloe.

"I see something," called Mojolo.

On the Onäis making their escape, Lilah was cut deep in her upper arm and Tethval was shaking uncontrollably from his encounter.

"It was colder than anything I've ever touched before," he told her.

"What were you thinking? I never suggested anyone take It on single handed."

"It injured you too," he pointed out.

"This is nothing. I am not even bleeding," she lied.

"I had to protect my men."

"That was a crazy manœuvre, you could have been cut in two," she said.

"This whole ambush was crazy manœuvre and he destroyed the äis," went on Tethval.

"The work of that bejal is done, the äis remaining still has good work to do." She stared at him and he looked deeply into her eyes.

"Did I worry you that much?" he asked.

"I have never seen anyone do anything like that before," she admitted.

"You've never fought with the Arvernat before," he reminded her.

"Something I obviously missed," she said.

Tethval rose as they closed upon Bofindle which was purposely coming to join them. The bejal slid into Lilah's hand and the blood vanished from her wound. He looked at the survivors.

"Not many to take back to Trecrogo," he said.

"We were close," she told him. "I did not think we could get that close. I am sorry for your people."

"Don't be. Since we met you we've all been waiting for death," said Tethval.

"I cannot help the times we are living through. I wish I could."

"You know your weapon felled the beast," grimaced Tethval, as his wound bit into him, "from how you talked I thought nothing could stop that thing."

"Nothing ever has yet," she told him.

A roar came from the battleground. The armada was close behind them, unbent and unyielding. Tethval was breathing heavily. None of them could guess who would get to Trecrogo first.

"That thing's unlike anything I've ever seen before," said Tethval. "You didn't exaggerate Its raw power."

She looked at the Arvernat. She sat back and bound his arm and pressed her fingers against the cuts to stem the bleeding. Quietly and without saying much she let a balm emanate from her finger tips that touched them all and gave them all some rest as they hurtled back to Trecrogo. Copret had always refused such balms. Scars, he used say, are honourable when they have been won fighting It. She hoped the loss of the Arvernat would be worthwhile as she thought about what Bofindle had planted upon Crilodach's back in that last moment. The second reason for their ambush and the one she told no one about. For a second she closed her eyes and reached back in her mind to a happier time. When Zananto had been a mother to her.

"We are taught in schools when we are children," she heard Zananto tell her, "but we never stop learning even as adults. Time is the true teacher but no one knows if there is time enough to reveal all that may be known. You will make the difference, if not you, who could there be, and if not in your time, then when?"

End of Book 1

Index

A descriptive index is downloadable from
www.footsteps.co/ruzniel